# Yesteryear

*Also by Dorothy Garlock*
*in Thorndike Large Print*®

Annie Lash
Wild Sweet Wilderness

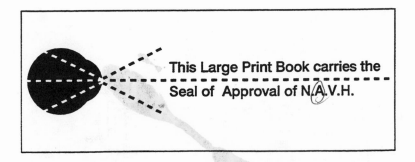

This Large Print Book carries the
Seal of Approval of N.A.V.H.

# Yesteryear

## Dorothy Garlock

Thorndike Press • Thorndike, Maine

Copyright © 1995 by Dorothy Garlock

All rights reserved.

Published in 1995 by arrangement with Warner Books, Inc.

Thorndike Large Print ® Americana Series.

The tree indicium is a trademark of Thorndike Press.

The text of this Large Print edition is unabridged.
Other aspects of the book may vary from the original edition.

Set in 16 pt. News Plantin.

Printed in the United States on permanent paper.

---

**Library of Congress Cataloging in Publication Data**

Garlock, Dorothy.
   Yesteryear / Dorothy Garlock.
     p.    cm.
   ISBN 0-7862-0542-3 (lg. print : hc)
   1. Frontier and pioneer life — West (U.S.) — Fiction.
2. Man-woman relationships — West (U.S.) — Fiction.
3. Large type books. I. Title.
[PS3557.A71645Y47  1995]
813'.54—dc20                         95-34855

This one is for the O'Haver clan
Betty and Louis O'Haver

Sally Nan and Mike Kenny
Missy and Beau

Michal and David Long
Eric

Rebecca and Shane Cloyde
Tyler

And . . . Gartett O'Haver

# CHAPTER

## * 1 *

Addie's eyes blared with anger.

"Get out of our way! It's no wonder the South lost the war with a vile creature like you fighting for it."

"Ya better watch who yore callin' names." The drunken soldier's face turned mean. He peered under the sunbonnet of the young girl standing beside Addie.

"L-looky here, Nate. Looky here. Ain't she a sight?"

"She's the nigger we heared about."

"I ain't carin' none a'tall. She don't look like it. She's pert nigh white."

Addie moved quickly between Trisha and the man before Trisha could get the knife out of her pocket.

"She yore nigger, ma'am?"

"If you've got a decent set of manners to your name, I suggest you put them to work." Addie tried not to raise her voice and draw attention.

"Wal, now. Ain't you high-tone, considerin' what ya are."

"Pay ya two bits fer a hour with 'er." The man put his face close to Addie's. His breath was so foul that it made her stomach churn. She put out a hand to shove him back, but he refused to budge.

"If I scream, every decent man on this street will be on you like a duck on a junebug."

"Quit yore play-actin' an' come ta terms. How much fer a half-hour? Come ta think on it, I'd not last a hour." He laughed. "I ain't had me no woman in a coon's age an' I'm 'bout ta bust my britches."

"Is they a-botherin' ya, ma'am?" A bearded man in a cowhide vest towered over them.

"Yes, they are."

"No, we ain't. She's storyin' is what she's doin'. We's tryin' to do some business, is all." It almost sobered the drunk when he looked up at the giant. To cover his fright, he put a cocky grin on his face. "We're a-wantin' ta use her nigger. We're willin' to pay. Hey . . . whatcha —"

The bearded man seized the drunk's shoulders with two large hands. He lifted him off his feet and shook him like a wet kitten before tossing him into the dusty street. Landing on his back, the drunk gulped in the air that

8

had been knocked out of him, shook his head to clear it, then scrambled to avoid the hooves of the horses tied to the rail.

"Ya had no call ta be doin' that." The second soldier began to back away.

The giant followed him and spoke so quietly that Addie had to strain to hear the words.

"I ain't a-arguin' with *horse dung*. Get that boozy bum away from these ladies or I'll make fodder outa both of ya."

The two men moved out into the rutted street, and when they had several horses and wagons between them and the man in the cowhide vest, the one who had picked himself up out of the dirt, yelled, "I ain't never heared of a nigger an' a whore bein' called *ladies!*" As soon as the words were out of his mouth, he ran.

Addie put her hand on the arm of their defender when he stepped off the porch to follow the two.

"Let them go. Please. We've caused enough commotion."

"Miss Addie!" Colin came running down the walk. "Ya all right?"

"We're all right, Colin. Did you give the horses water?"

"Yes'm. But —"

"This gentleman got rid of the trash for

9

us," Addie said calmly and smiled up into the man's warm brown eyes.

"It was pure pleasure, ma'am." The hat he removed was wide-brimmed, turned up in the front and held with a long silver pin that pierced the brim and the crown. Dark brown curly hair hung down over his ears and was chopped off straight as if it had been cut with a knife. He reminded Addie of a woolly bear, and she had to bite back the urge to tell him so.

The big man glanced at Trisha, who stood with her head lowered.

"You and the little lady ain't to worry. I'll keep a eye out for them weasels." He looked down at a small boy clinging to the woman's skirt and a girl a few years older holding on to him. He struck Colin's shoulder a playful blow. "I'm thinkin' I ain't even ort to a-stuck my oar in. This here feller could'a took on them hornswogglers. He was 'bout ready to wade in with fists flyin'."

"I'm aimin' to get me a knife." Colin straightened his thin shoulders.

"Using a knife to go at a man bigger than you ain't such a good idee. Remember this, boy. Take 'em by surprise. Use whatcha got and hit 'em where it hurts. Ya could've butted him with your head." He leaned down and whispered something in Colin's ear. "Do it hard and it'll lay 'em out cold. I seen it done by a lad not half yore size."

"Thanks, mister." Colin had a rare grin on his face.

"Good day, ladies," The man gave Trisha another long look, put his fingers to the turned-up brim of his hat, and walked away.

"He was a nice man. Wasn't he, Trisha?"

"I guess so," Trisha mumbled.

"What's a hornswogg-ler, Miss Addie?" Colin asked.

"I'll be doggoned if I know. It isn't anything good, I'm sure of that." She bent to straighten the hat on the head of a small boy and the bonnet on the head of the five-year-old girl who now held on tightly to Trisha's hand.

"I knowed it! I knowed I ain't ort ta a-come!" Trisha mumbled. "I should'a stayed home. Lordy! Oh, Lordee, mercy me! I wish I'd stayed home."

"Stop moaning and groaning, Trisha. Hold up your head and spit in their eye." Addie glanced at the three children, who were looking up at her and listening closely. "Oh, my. Fine example I'm setting. We'll talk about this when we get home."

"I ain't nothin' but trouble," Trisha muttered under her breath, but still Addie heard.

"Not to me! You're the dearest friend I

11

have in all the world. Now come on. Let's go to Mr. Cash's store. I have two pairs of men's socks to barter."

Addie settled the strings of her drawstring purse on her arm, straightened three-year-old Dillon's hat once again, and smiled down at the rest of her family. Crowds made Addie Hyde nervous and frightened Trisha half out of her wits. Addie glanced at her and saw that she'd pulled in her lips and held them between her teeth, and her large, expressive eyes swept from side to side as if she expected to be attacked at any moment. Addie knew the girl's fear and stayed close to her as they made their way down the crowded boardwalk with eleven-year-old Colin leading the way.

The main street of Freepoint, Arkansas, was little more than a narrow alley between two rows of frame buildings: some had false fronts, some had porches, and a few fronted right on the hard-packed dirt road. At the end of the street, facing the tracks, was a wooden building that served as the railway station.

The stores were always busy on the two days of the week that the train arrived, bringing not only mail but weary men coming home from the war. Today the streets were more crowded than usual. The two mercantile stores, the tonsorial parlors, the blacksmith and harness shops, and the taverns and eating places were overflowing with people. The boardwalk teemed with farmers, soldiers, bewildered, newly freed Negroes, drifters, and men in tattered Confederate uniforms. Women and children, for the most part, waited for their menfolk in wagons parked along the street.

John Tallman stood leaning against the wall of the store and watched the activity on the street. He saw the wagon come into town, saw the boy tie the tired, aged horses to the rail and then help the woman, the girl, and the two children down onto the crowded walk.

Eyes so dark blue that they at first appeared black surveyed the street. When the two Confederate drunks planted themselves in front of the women, John was on his way to buttonhole them. Then the bearded frontiersman had stepped in, and John stopped, doubting that his help would be needed. He stood back and chuckled as the oak tree of a man tossed one drunk into the street and backed off the other.

John was aware that he, too, was being observed, but he figured that was because not many men dressed as he was came to Freepoint. He was taller than average and wore his buckskin shirt outside his britches and belted about his waist. His hair, beneath his low-crowned, round-brimmed leather hat, was longer than most men wore it in the South. It was blue-black and turned under at his shoulders. To John, the face that looked back at him when he shaved — the narrow, straight nose, the full, wide mouth, and the mustache that curved down around it and reached almost to his jawbone — seemed un-remarkable. It was, however, a face remarked upon by others. His strong features and quiet assurance were matched by his bearing. Here was a man who moved with his head up, his back straight, assuming an air of apparent unconcern, yet whose eyes missed nothing. He wore that studied look of indifference when he followed the women and children into the store.

The little group had moved to a corner out of the line of traffic. The younger children held on to the skirt of the older girl, and the boy stood beside them ready to do battle if they were bothered. The woman in the round-brimmed bonnet smiled reassuringly at her family, then went to the counter to speak to the proprietor.

"Afternoon, Mr. Cash."

"How-do, Mrs. Hyde."

*Mrs.* Hyde. John moved behind the row

14

of goods where he could see and hear the woman and the storekeeper, who was also the postmaster. The man had a serious look on his face. He stood before the pigeonholes where the mail was kept while his clerk waited on the customers.

"Is Iola here?" Mrs. Hyde's question was in the softly slurred speech of the South. *Is Iola he-ah?*

"She's upstairs today. Got the misery in her joints again."

"I'm sorry to hear it."

"She asked me this morning if you'd been to town."

"We've been hoeing our cotton patch. Can't let the weeds get a head start on us."

"Mrs. Hyde, you don't have any . . . mail."

"I didn't expect any," Addie replied with a thin smile.

Although Addie knew the mail train had come in, she hadn't come to town expecting to find a letter from Kirby. The war had been over for almost two months, and her expectations had dimmed long before. He had not written her a single letter since joining the Arkansas Regulars almost four years ago.

"Will you step around here for a minute . . . please?"

Suddenly conscious of the troubled look on the man's face, Addie felt a sudden chill that

15

held her motionless for a few seconds. She looked over her shoulder at her family before following him around the counter.

"Is there something wrong, Mr. Cash? Have you changed your mind about trading goods for the stockings?"

"Lord, no. I'll take all the socks, scarves, caps, and anything else you bring me. It's not that at all."

"What is it, then?"

"Well . . . a man came through here yesterday. He was a Confederate officer, or had been. A few weeks ago he came onto a couple of fresh buryin' places over by Jonesboro. Care had been taken to mark them. A stick was poked in the ground at the head of each grave with a hat tied to it." The postmaster pulled out a handkerchief and wiped his brow.

"What's that got to do with me, Mr. Cash?" Addie asked, but she knew it had to do with Kirby. Her knees began to shake.

"I hate to be the one to break the news . . . especially like this. In one of the hats was the name Kirby Hyde, Freepoint, Arkansas. The captain asked me if the Hyde family lived in these parts; and, if it did, would I pass the news. I'm sorry, Mrs. Hyde."

Addie stared at the storekeeper, comprehension widening her violet eyes; then her heavy lashes shuttered her gaze.

"There's no mistake?"

"No, ma'am. The captain was careful to write the name down on a paper. I can get it for you if you like."

"There's no need." She placed her hand on his arm in a comforting gesture. "This wasn't easy for you. Thank you for telling me."

"Will you be all right? Do you want to go up and see Iola?"

"I'll be fine. Thank you for your concern."

The news was not unexpected. She felt none of the shattering grief she had felt when Kirby had gone away and left her alone and pregnant with his child. She had come to realize during that frightening time that the love she had had for him, if indeed it had been love, had died. Gradually over the years, when he hadn't written, she had tucked his memory somewhere deep inside her. Weeks now went by when she didn't even think of him.

She should grieve, she told herself. He was, after all, Dillon's papa. *I'll grieve later,* she thought.

Then she looked again at Mr. Cash and said: "The children and I will go home now."

"I'm sorry, Mrs. Hyde," he repeated. "Oh,

17

Mrs. Hyde," he called as she walked quickly down the aisle between the barrels and sacks of merchandise. "Just a minute. I owe you for the socks."

Addie returned to the counter. "May I trade them for sugar?"

"Of course. Some came in on the freight wagons this morning. Did you bring a sack?"

"Yes." Addie turned so quickly that she nearly bumped into a tall man in a doeskin shirt. She looked up into his dark face and even darker eyes. His shoulder-length hair was black as coal. He wore a felt-crowned leather hat.

"I beg your pardon." John's hand shot out to grasp her shoulders to steady her. Then he stepped back and put his fingers to the brim of his hat.

All that Addie heard was the murmured apology. She wanted desperately to get out of the store, out of town. She darted around the man and hurried to where her family waited. Colin was holding out the sugar sack.

"Miss Addie?" Trisha whispered. "Are ya sick or somethin'? Ya look . . . queer."

"As soon as I get the sugar, we'll go home."

"What we gonna do if them two shagnasties follow us?"

"Don't worry. We've got the rifle in the

18

wagon. Colin hid it under the seat . . . and it's loaded."

"Muvver, I wanna see the train." Dillon tugged on his mother's skirt.

"The train came in this morning. This is the end of the track. It switched engines and left again," she explained patiently.

"Wanna see it," Dillon whined.

"Next time. I tell you what — we'll make gingerbread when we get home and maybe bread pudding. Now be nice and stay by Trisha." Addie patted her son's head and went back to the counter. Mr. Cash took her sack and went to the back room to fill it.

John Tallman had moved back behind the row of goods where he had a clear view of the woman. From the concealing shadow of his hat brim, he surveyed the room. A down-at-the-heels former Confederate soldier in a ragged, dirty uniform leered at the girl who stood by the children. She kept her head turned away, her face concealed in the tunnel of her sunbonnet.

The town was alive today with women-hungry men, John decided, as his dark blue eyes returned to the woman by the counter, the intensity of his gaze markedly at variance with his relaxed attitude. He studied her as if reading a map. She was tall, slender, statuesque, a mature woman in her midtwenties.

19

Around her finely boned face were wisps of soft-spun hair of a light honey shade. He liked the proud lift of her chin and the free and easy way she moved. No stiff corset bound this woman. Though her body was thin to the point of appearing fragile, the set of her shoulders showed strength of character. She seemed utterly unaware that every man in the store was stealing glances at her. He had the sudden conviction that she was a person who met the trials of life head-on. In this backwater town, such a beautiful, desirable woman stood out like a rose in a weed patch.

Obeying an urge to see the woman up close again, to look into her remarkable violet eyes, caused John to move casually toward the counter where she waited. When he stood beside her, he noted that she was not as tall as he had at first thought. Her head came to just above his shoulder. Her erect posture and her slimness had created the impression of greater height.

Mr. Cash returned from the back room and placed Addie's sack on the counter.

"Ten pounds, Mrs. Hyde. Do you consider that a fair trade for the socks?"

"More than generous. Thank you." When she reached for the sack, a large hand grasped the twisted, tied top. She pulled her hand back and looked up.

"I'll carry it to your wagon, ma'am."

She met his gaze squarely. In her delicately drawn features there was a curious stillness. The faint color across her cheeks betrayed the fact that she was not completely at ease and was trying hard to remain composed. The fierce independence in her violet, thick-lashed eyes touched his innermost soul with a force that left room for only confused thoughts in his mind.

"It's kind of you to offer, sir. But I have help." The boy who had waited with the other children now was wedging himself between them. He wrapped both arms around the sack and pulled it toward him. The bulldog look on his young face seemed to dare the big man to object. "Tell Iola I'm sorry to have missed her," Addie said to the storekeeper.

"I'll do that, Mrs. Hyde." Mr. Cash watched Addie and the children leave the store, then looked up at John and shook his head. "Sure hated to break the sad news to that woman. She's got grit, I'll say that for her. She's had more trouble than fleas on a dog's back, but she holds her head up. Proud she is. Real proud."

John took the lid from a glass jar and removed two cigars. He placed a coin on the counter, and Mr. Cash scooped it up.

21

"Whatever the bad news was, she took it well."

"Addie Hyde is like that. Her man went off to war and far as I know she didn't get one single letter from him. She sent him one after the boy was born. I don't know if he got it or not. She didn't get no answer. Never figured out why she married up with him in the first place. He was one of them sugar-mouthed kind of fellers — all smiles and fancy talk to turn a woman's head. Iola, that's my wife, says Addie was just plain lonesome, living out there all by herself. A lonesome woman'll do foolish things." Mr. Cash shook his head, then fixed a questioning eye on his customer. "You ain't from around here, are you?"

John grinned. "How can you tell?"

"We don't get many dressed like you. You from out West?"

"You might say that. Are the socks for sale?" The stranger fingered the soft wool.

"Yes, but the price is high. She's got a couple special sheep. Shears 'em herself and processes the wool. Got a special way of makin' it soft."

"How much?"

"Two bits."

"I'll take both pair." The stranger placed a Yankee dollar on the counter. "Did you

22

tell her that her man wasn't coming back?"

"Yeah. Guess he come through the war and got hisself killed on the way home. Leastways his name's in a hat stuck on a grave over by Jonesboro."

"Too bad. A woman with that many younguns'll have a hard time of it."

"Only the little'n is hers. The other two is orphans shoved off on her by a do-little hill preacher. She's had that nigger gal with her for a few years. Looks more white than colored, don't she? Every horny piece of trash in the county finds his way to Miss Addie's door sooner or later to get a look at her."

Mr. Cash turned to a woman who was peering into the pigeonholes where the mail was kept.

"I'll get your mail, Mrs. Doubler. Your little Amy's got a letter here from her young man up in Des Moines. I hear there's gonna be a weddin' in the spring. My, how time flies. I remember when she was knee-high to a pup."

John turned from the counter and walked slowly out onto the store porch. His desire to see Addie Hyde again irritated him. He had gazed into her violet eyes for no more than a few seconds, yet the look in them remained in his mind.

He took off his hat and ran his fingers

through his hair. *Hell,* he thought. He had a week to kill before he had to meet the judge. As a special favor to his cousin Zachary Quill, he had consented to let Judge Ronald Van Winkle and his party trail along with him and his caravan of freight wagons through the Indian Nation, the Oklahoma Territory, and into New Mexico, where they would pick up the Cimarron Trail and turn south to Sante Fe.

His train of wagons, coming down from Saint Louis, would be at the rendezvous north of Fort Smith in another week. The teamsters would have a week to rest their animals and check their wagons before starting the journey west. Maybe he could arrange to run into Mrs. Hyde while he was here.

Addie held tightly to Dillon's hand and stayed close to Trisha as they followed Colin, carrying the sugar, to the wagon. They stepped off the boardwalk, crossed the road, and climbed the steps to the next porch.

The bearded man who had sent the drunken soldiers on their way sat on a bench in front of the eatery. He stared at Addie and her family. His bold eyes honed in first on Addie, then on Trisha, sweeping them up and down with a look of mingled lust and admiration.

Addie's nerves were taut already, and the

man's brazen appraisal broke the rein on her patience. When he didn't look away, Addie put her free hand on her hip and lifted her chin a little higher than she usually carried it. Her large violet eyes glared fiercely at the man. They did nothing to quell his interest; their color was unusual and they sparkled with the light of battle.

"Well, for heaven's sake! Haven't you ever seen a woman before?"

The faintest trace of amusement flickered across his face. He jumped to his feet, swept his hat from his head, and replied softly and respectfully: "I mean no offense, ma'am. It be such a pleasure to see womenfolk purty as ya are."

Addie blushed; then, realizing his sincerity, she laughed at him with her eyes, and her lips twitched.

"I'm sorry for being cross. And I thank you, sir, for helping us earlier," she said as they passed him.

Simmons had been known as Buffer for so long that he had almost forgotten that his first name was Jerr. He slapped his hat with its turned-up brim back onto his woolly head and watched the wagon leave town. The two small children were in the back, and on the seat, the girl sat at one side of the woman and the boy at the other. Although the boy was driving the team he kept looking over his shoulder as if he expected someone to follow.

A quick scan of the street told Buffer Simmons that his eyes were not the only ones following the woman and her family as they left town. Across the street, leaning nonchalantly against a porch post, was a tall, lean man in buckskins. Buffer squinted, the better to see the man, when, with the silent grace of an Indian, he stepped off the porch and crossed the street to the saloon.

Christ on a horse! What was a man like John Tallman doing in a sink-hole town like Freepoint? Almost as well known as Rain Tallman, his famous father, John was a long way from his mountain ranch in New Mexico Territory.

Buffer scratched his head. What he had thought was going to be a rather boring trip across Indian land now had the prospect of being a mighty interesting one.

# CHAPTER

## * 2 *

The wagon turned up the long lane to the weathered-plank house with its sagging porch and cobblestone chimney. Sitting on a rise amid a pecan grove, it was the only home Addie had ever known, and she knew every stick and stone in it.

She took pride in the front yard. It was almost as pretty now as when her mother was alive. The phlox and hollyhocks were in full bloom, as was the moss rose that covered the ground — red, white, yellow, and pink. Towering pecan trees shaded the house. Addie remembered watching her father as he walked along on the limbs, thrashing at the branches with a long pole. He was so nimble and quick, laughing and singing, while she and her mother picked up the fat nuts that rained down on them.

Both of her parents had drowned while trying to get their cows across a swollen creek. At sixteen, Addie had been left alone except

27

for an old uncle of her mother's who had lived with her until he died three years later.

A year of loneliness had followed his death — until Kirby had come. She could have married even before her uncle died. Suitors had come calling from twenty miles around. First they looked over the farm and, liking what they saw, looked over Addie, also liking what they saw. Addie couldn't bear the thought of spending the rest of her life with any of them. A few of her suitors were belligerent about being turned away and had spread the word that she was unreasonable and cold-hearted. She became known as a crotchety spinster — until Kirby came along.

When Colin stopped the wagon behind the house, Trisha jumped down and snatched off her bonnet. Her skin was the color of coffee after a generous amount of cream had been added. Her golden brown eyes were large, her nose was thin, and her chin was pointed. She whipped a piece of cloth from her pocket and tied it across her forehead to hold her black curly hair from her face.

"I ain't never goin' to town again!"

Addie understood the girl's fear and tried to allay it. "The war is over, Trisha. You don't have to be afraid someone is going to claim you. You're free to go anywhere you want."

"I ain't wantin' to go nowhere, Miss Addie. I want to stay right here with you an' the younguns. What's it mean to be free if you ain't got nowhere to go?"

"And I want you to stay. Lordy mercy! What would I have done without you these last few years? You were there when I needed you most. Then an angel put these two right down on my doorstep." Addie hugged Jane Ann and smiled at Colin. "And I've not been lonely a day since."

" 'Twarn't no angel!" Colin had begun to unharness the team. " 'Twas old Sikes. He was tired feedin' us and said other folks'd have to take a turn — like we was dogs. 'Tis a wonder he didn't just take us out and shoot us."

"You'll not be passed to anyone else, and that's that. You and Jane Ann are going to stay right here with me and Trisha and Dillon. Land sakes! Trisha and I would never have gotten the corn and cotton planted without you to help and Jane Ann to watch Dillon."

"An' I'd be deader than Jobe's turkey, is what I'd be, if'n you hadn't a-been there to chop that old rattler's head off with the hoe when I come on him in the patch," Trisha assured the boy and shuddered again at the memory.

"Go change into your everyday dress, Jane

Ann. And, honey, hang up your bonnet. Trisha just ironed it this morning." Addie reached into the back of the wagon for the sack of sugar.

"I'll bring the rifle," Colin called.

Addie had just walked through the house and opened the front door to allow the breeze to pass through when she saw a buggy coming up the lane.

"Oh, shoot! Here comes Preacher Sikes and Mrs. Sikes with him."

"I'm a-hidin' this here sugar." Trisha picked up the sack and dropped it behind the woodbox. "He see it, Miss Addie, and he'll start in on that tithe stuff he spouts when he wants somethin'."

The Sikeses had come to the Ozarks and established a church in the hill country at about the same time as Addie's parents had arrived to take up a homestead. Addie was sure that because of this longtime association with her parents they felt obligated to keep an eye on her. Preacher Sikes hadn't seemed such a religious fanatic in the early days, but now he blamed the world's woes on the sins of the people, claiming they had brought God's wrath down upon them.

He controlled his flock with a strong hand. If he learned that any of them had as much as sewn on a button on Sunday or splintered firewood for kindling, he was sure to chastise them publicly. He would preach a sermon declaring that they had failed to keep the Sabbath holy and were bound for the fiery furnace.

The buggy stopped beside the house, and Addie and Dillon went out into the yard to greet them.

"Come in out of the sun and have a cool drink."

"We can't stay but a minute or two," said Mrs. Sikes, a spry little birdlike woman. She climbed out of the buggy and was on the porch before her portly husband's feet touched the ground. "I was eager to know if Mr. Hyde had come in on today's train."

"No. He wasn't on the train. Sit here in the porch rocker, Mrs. Sikes."

"And how's that baby boy?" She pinched Dillon's cheek, her beady eyes bright with affection.

"He's no longer a baby. He's three years old."

"He is? My, how time flies."

"Afternoon, Preacher Sikes. Come up on the porch. I'll get a chair and a bucket of cool water. It's cooler out here than in the house."

"You gettin' along all right?" the preacher asked after he had drunk, dropped the dipper

31

back into the bucket, and sunk down on the chair Addie had brought from the house. She cringed, hoping the chair would survive when she heard it creak and groan under his massive weight.

"We're doing fine. Just fine," Addie replied.

"There's men on the road day and night, all of 'em fresh from the killin' and burnin' and rapin'. Town's clogged with deserters and free slaves that don't know what to do with themselves. You bein' out here without a man is the devil's temptation. 'Specially with that trollop here." His voice boomed in the quiet that was broken only by the buzz of junebugs and the caw of a crow high in a pecan tree.

"I'm not alone. I have the children and Trisha, who most certainly is no trollop," Addie said indignantly.

"Fiddle-faddle!" The fat preacher snorted. "That lazy nigger gal draws fornicatin' trash like flies to a honey pot."

Addie bit back the retort that came to mind. She controlled her temper and took a deep breath. She couldn't afford to anger the preacher. He was mean enough to take Colin and Jane Ann away from her just to "teach her a lesson." The flush that covered Addie's face did not go unnoticed by Mrs. Sikes.

"We worry about you, dear."

"We sit back from the road. We're not bothered." *(Forgive me, God, for this lie.)*

"You didn't come to service Sunday," Preacher Sikes said accusingly. It was not unseasonably hot, but sweat rolled from his forehead and down his cheeks.

"Daisy has a swollen fetlock and I didn't want to hitch her to the wagon. *(For this lie, too, God.)* It was too hot to walk and carry Dillon."

"Nay, my child." The preacher shook his head so hard that his jowls flopped. "Mere discomfort is no excuse for staying away from God's house. Them orphans should've been there to hear God's word," he said sternly, then added: "The boy's big enough to do a day's work to pay for his board, and he's been asked for."

"He works *here*." Addie felt an almost frantic uneasiness leap within her. "You needn't worry about Jane Ann and Colin. I'm going to keep *both* of them."

"You've done yore Christian duty by 'em. Ya kept 'em longer than ya ort to of. It's time someone else took on the burden."

"Colin and Jane Ann are not a burden," Addie said firmly. "When you brought them here, you said they had no close relatives to claim them. I have as much right to them as anyone."

"They ain't got no livin' kin that I know of. They was left to the church, and I took on the chore of seein' 'em raised. I'm thinkin' they be needin' a stronger hand than what they been gettin' here. The Lord says, 'Spare the rod and spoil the child.' "

Addie seriously doubted that the Lord meant to *beat* children, but she could see that arguing with Preacher Sikes would only make him more adamant. She choked down her anger and tried to speak reasonably.

"Have you seen the children misbehaving?" she asked, and went on before he could answer: "They're a part of my family now. A big part. Colin helps with the sheep and in the field. Jane Ann looks after Dillon."

"Ya ain't got the means to feed extra when ya ain't got no man on the place," he said stubbornly.

"I didn't have a man on the place when you brought them here. I've managed for almost four years. Now that the war is over —"

"Yore man will have a say when he comes home. Ya ain't heard that he's dead, have ya?"

"I've had no official notice," Addie said, trying to keep the tremor out of her voice.

"Well, looky here," Mrs. Sikes broke in, before her husband could continue the

argument. Dillon had placed a crudely made bow and arrow in her lap.

"Colin made it. Wanna see me shoot?"

"Sure do. But be careful you don't hit something."

"I hit a chicken once. Didn't hurt it." Dillon went to the edge of the porch, placed his arrow on the string, and pulled it back. When he let go of the string, the arrow went a good three feet out into the yard. He ran to get it. When he returned he was smiling happily.

"That was good. Very good. Wasn't it, Horace?"

"What? Uh . . . yes, good." The preacher was fanning himself with his hat. "Do you reckon Mr. Hyde'll want to live here on this place if he . . . when he comes back?"

"I imagine so. I see no reason to move."

The preacher's face always screwed up into disapproving lines when he spoke of Kirby. He had met him only once — the day Kirby and Addie had ridden over on his horse and asked Preacher Sikes to marry them. He had heartily disapproved of the hasty marriage and had tried to talk Addie out of it. When she refused to be swayed by his argument, he performed the ceremony with a deep frown on his face.

"If ya get a mind to sell the place, Oran

35

Birdsall is looking for a place for his boy. He's got cash money."

"I'll keep that in mind . . . should we decide to sell."

"Jist thought I'd mention it. Come on, woman." The preacher heaved himself to his feet and anchored his hat on his bald head. "We'd best be goin'."

"Come over, now." The birdlike woman hopped off the porch. "We're goin' to call on the Longleys. Sister Longley is down in the back."

"I'm sorry to hear it. Say hello for me."

"I'll do that. 'Bye, Sister Hyde."

"Goodbye."

" 'Bye," Dillon echoed.

Addie stood in the yard until the buggy was out of sight. She breathed a sigh of relief as she gathered her son into her arms.

She thought about what the preacher had said about the Birdsalls wanting to buy the farm. The Birdsalls and the Renshaws were the most prosperous families in the hills surrounding Freepoint. She had known for a while that the Birdsalls wanted to increase their holdings.

Addie had secretly longed to spread her wings. There was a big country out there, and she wanted desperately to see some of it. She had hoped that someday she could

sell the farm and start a new life in some other place where she could breed and raise her sheep, process her wool, and spin it into yarn. For the last few years the money she had earned from selling or trading the warm garments she and Trisha knitted had provided most of the necessities for her and her family.

But then Kirby, with his laughing eyes and dancing feet, had come into her life and turned it upside down. He had arrived one day and asked to sleep in the barn and work for his board. There had been so much to do, and he had seemed so eager to do it, that she had allowed him to stay. In no time at all he had helped her hoe her small cotton patch, mend the fences, and prune the peach trees. They had worked the vegetable garden together — and together they had picked the wild raspberries.

Kirby had nothing but disdain for her small flock of sheep and refused to have anything to do with them even though he liked the soft wool socks, warm gloves, and muffler she had knitted for him.

He had worked with a nervous energy that sometimes puzzled Addie. He had not been used to life on a farm, but once told what to do and how to do it, he had gone about the work as if his life depended on its being finished by sundown. And when they had

some leisure time, they had laughed, sung, and played games like two children let out of school.

One evening after many passionate caresses, Addie had given in to his sexual persuasion and allowed him to penetrate her. It had not been a pleasant experience for her, and afterward she had been riddled with guilt and fear. She had refused him further intimacy and they had quarreled. To Addie, conceiving a child out of wedlock was something akin to death. A week of misery went by before Kirby had agreed to go to Preacher Sikes and speak the vows. A month later he had gone to town to buy a well bucket and had returned as happy as a boy with a new slingshot.

*He had joined the Arkansas Regulars.*

Addie was left alone, pregnant and scared. Never would she forget that fall and winter. Knowing that she had no one to depend on but herself, she had worked tirelessly storing food for winter and dragging deadfalls from the woods for firewood.

During those painful months her dream of belonging to a large and loving family had died a slow, agonizing death. She had brought out and pondered the thoughts that had lurked in the back of her mind since Kirby had come into her life. He was not a staying

kind of man. Her brief time with him was over. Yet, she did not regret having let him into her bed, for he had given her the one thing she had desired above all others — a child to love.

It was during the last month of her pregnancy that Trisha had come out of the woods and hidden in the chicken house. Thin and sick, she had fallen on her knees and begged Addie to hide her from the man she believed was hunting her. She had been sold, she said, to a man who planned to place her in a brothel. To Addie, Trisha was like a gift from heaven. The two women had comforted each other, depended on each other, and come to love and respect each other. No one had ever come looking for Trisha, and Addie figured the girl must have traveled so many miles after her escape that her owner had given up tracking her.

Then, two years ago, Preacher Sikes had brought Colin and Jane Ann to the farm and asked Addie to take a turn at boarding them. She had taken the orphans to her heart, and, in a way she would never have imagined, she now had her family.

The two women, with Colin's help, had been able to raise enough food to see them through the winters. Addie and Trisha had brought down small game when they had the

shells to spare. Because Trisha was adept at robbing the hives of wild bees, they were never out of honey for their biscuits and wax for their candles.

Addie had managed to save two ewes and a ram. She taught Trisha how to wash the wool, card it, and spin the thread. She was surprised and pleased to discover how much the girl knew about drying the wool and how good she was at creating colors. From the yarn the women knitted socks, mittens, scarves and caps.

Thinking about it now, Addie realized that they had fared better than some. Thankfully, only minor skirmishes had taken place in their section of Arkansas, and they had been forced to give up to marauders only a hog, a few chickens, and some cabbages they had not had time to bring in from the field. On one occasion they had hidden the horses in a thicket and brought the sheep into the house.

The war was over — and now her worries were focused on keeping her family together and the riff-raff that prowled the countryside away from her door.

Addie waited until the family was gathered at the kitchen table before she told them the news about Kirby. She had fired up the cookstove and made a batch of gingerbread

while Colin and Trisha did the evening chores.

"I have something to tell you," she said from her place at the head of the table. She looked at each of the four faces that turned toward her. Dillon's little mouth was stuffed with warm gingerbread. Jane Ann and Colin stole frightened glances at each other as if they expected that what she was going to say would be bad news for them. Trisha, who had been unusually quiet since their return from town, left an unfinished piece of gingerbread on her plate.

"Mr. Hyde will not be coming back. Mr. Cash told me today that on his way home he was killed and is buried near Jonesboro."

Addie looked at her son, who continued to eat. The news had no effect on young Dillon, even though she had explained to him many times that his papa was away fighting the war. Colin and Jane Ann looked relieved. Addie knew that Trisha had been worried about what her place here would be when the head of the house returned.

"What will happen to all of us now, Miss Addie?" Colin asked.

"I guess there will be just the five of us from now on. We've worked hard and we've stayed together. There's no reason why we can't continue to do so."

"If'n old Sikes don't take a notion to take me over to old man Renshaw," Colin blurted, then hung his head.

Addie reached over and covered his hand with hers. "He's not going to take you or Jane Ann. You're going to stay right here with me and Trisha and Dillon."

"But, Miss Addie." Colin looked up, his eyes bleak, his voice raw. "Every Sunday Mr. Renshaw pinches my arm and says that I'm big enough now to work for my grub. He said he needs a stout boy — and he's tied up with Preacher Sikes."

"Damnation! I don't care how tight he is to Preacher Sikes." Addie never swore unless she were severely provoked. Now her eyes sparkled with anger. "You and Jane Ann are *my* children. *Mine,* by golly, and I'll be after Mr. Renshaw like a hive of stirred-up hornets if he tries to take you from me. He'll think he's in a tow-sack with a wildcat." She was hoping to get a smile from Colin, but he continued to stare down at his plate.

"And that ain't all," Trisha cut in. "I know ways've puttin' a spell on 'im that'll make his eyeballs bleed and his tongue dry up and pop open. I'll do it, if'n I don't kill 'im first." Emotion made her voice tremble and her remarkable eyes glitter like gold nuggets.

"Colin, have you been worrying about having to go stay with Mr. Renshaw?" Addie asked.

Colin didn't answer. As Addie met his gaze and saw the misery in his eyes, she felt her heart go out to him.

"We was goin' to run off." Jane Ann licked away the crumbs around her mouth. "We was going to get a horse an' ride to Calafornie."

"We was not!" Colin looked at his sister with disdain.

"We was too. You said we was, if you had to go to Mr. Renshaw. You said he didn't want me, and you'd promised Ma you'd take care of me. You said that, Colin."

"Forget about going to California or any other place. The two of you are going to stay right here — this is your home. I'll have a talk with Preacher Sikes and get this cleared up. Let's hear no more about it."

"Will you be our mama, Miss Addie?" Jane Ann asked.

"I told you not to ask her!" Colin shouted.

"I — I forgot." Jane Ann hung her head.

"Honey, if you want to think of me as your second mama and call me that, I'd be proud," Addie said to Jane Ann's bent head.

"You'd let me?"

"Of course. But you must not forget your own mama and hold her in your heart."

"I wish I could remember her. Colin does."

"I only remember a little bit," Colin murmured.

"Sit down, Dillon," Addie said firmly when her son stood on his chair in an attempt to reach the gingerbread. "Ask Trisha to pass the plate."

Dillon ignored his mother and leaned precariously over the table. Addie caught his hand and held it away from the plate. Dillon's face took on a stubborn expression.

"Sit down. If we all stood on our chairs to reach for things we'd . . . bump our heads!"

Jane Ann let out a peal of laughter. Even Colin smiled. Dillon sat down, folded his small arms across his chest, and stuck his tongue out at Jane Ann.

"See what he did! He stuck his tongue out at me!" Instantly Jane Ann's laughter turned to tears.

"I think everyone is tired." Addie got up to fill the teakettle from the water bucket. "Get the washtub, Colin. What's needed here is a bath and then to bed."

"Bath?" Colin grumbled on his way to the door. "I ain't takin' no bath."

Addie watched him leave. The promise she'd made to him lay like a yoke on her shoulders. Mr. Renshaw could provide a good portion of the money to build the new church, which alone would carry enough weight with Preacher Sikes that he might order her to give up Colin. She would somehow have to convince him that she needed Colin's help more than Mr. Renshaw did. She wondered if she could enlist the support of Mrs. Sikes. One way or another, she vowed to herself, she would keep her promise to Colin.

Addie was well aware that she was a different woman from the one Kirby had left pregnant and alone. She'd weathered the years in better shape than she had expected. She was grateful to the irresistible young man she had known for a few short weeks, and was sorry he had died, but she could not summon up the feeling of crushing grief.

She realized now how dreadfully lonely she had been and how vulnerable to his charm. She had been a young girl reaching for the stars and had unknowingly found the brightest of them all — her son, Dillon.

# CHAPTER

## * 3 *

"Ya know what, Miss Addie? If'n I ever marry up it'll be with the blackest man I can find. I want my younguns to be black as midnight in a graveyard so there ain't no doubt what they is. I'm thinkin' my granny's pa was white or part anyhow. Mama's was white, and mine was. White men done ruint us all."

"You're awfully pretty, Trisha. Your beauty attracts men like flies to a syrup bucket. Someday you'll meet a man who'll love and cherish you for what you are and not for what color your parents or grandparents were. I've heard about places where your Negro blood wouldn't matter."

"Hockey! I ain't never heard of no such place as that. That's just a bunch of windy is what it is." Trisha twisted the rag mop to remove the water. She was swabbing the kitchen floor with the children's bathwater.

"Ain't ya sad a'tall that your man got hisself killed?"

"I'm sad that Kirby is dead. He was so young and handsome and so excited about going to war."

"Lots of 'em was tickled to go fight to keep the poor stupid slaves from bein' free. They's so sure them poor niggers ain't got sense to stay outa the fire less'n white folk tell 'em."

"Kirby never took life very seriously, I'm afraid. Iola Cash said he was a charmer. He *was* charming, but he was also irresponsible."

"What that mean, Miss Addie?"

"He charmed his way into my heart, into my bed, and got me with child. The day after I told him he was going to be a father, he went to town and joined up. He left me here to provide for myself and to bear his child. He never wrote to me and never answered the letter I wrote him telling him that his son had been born. In all fairness, of course, he may not have received the letter. The only relative he spoke of was an uncle in Jonesboro, so I sent the letter there. His actions were more than irresponsible — they were contemptible! . . . Wait, Trisha, let me help you empty the tub."

"I ain't knowin' for certain what them big words mean," Trisha said, as they carried the tub to the end of the porch and emptied it onto the yard, "but I sure understand what ya feel."

"Now that I think about it, I think Kirby thought that going to war would serve two purposes: give him an excuse to get away from here and provide him with a great adventure." Addie hung the tub on a nail beside the back door and followed Trisha back into the house.

"Did ya love 'im?"

"Maybe for a few weeks. I was lonely. Weeks would go by and I'd not see another soul. But I can't put all the blame on Kirby. I wasn't a child."

"Ya warn't knowin' the ways of a horny man, is what," Trisha mumbled.

Addie was looking in the glass over the washstand and taking the pins out of her hair. She couldn't even visualize Kirby's face, she silently told the image in the mirror. She could remember other things about him: his restlessness, his evasiveness when she asked about his family, his refusal to talk about the future. At times, she had felt that he was with her in body, but the rest of him had always been in some faraway place.

She thought of what she would tell Dillon about his father when he was older. She would say that he liked to laugh, swim in the creek,

48

swing on the rope that hung from the pecan tree, and that he admired good horseflesh. She would also tell Dillon that his father was brave and went to war to fight for a great cause. Yes, she would tell him that. A boy had the right to believe that his father had been a brave man with principles, even if in truth he hadn't been.

As Trisha picked up Colin's shoes, a piece of cowhide she had cut to cover the hole in the sole fell out. She clicked her tongue and slipped the leather back inside before she set the shoes under the pegs where they hung their caps and bonnets.

"That boy's growin' plum outa them shoes, Miss Addie."

"I wanted to wait until the end of summer to buy him some new ones. I'm hoping we'll have a teacher for the school after harvest, and he and Jane Ann can go to school. Did you know that he was worried he'd have to go to Mr. Renshaw?"

"I knowed it. He don't like that man none a'tall. Said he pinches him ever chance he gets and puts his hands on his butt."

Addie turned in shock. *"Where?"*

"Ya know . . . back here." Trisha placed her hand on her buttocks.

"Why would he do such a thing?"

"Miss Addie! If you don't beat all. Yo're

green as grass 'bout the nasties that go on. Don't ya know why that ol' puke is botherin' Colin?"

"No, I don't. I declare! It's downright strange, a grown man doing that to a boy like Colin."

Trisha rolled her eyes to the ceiling. "Yo're the limit, Miss Addie. Don't ya know 'bout grown men likin' boys?" Trisha lifted her hands and let them fall to her sides. "If'n I gotta tell ya, I will. Miss Addie, that pig-ugly old fart's got more on his mind than workin' Colin in the field. He's a-wantin' to get him in bed."

"In bed?" Addie's eyebrows rose. "Why on earth would he want to do that?"

" 'Cause he's a nasty man, that's why. Ya been here on this place all yore life an' ya ain't knowin' what all is goin' in Orleans an' Natchez an' on them riverboats." Trisha threw up her hands. "If'n I spelled it out fer ya what all I seen with my own eyes, ya'd swear I was a-tellin' ya a windy, and then ya'd puke."

Addie studied Trisha's beautiful face. She had been no more than fifteen when she had come out of the woods, cold, hungry, and sick. Since that time she had been away from the farm not more than a half-dozen times. Addie wondered what she had seen to make

50

her so bitter about men.

Trisha seldom mentioned her former life, but once she had told Addie that her grandmother had been a beautiful quadroon, her mother an octoroon. Her father, a plantation owner, had loved her mother but couldn't marry her. Trisha and her mother had lived in a small house in New Orleans until she was ten years old. After her mother died, her father had brought her to the big house to work in the kitchens. When he went off to war, his wife, whom he'd married to get a heir, had sold her.

"Bad thin's go on. Badder than ya ever thought of." Trisha's long, curly hair framed her worried-looking face. "There's high-tone *gentlemen* that's worser than ruttin' hogs, an' there's them that'll steal women an' younguns for them high-tones to play with. Some of 'em tie up naked women an' whip their butts with a willow switch an' do nasty thin's to little boys like Dillon an' Colin an' little girls like Jane Ann —"

"Trisha!" Addie gasped, stunned. "I can't believe —"

"Ya better hear me. 'Tis what ol' Renshaw wants with Colin."

"But . . . how?"

"He'll make 'im . . . play with his . . . thing! He already made him touch it."

51

"Oh, dear God! Dear God!" Addie sank down in a chair and looked up at Trisha. "They do *that?* I never dreamed —"

"Course ya didn't know." Trisha was about to offer more details when she suddenly stopped speaking and tilted her head toward the door. "Shhh . . ." Then, fast as a cat, she sprang to the table and blew out the lamp. "Somebody comin'."

"I'll get the front door." Addie heard Trisha close the kitchen door and drop the bar. She thanked God for the girl's sharp ears, because Addie hadn't heard a thing.

She grabbed the rifle on her way to the door to pull it closed, leaving only a crack so she could look out. Now she heard the low murmur of masculine voices and saw the dark shapes of two riders coming up the lane. The sound of their horses' hooves were muted by the deep sand. The riders walked their horses up to the porch, allowing the animals to trample Addie's precious flower beds. She gasped in outrage and quietly eased the door shut.

"Tol' ya I saw a light."

The coarse voice that reached the ear Addie had pressed to the door was that of one of the men who had accosted them in town.

"If'n they think that li'l ol' door'll keep

us out, they's barkin' up the wrong tree. *Haw-haw!*" This voice was high with excitement.

"Ya can have the nigger gal. I'm goin' ta take the strut outa that hoity-toity woman what turned her nose up."

"She called ya horse-dung. *Haw-haw-haw!*" The man laughed as he pounded on the door so hard that it shook.

"Rotten, dirty drunkards!" Addie whispered.

The outside noise brought Colin running from his bed. "Miss Addie, what is it?"

"Some liquored-up swine, Colin. They'll leave in a little bit."

"Pur . . . ty la . . . dy. Open the door. Ya got comp . . . nee!" *Thump! Thump!* "We goin' ta give ya a real good time."

"C'mon, ma 'am. Ya ain't got no customers in there."

"You'd better leave before you get yourselves in serious trouble. You can find your pleasure in town," Addie called loudly through the closed door.

"We done rode all this way out here an' we ain't goin' back till mornin'."

"You're wasting your time here. Go back to town or wherever you came from." Addie was prepared to use the gun to protect her home and family.

"Open the door! Gawddammit! I ain't a-tellin' ya again." Anger was in the voice now. "Ya been puttin' the fellers ta that nigger gal fer worthless Reb paper. We got Yankee coin to pay."

Rage rose like a geyser in Addie. *Crude, vulgar beasts. How dare they come to my home and spout such filth!*

"Get away from here or I'll unload both barrels of this buffalo gun right through the door," she shouted.

"Ain't no reason to get all riled up. We's wantin' ta get our ashes hauled, is all."

"You low-life, chicken-livered polecats!" Addie yelled, her voice shrill. "Get your filthy, rotten carcasses off my porch."

"Git outta the way, Miss Addie," Trisha said as she moved to lift the bar. "I'll blow that trash clear down to the road."

"Don't open the door," Addie hissed.

"Ain't no hockey-head gonna talk ta ya that way —"

Trisha's words were cut off as heavy boots struck the bottom of the door, causing it to strain against the bar.

"If'n ya don't open this door we'll break out ever' winder in this house. We didn't ride out here ta be turned away by the likes of a whore and a nigger. If'n ya don't —"

*Bang!*

54

At the sound of the shot at close range, Addie froze and Trisha drew in a gasping breath. A hush followed; then a man's voice broke the stillness:

"The lady said you're not welcome. Get on your horses and ride out."

"Well . . . ah . . . by Gawd!"

"Who'er you?"

"A man with a gun pointed at that lump sittin' on your shoulders."

"If ya had pleasurin' in mind, mister, we can all take us a turn. Reckon the two of 'em could give us some sport."

"Who is it?" Colin whispered.

"I don't know. Shhh!"

"Ride out now or go with a few holes in your hide."

"Now see here —"

"He's a-wantin' 'em hisself!"

"I've no use for cowards who force themselves on women. Are you going or do I start shooting?"

"If'n yore wantin' the nigger an' the whore — yore welcome to 'em."

*Bang!*

"Ohhh, Gawd! Ya shot me!"

"This time it was your hat. Next time, your head."

"Why'd ya do that fer?"

"So you'll be more careful with your mouth

when talking about a lady."

"They ain't —"

"C'mon. Let's go. That crazy son of a bitch'll kill us over a couple of split-tails."

The sound of creaking saddle leather reached Addie, then fading masculine voices.

"They're gone."

"Who's that man?" Trisha whispered.

"I don't know."

"Did he leave?"

"I don't know that either." Addie eased the door open a crack. "Mister," she called. "Are you still there?"

"Yes, ma'am." On hearing the male voice, a sharp new pang of apprehension went through Addie.

"Thank you."

"Was a pleasure."

"Who are you?"

After a pause, he said, "Just a passerby. Do I have your permission to bed down in your barn?"

"Well . . . yes, if you want to."

Addie waited, and when he said nothing more, she motioned for Trisha to go to the back window.

"What do you think, Colin? Can we trust him?"

"Yes'm. I'm thinkin' so."

"I wonder who he is."

"Might be that big man that helped us in town."

"Could be."

"Why do men come here?" Colin asked.

"They want to come in and . . . drink, and . . . talk." Addie fumbled for words.

"When I get full-growed there ain't nobody goin' to bother you and Trisha."

"Oh, Colin. Your mama would be so proud of you, just as I am."

She put her arms around the boy and hugged him. He allowed the show of affection because it was dark. For a long moment he leaned against her. She held his wiry little body close and smoothed the hair back from his face. Her heart ached for him. He turned his face to her neck for an instant before moving away, then he took the rifle out of her hand and stood it by the door.

"That man put his horse in the pen. He's gonna bed down under the pecan tree by the porch," Trisha said as she slipped back into the room.

"It's so dark," Addie said, peering out the window. "For the life of me, I don't see how you can see anything."

"It's my nigger blood," Trisha said dryly. "It ort ta be good for somethin'."

"Trisha, for goodness' sake!"

"Goodness ain't got nothin' to do with it,"

Trisha replied with a nervous giggle.

"I suppose we might as well be in bed as sitting here in the dark."

"I ain't a-shuttin' my eyes with that 'passerby' out there."

"If he wanted to come in he would have tried it by now."

"He might get him a notion later on."

"It would take a battering ram to break down that door. Surely one of us would hear it or the breaking of glass if he tried the window."

Still grumbling, Trisha went to the room where she slept with Jane Ann. Colin, in his long sleeping gown, followed and lay down on the trundle bed. Addie lingered in the doorway.

"He ain't comin' in," Colin said. "I know he ain't, but if he tries it, I'll hear and come with the buffalo gun."

"You're a dear sweet boy. You have ears like a fox and Trisha has eyes like an owl. Do you reckon that stranger out there knows what he's up against?"

Fully dressed, Addie lay down on the bed beside her son. It had been an eventful day — the end of one important chapter in her life and the beginning of another. For the past few years she had been marking time, waiting to see if Kirby would come back.

In the interim she had learned a lot, grown stronger and more confident. It seemed to her that she had now been cut loose to decide which direction her life and that of her family would take.

She remembered a proverb often quoted by her father: "Yesterday will not be called upon again." A thought came to mind as her eyelids drooped and her mouth opened in a yawn. *Yesteryear is gone; tomorrow is a window waiting to be opened.*

John Tallman turned his horse into a split-rail enclosure where three sheep fled to the far corner and eyed him suspiciously and a black-and-white cow stood patiently chewing her cud. He carried his saddle and blanket roll to the tall pecan tree beside the porch and dropped them on the ground.

Sheep! The only thing he liked about them was what was made from their wool. They were stupid, smelly creatures that, when turned on their backs, would lie there and die because they didn't have the sense to roll over and get back on their feet.

John flipped out his blanket, sat down on the end of it, and removed his calf-high soft leather moccasins and his socks. He dug into his saddlebag and pulled out a pair of the wool socks he had bought at the store. His father had told him at an early age to take care of his feet: "You never know when you'll have to depend on them to save your life." Therefore, he wore good thick-soled moccasins and changed his socks every two or three days. Mrs. Hyde made a mighty fine pair of socks, he thought as he pulled them on. They were smooth and without the ridges that made sore spots.

He hadn't realized that the violet-eyed woman was so firmly entrenched in his mind until he became infuriated by the talk he heard about her in the tavern where he'd eaten supper.

"I heared that nigger gal eats at the table with 'em." The man spoke as if it was the strangest thing he had ever been told. "Now don't *that* beat all?"

The remark had caused John to stab his fork hard into his meat. He had no patience for ignorance and bigotry.

"Ain't no decent white woman I ever heard of allowin' that. Ya know what they say — water seeks its own level."

"— And birds of a kind flock together."

"No tellin' what they been up to out there. Could be they was runnin' one of them underground-railroad stops, helpin' slaves escape to the North."

"I just betcha that was what she was doin'."

"She ain't doin' it now. She's doin' somethin' else. We're goin' out there tonight, by golly damn."

"Stay away from Mrs. Hyde. Hear?" The bartender wiped a wet cloth over the bar and moved to wait on an impatient customer. "There ain't no truth in what you're saying about her."

The men continued to talk. "Heard her man ain't comin' back . . . that's if she ever had one. *Haw-haw-haw!*"

"Horse hockey! She's had one. Heard a feller say a slack-handed free-wheeler stayed out thar one summer and left her a-breedin' when he joined up."

"She ain't breedin' now, less'n one a them fellers that's been goin' out thar to see the high-yeller got in *her* drawers. Ya can have the snooty bitch. I aim to get me a juicy piece a that hot little colored twat."

"All yore goin' on is hearsay," the bartender said. "There ain't a man jack among ya that can stand here and tell me ya got a welcome from Mrs. Hyde . . . so hush yore mouths, else get outa my place!"

"What ya gettin' so het up for? Ya wantin' to go a-courtin' the widder Hyde an're 'fraid we'll muddy the hole? *Haw-haw-haw!*"

"Shut yore foul mouth. Better yet — get yore butt out an' don't come back!"

61

John Tallman finished his coffee and rose from the table. He wanted to plant his fist in the man's filthy mouth. But then he told himself that he didn't need to get into a fight over a woman with whom he had exchanged only a few words, and placed some coins on the table and walked out. He was standing on the porch when the two men came out bragging about the trip they were going to make to the widow Hyde's farm.

Now, lying on his blanket with his hands beneath his head, John was glad he had followed them. He looked at the dark shape of the modest house with its flower beds, carefully tended vegetable garden, and neat woodpile. The zigzag, split-rail fence had been mended with deadfalls. A piece of tin had been nailed over a hole in the barn roof. The cow stall was clean, the chickens penned for the night.

Addie Hyde was a woman of quality, just as he had thought her to be when he had seen her in the store.

"The first impression a person makes on you is oftentimes the correct one. Trust your own instincts; think your own thoughts; follow your own trail." That was the advice Rain Tallman had given his sons.

John touched the scab beneath his jaw. For the past ten years he had lived by the gun and become skilled at using the bowie knife. He had killed, swiftly and mercilessly, but only in order to save his own life. It had never been easy for him to kill, although he had lived among men who understood no other way of life.

John had come east to buy goods for the trading post his father had set up to serve the Indians and settlers coming down the Santa Fe Trail into New Mexico Territory. This was his third trip in as many years. This time he had made the side trip to Quill's Station on the Wabash River to visit his cousin, Zachary Quill. Now he was eager to get back to his ranch, to the cool, thick-walled adobe house he had built for the family he hoped to have someday.

John chuckled when he thought of how his mother nagged him to find a woman and fill the empty rooms in his house with children. He chuckled again and wondered what she would think if she could see him now, lying under a pecan tree, protecting a widow and a passel of younguns instead of sleeping on a soft bed in a hotel.

He was certain that he would never find a woman to equal the legendary Amy Tallman. In her midsixties, she still rode beside her husband, fought beside him, and loved him with a fiery passion. She, in turn, was the light of her husband's life. They had built a home in the mountains north of Fort Smith and raised two boys and two girls, of which John Spotted Elk Tallman, named for his Indian grandfather who had been killed during the great earthquake of 1811, was the youngest.

Six years before, realizing that soon their sons would be expected to fight for a cause they did not believe in, Rain and Amy Tallman had packed their family and worldly goods in three freight wagons, crossed the Indian territories and settled in northern New Mexico.

Birds fluttered in the branches above John's head. He fervently hoped they had emptied their bowels before roosting for the night. A yellow-white moon rose above the dark clump of trees, causing millions of stars to pale. An owl gave a mournful call; a wolf howled in the distance. All were familiar sounds to John.

Then a child coughed inside the house, bed springs squeaked, and once again his thoughts turned to a pair of violet eyes with dark lashes and hair the color of a buckskin horse he'd had when he was young. He turned and pillowed his head on his arm, suddenly uncomfortable by the sexual desire that swept over him.

Hell! Maybe it was time he took a wife.

# CHAPTER

## * 4 *

Addie awakened suddenly, lifted her head off the pillow, and listened. She heard the ringing blow of an ax. Through the window on the east wall she saw the light of dawn. Her son was sleeping soundly with his hand tucked beneath his cheek. Addie rolled to the side of the bed, got to her feet and hurried to the kitchen. She was lifting the bar from the door so that she could open it a crack and look out when Trisha appeared beside her, the rifle ready in her hand.

"Who is it?" she whispered.

"I'm about to find out."

Addie recognized the woodchopper at once. He was the man who had offered to carry their sugar to the wagon. Not many men wore flat-crowned leather hats. As she watched, his powerful arms lifted the ax and brought it down with enough force to slice through the log. He bent and tossed the stove-length stick onto a growing pile.

"Who's out there?" Trisha whispered.

"It's the man who was at the store, the one who wore a leather hat and shirt hanging outside his britches."

"What's he doin' out there at our wood-pile?"

Addie opened the door. "He's chopping wood."

"I know *that*. What for?"

"I don't know. For Pete's sake, Trisha, put the gun down."

"That's bugger's got somethin' on his mind or he'd not be doin' that. Ain't no man doin' choppin' work for womenfolk less'n he's wantin' somethin'."

"Well, let's just ask him. No use pretending he's not there."

"I'm holdin' this gun right on 'im long's he's on this place."

Addie took a string from her pocket, gathered her loose hair at her nape, and tied it. After she straightened her dress and made sure it was buttoned to the neck, she stepped out onto the porch.

"Good morning!" she called.

"Mornin'." The ax never missed a stroke.

"You did enough for us last night. You don't have to do that."

"I know." With one blow of the ax a chunk of wood fell. He picked it up and tossed it onto the pile.

"We appreciate what you did —"

With a wave of his hand he dismissed the deed as nothing, then he dragged another heavy tree limb to the chopping block.

"How we goin' to milk the cow with that . . . that buzzard out there?" Trisha hissed.

"I'd be obliged if you'd tell that girl to stop pointing the end of that rifle at me. It might go off." John tipped his hat back and wiped his brow with his shirt sleeve.

"If'n it does, you sure be a gone goose," Trisha yelled.

"That's what I'm afraid of," John said dryly, and swung the ax again.

"Miss Addie —" Colin came bounding out of the kitchen door with the big buffalo gun in his hands.

"Good Lord!" John stared. "You're about as helpless out here as a den of rattlesnakes."

Addie smiled. "We can pretty much take care of ourselves."

"I can see that."

"You're welcome to some breakfast."

"Miss Addie!" Trisha gasped. "Why you say that?"

John leaned on the ax handle and studied the trio on the porch before he accepted her offer.

"Thank you, ma'am."

"It'll be a little while before it's ready. We have chores to do first."

"I ain't goin' out and milk no cow with him out there," Trisha said crossly.

"Trisha, it'll be broad daylight in a few minutes," Addie said patiently to the girl. "If he meant to harm us he would have forced his way in last night. We'll *all* go do the chores. I'll gather eggs while you milk and Colin feeds the stock. Colin, put away the gun. You, too, Trisha."

"I'm a-keepin' hold of this gun, an' I ain't takin' my eyes off'n that . . . 'passerby.' "

"That's going to be hard to do when you milk. I'll get the bucket and hold the gun while you wash your hands."

John was still chopping wood when the women came from the barn. The chickens, free of the pen, were clucking and busily searching for grubs among the woodchips. Carrying the bucket of milk in one hand and the rifle in the other, Trisha gave him a wide berth on her way back to the house. Addie stopped to speak to him. She held the gathered end of her apron in one hand.
John stood looking down at her, waiting for her to speak. Time and space seemed to shrink to the spot where they stood beside the woodpile.

"The hens were good to us this morning. I can give you eggs with soda biscuits and gravy. We're out of fresh meat."

The thought crossed John's mind that he had seen prettier women, but this one drew attention because of the light way she moved: chin up, shoulders back, and a proud lift to her head. Her hair *was* the color of that buckskin horse. It was thick and fine, too, and wisps of it, stirred by the morning breeze, danced around her face.

He studied her with a determination to find some fault, some flaw that would prove that what had been said about her in the tavern had at least a sprinkling of truth. But the cool calmness of her eyes shut him out.

"Does this mean that you no longer think I came out here with . . . ah . . . less than noble intentions?"

Addie felt a blush flooding her cheeks. She hesitated, trying to think of an answer to give him, wanting to be honest, but unable to understand what had prompted her to invite him to breakfast. Her thoughts milled about in mild disorder, and in the end she shrugged, an oddly girlish gesture.

"No. It doesn't mean that we're not afraid of you. But there comes a time when one must take a chance. I'm gambling that you're an honest, decent man and have not come here to cause us grief." She tried to smile, but it didn't reach her eyes. Her gaze remained on him, intense, unfathomable, and, for an instant, disturbingly vulnerable.

John removed his hat and wiped his brow again with the sleeve of his shirt. He rested a foot on the chopping block, leaned his elbow on his thigh, and pointed to the house. His smile lent a fleeting warmth to his dark features.

"The girl wants to shoot me."

Addie's eyes never left his face. "She's had rough treatment. It's made her fearful."

"Do you get many callers like the ones last night?"

"Now and then. What brought you out here?" She gazed at him steadily, her violet eyes now openly inquisitive. "I know you weren't just passing by."

"I heard talk at the tavern. What they said didn't match up with the impression I had when I met you at the store."

"I have an idea what was said about me and Trisha. I want to thank —"

"Please don't thank me again, Mrs. Hyde. It isn't necessary."

"You know my name. I don't know yours."

"Tallman. John Tallman."

"How do you do." Addie offered her hand. John grasped it briefly and let it go.

"Miss Addie!" Colin yelled from the porch. "Preacher Sikes is comin'."

"Oh, fiddle! What a way to start the day." Addie turned toward the house, then back. "Mr. Tallman, would you mind staying in the barn until the preacher is gone? He would just *love* to find something . . . improper about your being here."

"Well, sure. But I'm not forgetting about the soda biscuits and gravy." His slow smile once more altered the stern cast of his features. Slapping his hat back on his head, he hurried to the barn.

Addie ran to the house, deposited the eggs on the kitchen table, and told Trisha and Colin to stay out of sight. She rushed out onto the front porch just as the preacher's buggy pulled to a stop in the front yard. Hoping to discourage him from coming into the house, she walked quickly down the steps to greet Preacher Sikes.

"Morning, Preacher. Isn't this a fine morning?"

"It is that, Sister Hyde."

"You're out early."

"Have business in Freepoint. I just stopped by to tell ya that Brother Renshaw'll be over in a day or two to get Colin. He has a need for him to pick bugs off'n his 'tater plants. Have the boy's stuff packed and ready."

71

The words hit Addie like a dash of icy water. For an instant her mind froze. Then she remembered what Trisha had told her about Mr. Renshaw, and the heat of her anger thawed the chill that had swept over her.

"I need Colin. I need him a lot more than Mr. Renshaw does. I thought I made it clear to you yesterday that he will stay here."

"Woman, ya got no say as to where that boy goes," the preacher said firmly, his small eyes going hard. "Ya can keep the girl."

"They are brother and sister and should not be separated. As far as they know, they have no other living kin. It would be cruel and unfair to separate them." Addie's tone reflected both her frustration and her determination.

"They don't *belong* to you, Sister Hyde. Ya just had the loan of 'em."

"They don't *belong* to you either. In case you've forgotten, the war is over. *Whites* as well as coloreds are free."

"Not in the case of minors. They do as they're told. Brother Renshaw has offered to feed and clothe the boy in exchange for work."

" 'Brother Renshaw has offered'?" Addie repeated with a curl of her lips. "Wasn't that generous of him!"

"He's doin' his Christian duty. He offered

72

to take a turn as others has done."

"Hell and damnation! I don't give a holy damn if that dirty old fool offered his whole dad-blasted farm. He will *not* have Colin! And, what's more — it's not your God-given right to take that child out of this home where he is loved and wanted." By now her voice had risen until she was shouting. "Dammit to hell! Admit it, Preacher — you're getting money for turning this child over to that pervert!"

"Blasphemy!" The preacher gasped, and his body went rigid. "Yore mama and papa would turn over in their graves to hear such comin' from yore mouth!" The man's cheeks swelled, his face turned the color of a turnip, and his jaws quivered. "That boy was put in my care. He goes where *I* say he goes."

"If it takes blasphemy to get your attention, so be it! I don't give a tinker's damn how much money that dirty old man is giving you or if he's building you a church the size of the capitol down in Little Rock. I'll not turn that child over to be mistreated by a degraded beast like Renshaw. Colin stays here, and anyone who comes to get him will be met with a load of buckshot."

"Well! That's settles it. Have the girl's thin's ready too. I'll find a *Christian* home for her. I been hearin' 'bout the goin's on out here. Never believed it till now. You're headed straight for hell, *Mrs.* Hyde."

"And so are you, you damned old hypocrite! You don't have Colin's interest at heart. You care no more for these children than if they were . . . dogs!"

"Cussin' like a riverman! Jesus, forgive her. Almighty God, this poor creature has been sucked down into the devil's snake pit!" The preacher's eyes rolled back in his head. He looked as if he were in a trance. Then, bright, hate-filled eyes glared into Addie's face. "I pray that God'll forgive me for leavin' poor innocent children in this den of sin. But no longer, God" — he looked toward the heavens — "no longer!"

"You'll have to kill me to get either one of them," Addie yelled.

Preacher Sikes snapped the whip against the horse's rump and the surprised animal leaped forward. Addie barely had time to jump out of the way.

"Did you hear me?" she screamed after the departing buggy. "If you dare come back here again I'll fill your fat hide with buckshot. You hypocrite! You — cold-hearted, nasty old bastard!" She shook her fists at the buggy careening down the lane. "Depraved old reprobate! Bible-spoutin' son of a bitch!"

Addie was so angry that words she had

never uttered in her life came boiling up out of the rage she had held back since her frank talk with Trisha about why old Renshaw wanted Colin. She was so frustrated that all she could do now was stand there and stamp her feet. Then she burst into tears.

"Miss Addie!" Colin and Trisha rushed to her side. "What that old toad say to you?"

"Oh, Miss Addie! Don't cry!" Colin's freckled face was a picture of despair.

"Someday I'm a-gonna shoot that ol' snot-nosed piss-pot right in the guts!" Trisha lifted the end of the rifle toward the departing buggy.

Addie's tears suddenly turned to hysterical laughter. She put her arms around Colin and the girl and held on to them because her knees were weak.

"Oh, aren't we a sight. I cuss 'em and you shoot 'em." Tears streamed down Addie's cheeks. "I said things I've never said before."

"Felt good to cuss 'em, though, didn't it?" Trisha said.

"I lost my temper. I've . . . ruined every-thing —"

"Is he . . . is he gonna make me go?" The desperate look on Colin's young face tore at Addie's heart.

"No, honey. You're not leaving us as long

75

as Trisha and I have shells to put in the gun."

"It's what he said, ain't it?"

"Yes, it's what he said." Addie couldn't lie to the boy even to make it easier for him. "But that doesn't mean you'll go."

"What about Jane Ann?"

"Mr. Renshaw wants only you. The preacher is mad at me because of some of the things I said. He said he'll find another place for Jane Ann. But he'll not take either one of you. I'll find a way. . . ."

The boy's proud little face crumbled slowly as realization sank in. The tears he had fought to hold back now rolled down his cheeks. Addie pulled him to her and felt the racking sobs that tore through his body.

"C-can't we go away? Can't we go to Cala . . . fornie?"

"Try not to worry, Colin. We'll do everything in our power to keep you right here with us. We'll think of something."

"I done thought a somethin'!" Trisha spoke in a choked voice. "I'll kill that . . . that ol' butt-pinchin' pile a horse shit!" For a moment Addie was frightened, for she was sure that the girl was capable of carrying out her threat.

Addie hugged Colin closer to her and felt the wetness of his tears on the front of her dress. Her heart ached for the poor little boy.

His arms were wrapped tightly about her waist, something he had never done before. It showed the depth of his despair.

Looking over Colin's head, Addie saw Mr. Tallman, the "passerby" as Trisha called him, standing on the porch. Dillon was on one side of him, Jane Ann on the other. Both children were still in their nightclothes. Addie's eyes met the man's intent dark blue ones and held. His hat was off and she could see the line of irritation that creased his brow.

"Oh, my! I forgot about him."

When she spoke, Colin stiffened, then tore himself from Addie's embrace, and bolted around the corner of the house. Addie watched him, then turned stricken eyes to the man on the porch.

"I'll fix your breakfast," she said in a dull voice.

Trisha took a step forward, but Addie put her hand on her arm. "See about Colin, Trisha."

"But —"

"Give me the gun. I'll be all right."

Trisha hesitated, then handed it over. "Ya holler if'n he makes a move."

"I will. Go on now. Colin needs you."

Trisha lifted her skirt above her bare ankles, then as she ran by the porch, she paused.

"White man, ya hurt Miss Addie, I shoot ya dead."

With the barrel of the rifle pointed at the ground, Addie went up the steps to the porch and into the house. John and the children followed.

"That girl seems determined to shoot me."

"She's distrustful of men. And I can't blame her." Addie stood the rifle in the corner. "Jane Ann, you and Dillon go get dressed, then come wash up for breakfast."

"Why is Colin cryin'?" Jane Ann pulled on Addie's hand.

"I'll tell you about it later, honey. Get dressed and help Dillon, will you?"

"Is me and Colin gettin' took away from here?"

"No, punkin." Addie hugged the girl to her side for a brief moment, then released her. "Now, scoot."

After the children were gone, Addie carried the teakettle to the washbench.

"Sit down, Mr. Tallman. I'll wash right quick, so I can start the meal." Addie soaped her hands, rinsed them, and splashed water on her face. After she used the towel, she emptied the washbowl and placed a clean towel beside it. "The water in the teakettle is hot."

"I washed at the well when I realized I'd

not be seen by your visitor."

"It'll take a little time to get the oven hot enough for biscuits." As she spoke, Addie opened the firebox and shoved in another stick of wood. Her motions were jerky and her hands shook as she put the flat pan on the stove, added grease, then brought the bowl she used for making biscuits to the work bench.

Trying to keep her back to the man at the table, she made a well in the flour in the bowl, then added salt, soda, and a spoonful of lard. After pouring in buttermilk, she worked the flour into the dough until it was stiff enough to pinch off, shape, and put in the pan.

Her heart was pounding. More than anything she wanted to crawl away to cry, but she worked swiftly and without unnecessary movement. Soon the gravy was bubbling in the skillet and she began to set the table.

John watched every move the woman made. Something was tearing her apart inside. She had not looked directly at him, but he caught the shimmer of unshed tears in her eyes.

"Dillon won't let me fasten his 'spenders. He runs off." The small boy, with Jane Ann behind him, ran into the room and wedged himself between his mother and the table.

"See there," Jane Ann said. "He's actin' up 'cause of the company."

"Dillon, please, behave now."

"Come here, you little sidewinder." John reached out and lifted the child onto his lap. "My sister's got a young scutter about your size. He's as frisky as a pup."

Surprised to find himself sitting on a man's lap, Dillon went stone-still, with his eyes locked on John's face.

"We had a dog."

"Was he big and mean?"

"He barked and pulled on the rope."

"What was his name?"

"Lincoln."

"Lincoln? I bet that would tickle old Abe —"

"Can I touch your mustache?"

"If you'll let me fasten your suspenders."

The boy's eyes were round and blue and solemn. "Me first?"

"Not until we shake on it man to man. I've got to be sure you won't break and run. A man keeps his word." John held out his hand. Dillon put his into it. "I promise to let you feel my mustache."

"Um . . . I promise to let ya hook my 'spenders."

As Addie watched her son sitting on the man's lap, a tear rolled down her cheek. She wiped it away quickly and turned to Jane Ann.

"Wash up. I'll brush and braid your hair after breakfast." Addie went to the door. "Trisha! Colin!" she called. "Breakfast is ready."

Addie was pulling the pan of golden-brown biscuits from the oven when the two came in. Colin went directly to the washbowl. Trisha scowled at Dillon as he sat on the passerby's lap, his chubby fingers fingering the mustache that drooped down on each side of the firm mouth. Jane Ann leaned against the man's knee and giggled.

"Get out a jar of plum butter, please, Trisha. We're ready to sit down."

Trisha brought the jar to the table, then backed off to the far corner of the kitchen.

"Take your places. That means you too, Dillon," Addie said when the child made no move to leave John's lap. "I'll pour the coffee." Addie wrapped a cloth around the handle of the granite coffeepot and returned to the table. Trisha remained standing, her back turned, looking out the open door. "Trisha, take your place and help Jane Ann."

John looked up, saw the worry in Addie's eyes, and realized that Trisha was afraid he would feel insulted if she sat at the table.

"I've not had biscuits like these in months,

miss," he said to Trisha. "I'll not be able to enjoy them if I have to worry about you shooting me in the back. And it's been longer than that since I sat at the table with *two* pretty ladies."

"Why you sayin' that, white man? You know I'm a colored," Trisha hissed as she spun around. Her golden eyes shone like those of an angry cat.

"So you've got a dab of color. I'm part Irish, part Scot, part French. My pa's stepfather was Shawnee. My grandmother married him because she wanted to, not because she had to. I'm named for him. John Spotted Elk Tallman. Is that the reason you won't eat at the table with me?"

"Ya know it ain't!"

"Then please sit down. I'm so hungry for these biscuits I could eat a sick dog."

"Ugh!" Jane Ann said, and stuck out her tongue.

Trisha flounced around the table and plopped herself down in her chair.

Addie hadn't realized that she was holding her breath until she let it out. She looked into the man's eyes and silently thanked him with hers.

The meal would have been eaten in silence had not Dillon and Jane Ann kept up a continual chatter. They were enjoying themselves. Addie had told them to hush up only once, when Dillon started to say something about going to the outhouse. John talked to Jane Ann and Dillon, knowing the others had troubles on their minds.

"When I was a boy, I found a baby skunk. I don't know what happened to its mother."

"Did it stink?" Jane Ann asked.

"Not at first. I carried it around in a pouch I hung around my neck. One day I climbed a tree and couldn't get down with the pouch. My mother stood under the tree and told me to drop it and she would catch it. I dropped it. We discovered then it was old enough to . . . you know."

The children laughed. Colin sat with his head bowed over his plate.

"What did she do?" Dillon asked, gazing into John's face.

"She made me take it to the woods and let it go."

"What was its name?"

"Rose. I guess I hoped she would smell like one." John caught Addie's eye and winked. Just a hint of a smile touched her lips before she turned away. "Thanks for the meal, ma'am. I don't know when I've had better. I'd like to repair that rail fence if the boy here would give me a hand. In a few places a good strong wind will blow it over."

Colin got to his feet without looking up. Addie rose too.

"Colin . . . if you'd rather not —"

"I want to. I can't spend my life hidin' behind your skirts, Miss Addie."

Addie stood in the doorway and watched the boy walk across the yard with the tall man. She was suddenly struck with the thought that had Kirby Hyde been more like this man, he would have survived to come home to her and their son, and now she wouldn't feel so alone and scared.

# CHAPTER

## * 5 *

By midmorning, six posts had been replaced and rails added to the fence where needed. Colin worked alongside John, speaking only when spoken to. The boy was a good worker, often anticipating what was needed and fetching it before John asked. When they finished with the fence, they stood back to survey their work.

"It wouldn't hold a herd of wild horses, Colin, but it'll do for a horse, a cow, and a couple of sheep."

"Daisy and Myrtle wouldn't run off if we left 'em in the yard."

John looked down at the boy. It was the first time he had volunteered anything.

"They're a couple of smart horses. They know which side of the bread the butter is on."

"What's that mean?"

"It means they know a good thing when they see it. In other words, they want to stay with folks that are good to them and feed them."

Trisha, working in the garden, was watching them. The rifle was never far from her hand. John wondered if the gun was intended as protection against him or if she was expecting someone else.

The scene he had witnessed in the early morning stayed in John's mind as a disturbing presence. He could still hear Addie Hyde's heartbreaking sobs and see the two women and the boy holding on to one another in their despair. When Addie had looked up and seen him, her pride had taken over. She had lifted her head high; and although her cheeks were wet with her tears, she had sailed by him and calmly gone about doing what she had to do.

"Let's get a cool drink, Colin. I think we deserve it, don't you?"

At the well, John loosened the rope and let it slide through the pulley until he heard the bucket hit the water. After it filled, he drew it up, set it on the plank platform around the well, and reached for the dipper hanging on the post. He offered it to Colin.

"That crosspiece holding the pulley is pretty wobbly. If you have a length or two of wire, we could strengthen it."

After Colin drank, he handed back the dipper and walked to the barn. John drank, then carried the water bucket to the chickens' watering trough and emptied it.

Colin returned with a piece of rusty wire and a pair of iron pincers.

"It's the section resting on this post that's loose," John said, moving around the side of the well. "If I hoist you up on my shoulders, you can reach it and wrap that wire around it and the post in a figure eight."

Colin nodded. John took off his hat and swung Colin up to sit astride his neck. Then he steadied him while Colin put his bare feet on his shoulders and stood. John held on to the boy's legs while he worked. When he was finished, John lifted him down.

"Good job. It'll hold until that wire rusts through." John picked up his hat. "Are you ready to tackle the hole in the wall of the chicken house? It's a wonder a fox hasn't discovered that loose plank."

Colin shrugged.

"I'll get a sheet of loose tin from behind the barn. Do you have any nails?"

Colin nodded and went into the barn. When they met at the chicken house, the boy had a dozen square, rusty nails.

"If you have extras, it's a good idea to stick them down in lard or goose grease.

Keeps 'em from rusting and they drive easier."

After they had repaired the side of the flimsy chicken house, John boosted Colin up on top to nail a piece of tin over a hole in the roof. Later, he followed the silent boy into the barn and they put away the tools.

"Colin . . ." When John put his hand on the boy's shoulder, Colin flinched away, as if the hand were hot.

"What?" he said crossly.

"Something's wrong here. It's not my way to butt in to other folks' business, but if there's anything I can do to help, I will."

"Ain't nothin' ya can do." Colin turned his back and leaned against a stall railing.

"There might be. I can tell that Mrs. Hyde is troubled. That preacher riled her a-plenty. Lordy, she's got a temper."

"I ain't never seen her so mad. That damned old Sikes is a . . . a mule's ass!" Sobs clogged the boy's throat.

"You're probably right about that. What's the old son of a bitch up to?"

"He's . . . h-he's gonna take me away from Miss Addie."

"Take you? How can he do that? Is he kinfolk?"

"No!"

"Were you left in his care?" John asked gently.

"He says . . . he says our maw left us to the church."

"How long have you been with Miss Addie?"

"Two years. She likes us —"

"There's no doubt about that. It's plain she thinks a heap of you and your sister."

"She s-says I'm *her* . . . boy. Old Renshaw's a . . . a bastard!"

Colin turned suddenly, threw his arms about John's waist, and pressed his face against him. Deep racking sobs shook the boy.

Stunned, John stood there with his hands on the boy's shoulders, not knowing what to say or do. He had once seen his mother cry like this, when his baby sister died. He was trying to think of comforting words to say when Trisha darted into the barn with the end of the rifle pointed right at him.

"Git away from 'im! I shoot ya dead, white man!"

Soft, tumbled black curls framed her face and cascaded about her shoulders. Her face could have been etched in stone except for her shining golden eyes. On bare feet, she stood poised and ready to strike. She was like the small, deadly copperhead snake so

89

common in the Oklahoma Territory.

"Trisha! No!" Colin turned, his back against John, and held out his arms as if to protect him. "He ain't done nothin'."

"He got hold of ya —"

"He might . . . could do somethin' to help —"

"Ha! Ain't no *passerby* gonna do somethin'. This here gun's gonna do somethin'."

John grasped Colin's shoulders and moved him aside. "You've been dead set on shooting me since I came here," he said far more calmly than he felt. "I'm getting kind of tired of it."

"I ain't carin' what yore tired of. Ya touch that boy and I blow yore head off."

Colin went to Trisha, put his hand on the rifle barrel, and pushed it down.

"He ain't done nothin'," he said again.

"You sure as hell need help, lady. I was thinkin' to offer," John said. "Now I'm thinking I'd better hightail it out of here while I can still fork a horse."

"Don't go!" Colin blurted.

Trisha rested the stock of the rifle on the ground and glanced from one to the other with a puzzled look.

"Why you say that?" Her eyes honed in on Colin.

"I don't know. Somebody's got to help."

"What's this about the preacher taking Colin to someone named Renshaw? Is that what upset Mrs. Hyde?" John asked.

"He ain't takin' 'im! I kill that sucker first!" Trisha drew in a deep, quivering breath. Her nostrils flared angrily.

"Has Mrs. Hyde talked to a magistrate?"

"I ain't knowin' nothin' 'bout that. I know preacher ain't givin' Colin to that ol' piss-pot hockey-head to diddle with."

"Diddle with?" John's dark brows drew together.

Trisha threw up one hand and rolled her eyes to the ceiling. Her expression was one of disgust.

"Are ya so dumb ya don't know what *diddle* is?"

John continued to look at the girl. Then suddenly his eyes hardened and narrowed. The anger deep within him caught fire and flared.

"If you mean what I think you do, I'd like to have a private talk with Colin." The dark blue eyes holding Trisha's did not waver. Neither did her golden ones.

"Ya hurt him, I kill ya."

"Fair enough."

"Miss Addie say come to dinner."

"We'll be there in a few minutes."

"Colin?"

"Yeah. In a minute."

Trisha turned and ran lightly from the barn.

"You will sit in your usual place," Addie said in answer to her son's question. "Mr. Tallman will sit beside Colin. Put the knife and fork alongside the plate, Jane Ann. Oh, Trisha, are they coming?" she asked when the girl came in from the porch.

"In a minute," she said crossly, and stood the rifle in the corner.

"Is something wrong?"

"Colin likes that . . . *passerby*."

"That worries you?" Addie came closer to murmur so that the children wouldn't hear.

"Yeah. Could be he ain't fittin' for crow-bait."

"Let's give him the benefit of the doubt. He did a lot of work here this morning. *Dillon!*" Addie caught her son's arm as he ran by her. "No running in the house. After dinner you and Jane Ann can chase yourselves silly — outside. You'd better go to the outhouse, then come in and wash up."

"You don't tell Jane Ann to go to the outhouse."

"Jane Ann is old enough to know when she needs to go."

"Me too."

"Not always. Sometimes you put it off until it's almost too late."

Grumbling, Dillon went out and Addie followed him to the porch. Just as she suspected, her son was pulling his suspenders off over his shoulders, preparing to let down his britches.

"Dillon Hyde! Don't you dare do it in the yard! Get to the outhouse or no bread pudding for you, young man. Hear?"

Addie was tired. The preacher's morning visit had drained her of energy. Too, she and Trisha had dug up a bucketful of little new potatoes, which she had washed at the well. They were now boiling on the stove, as were the collards, with a bit of smoked meat for flavor.

Lord, what would she do if the preacher and a group of men came to get Colin? She firmly intended to hold them off with the gun if necessary. But then what? Would Sikes go to the magistrate and demand that she turn Colin over to him? He wouldn't back down now and lose face with his flock. That much was certain.

The thought of selling out to Mr. Birdsall had been in the back of her mind since morning. It would be a miracle if she could collect the money, load her family into the wagon, and get away before Sikes took action. She would gladly leave this place if it would mean she could keep Colin and Jane Ann. The tears that had been close to her eyes since morning were about to appear once again. She tossed her head and willed herself not to think about it any more until she, Trisha, and Colin could sit down and plan what to do.

John took one look at the table and realized that Addie Hyde was serving him the best she had. After they were seated, Addie again said grace, then passed around a plate of hot cornbread squares. The children, he noticed, were well behaved. Their manners at the table were better than some he had seen in fancy hotel dining rooms and public restaurants.

"Mr. Tallman, we're obliged to you for fixing the fence and especially for repairing the chicken house," Addie said, after the plates were filled and they had begun to eat.

"I couldn't have done much without Colin. My back just happens to be stronger than his, or he could have done it without me."

"Do you have a little girl?" Jane Ann asked.

"No, but one of my sisters has two girls and the other has one. One of them is about your age."

"What's her name?"

"Her name is Tennessee, but she's called Tenny."

"What an unusual name," Addie said.

94

"She was named after Tennessee Hoffman, a little girl who saved my mother's life. The father of the child, Mr. Hoffman, was a Frenchman with a sense of humor; his wife was a Shawnee. They named their daughters after the states they were born in. Tennessee's two sisters were named Virginia and Florida."

"I believe there's a story here, Mr. Tallman. We'd be delighted to hear it, wouldn't we, children? But let's let Mr. Tallman finish his meal first."

Addie dished out the bread pudding and it was eaten quickly. The children loved a story. Sometimes during the long winter evenings Trisha and Addie took turns making up stories to entertain them.

"Are ya through yet?" Jane Ann asked as soon as John had taken his last bite.

"Yes, but . . ." He looked at Addie.

"Please. That is, if you don't mind."

"There's no secret about it. It's just that I'm not much of a talker."

"You seem to be doing just fine."

John shrugged and began.

"My mother and the rest of the family will be forever grateful to the little girl whose name was Tennessee for saving her from being carried off into the wilderness, possibly never to see her family again. It happened a long time ago; before my mother and my

95

father were married. My father, Rain Tallman, was escorting a lady from Quill's Station
on the Wabash to Fort Smith on the Arkansas.
My mother had gone along as companion to
the lady who was to marry the fort com-
mander.

"The party had stopped to rest for a day
or two at Davidsonville, a small settlement
on the Black River. Tennessee's father had
a trading post there. One day my mother
and the other lady went down to the river
to bathe and wash clothes. While there, they
were taken captive by a renegade trapper by
the name of Antoine Efant.

"Tennessee, who was about eleven years
old then, saw the women taken and saw Efant
and his party ride their horses into the river.
She knew they were doing this to make it
difficult for my father to track them. Keeping
to the woods, she ran alongside the river to
see where they would come out of the water.
Although her feet were cut and bleeding and
her face and arms scratched from going
through the brush, she followed for miles and
miles. Finally, when Efant and his party left
the water and took off cross-country, Tennessee ran back to the settlement.

"By that time my father had discovered
the women were missing. Tennessee was able
to tell him where the captors had come out

of the river, saving them hours of searching the riverbanks. Having been trained by John Spotted Elk, his stepfather, my father was able to follow. Both women were rescued the day after they were taken, thanks to Tennessee's quick thinking. My mother and father were married, right there in Davidsonville."

"What happened to the mean man?" Jane Ann asked.

"My father killed him."

"I'm glad!"

"He's mean like old Renshaw!" This, from Dillon.

Addie looked at her son in surprise. It occurred to her that he must be more aware of what was going on than she realized.

"And Tennessee?" Addie couldn't help but ask. "Did your mother see her again?"

"Oh, yes. Later she came to Quill's Station with Eleanor and Gavin McCourtney, the lady who had been captured with my mother. Tennessee married Mike Hartman, a friend of my father's. They still live in Quill's Station. I saw her only a month ago."

During the meal Trisha said not a word, but while John was telling the story, she kept her magnificent eyes on his face, judging him, he knew, for some reason of her own.

"Thanks for another really good meal, Mrs. Hyde. I'll be leaving, but first I'd like to

97

have a word with you alone." John got up from the table. "Miss Trisha can keep an eye on me from the porch," he added with a half-smile.

Colin stood behind his chair, his eyes on John's face.

" 'Bye, Mr. Tallman. I liked the story," Jane Ann said.

"He'll not be leaving for a few minutes," Addie said. "You'll have time to say goodbye." She followed John to the door, which he opened for her, then he followed her out. Addie went to the well, where she turned. "What's on your mind, Mr. Tallman?"

"The trouble you're having here."

"That's no concern of yours. I'm truly embarrassed that you witnessed . . . what you did this morning."

"The preacher wants to put Colin and Jane Ann in another home," he said flatly, leaving no room for denial.

"You've been talking to Colin."

"Yes. I'll help if I can."

"Why?"

"Because that boy is being torn apart."

"I know that. Trisha and I will take care of it."

"Have you talked to the magistrate?" he asked.

"No."

"For God's sake! Why not?"

"Because he won't turn the children over to me — a woman alone who at times can scarcely feed her own child! He'll be duty-bound to . . . do what Preacher Sikes wants."

"You're not going to fight to keep that boy out of the hands of a man like Renshaw?"

"You're damn right I'm going to fight!" Addie's temper flared.

"Then you have an idea of what kind of man he is?"

"Yes, I know." Tears filled her eyes, but she denied them and lifted her chin.

"I'll talk to the magistrate," John offered.

"Why would you do that?"

"For Colin."

"We don't know you, Mr. Tallman. We've gotten along quite well here on our own. We don't need your interference, well intentioned as it may be, in our affairs."

"You don't want to accept my help because you don't know me? That's the dumbest reason I ever heard. Lady, when you're in trouble you take help where you can get it."

"Don't get any ideas about taking Colin away with you."

"Christ!"

"When I was growing up, I dreamed of having a brother or sister. I never did. I intend to keep this brother and sister together until they're old enough to make plans for themselves." Addie's voice quivered, and her jaws snapped shut when she finished speaking.

For a long moment their eyes locked — blazing violet burning into dark blue fire. A thought came to John that immediately doused his anger and caused him to smile. He remembered his father saying that John Spotted Elk had said that a woman needed taming like a horse. Keep a strong hand on the bridle, pet them a little, and they would not mind the halter. But let them get the bit in their teeth, and they would make a man miserable and themselves too.

His smile seemed to make Addie all the more angry. Silence swirled around them as their eyes did battle.

"I'm sorry if I riled you, Mrs. Hyde. It isn't often that I offer my services to a lady. If they're not wanted . . ." He turned to walk away.

"Wait!"

John turned back. Color had drained from Addie's cheeks. Her eyes were wide with distress, but she looked steadily at him. Oh, God, but she was pretty. He realized that suddenly he was feeling things he had never felt before, had never dreamed of feeling. His heartbeat surged as a fierce wave of longing, an enormous desire, washed over him.

"You want to say something more?" he said gruffly, because he felt that reality was slipping away.

"I'm sorry —" The words came in a tormented whisper from her tight throat. "It's just that I've not had time to sort things out."

"I'm thinking you don't have much time."

"I . . . know."

"I'll speak to the magistrate. I can tell him better than you can what kind of man Renshaw is."

"Thank you."

# CHAPTER

## * 6 *

John rode away from the farm cursing himself for a fool for allowing the warm feeling of joy to come over him when he held Addie Hyde's hand as they said goodbye. She had awakened something in him that had not even been stirred before — something that left him restless and excited. John had been intimate with a few women. He had never felt the urge to go back to any of them.

He remembered the clear, honest way Addie had looked at him when she thanked him, the graceful movements of her body when she had moved back from the horse and taken her son's hand. There was quality to Addie Hyde; she was like a sleek handsome Thoroughbred.

Hell, he thought. He couldn't afford to be interested in a woman a thousand miles from home. Her roots were here on that farm where she had lived all her life. Why couldn't he have met such a woman in Santa Fe?

He kicked his horse into a canter. He would forget her once he was on his way home. He would do what he could to help her keep the orphans, then he would ride on.

*My obligation will be over.*

At the livery, John unsaddled his horse and put him in a stall.

"Give him a little grain," he said to the old man sitting outside the door with his feet on a stump. He flipped a coin, which the old man failed to catch but bent to pick up out of the dirt.

A rider came from the corral side of the livery.

"You leavin'?" the old man asked.

"Nope." The rider's eyes were on John. "You John Tallman?"

"Yeah."

"Thought so. Met ya once over at Fort Gibson in the Nations."

John studied the man. He wore a brown and white cowhide vest even though the day was hot. His hat was wide-brimmed and turned up in front. He was big, thick-chested, and had legs like tree trunks. He was so tall that his stirrups hung below his horse's belly.

"Don't recall," John said.

"Been five or six year." The man leaned over to spit on the other side of the horse. "Didn't have all this face hair then. Name's

Jerr Simmons. Ya might of knowed me as Buffer Simmons."

"Hunter?"

"Yeah."

"Well, good day to you." John stepped around the horse and headed for the main part of town.

"Strange feller," the liveryman said. "Ain't much of a talker."

"But a hell of a fighter."

"What's he doin' here?"

"Damned if I *know*, but I got me a idee." The big man put his heels to the horse and rode away leaving the curious liveryman disappointed that he wasn't going to have news to pass along that night at the tavern.

Usually in the afternoon Colin took the sheep out to the meadow behind the farm where there was no nightshade weed to poison them. Today, however, Addie went with him, leaving Trisha at the house with the younger children. The ram, Mr. Jefferson, and the ewes, Dolly and Bucket, were family pets. They knew the sound of Addie's voice when she called them and knew that she usually had a little tidbit in her pocket to feed them. The ewes were especially docile. Mr. Jefferson got stubborn at times but obeyed the long stick Addie carried.

Bucket had been born during a late spring storm. Her mother had died, and Addie had brought the small lamb to the house to feed. Dillon was allowed to name her as Jane Ann had named the other lamb. As he was being pressed to come up with a name, he looked around the kitchen for inspiration. When his eyes had come to rest on the water bucket, he had smiled.

"I'm gonna call her Bucket," he had announced.

"Is that your final choice?" Addie had asked seriously, while the rest of the family had snickered behind their hands.

"I'm gonna name her Bucket."

The meadow was a long, narrow strip that ran between two steep hills covered with a heavy growth of pine trees and scrub. The grass grew deep and lush. Today Colin and Addie would fill bags of cut or pulled grass to take back to use on days they couldn't bring the animals out to graze.

Addie loved to come here. It was peaceful and quiet. The air was still, the sky impossibly clear. She sat now on a large rock that had been her special spot since childhood. She could remember when she had to climb to get up onto it. Now she just sat down. The sun felt warm on her back.

While Addie rested, questions dogged her

mind. Why had John Tallman followed the men out to the farm? Curiosity, maybe. After that was satisfied, why had he stayed the night? He might truly have wanted to guard against the men's returning, Addie reasoned. But why had he done all that work this morning? And why the offer to help Colin? Addie mulled it over and the only conclusion she could come to was that he was from a close-knit family and Colin's plight had somehow touched a soft spot in him.

"Do ya think Mr. Tallman'll come back, Miss Addie?" Colin asked, as if he had been reading Addie's mind.

"He said he'd speak to the magistrate. I think he'll come and tell us what was said."

"I want to be like him when I grow up."

"What makes you say that? You don't know him. He could be just putting on a show."

"He ain't puttin' on a show. He got real mad while I was tellin' him 'bout . . . old Renshaw."

"You have to be with someone longer than just a few hours before you *know* him. Sometimes it takes months to find the real person under a nice facade; and when you do, you realize he didn't really care about you at all." There was a wistful tone in her voice.

"I don't think Mr. Tallman is like that."

*Colin, honey, you are more trusting than I. He could be a rascal for all we know.*

Addie sat on the rock and looked out over the valley. She needed this quiet time. It seemed to her lately that her life was passing too fast, that soon she would be old and would not have done the many things she had dreamed of doing nor seen the things she had dreamed of seeing.

Besides giving her Dillon, Kirby had opened doors to her imagination with his stories of places and things. Poor Kirby. She would always wonder if he had been heading back to her when he was killed, or if he had dismissed her and Dillon from his mind to seek his own dreams.

Several hours slipped by. Colin went out to drive the sheep back when they strayed too far down the valley and then returned to stand beside Addie.

"Miss Addie, don't turn your head now, but over yonder where lightnin' split that big cedar, there's a man on horseback. I think he's lookin' at us through a spyglass."

"Oh, Colin —" Addie's fear sprang to life.

"Let's go back to the house."

"Why don't we just start filling the bags with grass and work our way back toward the house. I'll look as soon as I can."

Colin began to swing the short hand scythe.

While she waited to scoop up the grass and stuff it in the sacks, Addie looked around as if watching the sheep. She lifted her eyes and saw the man. He and his horse blended into the shadows so well that she would never have noticed him. Colin was right: he was watching them through a spyglass.

"We'll fill this one sack, Colin. Move slowly. We don't want him to think we're leaving because of him. If he thought we were running, he could be over here before we got halfway to the house."

"Who is he?"

"He's not one of the preacher's flock. If they come, they'll ride up to the house bold as brass. It's someone from town trying to get a look at Trisha."

"I wish Trisha wasn't a nigger."

"Colin, that word just sets my teeth on edge. Please don't use it. Trisha has some colored blood. Goodness! A hundred years from now, the way these southern *gentlemen* are begetting children, there won't be a white person in the South who doesn't have a little colored blood."

"But she's . . . white as me." Colin held up his suntanned arm.

"I know. But it seems that if she has even a little Negro blood, she's considered a Negro and treated like . . . property."

"Men don't grab at white girls."

"No." Addie slyly watched the watcher while they worked.

"Mr. Tallman didn't care if Trisha was a Negro."

"Mr. Tallman was raised among Indians, or rather his father was. In some places Indians are treated worse than Negroes."

"Why do white people do that, Miss Addie?"

"Not all whites do it. Colin, he's moving away. Now he's stopped and . . . he's looking at the house. He can see it from there. Get the sheep." Hurriedly, Addie began to fill the sack with the grass Colin had cut.

As soon as they rounded the knoll and headed down the lane to the farm buildings, Addie searched the hillside again and located the outline of the horse and rider.

"He's still there, watching the house. Trisha is in the garden. Dillon and Jane Ann are on the porch."

"What we gonna do?"

"Stay close to the house."

Trisha came to meet them as they were putting the sheep in the pen.

"Ya didn't stay long."

"There's a man on horseback watching the house with a spyglass."

"What's he doin' that for?"

"Don't look. Act like we don't know he's there."

"Horse hockey is what he is. I wish I had me one a them glasses so I could look at *him*."

"I wish I was growed up, is what I wish." Colin kicked the dirt with his bare feet.

As soon as supper was over, the younger children were washed and put to bed. After Addie doused the lamp, they sat in the dark and talked.

"We need a dog," Addie said. "Then we'd know when someone was nearby."

"Geese is good watchers too. A lady I knowed in Orleans had two geese. Anybody come on the place, they'd squawk."

"We'd have better luck finding a dog than we would geese."

"Ya reckon Mr. Tallman will come back?" Colin's voice came out of the darkness. It was the second time in the past hour that he had asked that question.

"I think he will," Addie said. "But we can't count on it. If the preacher insists on your going to Mr. Renshaw, I'll visit all the church members and tell them what kind of man Ellis Renshaw is."

"They'd not believe ya," Trisha scoffed. " 'Sides, ya can't talk nasty, Miss Addie, and ya know it."

"There's another thing we can do. Pack up and leave in the night. We could go to another town, maybe Fort Smith, and start us up an eating place. We could do that, but we won't have any money until I sell the farm."

"Sell the farm?" Colin's voice croaked with disbelief. "It's yore home, Miss Addie."

"It's just a place. We could be at home in a wagon, or anywhere, as long as we're together."

"Ya'd give up this to . . . keep me and Jane Ann with you?"

"I'd do a lot more than that, honey."

"But you said you loved the farm."

"I said that. But the truth is . . . I love you more."

John left the magistrate's office with his face set in lines of anger and frustration. He had gone there the afternoon before only to be told that the magistrate was away for the day. He had returned this morning and waited for the man to show up. When he finally did, he was bleary eyed from a night of heavy drinking.

"Worthless piece of trash," John muttered to himself as his long legs ate up the distance to the livery.

The South was in a hell of a mess, he

thought, if they had to put the dregs of society in positions of authority. As soon as he had mentioned the reason for his visit to the magistrate, he had been informed that Renshaw had filed for legal custody of the orphan Colin Harris. No, Renshaw had not asked for the boy's sister, the magistrate had said, because he did not have a woman living in his house.

After that announcement, everything John tried to tell the man about Renshaw had fallen on deaf ears. The magistrate had scoffed at the suggestion that Renshaw was a sexual deviate. He hadn't even understood the meaning of the word until John had bluntly explained that there were some men, a very small number, who got their pleasure from young boys.

The magistrate had declared that Ellis Renshaw was an oustanding citizen of the county and had countered the charge against him with one against Addie Hyde. He'd said that when Mr. Hyde went off to war, she had not only harbored a runaway slave but had turned the farm into a place of prostitution. A house of ill-repute was not a fit place for children. He had even hinted that now that Mr. Hyde had been reported killed and so would not be coming home to take charge of the boy Dillon, Preacher Sikes was going to petition for guardianship of Mrs. Hyde's son.

It was then that John was no longer able to contain his rage.

"You let that happen," he had said softly, as with fists clenched he towered over the man, "and I'll nail your mangy hide to a tree and your bones'll not be in it."

The cowering magistrate had looked into eyes blazing with anger and realized that this stranger dressed in the clothes of a frontier scout could kill him in an instant with the bowie knife stuck in his belt.

"I got the law behind me."

"The *law?*" John had answered with a wintry sneer. "The law around here is about as useless as tits on a boar. You're a hell of a lawman. You're nothing but a drunken sot!"

"I can arrest you for threatening me."

"Try it, and you'll get more than threats. When a snake needs killing, I kill it, and it makes no never mind to me how it's done. I lived three years with the Shawnee, and sneaking up on a man and putting a knife in his back is one of the things I do best. Remember that!"

Jerr Simmons, known throughout the Indian Nations as Buffer, had watched John leave the magistrate's office and head for the livery. The scout's face had had the look of

113

a snarling wolf. He was sure sour-mouthed about something. From the doorway of the harness shop Simmons had seen John come out of the barn, swing into the saddle, and ride out of town in the direction of the Hyde farm.

Why would a well-known scout and cattleman have need to see the law in this one-horse town? Simmons had made a midnight visit to the livery stable. Tallman's horse had been there. It had not been in the stable the night before. Had he spent the night at the Hyde place? The only things of interest out there were the women. Which one had caught the scout's fancy?

The blond woman was pretty enough, Simmons thought now. But she had three young-uns hanging on to her skirts. A man would have to be really smitten with her to take them on. He couldn't see John Tallman loading himself up with that. He had to be after the girl, Trisha. It hadn't been hard to find out her name. Almost every man in town knew it. None of them knew where the girl had come from or how she happened to be at the Hyde place. All seemed to know she had Negro blood, and that made her fair game.

"Trisha, Trisha . . ." Buffer liked to say her name. The fact that she had a drop or two of Negro blood mattered not at all to him. She was the most beautiful creature he had ever seen, and she had been constantly in his thoughts since he had caught a glimpse of her face beneath the sunbonnet. Yesterday, when he had watched her through his spyglass, he had become as excited as a boy seeing a naked woman for the first time. Her movements were wild and free, leaving him to wonder if she wore anything at all beneath her loose shift. She had seemed docile in town, but he'd bet his jackknife that when cornered, she'd be wild as a bobcat with a fresh batch of cubs.

He chuckled.

Buffer Simmons had made up his mind when he left the buffalo-hide–covered shack on Wolfe Creek in Oklahoma Territory that he was not going back. Pretty Flower, the Kiowa who had cared for him after he had eaten tainted meat and almost died, had gone back to her people. She had been pretty and the only female he'd seen for the better part of a year.

Thank God there had been no younguns to tie him to her. He remembered how willing she had been, and how he had ached for a woman. He felt no guilt about pulling foot without telling her he wasn't coming back. She had understood that from the first. Her people would take care of her. The Kiowa always took care of their own. In time, a warrior who needed a woman to do for him would take her to his lodge.

All of Buffer Simmons's thoughts now were fixed on the young black-haired girl with the catlike eyes. He wanted her more than he had ever wanted anything in his life. He had to figure out a way to get her alone. He didn't want to take her by force if he didn't have to. The thought was insane. They would have to strike off into Indian territory alone. That part didn't bother him, but if he could persuade her to come with him, he could still join Judge Van Winkle and do what he had been hired to do — provide fresh meat for the party traveling to Sante Fe. The money would give them a start.

John Tallman, known as Spotted Elk by the Shawnee, Cherokee, and Kiowa, was a problem to be reckoned with if he too had his sights set on the girl. All hell might break loose if he took Trisha by force and she was the one Tallman wanted. He sure as shootin' didn't want to fight the New Mexico scout for her, but he would if that was the only way.

Buffer Simmons drew from inside his vest a long thin knife, razor-sharp on both sides of the blade, and began to shave the hair from the back of his hand. In his mind he pictured a fight to the death with John Tallman. He sure as hell hoped it wouldn't come to that. Buffer was confident that he could take care of himself. Tallman was a man like any other and bled like any other. He might be the best scout in the territory, but he, Buffer Simmons, was the best hunter. One thing bothered him, though: There were no rules of fair play when it came to stalking and bringing down game, but a man like John Tallman was another matter.

# CHAPTER

## * 7 *

The sun was a bright ball of fire coming up over the eastern horizon. This morning promised to be no different from other bright sunny mornings, yet in the years to come Addie would look back on this day not only as the most frightening day in her life up to this time, but as a turning point for her and her family. Every detail of this day would be etched in her memory forever.

As usual, Trisha got up as soon as she heard Addie in the kitchen. Dressed in the loose shift she favored, her feet bare, her hair hanging in ringlets down her back, she stopped just inside the door and tied the cloth sash around her head to keep her hair away from her face.

"Mornin', Trisha." Addie noticed that the girl had dark circles beneath her eyes and that her mouth drooped. "Did you stay awake most of the night?"

"Yes'm. I jist couldn't get it outa my mind

'bout old Renshaw comin' for Colin. I kept tellin' me he'd not come at night, but ever' time I heared somethin', I feared it was him. What we gonna do, Miss Addie?"

"I don't know. I thought about it all night too. If we can't get help from the magistrate, the only other thing I can think of is to try to get Mr. Birdsall to buy the farm; then we'd take the children and leave. I don't know where we'd go, though. It would have to be someplace where we could do something to earn a living."

"Colin thinks that . . . passerby is gonna help."

"He offered to talk to the magistrate." What Addie didn't say was that she was counting desperately on his being able to convince the official that Renshaw was not a decent man and therefore was unfit to have control of a young boy.

Trisha shrugged. "I be mighty surprised he come back." She emptied what water was left in the bucket in the stove reservoir and went out to the well. "Are we gonna do washin' today?" she asked, when she returned.

"Do you think we should? Yesterday was wash day; but after the preacher came, I didn't even think about it."

"I say we wash 'cause a nice warm wind

is blowin'. Might be we get rain next washin' day."

They ate mush laced with honey and left-over biscuits that had been buttered and browned in a skillet on top of the stove. Colin and Trisha drew water from the well to fill the wash and rinse tubs. Then Addie added the hot water from the reservoir, gathered the soiled clothes, and put them in a pile on the porch.

The morning passed slowly. They had plenty of work to do, but it did little to keep their minds off the dread that hung over them. Washing one of Dillon's shirts, Trisha scrubbed it so hard on the wash board that she tore a hole in it. Addie, catching Colin as he looked toward town with an expression of longing on his face, hoped that John Tall-man would not disappoint the boy.

By midmorning the clothes were flapping on the rope strung between two trees; wash water had been carried from the porch and dumped. Colin had taken the cow to be staked out in a grassy meadow until milking time.

Addie was kneading bread dough when Jane Ann ran into the kitchen, her eyes wide with fright.

"Miss Addie! Miss Addie!" she screamed. "Old Renshaw's comin'."

"Lordy mercy!" Addie felt as if the breath

had been knocked out of her. She wiped her hands on her apron and hurried to the front door as the wagon passed the side of the house heading for the back. She ran through the house and out onto the back porch. Mr. Renshaw had pulled the horses to a halt in the open space between the house and the barn and was climbing down from his wagon.

"Ya know why I'm here," he said with no pretense at civility.

Although Addie and the children referred to him as "old" Renshaw, he was only a little older than Addie's twenty-five years. He was a small man, wiry and bowlegged, with light-brown, sun-streaked hair. His most prominent feature was his large, bucktoothed mouth.

He stared at Addie with hard, cold eyes. "Ya heared me, woman. Get 'im."

The memory of what Trisha had told her about how this man planned to use Colin filled Addie's mind, and a red-hot rage washed over her as she looked at him. At that instant she fervently wished that she were a man so that she could beat this sorry piece of humanity to a pulp and smear what was left of him into the muck of the barn lot, where he belonged.

"Air ya deaf and dumb? Air ya so addled ya ain't knowin' what I'm sayin'? I said I come fer the boy. Get 'im! I ain't got all day."

"Get back in the wagon and leave. Colin is staying right here." Addie's voice shook; her throat was so tight she could scarcely speak.

"Preacher said ya'd got full of sass all a sudden. Don't ya be spoutin' off at me, 'cause I ain't gonna stand fer it. Give *me* some of yore sass and I'll slap yore jaws."

"No ya won't! If'n ya hurt Miss Addie, I'll . . . I'll cut yore heart out." Colin's voice shook with fear, but he stood erect, shoulders back, head up.

Addie looked down at the small boy whose head hardly came to her shoulder. He was so helpless to defend himself. His life, his well-being, was being decided by an ignorant, uncaring, self-serving hill preacher.

Colin had seen the wagon and knew who had arrived. His fear was so great that his first thought was to hide where Renshaw couldn't find him. Then in the night he would run away. But that would leave his dear Miss Addie to face old Renshaw and the preacher with only Trisha to help her and he knew he couldn't do that. He had run all the way in from the meadow. He felt his skin crawl now as the man's eyes bore down on him.

"Shut yore mouth and get in the wagon.

122

Ya can get yore things later."

"I thought I had made it quite clear," Addie said, her voice rising. "He's not going with you. Ever! And I want you off my property right now." She was immensely relieved that her voice didn't reflect her fear.

"Preacher said ya'd be stubborn. It makes me no never mind how hard ya got yore head set on keepin' 'im. I come for the boy, an' I ain't leavin' without 'im. Preacher said he was to work for me."

"*Work* for you? Is that what you call it? You lecherous old billy goat!" Addie's control broke. She lifted her hand as if to strike him, and her voice rose until she was yelling. "You shameful defiler of children! You're worse than a rutting boar! The lowest male beast doesn't do to the young what you do! Get off my land now, or God help me, I'll shoot you down like the mad dog you are!"

"Don't raise a hand agin' me, bitch! I come for this boy an' I'm takin' 'im." As quickly as a striking snake his hand lashed out and grabbed Colin's arm. "Get in the wagon, ya gawddamn by-blow of a whore, or I'll switch yore ass good when I get ya home."

"*I ain't goin'!*" Colin struck out with his free hand and tried to kick the man.

Renshaw gave the boy a resounding, open-hand slap across the face. The blow rocked

Colin's head back.

"Nooo!" Addie screamed. She dived for Colin, grabbed him around the waist, and the two of them fell to the ground, breaking Renshaw's hold on the boy. Addie rolled with Colin, keeping her body between him and Renshaw. She felt a vicious pain in her ribs when the man kicked her with his heavy boot.

"Ya damn bitch! I'll learn ya —"

*Bang!*

Renshaw screamed, staggered back, and sprawled on his back in the dirt, his hands clutching his private parts.

Startled by the sound of the shot, the wagon team lurched, ran a small way, came up against the barn, halted, and danced nervously in their traces.

Addie scrambled to her feet. Trisha was standing, bare feet spread, with the gun pointed at the fallen man, a stream of curses pouring from her mouth.

"Bastard! Son of a bitch! Horny old goat! Shit-eatin' dog!"

"Ah . . . Gawd! Lord help me —" In pain and panic, Renshaw continued to scream and curse and hold his crotch.

"The *Lord* ain't gonna help ya now!" Trisha shouted. "Ya ain't fit ta live nohow. Yore a suck-egged, pig-ugly ol' bastard, is what ya are! I'm gonna shoot that *thing* off'n ya and ya'll not be pokin' it at little younguns no more. Then I'm gonna shoot ya so full a holes, ya'll look like a flour sifter."

"Trisha, no!" Suddenly reality began to filter into Addie's mind.

*Dear God! Trisha has shot a white man! It doesn't matter if he dies or not, the Renshaws will come for her and hang her!*

Addie grabbed the rifle out of the girl's hand.

Trisha was like a coiled, deadly snake. It was as if she had suddenly gone wild. Her lips were pulled back from her teeth in a vicious snarl. Her eyes glimmered.

"Let me kill 'im! Let me kill 'im!"

"I hope ya did," Colin said, tears streaming from his eyes.

Addie looked down at Renshaw sprawled in the dirt, glaring up at her with hate-filled eyes. The bullet had missed his private parts and slammed into his hip joint.

"The nigger bitch shot me!" he said with disbelief. "Gawd help me!"

"It was *me* who shot you, you filthy scum!"

All of Addie's attention was focused on the man on the ground. She didn't hear the frightened cries of Dillon and Jane Ann or the sound of a running horse. In a daze, she turned to see John Tallman leaping from his horse.

John went by her and knelt beside the fallen man. "Who is he?"

"Ellis Renshaw. I shot him."

"Miss Addie . . ."

"*I* shot him," Addie repeated firmly, looking directly into Trisha's eyes and shaking her head almost imperceptibly.

"I hope he die!" Trisha said. "I hope he die."

"Colin, run get one of those towels off the line," John said calmly, as he used his bowie knife to cut Renshaw's britches from waist to thigh. "No doubt he deserves to die, but it'd cause a lot of trouble right now. You women back off unless you want to see his privates."

"I goin' ta get me a knife," Trisha hissed. "I goin' to *geld* that sucker!"

"Take Trisha and the children to the house, Addie. Colin and I will take care of this."

It didn't occur to Addie not to obey the softly spoken order. She took the children by the hand and together they sat on the edge of the porch. Trisha followed reluctantly, muttering and looking back over her shoulder at the man on the ground. Dillon climbed into Addie's lap as soon as she sat down and framed her face with his two small hands.

"Love ya, Muvver." There was an almost

desperate look on his little face. Addie felt like crying.

"I love you too, my darlin' boy."

"Love Trisha too."

"I know, and Trisha loves you too. Now, you and Jane Ann are not to worry. We have some trouble here, but we'll work it out."

"Colin said Mr. Tallman wouldn't let old Renshaw take him away," Jane Ann said from where she sat on Trisha's lap, her fingers twisting a strand of hair on the top of her head as she often did when she felt confused.

"I ain't countin' on that *passerby*. I'm countin' on that gun to keep old Renshaw 'way from Colin," Trisha said in a deadly calm voice.

Addie's thoughts raced in wild confusion. She was sure that Renshaw's relatives would come for Trisha; and because she was colored, they would hang her without giving it a second thought. She had to convince Renshaw that she — Addie — was the one who had shot him. She would claim that he had accosted her. They wouldn't dare hang *her* without a trial.

"Stay here, honey, and take care of Trisha and Jane Ann," she said to Dillon and set him on the porch beside Trisha, who placed an arm about him and hugged him close.

Addie walked rapidly across the yard to

where John squatted beside Renshaw. Colin had guided Renshaw's team and wagon close to where the man lay on the ground, still moaning and cursing.

"The bullet busted his hip," John said to Addie. "We need a flat board to put him on so we can lift him into the wagon."

"There's an old door in the barn. Colin and I will get it." As she passed Renshaw, she paused and looked down. "I'm not one bit sorry I shot you. If the decent men in this county knew what a filthy cur you are, they would take you out and hang you."

"That nigger bitch is the one who shot me!"

Addie's lips curled, and when she spoke her voice dripped with sarcasm.

"All the Renshaws are stupid, and you're the stupidest of all. You're so dumb you don't even know who shot you. I did, and I'm proud of it. I only wish I'd killed you."

Addie was aware that John had stopped working on Renshaw and was looking at her.

"Get the door, Addie."

Addie and Colin carried the old wooden door from the barn to where Renshaw lay, his hand protectively shielding his privates. John shoved it close to him.

"Tilt to the side if you can."

"I . . . can't, gawd damn you!"

John shrugged. He moved the man's shoulders. Then, with his hands beneath his hips, he dragged him onto the board. Renshaw screamed in agony.

"Can you and Colin lift one end of the board?" John asked.

Addie nodded. "Where are you taking him?" she asked, after they had lifted and then slid the board onto the bed of the wagon.

"Home. He told me how to get there. Get my horse, Colin, and tie him to the tailgate." John took Addie's arm and led her away from the wagon. "This is going to cause plenty of trouble. Your taking the blame is not going to help. He knows Trisha shot him, and he swears she'll hang for it. I'll take him home, then I'll be back. While I'm gone, keep Trisha and the children close to the house." His voice was low and even, but his tone left no doubt that he expected to be obeyed.

"All right." She stared at him, trying to read his thoughts. A flush tinged her cheeks, but her wide violet eyes didn't waver. Shyly, she placed a hand on his arm. "Mr. Tallman, I thank you; Colin and Trisha thank you too."

John's mind seemed to grind to a halt. He felt the warmth of her hand on his arm even after she had removed it. He was confused by the depth of his desire to take care of this woman and those she held dear. He forced his lips to smile and to speak lightly.

"I'll say one thing for you, Addie. You've got more than your share of spunk."

Addie's eyes fastened to his. "You do what you have to, Mr. Tallman."

"This is serious business."

"I know. What did the magistrate say?" She couldn't help asking; it had been on her mind all morning.

"We'll get no help there. If someone rides in, Addie, stay in the house. Don't let anyone in. I'll be back as soon as I can."

Under his dark, steady gaze, her heart began to hammer. Right at this moment he didn't seem a stranger she had met only a few days before. He seemed a trusted friend. After a long, searching look, he turned and climbed up on the wagon seat.

She watched the wagon go down the lane to the road. He'd said "we." He'd called her Addie, too. Suddenly she didn't feel so alone.

"Colin, get the cow. Give her some of the grass we cut yesterday." Addie hurried to the porch where Trisha sat with Dillon and Jane Ann. "We've got to get Mr. Jefferson and the ewes back in the sheep pen."

"I'll help Trisha!" Jane Ann jumped off Trisha's lap.

"Thank you, sweetheart. Dillon and I will

see to my bread dough."

"What that passerby say?"

"He said he'd be back as soon as he could. He's going to help us, Trisha. Lord knows we need all the help we can get right now."

"Why ya say ya shoot that old shithead for?"

"Shhh . . ." Addie glanced at the children. They were interested in a horned toad that had come out from under the porch. "You know as well as I that Mr. Renshaw will stir his folks up to come get you. But they'll not dare touch me without having a trial."

"I ort to a killed 'im. It wouldn't a been no worse." Big tears came into Trisha's golden eyes. She looked like a small, frightened child. Addie hugged her, and the girl clung tightly.

"You're as dear to me as if you were my own. I'll fight with my last breath to keep you safe. Think of all we've been through the last few years and how we've managed to stay together. We're not alone now. Mr. Tallman will be back, and he'll tell us what's best to do. I know one thing — I'll shoot every damn Renshaw on that hill before I let them put their hands on you."

Time passed slowly. A meal was prepared, the children were fed and something was put by for Mr. Tallman in case he wanted it. Addie's mind had been busy mulling over the idea of going to Birdsall and offering the farm for cash. They had to get away from here not only for Colin's sake but now for Trisha's, too. The more Addie thought about it, the more convinced she became that it was the only thing to do, and that it would have to be done as soon as possible.

"Trisha, would you and Colin be afraid to stay here alone for a while? I'm going over to see Birdsall and ask if he was sincere about buying the farm."

"I ain't afeared o' them no-good Renshaws." Trisha tossed her black mane and glared defiantly, but Addie wasn't fooled by her brave show; her lips trembled and her hands shook. The girl was terrified.

"If they do anything, it will be later this evening; and Mr. Tallman will be back by then. I shouldn't be gone more than an hour. I think it best to talk to Mr. Birdsall before he finds out the trouble we're in. Colin, help me hitch up the team." Addie took off her apron, smoothed her hair, and picked up her sunbonnet.

"Don't ya worry none 'bout these young-uns. I take care of 'em. Guess I showed old Renshaw we ain't ta be messed with."

"When I get back, we'll load the wagon

with as much as we can take. Sort out the foodstuffs, the clothes and blankets, Trisha. We've got to take that whether or not we take anything else." Addie bent down to hug Dillon and Jane Ann. "You two help Trisha while I'm gone. Hear? And mind her."

Addie hurried out the door before the children saw the mist in her eyes. Colin stood at the head of the sway-backed team.

"Ain't ya wantin' me to go with ya, Miss Addie?"

"I'd love to have you with me, but you're needed here to take care of Trisha and the little ones. Get a handful of cracked corn and scatter it in the chickens' pen, then pen them up. We'll want to take some of them with us when we go."

"Where we goin'?"

"I don't know yet, but we're leaving here as soon as I get back. You and Trisha can start getting things together."

She was climbing up onto the wagon seat when John rode up the lane to the house. He came to the wagon, a look of irritation on his face.

"Where the hell are you going?"

A flush of color came to Addie's cheeks and the light of battle to her eyes.

"To the Birdsalls'. Mr. Birdsall once offered to buy the farm."

"I told you to wait here."

"We can't stay here. We've got to leave, with or without the money for the farm. The Renshaws will never rest until they get their revenge. They'll hang Trisha" — Addie's voice quivered — "and no one will lift a finger to help us."

"I told you to stay near the house. You don't take orders well, do you, Addie?" When she didn't answer, he asked, "How far to the Birdsalls'?"

"A couple of miles. Maybe a little more."

"Anyone been around?"

"We haven't seen anyone."

"The Renshaws are plenty riled. I figure they'll sneak in here around midnight to get Trisha and to burn you out."

The flat, unequivocal statement gave her a glimpse into the man's character. He was not one to play with words. He said what had to be said straight out.

The bone-chilling fear that pierced Addie was as sharp as a knife. She took a shaky breath and tried not to let him see how frightened she was. She lifted her chin and reached for the reins, only to have them taken out of her hands and given to Colin.

"Unhitch the team, Colin. Feed and water them, and give them some grain. They'll get a hard workout tonight. Tell Trisha to stay in the house and keep the little ones with her. Someone could be watching with a spyglass."

Strong hands reached for Addie and grasped her about the waist. Before she realized what was happening, she was lifted from the wagon seat. When she recovered from her surprise, she found herself sitting in front of John on his horse, the man's hard thighs cushioning her bottom, his arms around her as he turned the horse toward the road.

# CHAPTER

## * 8 *

"Which way?" John asked when they reached the road.

It was a moment before she could collect herself, and even then she found it difficult to speak.

"To . . . the left."

Never before had she ridden in this fashion, sitting on a man's lap with his arms around her. When she and Kirby rode one of the work horses to the church to be married, she had sat behind him with her arms around *him*.

"Take off that damn bonnet. It's poking me in the eye."

Without hesitation Addie pulled on the tie beneath her chin and removed the bonnet, even though she couldn't see how the soft crown could be bothering him.

"That's better. You have beautiful hair. It's a shame you keep it twisted up in that knot."

"I'm not a girl to . . . go about with my

136

hair hanging down my back," she said testily.

"Why not?"

"Because I'm not a hussy, that's why!"

"What's not being a hussy got to do with it? I've seen hussies with hair pinned up so tight it squinted their eyes."

She knew he was teasing her and refused to take the bait.

"Have you always been this serious, Addie?"

On hearing his softly spoken question, Addie was jolted by an instant flash of memory: *Playing hide and seek in the barn, running toward the creek, her hair loose and streaming out behind her, Kirby reaching for her, pulling her down onto the grassy bank.*

*No!* her mind screamed. She had not always had this heavy burden of responsibility on her shoulders. She had let her hair hang down and acted the fool over a man who had used her, then left her to chase his dream of adventure. She would not be so foolish again. Addie didn't even pretend to herself that Kirby had gone to war to fight for a cause. He'd gone to get in on the excitement and to rid himself of her and their son.

Realizing that John was waiting for an answer to his question, and not knowing how to respond, Addie said the first thing that came to her mind:

"I've not given you permission to call me by my first name."

He laughed.

Not only did she hear the soft chuckle, but she felt his movement against her upper arm and his warm breath on her neck. She was very aware that her buttocks were nestled in the V of his crotch and tried to keep her back stiff and her shoulders away from his chest. She looked down at the hands holding the reins. His fingers were long, the nails short and lean. Fine black hair covered the backs of his hands.

For some crazy reason she was having difficulty breathing, and her silly heart was beating as hard as if she had run a foot race.

"Turn right," she said when they came to a wagon track that led up through a thick stand of cottonwood.

The track passed through a thick grove. Overhead the sun shone bright in the green foliage. It was extremely quiet except for the *tunk, tunk* of the horse's hooves on the deep-cushioned humus.

*Caw! Caw!* A crow, flying above them, wheeled and dipped. *Caw! Caw!* it challenged them saucily. After the scolding from the crow, a concerted chorus of profanity came from a flock of bluejays in the treetops. Then it was quiet again until the song of a mountain thrush came from far away.

A doe with a fawn close to her flank ran out of the forest and on down the trail ahead of them, disappearing into the shelter of a thicket.

"I thought game would be hunted out this near to town."

"This is Birdsall land. No one hunts on it but Birdsalls."

"What kind of man is Birdsall, and how come he offered for your place?"

"He's a far cut above the Renshaws —"

"That wouldn't take much," John said dryly.

"He was one of the first to settle in this area. My father came later and took up land next to his. Mr. Birdsall has two sons and wants a farm for each. And . . . he doesn't want the Renshaws to have my land. One of his sons, the one who just came home from the war, had trouble with a Renshaw over mistreating a darkie. The Birdsall boys went to war because they didn't like the idea of the Yankees coming down here and telling them what to do, not because they believed in slavery."

"Does Birdsall know about the preacher wanting to give Colin to Renshaw?"

"I don't know. He doesn't kowtow to Preacher Sikes as some of the others do."

Barking dogs of various sizes and breeds came out from under the house and surrounded them when they approached it. A word from the white-haired, white-bearded man who sat in the chair on the porch sent them scurrying away, but they didn't go far — they sat in the yard eyeing the visitors suspiciously.

The log house, which looked as if it had been there forever, was wide and boxy with a sloping roof that covered porches both in the front and the back. Rock chimneys on each end towered above the roof top. To the side of the house was a peach orchard and a well-tended garden with string suspended across it from end to end with tiny bits of fluttering cloth tied to it to scare away the birds.

John stopped his horse at the split-rail hitching post, helped Addie down, then stepped from the saddle. He followed her to the porch.

"Afternoon, Mr. Birdsall."

"Howdy, Addie," the old man replied, his eyes going beyond her to John.

"This is Mr. Tallman, a . . . friend."

"Howdy." John stepped forward and extended his hand.

"Don't meet many people by the name of Tallman. Met a feller by that name once over

140

near Fort Smith. 'Twas a long time ago."

"It could have been my father, Rain Tallman. He came into this country forty years ago."

"Yup, guess it was. Ya favor him some, now that I think on it. Sit down, sit down." After indicating the well-worn cane-bottomed chairs, he turned his head and yelled into the house, "Cloris!"

A chubby, pleasant-faced woman stepped out the door so quickly that it was apparent she had been lurking there.

"Hello, Addie."

"Hello, Cloris. This is Mr. Tallman." Then, to John: "Cloris is married to Alfred, one of Mr. Birdsall's sons."

"Would ya like a cool drink?"

"That would be nice," Addie murmured.

"I know this ain't no pass-the-time visit, Addie," Mr. Birdsall said as soon as Cloris had left the porch. "What's on your mind?"

Addie took a deep breath. "Are you still interested in buying my farm?"

"Are ya ready to sell, or just dillydallyin' 'round 'bout it?"

"I'm ready to sell. Today."

"Why today?"

"Well . . . I just —"

"She's getting married," John said smoothly; then, to Addie when she turned startled eyes to him: "I think we should tell him the truth, honey. Mr. Birdsall, Addie's afraid folks will look down on her for marrying again so soon after hearing about Kirby."

Cloris came out with a bucket of water. After Addie drank, she handed the dipper to John.

"Mighty good water," he said after a few gulps.

"Best in the Ozarks." Mr. Birdsall waited until Cloris went back in the house before he asked again: "Why today?"

"I'm leaving to go back to my ranch in New Mexico and I want to take Addie with me. I've contracted to act as scout for a wagon train that's waiting for me."

Addie was speechless. The man could lie so glibly.

"Envy ya some. When I come here it was new country. Orbie Johnson, that's Addie's pa, come a few years later. Fer a spell we was the only ones. Then others came. Trash with 'em," he grunted. "Good hard worker, Orbie was. He helped me plant them peach trees just before he was took. Orbie'd be glad to know Addie's gettin' a good man. That other feller she wed didn't 'mount to a hill of beans."

For crying out loud! How did Birdsall know

John Tallman was a *good* man? Addie asked herself. And how did he know that Kirby didn't amount to a hill of beans? She opened her mouth to ask, then closed it when she saw John looking at her intently, his dark blue eyes warning her to keep quiet. She clamped her mouth shut, but her violet eyes were resentful.

"Guess Sikes'll be 'long to take them orphans off yore hands. Hear Renshaw'll take the boy. Cloris's been askin' 'bout the girl. Don't know, though, she'd have to grow some 'fore she'd be much help."

"Colin and Jane Ann are going with me," Addie said firmly. "I . . . ah, explained to Mr. Tallman that I couldn't part with them. Mr. Birdsall, about the farm —"

"Sir, we've talked it over," John interrupted smoothly. "There's fifteen acres in cotton, ten in corn. An acre of broom straw and a acre of garden. Barn's in good shape and there's a good water well. Addie will leave what household furniture we can't take with us, as well as the milk cow and the sheep."

"Not the sheep!"

"Now, honey —"

"Not the sheep!" she insisted.

John winked at Mr. Birdsall. "We figure six hundred cash money a fair price."

*Six hundred?* Addie almost choked. She had meant to ask only three hundred.

"That's a mighty steep price for cash money."

"Not the way things are going. By this time next year you'll be able to get twelve hundred for that farm. I'll tell you what we can do. Throw in a heavy wagon and a couple of good mules to pull it, and we'll come down to four-fifty cash money."

"I don't know —"

John was silent. His eyes caught Addie's and held them. The silence built. Birdsall rubbed the whiskers on his chin.

"I don't know," he said again.

"There's another fellow that's interested, but Addie —"

"Four."

"Four-twenty-five, and I pick the mules."

"Done." Mr. Birdsall stretched out his hand to John, then heaved himself to his feet and stepped off the porch.

Addie was amazed. The two men had completely disregarded her during the whole process of selling *her* farm.

She and John followed Mr. Birdsall to the barn lot in back of his house. John took Addie's elbow and squeezed it briefly before he went to look at the mules.

A half-hour later, Addie sat on the wagon

seat while John tied his horse to the tailgate. After she had signed the farm over to Mr. Birdsall, he had given John a bill of sale for the wagon and the mules, plus a bag of money, which John had counted and then put in his inside vest pocket.

Cloris Birdsall came out to the wagon. "Good luck, Addie. Pappy said Alfred and I can live on your place. I'm so excited . . . and tired a sharin' a place with kinfolk," she added in a whisper.

"Take care of the moss rose," Addie said in a choked voice. "The hollyhocks come up each year, but I scatter seed anyhow. Daisy's a good cow, but sometimes you have to poke her in the side with your . . . head —"

"Ready?" John put his foot between two spokes of the wheel and jumped up onto the seat beside Addie, where he took up the reins.

She nodded, too emotional to speak.

Mr. Birdsall came to the wagon and extended his hand.

"It ain't gonna be like strangers takin' over your place, Addie. Orbie knew I was fond a that place."

"Papa'd be glad you have it. Goodbye, Mr. Birdsall."

"We're obliged to you," John said. Then: "You might want to send some of your boys down to the farm tonight. We'll be leaving about dusk. I'd not put it past the Renshaw outfit to come in and shoot things up if they hear we've gone."

"By golly, it'll be the last place they shoot up if they do. Them Renshaws ain't got enough brains between 'em to fill a gnat's eye."

"I agree with you there. Good day to you."

John sailed the whip out over the backs of the mules, and the wagon rolled away from the homestead. Addie sat beside him, stiff as a poker, her eyes straight ahead. As soon as they were out of sight of the Birdsall house, she whirled to face him.

"Why did you tell him *that?*" she demanded. Her eyes burned with resentment, and her voice rose despite her wish to stay calm.

John's dark brows drew together as he looked searchingly into her eyes. Ignoring her anger, he spoke gently.

"Tell him what?"

"You know!"

"That we were going to marry? Is the thought of marrying me so terrible?"

"But . . . it's a lie."

"Maybe; but it worked, didn't it? We came out far better than I thought we would. I saw this wagon when we first came up the lane. You'd play hob, trying to fit your stuff

146

in the one you have. Let's hope it doesn't rain before we can get a set of good strong bows and a wagon sheet."

"It wasn't right to lie to Mr. Birdsall," Addie insisted. "You just took over and — sold my farm. I didn't have any part in it."

Surprise altered John's expression. "Is that what's bothering you? You've got to be the one who wears the pants in the family?"

"We're not a family!" Addie almost shouted.

"Mr. Birdsall thought we were. Could you have made a better deal? What were you going to ask? Two, three hundred?"

His guess was so close that it took away some of Addie's resentment. Her violet eyes flicked up at him. His face had a harshness that made her shiver. Addie prided herself on being fair-minded. In spite of his arrogant attitude and domineering style, she owed him a debt of gratitude.

"I thank you for what you did, Mr. Tallman. Please forgive me for being touchy." She lowered her eyes to her hands, which were clasped tightly in her lap. She felt his eyes on her and it made her nervous.

"Don't pull such a long face. You got what you wanted and a wagon and team to boot."

"I know, but it isn't every day I . . . sell my home." Her voice cracked. To hide her humiliation she concentrated on holding on to the side of the wagon seat because the team had picked up speed.

"Then why did you? You could have sent Trisha up North; Colin could have gone with her, and your troubles would have been over."

It was the wrong thing to say, he realized. Addie's face turned a dull red, her eyes blazed angrily, and she completely forgot her feeling of gratitude.

"Get rid of my troubles? Just send them away without a thought of what would happen to them? Is that what *you* do with your troubles, Mr. Tallman? Out of sight, out of mind? Well, I take my responsibilities more seriously than that."

He smiled. "You're quite a woman. I'm going to enjoy getting to know you." He placed his foot on the front board and pulled back on the reins to slow the team. They were coming to a sharp bend in the trail.

"Bullfoot! You know me now as well as you ever will."

His smile broadened. Such admiration and implacable determination shone in his dark blue eyes that Addie shivered, even though she was sweating with anger.

"You need me, Addie. I'm all that stands between you and the Renshaws. For some reason that God only knows, our paths crossed. It may be that fate intends for us to know each other . . . very well." He spoke calmly, as if he really believed such a ridiculous notion.

It was quiet except for the creak of the wagon and the jingle of the harnesses, but John's words roared loudly in her head: *know each other very well.* Why, the nerve of him! *He's got mush for brains,* she thought wildly.

"Fate indeed!" she sputtered. "You're out of your mind if you believe that poppycock!" She'd wanted to say something that would really cut him down, but she realized she had failed when she looked into his laughing eyes. "You're crazy as a bedbug."

"Maybe. Climb down off your high horse and tell me about your husband. Mr. Birdsall didn't seem to think much of him."

"My husband is a subject I'll not discuss with you, now or ever."

Somehow, Addie felt strangely alive. She put it down to the fact that she hadn't conversed with an interesting man in months, even years. She begrudgingly admitted that she enjoyed talking to him; but this other thing, this feeling of being alive when she was with him, this seeing his face behind her closed eyelids, disturbed her. And, Lord help her, she was glad, oh so glad, that he was with her.

John wasn't sure why he had said those things to her. He didn't even believe them himself. He had been taught to believe that a man made his own track through life. It was up to him whether to cut a straight one or a crooked one. He also believed that there was no such thing as luck. A man made his own.

He glanced at the woman beside him. It irritated him that he liked to look at her. She was delicate and elusive, yet strong. She had backbone, all right, and would buck a man every step of the way if she believed herself to be right. He admired her deep loyalty to Trisha and the boy, and even to her husband, who Birdsall had said wasn't worth a hill of beans.

John wondered if she would be a passionate lover. Abruptly, he felt bitter resentment rising in him. Hell! He hadn't planned to be interested in a woman for a long time, especially a woman with extra baggage. Her own son was one thing, but there was also the boy, his sister, and Trisha — a ready-made family to fill that big house of his out on his ranch. *Now where the hell did that thought come from?* In his mind's eye he saw Addie there in the shaded courtyard — a

150

full skirt swishing around her bare ankles, her hair hanging to her waist, and a dark-haired babe astride her hip.

Holy damn! This was serious business that was going through his mind. Was it just that he needed a woman? He had always been choosy about the women he was with and had gone for long stretches without finding relief with any of the bangtails that were so readily available at most saloons.

He was certain of one thing: The sight of Addie Hyde made his heart jump as no other woman had ever done, and he was stunned by the intensity of his desire to take care of her. She was a full, mature woman, fiery in character, bright in mind, and high in spirit. Her body was straight and strong, yet incredibly soft. It would be very easy to care for her a great deal.

"Ohhh!" The exclamation that burst from Addie jarred John out of his reverie. His strong hands on the reins had turned the mules up the lane to the house. "Oh, my! I just realized that . . . I can't possibly handle these mules!"

"Stop worrying. You'll not have to handle them."

"But —" Addie stopped suddenly and looked at the man beside her. He sat as still as a stone, his eyes searching each side of the lane and ahead. He was as alert as a stallion protecting his herd. "What is it?"

"Someone's here. If I tell you to get down, do it, and don't argue."

"How do you know? I don't see —"

"My horse. There's another stallion here."

Addie glanced back at John's horse, tied to the tailgate. His ears were up, his nostrils flared, and he was uttering little snorting sounds.

"Oh, I shouldn't've left them!" Addie's eyes searched the house for a sign of Trisha or the children. The front door was closed and not even a chicken stirred in the yard.

John said not a word as he hurried the mules up the lane and around to the back of the house. Addie's heart was pounding with fear and dread. The first thing she saw was a big spotted horse tied to a rail beside the watering tank. Then she saw Colin and a bearded man sitting on the edge of the porch. Colin had a spyglass in his hand. John cursed, stopped the mules, and tied the reins to the brake handle. Addie climbed down over the wheel before he could get around to help her and hurried toward the porch.

"Is everything all right?" she asked. Some of her anxiety left her when she saw the smile on Colin's face.

152

"Remember Mr. Simmons, Miss Addie? He's been lettin' me look through his spyglass." Addie glanced at the closed door. "Trisha won't come out."

"At least *she* can obey orders." John had come up behind Addie. "What are you doin' here, Simmons?"

"Howdy, Tallman." The bearded giant grinned. He was as tall as John, and much heavier. "Just passin' by."

"Like hell. I saw your horse's prints on that knoll up there. You've been watching with that spyglass."

"By Jupiter, you're better'n I thought. Heard ya could track a bird through the sky but didn't believe it."

"It wasn't hard. Not many horses wear that size shoe. If you plan to do much sneaking around you better get another horse."

Simmons acknowledged that with a tilt of his head and a grin.

Colin, watching both men, had an uneasy look on his face.

"Good day to you," John said by way of dismissal. And although he took Addie's elbow as she stepped up onto the porch, his eyes never left the other man.

"You takin' over here, Tallman?" Simmons asked.

"You might say that. I'm marrying Miss

Addie." As John spoke he squeezed Addie's elbow. Hard.

"If that's the way the wind blows, I'd like a private word with ya."

"Wait over by your horse. I'll be right out." John opened the back door and pushed Addie in ahead of him before she could sputter a protest.

"Why did you tell him that?" she whispered angrily.

"Use your head. You'll not be hassled by men like him if he thinks you've got protection."

"But —"

"We've no time to argue." He grasped her shoulders. "You and Trisha pack up what you'll need. Cooking pots, food, bedding, and clothing first. Then we'll see how much room is left for other things. We're leaving here in two hours, so don't waste time."

When he went out, he left the door open. Addie turned and saw Trisha and the young children standing in the corner behind the packed washtubs. It was then that she noticed the kitchen had been stripped of almost everything but the furniture.

She blinked the tears from her eyes.

# CHAPTER

## * 9 *

John didn't know much about Jerr Simmons, the man known as Buffer. He hadn't heard anything bad about the man, but then he hadn't heard anything good, either.

Only this morning he had discovered that someone had been watching the house. The prints were deep, which meant that that someone was a big man on a big horse. When he saw Simmons and the spyglass, it had not been hard to put two and two together. He didn't have much respect for a man who would hide out and spy on women.

"Colin," he called when he saw the boy talking to Simmons. "Miss Addie needs help."

" 'Bye, Mr. Simmons. Thanks for lettin' me look in your spyglass." Colin gave John a worried, puzzled glance as he ran past him.

"Well, Simmons, what were you doing? Picking the boy for information about the women?"

"Yeah," Simmons admitted. "But didn't

get much. Kid's as closed-mouthed as a snappin' turtle."

"Say what you've got to say. I have things to do."

"Why'd ya say ya was marryin' that woman? She 'peared surprised to hear the news."

"Not that it's any business of yours, but I am going to marry her. She just doesn't know it yet."

Buffer Simmons chuckled. "Figured ya fer a man who took what he wanted."

"I don't *take* a woman unless she wants to be taken!"

"Meant no offense to ya . . . or the lady. C'mon. I got somethin' ta show ya."

John followed the man into the barn and on through to the back. When he stepped out the back door he saw Buffer standing, hands on his hips, grinning.

"Found me a little ol' dried-up turd."

The man sitting on the ground in a pile of cow manure was short, wiry, and had almost as much hair on his face as on his head. His feet were securely bound, a gag was in his mouth, and his hands, wrists tied together, were pulled up and fastened to a branch over his head. Judging by the softness of the cow-piles he sat in, the cow had just recently been chased from her favorite shade.

Hard, watery blue eyes glared at John and then at Buffer from beneath sparse, straw-colored hair.

"Purty, ain't he?"

"Looks like a pile of shit to me," John said dryly. "Where'd you find him?"

"Sneakin' 'round with a rifle. Saw him through my spyglass. Knew ya wasn't here 'cause I saw you ride off with Miss Addie. Figured I'd better see what he was up to."

"He's a Renshaw."

"Yeah. Shot off his mouth aplenty 'fore I stuffed it with that rag. Course, I had to wipe the cow shit off my boots with it first." Clearly, Simmons was enjoying himself.

John picked up the rifle that leaned against the side of the barn, jacked out the shells, then grasped the barrel and swung it against the tree trunk with such force that the stock splintered; the firing mechanism broke and fell off.

The man on the ground kicked his feet in rage. They slid back and forth in the soft manure. Grunts of fury came from behind the gag.

"You son of a bitch," John snarled. "I ought to kick your teeth out. Simmons was easier on you than I'd have been. I'd've hung you up by your thumbs after I took some skin off your back. When your kinfolk find you, tell them that if they come looking for the women here, I'll get them . . . one by one . . . in the back . . . when they least expect it."

It was John's intention to intimidate, and he succeeded. The man's face turned a chalky white. He watched fearfully as John threw the broken rifle far out into the barn lot and went back into the barn.

"Does the boy know about him?" he asked as soon as Buffer entered the barn.

"No. Didn't see no need to tell him."

"What did Renshaw tell you?"

"That he was gunnin' for the wench who crippled his cousin."

"That's about the truth of it. She crippled him. He'll not plow another field. Probably not straddle another horse."

"I heard about them Renshaws in town. There's a whole passel of 'em. Some of 'em are meaner than a peed-on snake. They'll be comin' with blood in their eye."

"Yeah."

"Ya need help loadin' that big wagon? The boy's gathered up the tools, ropes, and harnesses."

"You've got it all figured out, haven't you?"

"Yeah. Renshaw spilled his guts. His cousin wanted the boy; the girl shot him. The clan'll

158

be here to burn 'em out, so you're gettin' 'em outa here. I figure that's a tall order fer one man. Two could handle it jist fine."

John eyed him suspiciously. "What do you want out of it?" When the giant shrugged, John said: "You're out of your territory, Simmons. Last I heard, you and a Kiowa woman were shacked up down on Wolfe Creek."

"Didn't know I was so famous that a Tallman would be keepin' tabs on me."

"What brought you here?"

"Same as what brought you, I'm thinkin'."

"That is?"

"Waiting for Van Winkle. I signed on to hunt for his party."

"Hell!"

"You scoutin' for him?"

"He's following my outfit across the territories. If you've signed on with him, he doesn't need me."

"Tell it to Van Winkle."

"I'll do that." John untied his horse, led him to the watering tank, then exchanged the bridle for a halter and staked him in a patch of grass.

When he returned, Buffer had unharnessed the mules and was leading them to the tank. John went into the house. Everyone was working. Addie had given Dillon and Jane Ann each a pillow slip to hold their clothes.

Trisha and Colin were bringing food up from the cellar. Nodding his approval, John went into a bedroom and came out with a straw mattress, which he carried to the wagon. He then returned for the other mattress and a feather bed that he was sure Addie would not want to leave behind.

Buffer brought the essentials from the barn. He seemed to know what to take and what to leave. He worked quickly, as if this was something he had done before, and he came to the porch when called and helped John carry the trunk and the walnut chest to the wagon.

"We'll take all this out later and rearrange it," John promised when he saw Addie's worried look. Her spinning wheel was perched on top of a tub full of utensils. "We'll have to travel all night, Addie," John said as he arranged the mattresses. "We need to make a place for the little ones to sleep tonight."

"My sheep can ride in the other wagon."

John jumped down off the wagon and looked at her as if she had suddenly sprouted horns in the middle of her forehead.

"Did you say what I thought you said?"

"You did, if you thought I said my sheep can ride in the other wagon."

"Addie, you are *not* taking those sheep!"

"Yes, I am. They are my sheep; this is my wagon."

"You can buy more sheep where you're going."

"Not this kind of sheep. It took me years to get my hands on this pair of merinos. They will ride in the back of the wagon with the tools and other things. We'll put some straw in so they can lie down."

"Addie, be reasonable. We're going to travel all night and all day tomorrow. We've got to get away from here as fast as possible. My men are waiting over near Van Buren with my freight wagons. If we can get to them before the Renshaws catch us, a whole battalion of Renshaws, or lawmen for that matter, will not take Colin or Trisha." He spoke in a conversational tone meant to calm her.

"Please, John." She placed her hand on his arm and looked beseechingly into his eyes. It was the first time she had said his name aloud or voluntarily touched him. "I can make a living for me and my family with these sheep."

"Addie, you don't have to do that. I'll take care of you, and the children, and Trisha."

"No!" She removed her hand as if his arm were hot. "We're not beggars. I'm grateful for what you're doing now, and I hope that someday I can repay you. I'll use the money from Mr. Birdsall to buy a little place, and with the wool from the sheep, I can do what I've been doing for the past few years — sell my knit goods."

A flood of tenderness for the spunky woman washed over him. Her eyes pleaded for understanding. He lifted his fingers and smoothed a strand of hair back over her ear. His brain pounded with a million vague thoughts he couldn't voice.

He turned away and yelled at Buffer Simmons: "Fork some straw in the back of Colin's wagon and load the sheep."

Addie walked through the house one last time. She trailed her fingers over the kitchen table, the back of the rocking chair, the foot of the iron bedstead. Her humpbacked trunk was no longer at the foot of the bed; she had filled it with bedding and keepsakes, including her mother's clock, her parents' wedding picture, and the ivory-handled comb, brush, and mirror set they had given her the year before they died. John had carried the trunk to the wagon.

She was taking two kitchen chairs and leaving four for the Birdsalls. The table, with the deep gouge Dillon had made with the butcher knife, the stove, and the workbench were all that remained. Cloris wouldn't know that one side of the oven was hotter than the other and that the long stovepipe going up through the roof had come down a few times, scattering soot all over the kitchen.

*Goodbye, house. Within your protecting walls I spent my childhood, grieved for my parents, conceived and gave birth to my son. I'll never forget the way you sheltered me that cold, rainy night. You've shared my joys and my sorrows. Now it's time for me to move on.*

"Addie," John said from the doorway.

She turned quickly, her violet eyes bright with tears.

"We're ready to go."

She lifted her head with fierce determination. "Then let's get started."

John closed the door behind her, walked beside her to the wagon, and helped her up onto the seat. He went around checking the tarp he had tied over the back half of the high-piled wagon bed. Dillon and Jane Ann were in the nest he had made behind the wagon seat. They were so excited they could barely contain themselves.

Wearing a brown linsey dress and a dark sunbonnet, Trisha sat beside Colin on the seat of the second wagon. She had worked harder than any of them, and during that time she had uttered scarcely a word. That she didn't like or trust Buffer Simmons was evident.

She neither looked at, spoke to, nor acknowledged him.

Buffer mounted his horse and moved up to where John was tying his stallion to the back of the mule-drawn wagon.

"I'll hang 'round. I don't figure they'll come straight on. They'll sneak in and find Cousin. That'll take some time."

"These wagons'll be easy to track."

"Hellfire! If the rest of 'em is dumb as their cousin, they ain't got nothin' but clabber for brains. They'll forget 'bout the wagons and take out after me. Cousin'll be wantin' a piece a my hide, and I'll show 'em jist enough of it to keep 'im comin'. 'Fore they know which end is up, they'll be halfway to Little Rock."

"Do what you can and I'll be obliged."

Buffer Simmons turned his horse and rode the few yards to where Trisha sat beside Colin. He stopped the horse and tipped his hat.

"Ya ain't to worry none, Miss Trisha. Them Renshaws ain't gonna catch up with ya. Tallman knows what he's a-doin'. I'll be a-catchin' up tomorry sometime."

Trisha looked at him. Her face was pale above the dark collar of her dress. Her jet-black hair, honey-colored eyes, and small, petallike lips made her a thousand times more enticing than any other woman he had ever seen. For a long, stunned instant Buffer Simmons's mind absorbed her image like a sponge and he was struck speechless, as tongue-tied as a smitten boy.

And then, as fast as a flicker of her long lashes, the moment was gone. Simmons regained his senses. With a slight bow of his head, he gigged his horse sharply and rode away.

John lingered at the end of the wagon until Simmons rounded the barn and was heading toward the knoll behind the house, then he walked back to speak to Colin.

"We'll start off at a good clip because the horses are fresh. Then we'll settle down to an even pace." He glanced at Trisha. She was looking straight ahead. "Let Trisha drive some. I don't want you to wear yourselves out; you might need your strength later on. Keep as close as you can, without letting your team get too close to my horse, Victor; and sing out if you need help. We'll keep going until after dark, then find a place to rest until the moon comes up."

"Do ya think they'll come after us?" Colin asked.

"Yeah," John said honestly. "If nothing else, they've got to make a show of it in order to save face. But Simmons will lead

165

them off and give us a chance to put some miles between us."

"Where we goin', Mr. Tallman?"

Not even Addie had voiced that question.

"I've got men with freight wagons waiting west of here. We'll head for them. The Renshaws will think it's Shiloh all over again if they come up against that outfit."

John circled Colin's wagon to see that everything was tied securely before he climbed up onto the seat beside Addie.

"Well, here we go." He cracked the long, snaky-looking whip out over the backs of the mules. The wagon lurched, steadied, and moved forward. John glanced at the woman beside him. "Don't look so sad. You can come back sometime."

"I don't think I want to."

With her eyes on the house, Addie held fast to the side of the wagon seat. Her throat was dry. Her heart felt like a lump in her chest.

*Goodbye . . . goodbye . . . goodbye . . .*

The wagon lurched on.

They left the homestead at dusk. Addie didn't look back. Her tear-misted eyes stared westward. She didn't even hear Dillon's and Jane Ann's shrieks of laughter coming from behind the seat. They were having the time of their lives; she was starting a new one, putting her trust in a man she had met not much more than three days ago.

Addie had always liked the early evening hours. She loved to watch the soft sunlight change the colors of the sky and to inhale the cool, fresh air with the smell of cedar in it that swept down from the Ozarks. She supposed that it was fitting that she start this new life in the evening and not in the morning when she would have a full day before her.

When she was young and her parents were alive, Addie thought now, everything had been easy, and life was forever. She had never imagined that life would be so hard, so lonely, and so full of disappointments. Like any young girl, she had dreamed of sharing her life with a man. His image had changed from time to time as she grew older, but he was always strong and loving. He would build his life around her and the children they would have.

That summer almost five years ago, she thought she had met such a man when Kirby came to the farm. There had been an emptiness within her, a yearning that begged to be fulfilled. She was a woman with a woman's love to give, and she had needed someone to reach out for it.

She had been blinded by loneliness.

* ★ ★

The light was leaving the sky.

Addie hadn't said a word since they had left the farm, nor had the man beside her. The children lay on the mattress whispering and giggling.

"Mr. Tallman, you still have the money Mr. Birdsall paid me for the farm."

"It's in that tobacco can under the seat if you want it. I suggest you not carry it on you."

"I want to pay you for what you've done."

"You will."

"Name your price," Addie said tersely.

"Well, let's see. I left a perfectly good change of clothing and an unpaid bill back at the hotel in Freepoint. If the proprietor refuses to keep the clothes in exchange for the bill, he'll be sending the law after me."

"I don't know what I can do about that."

"You can take me under your wing and take care of me like you did the other orphans."

"You're not an orphan!" Addie said crossly. "Or . . . helpless to defend yourself in a world of grown-ups who consider children no more than property."

"No, I'm not. Calm down, Addie. I know it's a shock to leave your home so suddenly, and I don't blame you for being up in the air about it. The only other thing you could have done was stay and fight it out with the Renshaws. They had the law on their side, even if Trisha did have a good solid reason for shooting the bastard." He looked at her then. She had removed her bonnet and the breeze was blowing her hair. Her slender body was as stiff as a ramrod. Then, as he watched, her shoulders slumped ever so slightly.

"I realize that, and I'm terribly grateful —"

"Even if she hadn't shot Renshaw, your troubles were just beginning. The magistrate said that Renshaw had filed papers to adopt Colin —"

"Oh, good Lord!"

"That's not all. Preacher Sikes was going to try to take Dillon away from you."

The words hit Addie with the force of a cannon ball.

"Take Dillon? Preacher Sikes would . . . take Dillon away from me because I didn't want to give up Colin?"

"No, that's not it. I guess you set the old man off the other morning with your cussing and calling him a hypocrite. Now he's sure that the boy should be removed from the home of a fallen woman. In other words,

169

taken out of a whorehouse."

"A whorehouse?" Addie gasped. When she was able get her breath, rage roared through her like a tidal wave. Her anger was so great that she choked on her words. "Why, that . . . that old son of a bitch!"

"Addie, watch your language! You're cussing again." There was laughter in John's voice, but it did nothing to allay Addie's anger.

"Take my son? I'd kill him first! He's nothing but a fat, overbearing, Bible-spoutin' hypocrite! A toad is what he is. If I ever see him again, I'll spit in his face. He's crow bait! A yellow, stinkin' coward! He wouldn't dare try to take a boy away from his father even if he was the sorriest man alive!" Addie was so agitated that the angry, bitter words flowed from her mouth like a fountain. She wadded up her sunbonnet and twisted one of the ties around and around her wrist until it broke.

John turned his face away because he couldn't keep from grinning. He had jarred her out of her doldrums. She was riled aplenty. He was glad that he had saved that part of the news until now. It had taken her mind off leaving her home.

Addie was still muttering.

"That pompous know-it-all horse's ass will

never get his hands on my son, and that dirty son of Satan, who old Sikes said was such an 'upstanding' pillar of the church, will never get his filthy hands on Colin or Trisha. I'll blow his damn head off first!"

John whistled through his teeth. "I sure hope you never get mad at me, honey. I'd not stand a chance."

Addie was so angry that the endearment failed to register in her mind. She turned to face him.

"I'm so damn tired — of being run over, knocked down, disregarded, and looked down on because I'm a woman and don't have any-one to stand up for me. Tired of it. Do you hear? *Tired of it!*"

"Yes, I hear. Don't blame you a bit," John said evenly.

"It's going to be different from now on. You can bet your bottom dollar on that."

"Good for you."

"Don't placate me, Mr. Tallman."

"I'm not, Addie. I'm just agreeing with you."

She glared at him. "You don't know what it's like being a woman alone. Damn men! They don't give a woman credit for having any brains at all." She turned to look at the wagon behind them. "Where's Mr. Sim-mons?"

"He hung back to see what the Renshaws would do."

"That was good of him. I'll pay him something too."

"No, you won't."

"Why not?"

"Because he didn't hire on. He *offered* his help." He spoke in a crisp, almost angry tone.

Addie sat quietly wondering why in the world she had let her tongue run away with her. As she gathered her scattered thoughts, questions began to pop into her head.

"How far ahead are your men, and why are they there and you here?"

"If we keep going, we'll meet up with them by late tomorrow. They're there because they brought the freight wagons down from Saint Louis, and I'm here because I'm trying to get you and your family away from the Renshaws."

"Why are you not with your men and the freight wagons?"

"I went to Saint Louis, ordered my goods, and left my men to load it and head back while I visited my cousin Zachary Quill at Quill's Station, a small place up on the Wabash River."

"That doesn't explain why you were in Freepoint," Addie said pointedly.

"My cousin asked, as a special favor, if I

would allow a friend of his and his party to trail along with us through the Indian Nations and the Oklahoma Territory. He's coming down from Springfield and will rendezvous with us five days from now. Does that answer your questions?"

"That still doesn't explain why you were in Freepoint."

"I had time to kill. Wanted to see the sights, maybe take a bath, visit the . . . taverns."

"Oh."

"Are you satisfied that I'm not an outlaw or a spy, or a renegade? Speaking of renegades, there are plenty of them now that the war is over."

"Do you think we'll run into any?"

He shrugged "Maybe; maybe not. But that's another reason why I want to reach my camp as soon as possible. To some bands I've seen, you and Trisha would be worth more than money."

"Are you trying to scare me?"

"No, Addie. I'm trying to be truthful."

After a brief silence, Addie asked, "Is Van Buren a good-sized town?"

"About the size of Freepoint."

"We've got to find a place to settle."

"Don't worry about it now. We'll talk about it tonight."

"Muvver." Behind her, Dillon stood and

pulled on her arm. "I gotta wet!"

"Dillon, please —"

"Can't help it," he said urgently, holding himself and moving restlessly.

"I gotta pee too." Jane Ann's announcement was even louder than Dillon's.

"In a little while."

"But I *need* to, Muvver."

"Can you two wait just a little bit longer?" John asked, as though he dealt with such situations frequently. "After we round that bend and go just a little farther, we'll stop and rest the teams. You can get a drink of water and go to the bushes."

"I'll wait," Dillon said.

"Me too," Jane Ann echoed as she and Dillon sank back down on the mattress.

How odd, Addie thought, to be discussing bodily functions with this strange man and not even feel embarrassed.

# CHAPTER

## * 10 *

Uneasiness touched Addie as she watched John untie his horse from the back of the wagon.

"I'm going to backtrack a mile or two to see if we're being followed. Give the horses and mules a bucket of water each and no more." He sprang up onto the horse's bare back. "Addie, fire two rapid shots if you need me."

They all stood motionless for a few seconds after he left. Then Colin took two buckets from the back of the wagon, handed one of them to Trisha, and walked down to the stream that ran alongside the trail.

"Be careful of snakes."

"Miss Addie, why'd ya have ta go say that for?" Trisha grumbled.

"Muvver —"

"Go to the other side of the wagon, Dillon, and do what you have to do. Jane Ann, go down to the stream with Trisha."

Addie waited until her son was in sight once again, then went to the end of the wagon bed to check on her sheep.

"You all right, Mr. Jefferson?" she asked, rubbing the spot between the ram's eyes. "Are you watching over Dolly and Bucket?" The sheep had risen shakily to their feet. "You'll get a drink of water in a minute."

After the sheep had been watered and the horses and mules rubbed down with a couple of tow-sacks, the little group quietly ate the biscuits and meat Addie had wrapped in a cloth and stored under the wagon seat.

Standing with Colin and Trisha on the dark, lonely roadside, Addie suddenly realized how much she had come to depend on the tall, dark man who had thrust himself into her life. He had swiftly become her strength and her courage. How was she going to cope without him? Cope she would, she knew that, but it was different now. She'd had a taste of how it was to have a strong man to share her troubles.

"Miss Addie, do ya feel bad?" Trisha had come up close to her after she had helped Dillon and Jane Ann back up into the wagon so they could lie down.

"I don't feel *bad*," Addie whispered. "I just feel kind of lost out here all by ourselves."

"I mean, do ya feel bad 'bout leavin' the

farm? I do hates it, Miss Addie. If'n I hadn't a-shot that polecat —"

"I don't think we could have kept Colin away from him otherwise. And no, I don't feel bad. I did at first, but it was just the breaking away. I've always wanted to see something else, do something else. I didn't want to live there on that farm until I died."

"Ya ain't blamin' me?"

"Of course not!" Addie put her arm around the girl. "Don't even think such a thing!"

"What we gonna do? Is that *passerby* takin' us to a town where them Renshaws can't find us?"

"I asked him about that. He said we would talk about it tonight. I keep telling myself that he's an honorable man. He must be. Why else would he be taking the risk to help us?"

"That other'n. That Simmons. What's he hangin' 'round for?"

"What do you think, Colin? You seem to know Mr. Simmons better than Trisha and I do."

"He's a hunter," the boy said, and Addie felt a surge of sympathy for the boy who had been deprived of a normal, carefree childhood. "He said he was gonna hunt meat for a wagon train that's crossin' Oklahoma Territory to New Mexico. He ain't a bad man, Miss Addie, but I'm thinkin' that Mr. Tallman don't like him much."

An owl hooted. They stopped talking and listened. The owl hooted again.

"It's quiet, ain't it? It's nights like this that haints come out. I betcha there's a buryin' place 'round here," Trisha whispered fearfully.

Addie looked toward the eastern sky and saw the moon coming up over the hills.

"Mr. Tallman said that we'll travel all night and should reach his men by tomorrow evening."

"Then what'll we do?" Colin asked.

"To tell the truth, I don't know. Right now we've got to trust Mr. Tallman."

"He might'a jist pulled foot and took off," Trisha murmured. "Took his horse. Ain't no reason he *got* to come back."

"He left his saddle," Colin said quickly. "He'd not leave for good without that."

"Not that I'm scared or nothin' if'n he don't come back. Long's I got this here gun in my hand, I ain't scared a nothin' but . . . haints." Trisha attempted a brave front, but her voice quivered.

The three waited silently by the wagon where Dillon and Jane Ann lay sleeping. Addie's eyes swept the darkness for movement. She shivered in the night air and hugged herself, rubbing her hands up and down her arms. The quiet became almost absolute, broken only by the occasional flutter of a bird or the distant call of a coyote. A cloud floated over the three-quarter moon.

"Addie, it's me." John's voice came from the direction of the stream. Then the sound of horse's hooves on the rocky bank reached them.

Addie felt tremendous relief when he came in sight leading his horse.

"You all right?" he asked.

"We're fine. The animals have been watered and rubbed down. Did you see anything?"

"No. Simmons said he could lead them away; I guess he did. But come morning they'll be on the trail again. They'll not give up easily," John said, recalling the trussed-up Renshaw cousin sitting in the fresh cow manure. He retied his horse to the back of the wagon. "Let's get started. Pull out and go ahead, Colin. Give the team their heads, and they'll stay on the track. Move them along at a good clip. You got the rifle?"

"Yes, sir."

"I could ride with Trisha, and Colin ride with you, for a while," Addie suggested.

"No. Colin's a good hand with the horses and Trisha with the rifle. They make a good team." He put his hand beneath Addie's elbow and urged her up onto the wagon seat. "Younguns asleep?"

"It's way past their bedtime. Even the excitement of the trip couldn't keep them awake." Addie unrolled the food she had saved for him, and after he put the team in motion, she broke open a biscuit, put a piece of meat inside, and handed it to him. "I didn't have time to cook up something to bring. I hope this holds off your hunger pangs for a while."

John took a bite. "It fills that hollow spot that's been nagging at me."

"There's a churn full of milk back there. We may be making butter." She laughed softly. "I baked three loaves of bread this morning. We have jam and honey to go with it, so we'll not go hungry. Dillon and Jane Ann were too tired to eat much tonight, but they'll make up for it tomorrow."

John finished off two more biscuits before he spoke. His mind grappled with how to approach Addie with his proposition. The more he thought of it, the surer he was that he wanted Addie and her family to fill the empty rooms in his hacienda. That he had taken responsibility for their safety didn't enter into this decision at all. He could almost guarantee that if he put them in the care of a friend of his in Fort Smith or sent them north to Quill's Station, they would have protection from the Renshaws; but he wasn't sure whether the magistrate had the authority in Fort Smith to take the orphans.

He turned to look at the fair-haired woman with the violet eyes who sat beside him. Her face was turned toward him, as if she were studying him. The moon shone on her face. Courage was there in plenty, and strength. She was exactly the kind of woman he had been waiting for, one who wouldn't buckle at the first sign of trouble. Looking at her now, he recalled words he had read somewhere before: *There are in a man's life certain ultimate things, and just one ultimate woman. When he finds her, he does not pass on unless he is a fool.*

"I'm no fool." He realized he had spoken aloud when he heard a small sound from Addie. "Talking to myself," he said quickly and grinned. "It means that I spend too much time alone."

Addie nodded thoughtfully. "I did that when I was alone."

"When was that?"

"Off and on for the past eight years — after Mama and Papa died. Then, even before Dillon was born, I talked to him and my sheep. Of course, I didn't know then that Dillon was a *him*." She laughed nervously.

With the moon lighting the trail, they could clearly see the other wagon. It was quiet except for the jingle of the harnesses, the creak of the wagon and the sound of the horses' hooves.

"Why did you tell Colin to go ahead?"

"I was afraid his team might get too close to my horse and get kicked. Victor is a mountain-bred horse with strong survival instincts. He'll let me know if another horse is coming up behind even before I can hear it."

"Mr. Tallman —"

"Can't you make yourself call me John?"

"I really don't know you that well."

"How long will it take?"

"Well . . . I don't know the answer to that. But I do want you to know how much the children, Trisha, and I appreciate —"

"Addie, if you tell me one more time how grateful you are, I just might dump you off that seat and drive on without you."

"Oh, you!" She laughed. "All right. I'll not say it again . . . tonight."

"Not tomorrow, not tomorrow night, not ever again."

After a few moments of silence, Addie said: "Trisha and Colin are anxious about what we're going to do. So am I. I only know that we're headed west and Fort Smith and Van Buren lie in that direction."

"— And my freight wagons."

It occurred to John that Addie knew nothing about him except what little he had told her the first day at her breakfast table and the little bit more he had told her just after they had left the farm. She needed to know him and his way of life in order to make a decision that would so drastically affect her and her family.

"Do you trust me, Addie?"

"Heavens! If I didn't, I certainly wouldn't be here now."

"Why? Why do you trust me?"

"I guess . . . because you helped us that first night. And, well . . . you *seem* trustworthy."

"That's not much of a reason."

"I didn't have much choice, now did I?"

"No, I guess not. I'm not much of a talker, especially about myself. But in view of . . . well, what I plan — concerning you — I think it only fair that I tell you a few things."

"Concerning me? What do you mean?"

Ignoring her questions, John began: "I'm thirty years old. I come from good stock. My father and mother are well respected in both Arkansas and New Mexico Territory. My father refused to take sides during the war, and my brother and I shared his beliefs. On my ranch in New Mexico Territory near what's known as Elk Mountain, I run five hundred head of cattle and almost that many head of horses. My men and I break them for the army."

John had talked rapidly, as if he wished to get the ordeal over with, but now he slowed as he began to describe his home.

"The ranch buildings sit on the long, gentle, easterly slope of a wide shallow valley. A clear spring-fed stream flows near by. Peach-leaf willows and cottonwoods border the stream. Also nearby are tall lily plants called yucca. Soap is made from the yucca roots. To the south and west of the valley is a sweeping view of grassy plains and in the distance the Continental Divide.

"My house, or 'hacienda' as the Spanish call it, is built of stone and adobe in the shape of a U. The walls are two feet thick, the roof flat. It's warm in the winter and cool in the summer. The center of the U is a courtyard; it has a deep well and is shaded by pinon trees."

John grew silent and seconds passed.

"It sounds lovely," Addie said, to fill the void.

"Most of the rooms are empty," he said softly. "There are no children playing in the courtyard. A Mexican couple lives there while I'm away, and my father rides over once in a while to keep an eye on things."

Silence.

Addie glanced at him. He was looking straight ahead, his elbows resting on his thighs, the reins held loosely in his hands.

"Do you know what I'm leading up to, Addie?" When she didn't answer, he said: "I'm asking you to come with me to New Mexico, live in my house, fill those rooms with children. You need someone to protect you. I need someone to share my home."

Addie was stunned. She couldn't have spoken if her life depended on it. The silence between them lengthened. He was obviously waiting for her reaction. Addie cleared her throat. She felt the intensity of his gaze focused on her and suddenly grew quite warm and breathless.

"I had hoped, Addie, that you might consider a liaison between us as beneficial."

His cold, impersonal words unlocked her mind and jarred her back to reality. Determinedly, she raised her chin, looked him in the eye and spoke coolly.

"Are you suggesting an indecent liaison?"

"Not unless you consider marriage to me indecent," he said with the same coolness in his tone.

"Why would you even consider marriage to a woman you don't know? Especially me, with three children and a dear friend who will have a home with me for as long as she wants."

He answered her question with one of his own.

"Would you consider traveling almost a thousand miles across Indian Territory to live with me on my ranch without marriage?"

"Of course not! What do you think I am? A . . . trollop?"

"If I thought that, I'd not have asked you to take my name." His tone was firm and decisive. The tension between them intensified.

Addie swallowed bravely and looked him in the eye. "Mr. Tallman, I am honored . . . I guess, that you consider me a candidate to be your life's companion. I must, however, refuse your proposal. As soon as we reach our destination, you must feel free to go your own way. You have more than fulfilled your gentlemanly duties."

When John laughed, Addie's mouth snapped shut and a flush covered her face.

"I'm glad you find my decision so . . . entertaining."

When he said nothing, she turned to look at him. A broad grin splashed across his face. He let his gaze drift over her smooth forehead, the curve of her brows, her sweet rosy cheeks.

When his eyes focused on her lips, she parted them and drew in a quivering breath.

"You're a prize, Addie. So prim and proper, yet when you get your dander up, it's as if you were bred back to a wildcat."

"That's a compliment?"

"I meant it as one. Let me set you straight about a few things. I don't consider myself a *gentleman*. I didn't help you because it was the *gentlemanly* thing to do. I was brought up in a hard land that breeds hard men and was taught to use my instincts. I knew the instant I saw you in the store that you were a woman with high moral standards. I respect women and children and despise cowards and bullies. That's all there is to it."

No words came to Addie's mind. She was still reeling from his proposal of marriage.

"Well, what do you say? I've already told you more about myself than I've ever told another woman. There it is, take it or leave it."

"I'll leave it, but thank you very much."

"You've not only yourself to consider," John went on as if she hadn't spoken — "but the children and Trisha. There is a deep-seated desire for revenge in hill people. That's the reason for so many feuds among them. I don't doubt that the Renshaws will make it their primary aim in life to avenge what was done to a Renshaw. I can leave you in Fort Smith, a mere two-day ride from Freepoint, where the Renshaws will find you in less than a week; or I can take you with me out through the territories to New Mexico, where you and the children will have not only my protection but that of my men. The choice is yours."

"I already told you —"

"Then consider Colin and Jane Ann. Renshaw filed to adopt Colin. That crazy hill preacher thinks you're unfit to raise Dillon."

"Oh, my goodness. Every time I think of that, I feel like I'll shatter into a million pieces."

"Are you still grieving for Kirby Hyde?"

There was a moment of astonished silence; then: "No!"

"Did you love him?"

"No! Er . . . yes! It's none of your business."

"Tell me about you and Kirby."

"There's nothing to tell. I married him; he went to war and didn't return."

"That's all?"

"That's all."

"Hummm . . ."

There was a long silence between them after that. Both were wrapped in their own thoughts. The air grew cool. Addie knelt on the seat and spread a cover over the children sleeping on the mattress. When she sat down again, she pulled her apron up to cover her arms and locked her eyes on the outline of the wagon ahead.

In her mind she replayed the events of the day, from early morning to the last word uttered by the man sitting beside her. After she had explored every possibility for preserving her independence and safeguarding her family, she could come to only one conclusion. The four people who depended on her were her first concern. To keep them safe, she would sacrifice her dream of meeting a man who would love her for herself alone.

Having made her decision, she tried one last time to retain some control of their future.

"Mr. Tallman, I will go with you and work as a housekeeper in your home —"

"Addie, that isn't what I had in mind. I can hire someone to cook and clean."

"But if we are wed, and later you should meet someone else, you might be sorry you're tied to me."

"Or it could be the other way around. Are you thinking you might meet another man and wish to be rid of me?"

"No. I'm just trying to tell you that you don't have to marry me in order to fill your house with the children."

"You'd sleep with me out of wedlock?"

"No! I meant Dillon, Jane Ann, and . . . Colin."

"I'll consider them mine. They'll carry my name. But I want other children too, and I don't intend for them to be *bastards*." His tone was abrupt, almost angry.

Once again Addie was shocked into silence.

"Is the thought of being with me . . . like that . . . repulsive to you?" When she didn't answer, he added: "I don't intend to jump on you the minute the vows are spoken." Silence. "And I don't intend to have *two* unattached women on that train. Trisha will be trouble enough."

Addie thought of what he had said for a long while before she spoke.

"When do you need an answer?"

"By daylight. There's a town of sorts ahead. They'll have a church and a preacher."

He appeared to ignore her after that. Tired, and too numb to think, Addie sat hunched on the seat and tried not to cry. She was fully aware of how fortunate she and the children were to have a man like John looking after them. She blamed her need to weep on the fact that she required time to adjust to the drastic turn her life had suddenly taken.

The moon was directly overhead when they stopped the second time to rest the teams.

190

John shouted to Colin to pull up. When both wagons had stopped, John jumped down and took the buckets to the stream. Addie and Trisha wiped the sweaty horses and mules down with the tow-sacks. After both teams were watered, John and Colin carried water to Victor and the sheep.

"Muvver . . ."

Before Addie reached the wagon, John was there.

"What are you doing awake, tadpole?"

"Gotta go!"

"Again? C'mon." As he lifted Dillon out of the wagon, the child wrapped his arms around John's neck. "You must have drunk a tank of water today," he said as he walked off into the darkness carrying the little boy.

Addie felt a queer stirring in her heart at the sight of her child in John's arms.

"Mama —"

"Do you have to go too, Jane Ann?" Addie asked.

"I'm cold. This ain't fun no more. I want my bed . . . with Trisha."

Trisha climbed up on the wagon. "Trisha's here. I'll get more cover for my purty sugar-plum. Ya lay down and sleep. Tomorry, ya can sit with me an' I'll tell ya 'bout a princess name of Jane Ann." Trisha put a quilt over the child and tucked it around her.

She climbed down off the wagon just as John returned with Dillon nestled in his arms, the child's head on his shoulder. He laid Dillon beside Jane Ann and covered him.

"There's room there for Colin. He should get some sleep," Addie said. "I'll take over the team for a while."

Colin started to protest but stopped when John spoke up.

"She's right, son. You're going to need all your strength tomorrow. A man takes his rest when he can. Climb up there and snuggle down by Dillon. You needn't worry he'll wet on you. He just emptied out enough to raise the creek."

Addie didn't realize that John was behind her until she put her foot on the spoke of the wheel to pull herself up onto the seat. He took her hand, then continued to hold it tightly after she was seated. His grip was warm and hard. She felt a strange and unexpected sense of being cherished, and her throat constricted.

"Would you rather follow?"

"It . . . doesn't matter."

"If you need me, just pull up and stop." He squeezed her hand, then let it go. She loosened the reins from the brake handle. "You've got a good partner riding shotgun," he said as Trisha seated herself and picked up the rifle.

Addie looked at him then and saw the flash of white teeth beneath his dark mustache. *The future will be good,* she thought. *I'll make it be good. He may not love me, but he'll not go off and leave me as Kirby did.*

# CHAPTER

## * 11 *

The wagons slowed to allow the teams to walk up the long grade to the town that lay quiet in the morning sun. At the hitching rail in front of the saloon were two horses; at the mercantile, a wagon and team.

Addie, on the seat beside Colin, tried to poke the strands of loose hair into the knot at the back of her neck and then smooth some of the wrinkles out of her skirt. At the last rest stop Colin had insisted on driving so that Addie or Trisha could get some sleep. Trisha had gone reluctantly to lie beside Dillon and Jane Ann.

During their time together, Addie had explained their situation and told Trisha that she was considering marrying Mr. Tallman and going with him to his ranch in New Mexico. At first the girl was adamant in her objection to Addie's marrying the "passerby" in order to save her from the Renshaws. But then Addie had explained that Ellis Renshaw

194

had filed a legal claim to Colin and that Preacher Sikes was going to try to make Dillon a ward of the church because he considered her an unfit mother.

"Trisha, it will be a long, dangerous journey."

"I ain't carin' 'bout that. I'm goin' where yo're goin'."

"You think it's the right thing to do?"

"I don't see no other way out, Miss Addie."

Addie put her hand in the small of her back and blinked her dry, dust-rimmed eyes. She could remember only one other night that she hadn't slept at least a little while, and that was the night her parents hadn't come home and the next day their bodies had been found downstream.

When John whistled, Colin stopped the team on the edge of town near a livery where a watering tank was being filled with a hand pump. After motioning for them to sit still, John walked over and spoke to the man for a few minutes, then he came back to the wagons.

"I've made arrangements for the teams to be watered and fed." John held his hand up to help Addie down. "The liveryman didn't want anything to do with the sheep" — he smiled — "but we'll take care of them later."

Addie stumbled while climbing down. John

caught her around the waist and eased her to the ground.

"Thank you."

"My pleasure, ma'am." He seemed in amazingly good spirits for a man who had passed the night without a wink of sleep. "There's an outhouse for you ladies over there." He pointed to a plank building. "Dillon, Colin, and I will go behind the livery. We'll meet you back here."

Trisha had climbed down off the wagon when John reached it. He helped Jane Ann down, then Dillon. He took the boy's hand and walked toward the livery.

"Dillon's sure took to that passerby, Miss Addie."

Trisha had put on her bonnet and tied the strings beneath her chin. Addie had let hers hang on her back. John and the boys were waiting when they returned to the wagon.

"We've only an hour and we have lots to do." John pulled a bag from inside his shirt and handed Colin some money. "Addie and I have some business to attend to. While we're doing it, take Trisha and the children to the mercantile. Trisha, pick out some food to eat on the way: raisins, dried peaches, cheese if they have it, and candy sticks."

"I have money . . ." Addie started to climb up onto the wagon to look for the tobacco can that held the money from Mr. Birdsall, but then she felt two hands at her waist and was lifted aside.

"Not now, Addie."

"Oh, but —"

"Shhh . . . Isn't that what you say to Jane Ann when you want to hush her up?" His hands were still at her waist, and his eyes held hers.

*They are blue, not black.* The thought came to Addie's mind as if it were of great importance. He continued to look at her, and both of them knew what he wanted to know but didn't want to ask in front of the others. After a moment, she nodded.

His eyes narrowed and his brows raised. His mouth worked and the word that came out on a breath was, "Sure?"

She nodded again.

He took a gulp of air as if he had been holding his breath. His hand moved to hers and held it tightly.

"If you get back here before we do, Colin — and I'm sure you will — let the sheep down to graze awhile."

"Can I go with ya?" Dillon tugged on John's hand.

John put his free hand on the boy's head. "Not this time, tadpole. Go with Colin and Trisha."

Addie walked with John down the dusty road. When he realized she was taking two steps to his one, he slowed his pace.

"Where are we going?"

"To the hotel. The liveryman said there's a judge staying there. He can marry us. It's either him or the magistrate, and if this one is anything like the one in Freepoint, I'd rather have the judge."

"Why are you in such a hurry? We could be married in Fort Smith or —"

"We'll not be going to Fort Smith. And I want us to be married before we meet my men."

"Why?"

"Because I want to introduce you as my wife." *Or before you change your mind.*

"I'm not dressed for a wedding," Addie protested. "My face is dirty and —"

"I'll ask at the hotel for a place for you to wash and comb your hair while I talk to the judge. And, Addie, don't screw your hair up in a tight wad on your head. Put it in a loose braid and let it hang down your back."

"Why, I never!" she sputtered.

"I know you never, but do it for me. It'll be your wedding present to me."

They stepped up onto the porch of the hotel and entered through the bat-wing doors. The man at the desk looked up from his led-ger. His mouth formed an O. The big black-haired man in buckskins was an intimidating figure; his hair hung to his shoulders, and his naturally dark face was darker with several days' growth of whiskers. But it was the man's eyes and attitude that caused the clerk to jump to his feet.

The woman looked pale and tired. She had a dirt streak on her face, and strands of hair had come loose from the knot and hung down over her shoulders. She had magnificent violet-colored eyes, but they looked flat and bloodshot.

The clerk took all this in at a glance because when the man spoke, he demanded attention.

"Judge Carlson. What room is he in?"

"Why . . . ah . . . number two. Right down the hall."

"I want a room where this lady can have some privacy for a few minutes."

"Yes, sir. Right this way. Room number one."

They followed the clerk to the end of the lobby and into a short, narrow hallway. He opened a door and stood aside. Addie and John went into the room, which held a bed, a chair, and a washstand.

"I'll knock on the door in a few minutes," John said. He looked as if he would say more, but after glancing at the clerk, who was watching with undisguised curiosity, he squeezed her arm and left the room, closing the door behind him.

Addie groaned aloud when she saw her image in the small cracked mirror that hung above the washstand. She looked far worse than she had thought. Leaning forward for a closer look, she could see why her eyes felt so scratchy. A film of dirt covered her face and had settled in the corners of her eyes. After pouring water from the pitcher into the bowl, she wet the end of a towel and held it to her face.

*Oh, my. It feels so good.*

Trying not to think about what lay ahead, she rolled her sleeves up to her elbows and washed her face, neck, and arms as best she could without soap, then took the pins from her hair and put them in her pocket as she pulled out the piece of comb she carried. Remembering John's request that she let down her hair, she smoothed the tangles with the comb and braided it in one long rope. She was holding the end, wondering what to tie it with, when she heard John's knock.

He stepped eagerly into the room as soon as she opened the door. He had removed his hat and was carrying it under his arm. Without a word, he took his knife from its scabbard and sliced a thin strip from the end of his doeskin shirt. He replaced the knife, then carefully tied the strip around the end of her braid.

Addie felt her heart thumping like a wild thing in her breast, and a shudder rippled under her skin. She raised gold-tipped lashes and immediately became lost in the narrowed pools of his dark blue eyes. He was so tall, his shoulders so broad that she felt that if she leaned against him she would be protected from the world. For an endless moment their eyes held, their faces so close that his breath was warm on her damp face.

"You won't be sorry, Addie. I'll do my best to see that you're not sorry you married me."

"You're the one who may be sorry —"

"No, I won't. When you get to know me better, you'll find out that I don't act on impulse, especially about something as important as this."

"You should wait until you get to know me. The children . . . you may hate having them in your home."

For a fleeting moment this morning he had felt that she was with him, that she felt as he did, that she responded to him. Now he felt tied up inside. Words did not come easily to him when he felt most deeply, and somehow he always found himself saying the things that meant nothing, leaving unsaid all the things he wanted to say.

He wanted to speak his heart now but found himself wordless when he looked into her eyes. There was much that was fine in her — the way she carried herself, the lift of her chin, the curve of her lips when she smiled. The way she had come through the last twenty-four hours had convinced him more than ever that she was the woman he wanted.

"Judge Carlson will be here in a few minutes. I need to wash before he gets here. I have ten pounds of dirt on my face."

He moved away from her and went to the washstand. On the way he hung his hat on the bedpost. Addie had poured the water she had used into the slop jar. John filled the basin, cupped his hands in the fresh water and splashed his face and neck. While drying his face with a towel from the rack, he looked intently at Addie.

*This woman will be my woman to love and to cherish until death us do part.* The thought filled his mind with gladness. He had no doubt that once they were married she would be a loyal wife; and maybe, just maybe, she would become fond of him, perhaps even love him as his grandmother had loved the first John Spotted Elk and as his mother loved his father. Then he dismissed the idea immediately. It was too soon even to contemplate such a miracle.

He looked at her for a long moment, then walked to her, tilted her face up by putting his fingers beneath her chin, and kissed her gently on the lips. It was a soft, lingering kiss. When he lifted his lips, his face was so close to hers that they were breathing the same air, so close she couldn't look into his eyes.

"You look like a scared little rabbit caught in a trap. Don't worry, I'll not demand anything of you. When we come together as man and wife, it will be because *both* of us want it."

"Thank you," she whispered, blinking rapidly to keep her tears at bay.

"You don't happen to have a comb, do you?" he asked, stepping away from her. She held out the piece she had used. He had to stoop to see himself in the minor. "One of these days you'll have to cut my hair, or else I'll have to braid it."

Addie was still rattled from his kiss, from the unexpected sweetness of it. She had not known that kisses could be so gentle. Kirby's had been soft at first, but later they became hard and demanding and not at all to her liking.

*Oh, Lord, am I making another mistake?*

Addie suddenly remembered something her mother had told her many years ago: "Don't make yourself miserable over the mistakes you made yesterday. Each morning is a new beginning. Start fresh from there."

The rap on the door sounded like a thunderbolt. Addie jumped, and her heart began to hammer. John opened the door to admit a small man with white hair and a mustache and goatee to match. He wore a dark serge suit and a white high-collared shirt. He looked exactly the way she pictured a judge would look. The small man closed the door behind him with a loud bang.

"We got papers to fill out." Judge Carlson picked up the chair and carried it to the washbench. "Get rid of these things, son. I need something to write on."

John removed the bowl and the pitcher while the judge pulled papers, a pen, and ink bottle from his satchel.

"Well now, young lady. Your full name."

"Addie Faye Johnson Hyde."

"Widow?"

"Yes, sir."

"Age?"

"Twenty-four."

Judge Carlson took pride in his penmanship, which featured many curves and curlicues as if the document were to be framed and hung on a wall.

"Now you, young man. Full name."

"John Spotted Elk Tallman."

The judge looked up. "Any kin to Rain Tallman?"

"My father."

"Hmm. Widower?"

"No."

"First time you've jumped the broomstick, huh? Age?"

"Thirty."

They waited for what seemed hours to Addie but could only have been minutes, while Judge Carlson filled out yet another paper; then he set the documents aside and stood.

"Take her hand," he said to John. Then: "Come to think on it, you look like your pa did thirty years ago."

"Did you know him?"

"Everybody in the territory knew Rain Tallman. If this boy is anything like his pa, girl, you got yourself a good man."

At the judge's use of the term *boy* when referring to John, Addie's eyes sparkled. Imagine calling the tall man beside her a boy!

The ceremony was so short that it was over almost as soon as it began. Judge Carlson didn't believe in wasting time.

"Do you take this woman to love and to protect?"

"I do."

"Do you take this man to love and to obey?"

"I do."

"I now pronounce you man and wife. What God has united, let no man put asunder. You may kiss the bride. Here's your paper, Mrs. Tallman. Keep it in a safe place, and if this stud gets to roaming, wave it under his nose. I'll file the legal document with the proper authorities."

All of this was said with the man scarcely pausing for breath. A second later he had returned pen and ink bottle to his satchel and headed for the door, where he paused and looked at John. There was a twinkle in his eyes, and he smiled for the first time.

"Don't reckon you want me hanging around now."

"Thank you, sir."

"Harumph!" he snorted just before the door shut with a loud bang.

John looked down at Addie's red face. "I guess we're married."

"I guess we are."

"He told me to kiss the bride."

Addie lifted her shoulders in a noncommittal gesture that belied the fact that she was almost afraid to breathe.

John lowered his face to hers. When she felt the soft brush of his mustache on her cheek, she wanted to cry. She meant no more to him than a woman who would give him children, keep his house, and work beside him in return for protection for her and her family. As his lips touched her, she closed her eyes.

He settled his mouth against hers and breathed. "Addie . . . Addie — don't act as if I'm torturing you. Open your eyes and look at me." He lifted his head and she gazed up at him. "We'll have a good life together."

She nodded and slipped her arms around his waist. When his lips touched her again they were warm and gentle as they tingled across her mouth with fleeting kisses. The arms that held her tightened when her mouth moved against his. Addie felt herself being drawn tightly against hard, muscular thighs, yet in no way did she feel threatened by his strength. She was breathless when he pulled his mouth from hers and raised his head only a fraction.

"I don't take my vows lightly, Addie."

"I know."

She felt the strong thud of his heartbeat, smelled the tangy smoke on his doeskin shirt, felt his breath warm on her forehead. He stroked the nape of her neck, then trailed his fingers along the braid that reached the curve of her hips.

"I like your hair like this. A lot of women in New Mexico wear their hair down," he murmured softly.

It was comforting to lean against him, to be sheltered in this man's arms. She rested her forehead against his shoulder. It had been so long since she'd had anyone to lean on.

"I know you're tired," he whispered against her ear. "But we must go."

Addie lifted her head and stepped back. John took his hat from the bedpost and opened the door. With his hand beneath her elbow, he held Addie close to his side as they went back into the hotel lobby. The man at the counter stood up as John slapped a coin onto the registration book.

When they stepped out into the sunlight, John's eyes scanned the street. The same horses were in front of the saloon, the same team and wagon in front of the mercantile. The strong smell of coffee wafted from the eatery when they passed. John paused and looked down at Addie.

"Mrs. Tallman, do you think we dare take the time to bring our family up here for breakfast?"

"You're the wagon master, Mr. Tallman."

Addie surprised herself with her retort. Then she remembered. "Oh. We can't leave Trisha. They wouldn't permit her to eat here."

"Yes, they will. Trisha looks Indian or Mexican. It's only back in Freepoint, where they know she has colored blood, that they'd refuse her."

"All right." Addie grinned up at him. "Let's do it. That coffee smells wonderful."

"I like a woman who's willing to take a chance."

He smiled and hugged her closer to his side as they walked companionably down the boardwalk.

His smile made him look younger, less harsh. Addie realized what a fine figure of a man her new husband was.

Dillon and Jane Ann were chasing each other around the wagons. Trisha and Colin leaned on the end, watching the sheep graze on the short grass beside the roadway.

"Muvver! Muvver!" Dillon ran to them. "I'm hungry. Trisha told us to wait."

John picked the boy up and set him astride his hip. Jane Ann clutched Addie's hand.

"We're going to eat in that restaurant over there," John said. "Trisha, put the rifle under the wagon seat. It'll be all right. I'll be able to see the wagons from the window."

Addie saw the look that came over Trisha's

face and her heart ached for the girl.

"Y'all go on. I'll watch the sheep."

"We're not going without you, Trisha." John reached for the rifle. "I know what you're thinking. But trust me in this. The farther west you go, the less your skin color will matter."

"I is what I is, Mr. *Passerby*." Trisha tried to act flippant, but Addie saw her lips tremble.

"Yes. You're a very pretty young lady. One of the prettiest I've ever seen. That's what makes men look at you. You're allowing a few drops of Negro blood to color your whole life. Now come on. With your black hair and my black hair, they'll think you're my daughter."

Trisha looked at him in astonishment. "Won't ya be mad?"

"Mad? Hellfire!" John laughed. "I'll be tickled if my girls are half as pretty as you are."

At that moment Addie fell a little bit in love.

# CHAPTER

## * 12 *

They were on the road again. The town where Addie and John had married, and where they had eaten in the restaurant as a family, was behind them now.

Suddenly John laughed aloud, then smiled at Addie, looking terribly pleased with himself.

"Colin's mouth dropped open a foot when we told him we had married and were going to my ranch in New Mexico."

"Poor child. He wasn't sure what that meant for him and Jane Ann and Trisha. He and his sister have been shuffled from one place to another since their folks died."

"He'll be all right now. In less than a half-hour I got myself two boys and a girl."

"That pleases you?"

"Hell, yes. Every man wants sons . . . and daughters."

Addie was mystified by his exuberance over taking on the responsibility of children who were not his.

"But they're not . . . yours."

"Yes, they are. When I married you, they became my stepchildren." His dark brows came together in a frown. "Are you thinking I'll not be a good father to them?"

"No, I wasn't thinking that. I'm glad for Colin that you'll take an interest in him. He's such a good boy."

John smiled again. "Amy will be surprised."

"Amy is your sister?"

"My mother. She's quite a gal. You'll like her."

"Will she like me?"

"Of course. She'll love you if you're good to *me*, and if you give her grandchildren. You've already given her three."

"Will she accept them?"

"Sure she will. I'd like to change their names to Tallman, though, if it's all right with you."

"I can decide for Dillon, but we'll have to ask Colin and Jane Ann."

After a brief silence, Addie said: "Thank you, John." It was the second time she had called him by his first name.

"For what?"

"For accepting my children and for the way you've treated Trisha."

"Trisha's part of your family — *ours,* now."

"How is it that you overlook her Negro blood while other men seem unable to?"

"My father taught me and my brother and sisters that all men are equal under the sun. I was brought up with Indians and Mexicans in our home. My father tells stories about a Negro named Mr. Washington who ran the ferry on the Wabash below Quill's Station. He was a friend of Tecumseh, chief of the Shawnee. His wife was a Shawnee named Sugar Tree. Mr. Washington was treated with great respect at Quill's Station."

"Trisha has never been treated as an equal by whites because of her Negro blood, and not by Negroes because she looks so white. She's been stomped on, used, and humiliated all her life. You've made her feel one of us."

"Has she been with you a long time?"

"A little while before Dillon was born I found her in the barn, cold and weak from hunger. She was a runaway. She told me that her mother was a beautiful octoroon. When she died, Trisha's father brought her to live at the big house. Then he went to war, and his wife sold her when she discovered her working in the kitchens."

Addie told him how Trisha had chopped wood, done the chores, and taken care of her and Dillon when he was born.

"I doubt if the baby and I would have survived without Trisha."

"You've had a pretty rough time."

"It could have been worse. We had a house and food, which is more than some had. All over the South the Yankees burned homes and stole food and animals."

"The Rebs probably did the same in the North."

"Thank God it's over."

Although it was pleasant to sit beside John and discuss things that were important to her, she was aware that he was constantly on the alert. One time, Victor, his stallion, warned him of an approaching horse. John took his rifle from the floor of the wagon and placed it across Addie's lap. Then he shifted so that the gun strapped to his waist could easily be pulled from its holster. As the horseman approached, John handed Addie the reins.

"Howdy," the man said as he passed. He tipped his hat to Addie and again to Trisha in the wagon ahead.

John eased the rifle back to the floor and took the reins.

"I didn't think it was Renshaw. He was riding too good a horse. It was a Tennessee Walker, if I'm not mistaken."

In the middle of the afternoon they came to a plank bridge over a stream. Addie's horses, pulling the lead wagon, walked right across, but the mules balked. The sound of their hooves on the planks frightened them. Only John's strong, experienced hands on the reins and the sting of the whip on their rumps forced them over the planks.

Colin had pulled his team to a stop on the other side of the bridge. John stopped behind him and wound the reins around the brake handle.

"We'll water the teams here. That'll hold them until we reach the freight camp."

John stepped down off the wagon and reached for Addie. His hands at her waist swung her easily to the ground. He reached for Jane Ann and then Dillon.

"Stay on the road until I beat the grass with a stick," he cautioned. "Most likely there are snakes this close to the creek, and they'll be lying out in the sun. We'll take a fruit jar and get you a drink of fresh water."

Colin, carrying the buckets, followed John as he beat a path to the creek. Trisha carried a jar, along with a bucket for the sheep.

Jane Ann tugged on Addie's hand. "I gotta pee."

"Do it here while John and Colin are down at the creek. Do you have to go, Dillon?"

"Naw." He ran to pick up a small terrapin that had started to cross the road but was now closed in its protective shell. "Looky. I got me a turtle."

"Leave it be, Dillon. You can get it when you've finished. Come up ahead of the horses and give Jane Ann some privacy. You do your business too, young man. We'll not be stopping for you later."

"Ah, Muvver!"

They all drank thirstily from the jar and ate a handful of raisins while the horses each had a bucket of water and the sheep shared one. Dillon picked up the turtle and showed it to Colin and John.

John was cautioning the boy not to put his fingers between the shells when Victor whinnied and began to dance nervously. The stallion's ears peaked, and John was instantly at the ready.

"Someone's coming fast. Put the children in the wagon. Get your rifle, Trisha. Addie, get mine. Colin, stand behind the big wagon with that buffalo gun. Let it be seen, but for God's sake don't shoot it, or it'll knock you clear back to the creek. Just seeing it is threat enough. I should've bought a shotgun back at that town," he mumbled.

The sound of a running horse reached them. The rider rounded the bend in the road and crossed the plank bridge.

"It's Simmons," John said, stepping out

from behind the wagon. The hunter's horse was wet with sweat, and its sides were heaving. "You been riding hard."

"Yeah. The Renshaws are about three miles behind. I cut cross-country to get ahead of 'em."

"How many?"

"Four."

Addie made a little moaning sound. All eyes were on John. He had made his decisions in the time it took Buffer Simmons to step from his horse.

"Addie and Colin can't handle the mules. Get the sheep out of the wagon to lighten it." He hurried to the wagon and let down the tailgate. He and Buffer lifted out the sheep, which bleated, then began to eat the grass alongside the road.

"Get in here with your rifle, Trisha." John swung her up into the wagon, fastened the tailgate, then hurried to the other wagon. He lifted a whimpering Jane Ann and handed her to Buffer, then picked up Dillon. "Put them up front where they can hunker down behind the seat. Trisha," he said in passing, "shoot anything coming down that road that looks like a Renshaw. Shoot at the horse. Maybe a Renshaw'll break his neck when he falls off."

John put his hand on Colin's shoulder.

"Son, you're the man here. I'm depending on you to get the women and children on down the road. Understand? Keep going until you see the freight camp. It'll be off to the right on a knoll."

"Yes, sir."

"Addie, this is as good a place as we'll find to stand them off." He grasped her shoulders. "Simmons is with me, or he'd not be here."

"Can't we all make a run for the freight camp?"

"No, ma'am," Buffer said. "Ya got no chance of outrunnin' 'em."

Addie appealed to John: "Then let Colin take the children. I can shoot and so can Trisha."

"No. You're going with Colin. When you get to the camp, tell my men who you are." He grasped her at the waist and lifted her up into the wagon. "I don't want to kill Renshaws if I don't have to. What I'd like to do is dump them in that cold creek and drive off their horses."

"Good idee." Buffer laughed gleefully and eyed two tall trees, one on each side of the road. "I know just how we can do it."

"Be careful," Addie called as the wagon lurched and the horses took off at a run. She turned to look back and saw Buffer Simmons leading his horse and John's back to the plank bridge and John pulling a coil of rope from the wagon bed.

The wagon had covered several miles before Colin braced his feet against the footboard to slow the running horses first to a trot and then a fast walk. Addie wondered where the young boy got his strength. Jane Ann was whimpering and Dillon was crying loudly. Addie looked back to see Trisha hunched against the tailgate, watching the back road through the dust raised by the speeding wheels.

"Shhh . . . Dillon, don't cry. Jane Ann, honey, are you all right?"

"I hurt my bottom . . . when I fell back."

"You and Dillon climb up here with me and Colin. Trisha," she called after she had settled the children on the seat, "you all right?"

"Yeah, 'cept I'm settin' in sheep do-do. If'n I catch me a Renshaw, I gonna make him eat it!"

Addie laughed, then began to cry. She turned away so that the children couldn't see the tears streaming down her face. The night without sleep, the tension of the morning, the anxiety, and the rough ride were taking their toll on her nerves.

"Do you want me to take the reins awhile, Colin?" she asked, regaining her composure.

"No, ma'am."

"Have you heard . . . shots?"

"No, ma'am. Don't worry, Miss Addie. Them Renshaws ain't no match for Mr. Tallman."

"Do you like him, Colin?"

"Yes, ma'am!" The boy turned to her with a broad grin. "He's gonna get me my own horse. He says nobody but me can ride 'im, and nobody but me will take care of 'im."

"It's a long way to New Mexico. More than likely we'll never come back."

"I ain't ever wantin' to go back to that place. You sad, Miss Addie?"

"Not sad exactly. Anxious, perhaps. We've put ourselves in the hands of a man who is almost a complete stranger."

"Didn't ya want to wed up with Mr. Tallman?"

Addie was sorry she had put their situation so bluntly when she saw the worry on Colin's face.

"I believe Mr. Tallman to be a good, decent man. He has a house and wants a wife and children in it," she hastened to say, and was relieved to see that Colin was satisfied with her answer.

Colin stung the horses with the whip and

220

got them moving faster. Addie strained her ears for the sound of gunshots but heard none. Dillon went to sleep on her lap and Jane Ann against her shoulder. Her back ached and her eyes stung from lack of sleep. The wagon bumped along for what seemed to Addie an eternity before, in the distance, she saw an awesome sight.

A string of freight wagons was parked on a grassy knoll. Dark canvas covered the loads that rose above the six-foot sideboards. Two covered wagons were parked nearby, and inside the circle a large number of mules and oxen grazed on a grassy plain.

Colin turned the horses off the road and up a rutted track to the camp. Several men were waiting for them by the time they stopped beside one of the covered wagons. One of the men stepped out to stand at the head of the sweating, heaving team.

"Ya tryin' to run these horses to death, boy?"

"Is this John Tallman's freight camp?" Addie asked.

"It is."

"Mr. Tallman is eight or ten miles back. Four men were chasing us, and he's trying to stop them. He needs help."

"Four, ya say?"

"Yes. Four men who are . . . evil."

A bandy-legged man with a face full of whiskers came to the side of the wagon. His bright blue eyes strayed over the group.

"Wal, ma'am, John ain't needin' no help if'n thar's only *four*. If'n thar was eight or ten of 'em we might ride on down thar and take a look-see."

"You're not willing to help him?" Addie stared at the man in astonishment.

"He won't be thankin' us fer buttin' in on his fight, less'n he's outnumbered by more'n that."

"There are *four* of them, you — you jelly-head!" Addie shouted. "Don't you understand English?"

"Yes, ma'am."

Dillon woke and began to cry.

"Whatcha think, Rolly?" the bushy-faced man asked the one standing by the horses.

"Naw! It'd be over by the time we got the horses saddled."

Addie moved Dillon off her lap and stood. "I can't believe what I'm hearing. You are refusing to help your employer? Why, I never heard of such a thing!"

"Who might you be, ma'am?" Bill asked.

"I'll tell you who I am." Addie was so angry, she was shaking. "I'm *Mrs.* John Spotted Elk Tallman, that's who I am." She bent and snatched the horse whip. "You men get down the road and help him, or — by all that's holy, I'll take a strip of hide off your backs." She was unaware of it, but tears were making roads through the dust on her face.

The grins on the men's faces broadened.

"What ya tryin' to pull here, ma'am? Ya thinkin' to draw us away from camp so yore friends can steal the goods here? Ya ort to a made up a better tale than that. It ain't likely John'd sign up to travel in double harness, 'specially with a woman with a flock of younguns."

Addie was so shocked at what he was saying that she was unaware of the man who rode up on a big gray horse until he spoke.

"What's goin' on, Bill? Who's this?"

"Says she married up with John. Says John's in a little skirmish eight, ten miles down the road. Wants us to go down thar. Thar be only four of 'em."

"They've followed us from Freepoint," Addie explained. "Mr. Tallman sent us on ahead and was going to wait for them."

"Did he send word for us to come?"

"There wasn't much time for him to tell us anything."

"John knows what he's doing. He can take care of himself."

Addie looked at the man on the horse, at the amused look on his face, and on the faces of the others. It occurred to her that what they saw were a ragtag woman with a flock of children in a rickety old wagon. They didn't believe that their boss, John Tallman, would marry her! They believed she had some ulterior motive for coming here.

It was more humiliation than she could endure. Tears she could no longer control erupted suddenly and harshly. She sank down on the wagon seat, covered her face with her hands, and sobbed as she had not done since her parents died.

"Muvver! Muvver!" Dillon was terrified. He'd never seen her so distraught. He burst into a fit of crying and tried to put his small arms around her. Jane Ann cried against Addie's shoulder.

"Get away from that horse!" Colin shouted, and sent the whip sailing out over the backs of the tired team. They lurched forward. He wheeled them in a sharp arc and headed them back down the track to the road.

The man on horseback followed. He rode up beside the wagon.

"Hold on!" he shouted.

*Bang!* Trisha shot the rifle in the air. "Get!" she yelled. "Get, or I shoot yore ugly head off!"

"Gawddamn! Stop this wagon, boy!"

They had reached the end of the track and

224

turned down the road before the man was able to grab the cheek strap on one of the bridles.

"Whata ya want?" Colin demanded. "We ain't stayin' here and havin' *them* back-talk Miss Addie and makin' her cry. We'll wait right here till Mr. Tallman comes . . . if he comes."

"Get yore hands off that horse, sucker!" Trisha stood in the wagon bed, her feet spread, the rifle at her shoulder pointed at the man on horseback.

He looked at her with narrowed eyes and a set, angry face.

"Put the gun down, girl."

"Ain't puttin' it down, *boy*, till ya back off. Mr. Tallman say shoot the horse if a pig-ugly polecat comes after us. Reckon that's you, pissant." She moved the barrel until it pointed at the horse's head.

"Gawdamighty!" The man wheeled the horse, moved back from the wagon, and sat looking at them.

Addie dried her eyes on the end of her skirt. She felt as if she had been hit on the side of the head with a club. Her body ached, her head hurt; but most of all there was an emptiness inside her. How could she ever again face those men who held her in such low esteem?

"Don't cry, Muvver." Dillon, still whimpering, wrapped his arms and legs around her.

"I won't. I promise. What we need is a drink of water." She turned to look behind her. "Trisha, is there a jar of water back there?"

"Put Jane Ann back to get it." Trisha never took her eyes off the rider.

"Put down the rifle, Trisha. He isn't going to hurt us. He isn't going to help us either." Addie lifted Dillon off her lap and climbed down over the wagon wheel.

"Shall we go on, Miss Addie?" Colin's young face was troubled.

"The horses are awfully tired." She lifted down first Dillon and then Jane Ann. "Just ignore him, Colin," Addie said, when she saw the boy looking belligerently at the man who watched them. "I'll give the children a drink, then we should rub down the horses. Poor beasts. They've worked hard the last two days."

John and Buffer Simmons were ready for the Renshaws before they heard the sound of their voices and the clip of horses' hooves in the quiet afternoon air. The rope had been tied to a tree on one side of the track, left to lie in the dirt until it reached the other side, then pulled up over a low limb. The end was tied to Buffer's saddle.

Astride his horse, John waited behind a screen of bushes on the other side. He couldn't believe the Renshaws would be so stupid as to fall for the old trick. Any ten-year-old boy on the frontier would know better than to ride bunched up, without hand-guns, and with their only weapons in the saddle scabbards. Simmons had watched them and said that unseating them would be as easy as falling off a log. He was gleefully looking forward to bashing their heads.

John left nothing to chance. He checked his handgun, then took a good grip on the three-foot piece of deadwood he had chosen to use as a club.

As Simmons gigged his horse and the rope came up, he let out a bloodcurdling yell. Two men were swept from their saddles by the rope. One horse reared, throwing its rider into the creek, and in the confusion, one horse went to its knees.

John charged out of the bushes and swung the club. The man still in the saddle was knocked off his horse and fell backward into the stream. Still yelling like a drunken Indian, Simmons sprang into the fray and with a well-placed kick sent another Renshaw over the edge and into the cold water.

"I get Cousin!" Buffer yelled, and picked the man up by the back of his shirt and the seat of his pants. "Phew! You still smell like cowshit," he said, and tossed him into the creek.

"Get in there," John said to the remaining Renshaw.

"I . . . can't swim!"

"Too bad." John punched him in the stomach with the club. The man staggered back and toppled off the bridge.

"I can't swimmmm. . . ."

"Sit the dumb ass up," Buffer yelled. "We ain't wantin' 'em to drown — yet." One of the men hurried to the man lying on his back, his arms and legs thrashing in the water, and pulled him to a sitting position.

"Stay right there." John pointed his gun at a man who tried to get to his feet. He sank back down into the cold water that reached his chest.

"What ya gonna do?" the youngest of the Renshaws demanded.

"We're thinking on it," John replied. Then: "What do you think, Buffer? Isn't that a pretty sight?"

"By golly bum. Nothin' purtier! Hain't we ort ta go on ahead an' shoot 'em?"

"We might as well have some fun first. Wasn't any fun catching them. A blind man could have done it. I've never seen grown men stupid as these Renshaws."

"Go on, have yore fun. Our day'll come. Us Renshaws ain't forgettin' what that bitch done."

"And I ain't forgettin' what ya done to me," Cousin shouted.

"As long as they're not forgetting, we better give them something to not forget." John took his gun from its holster and cocked it. "I get the first shot. Hey, you. Stand up so I can get a sight on your kneecap."

"No! Please! Don't . . . Pa . . . lea . . . sse —"

"Shut up beggin'," an older man snarled.

"Shoot that'n in the head," Buffer suggested.

"Reckon it would splatter like a pumpkin?"

"Reckon it would, but it ain't Christian ta send 'em up to the Pearly Gates dirty as they is. Let 'em sit there a spell and soak that Renshaw stink off 'em."

"Good idea. You watch for zitter snakes. That's a hell of a way for a man to die. I'll take care of the horses."

"Zitter snakes? Yeah, I heard they was in the creeks over this way. They come outta them stinkin' springs down by Rock Cave. It's said they like water and breed like rabbits."

"Snakes! Gawd damn ya!" The Renshaws began to beat the water with their hands.

"They're just little-bitty," Buffer said. "Ya won't even know they've bit ya till ya start ta swell all up an' blood starts comin' outta yore nose and ears. Haw-haw-haw!" He pointed at the youngest Renshaw. "That little'n will be right purty when he gets swole up some."

# CHAPTER

## * 13 *

The sun had gone down.

The days were long at this time of year, but for Addie nighttime was approaching far too fast. It had been more than six hours since they had left Mr. Tallman back at the bridge. It was still too soon for Addie to think of him as John, her husband. The last two days had passed like a dream that was happening to someone else and that she was watching from afar.

Colin and Trisha had unhitched the horses and staked them out to crop the grass beside the road. Colin had brought water from a nearby creek, and from it Addie had wet a cloth and they had all been able to wash the road dust from their faces and hands.

She was worried. Tears that she attributed to exhaustion, from having gone so long without sleep, were never far from her eyes. How could she live with the guilt if something had happened to Mr. Tallman? He had taken on her troubles. He could be hurt and bleeding and at the mercy of the ruthless Renshaw family.

Another thought occurred to her. She and the children might have to spend the night here with just one blanket and a shawl among them. Thank goodness for the raisins and dried peaches Trisha had bought that morning. They had been enough to stave off the children's hunger pangs.

At the freight camp on the knoll above the road a fire was burning, and the smell of cooking meat drifted down to them. At one point the man on the gray horse had approached, asking to talk with them. They had turned their backs and gone to the other side of the wagon, ignoring him. Finally he had left to join what seemed to Addie an army of men gathered around the cook wagon.

Addie had no doubt who was the topic of conversation.

"What we gonna do if Mr. Tallman don't come?" Trisha asked. It was the first time any of them had voiced that almost unthinkable question.

"He'll be along. If he was hurt, Mr. Simmons would come tell us."

"I ain't likin' that bushy-face man none a'tall. He keeps a-lookin' at me like a cat lookin' at a bird."

"Has he said anything disrespectful?"

"No. But he heard the talk in town an' knows I'm colored. He's a-thinkin' like all them other horny billy goats that I'll be easy to get in bed with."

Addie looked around to make sure the children weren't listening. Colin had brought a tadpole up from the creek. They gathered around the bucket while Colin tried to explain that it would turn into a frog. For a moment Dillon forgot the turtle he had left behind.

"Maybe Mr. Simmons isn't thinking that at all."

"Then why'd he watch us with that spy-glass for?"

"I don't know. But I do know that he helped us get ready to leave and that he delayed the Renshaws to give us a head start. And he came to warn us."

"He's wantin' somethin'," Trisha insisted stubbornly. She had wrapped a shawl about her shoulders. Her hair curled around her face and down her back. She brushed it back impatiently. "If we go to New Mexico, will it be with them?" She jerked her head toward the freight camp.

"I imagine so. They certainly aren't what I thought they would be." Addie wondered if Trisha would ever get over her distrust of men.

"We could run off . . . now. To a town."

"It's too late for that now. I *married* Mr. Tallman. I spoke the sacred vows."

"Why ya reckon he want to marry ya for?"

"As I told you last night, he thinks it's time he settled down with a family. He wants children in his house."

"I ain't children." Trisha's voice held a note of suspicion.

As darkness fell, Addie's worries about Tallman increased. Had the Renshaws managed to sneak up and ambush him and Mr. Simmons? She began to pace up and down, always keeping out of sight of the freighters by staying on the far side of the wagon. She was almost afraid to turn her eyes from the road they had come down so many hours ago.

Trisha was sitting on the tailgate of the wagon, swinging her feet, then suddenly she jumped down.

"Listen," she hissed. "I hear sheep."

Addie stopped pacing and listened, her gaze fastened on the road.

"Baa . . . baa . . ."

"I heard it too. It's the sheep!"

They gathered at the end of the wagon and waited. Then in the dim light they saw the wagon round a bend in the road, and the bleating of the sheep sounded louder. Addie's heart thumped with relief when she saw the flat-crowned leather hat on the man on the wagon seat. The children drew closer to Addie and Trisha as the wagon neared.

Colin, with a welcoming grin on his face, stepped out and greeted John.

"Glad ya got here, Mr. Tallman. Ya all right?"

"We're all right. You?"

"The same."

John pulled the mules to a halt, and Buffer Simmons, with one of the ewes resting across his thighs, rode up beside the wagon.

"Take this here dad-blasted sheep 'fore I pull its bleatin' head off. Ain't nothin' stupider than a sheep, less'n it's a Renshaw."

John lifted the sheep down. It ran to Addie.

"Where are the others?"

"Tied up behind the wagon seat. Had a hell of a time catching them. That's why we're late. What in thunder are you doin' here? Why aren't you up at the camp?"

"We decided to wait for you here. Did the Renshaws —"

"They didn't give us any trouble to speak of. Why are you down here and not up at the camp?" John asked again. He put his hand on her shoulder and gave it a little shake.

"We *went* up there. Them pissants laughed at Miss Addie."

"Trisha! That's enough!"

"— An' said you'd not marry up with a woman with a 'flock' of younguns." Trisha tossed her head angrily. She had moved protectively close to Addie.

"They made Miss Addie cry," Colin blurted. "And I brought her down here."

"I hate 'em!" Jane Ann wailed and hid her face in Addie's skirt.

"That's enough. All of you." Addie looked up at John's scowling face. "The men we talked to didn't understand. I asked them to go help you, but they were sure that you would be able to handle what was happening back there."

"They said we'd come to draw 'em off so somebody could steal the goods in their wagons."

"Colin, I swear! You're getting to where you run off at the mouth just like Trisha."

"It's the God's truth, Miss Addie." Colin hung his head.

Looking at the boy, Addie failed to see the smoldering anger that came over John's dark face. When she did look up, she became immediately aware of it. His hand on her shoulder squeezed almost painfully. He had stopped breathing. His lips were pressed together, his jaws hard-clamped, and his eyes mere pinpoints between his dark lashes.

Addie put her hand on his arm. "John, we don't want to be the cause of trouble between you and your men. The way we looked, this rickety old wagon — I can't blame them for thinking we were some ragtag outfit —"

He moved his hand back and forth across her shoulders, then pulled her close to his side in a protective embrace.

"It will not happen again," he said softly, looking into her tired, violet eyes circled with dark bruises. "What is mine is now yours. What is yours is now mine."

He left her abruptly and climbed up on the wagon. One at a time he lifted the sheep down to Buffer, who set them on their feet. Like children they ran to Addie. She bent and rubbed each head.

"Are you all right, Mr. Jefferson? Run along and take care of Bucket and Dolly."

"Hand up the babes, Simmons." John reached for Dillon and Jane Ann and set them on the seat. Then he climbed down off the wagon. "The team and the wagon will be all right here, Colin. Do you and Trisha want to crowd in behind the seat or walk up to the camp?"

"They can ride with me." Buffer climbed

back onto his horse and leaned on the saddle horn, a wolfish grin on his face.

"I ain't ridin' with that warthog." Trisha gave him a scathing look, climbed up into the wagon, and wedged herself behind the seat.

"John" — Addie put her hand on his arm — "why don't we camp down here tonight and . . . give them a chance to —"

"No. You and the children will have a hot meal and shelter." He grasped Colin and swung him up behind Buffer, then helped Addie climb the wheel to the seat.

"I'd rather you didn't make a big to-do over this. The men will resent us all the more."

John didn't answer but sailed the whip out, stung the mules to get them started and turned them up the heavily rutted track to the freight camp.

Addie tried once again to cool John's anger. "It could have been the way I demanded they go help you that raised their suspicion. A man on a big gray horse did come down and try to talk to us."

"What did he say?"

"Trisha ran him off with the rifle."

"Good girl, Trisha. I'm going to teach you to shoot that thing and hit what you aim at."

When they reached the camp, John drove

right up into the circle of light made by the large campfire. A half-dozen men stood around. One walked to the wagon.

"Howdy, John. See ya made it."

Ignoring the greeting, John came around and lifted Addie down, then the children and Trisha. Buffer rode up and Colin slipped down from behind him.

"Put your tucker where you want to bed down, Simmons, and help yourself to whatever Bill's got in the cookpot. Rolly," he said to the man who had stepped forward to greet him, "take the wagon over there and park it under the trees, unhitch the mules, and put them on a picket line until the other stock gets used to them. Paco, you and Huntley get extra canvas and throw up a couple of tents over there by the wagon for my wife and the children. And get out enough canvas to cover what's on the wagon after it's removed and piled in a high, dry place. There are a couple of mattresses on the bottom of the load. Put them in the tents."

The men hurried to obey the orders. When the wagon moved out from behind Addie, she felt naked and exposed to all eyes. She knew that Trisha felt the same when the girl moved over behind her.

"John —" Addie was sure it was the man who had ridden the gray horse who spoke, although he was hatless now.

"Later, Cleve."

"We didn't —"

"Later." John spoke in a tone that brooked no argument. He picked Dillon up and set him astride his hip. The boy whispered in his ear. John paused for a minute, then whispered back: "The turtle is in the wagon. We'll find it tomorrow." He led the little group around the fire to a couple of benches.

"Dish them up some supper, Bill."

"He doesn't have to wait on us. I can dish it up," Addie protested.

"You're so tired you're about to drop. Sit down. Where's your helper, Bill?"

"Wal . . . he's —"

"He's what?"

"Drunk."

"Too drunk to work?"

" 'Fraid so."

John looked at Cleve. "When he sobers up, pay him off and send him down the road."

John lowered Dillon to the bench beside Addie. Trisha sat down close to her. Addie could feel her trembling. Refusing to be intimidated by the stares of the men who had moved back out of the light and lingered in small groups, Trisha lifted her chin and stared back at them. Only when Jane Ann moved close to lean against Trisha's knees did she turn her face away.

Standing in the darkness, Buffer watched Trisha and admired her courage. Puzzled by his protective feeling for her and by his resentment of the men ogling her, he led his horse out to be tied to a picket rope.

The tension around the campfire was profound. Addie had never been so uncomfortable in her life. She felt as if she and her family were sitting in a store window for people to gawk at. Even the children were quiet and cast fearful glances at the men lounging back out of the light.

John carved slices from a haunch of meat roasting over the hot coals of the campfire. He placed them on a plate. Bill added beans and carried them to a table he had let down from the side of the wagon. He didn't speak or look at the tight little group sitting on the benches. Addie got up to help. It wasn't natural for her to sit and be waited on.

"Sit and eat, Addie," John said as he carried the last two plates to the table.

"Are you going to sit down?"

"In a minute." He filled a plate for himself and came to sit beside Colin.

"Baa-a . . . baa-a . . ." Addie was taking her first bite when she heard the sheep.

"What the hell?"

"Gawdamighty —"

"Name of a cow!"

"Cow, hell! It's gawddamn sheep!"

Bleating loudly, Mr. Jefferson, followed by Dolly and Bucket, came into camp and made a beeline for Addie. They brushed against Dillon. The beans on his plate slid into his lap and he began to bawl, his mouth open and full of food. Over his cries, Addie heard snickers from the men in the shadows. John picked the child up and set him on his lap. Red-faced and wishing she were anywhere in the world except where she was, Addie got up quickly. The sheep followed her out of the circle of light.

"Gregorio," John yelled.

"*Sí, señor.*"

"You know about sheep. Take care of them so Mrs. Tallman can eat her supper."

The Mexican youth who came out of the shadows had a large hat, riding on his back, held there by a string about his neck.

"*Señora,* wait. I get some corn and they come with me."

Addie rubbed the heads of the sheep and murmured to them while she waited, knowing that they were as confused by their surroundings as she was. Gregorio came back with a shallow pan. He held the ground corn under Mr. Jefferson's nose and let the ram smell it. Then he backed away and the sheep followed. Addie waited until the sheep disappeared in the darkness before she went back to the table.

Dillon was asleep on John's lap.

Addie was tired in body and spirit. She was sure that once she closed her eyes she would sleep like the dead, but she could not. Behind closed lids she saw the face of a tall man with dark shoulder-length hair and dark blue eyes. Her mind whirled in confusion as she lay on the mattress beside Jane Ann and Trisha.

This was the first night since Dillon's birth that he had not slept beside her, and she wondered why she had given in so easily to John's request. No, she thought now, it had not been a request; it had been a decision.

"You and the girls can sleep here." With Dillon sleeping on his shoulder, John had led the way to the tents that had been set up a short distance from the main camp. "Colin, Dillon, and I will sleep in the other one."

"Dillon can sleep in here with us. There's room."

"There'll be more room if he's with me and Colin."

"But . . . he's never been away from me at night. He'll wake up and be scared."

"If he is, I'll bring him to you."

243

"He may have to . . . go to the bushes."

"Colin and I will take care of him. Get some sleep, Addie. Tomorrow we'll start getting ready for the trip."

Trisha and Jane Ann fell asleep immediately. Addie lay with her face toward the open end of the shelter so that she could see the tent where her son lay sleeping. She had mentally prepared herself to sleep with her new husband if he demanded it. She was Addie Faye Tallman now. Kirby Hyde was no longer her husband. John Tallman was. Would he insist on his *rights* morning, noon, and night, as Kirby had after they had wed? She had come to detest that part of marriage but had resigned herself to it as she had to other unpleasant duties.

She had watched John enter the shelter with Dillon and Colin. She watched him a short time later when he came out and walked back to the cook wagon where a small fire was still burning.

*Tomorrow we'll start getting ready for the trip.* The words her new husband had spoken ran repeatedly through Addie's mind along with the thought that time was rushing by too fast. She wanted to stop it for a little while until she could think about and become accustomed to all that had happened to her.

*Do you take this man to love and obey?* Obey?

Other than the two short months she had lived with Kirby, she had not had to obey anyone since her parents died. Now this man was her lawfully wedded husband and she had promised to obey him.

*John Tallman, who are you? I don't know you!*

John laid the sleeping child down on the mattress and removed his shoes. The little bugger was tuckered out, but no more so than his mother. Her violet eyes were glazed with fatigue and ringed with dark shadows. She had made a brave effort to hold her shoulders back and her head up, but as she walked beside him to the tent, she had almost staggered. A few more hours without sleep and she would collapse.

Looking down at the sleeping child, John thought briefly of the man who had sired him. Kirby Hyde might have sown the seed, but *he* would nurture it, teach this boy to be more of a man than the one who had fathered him. Dillon was his son, now, in every way that mattered. John covered the boy and stroked his chubby cheek with the back of his hand before he got to his feet.

"I'll be up by the cook wagon for a while, Colin."

"We'll be all right, Mr. Tallman. I'll take care of Dillon."

"You don't have to call me Mr. Tallman, Colin."

"Ah . . . I . . . Miss Addie don't let me call grown-ups by their first names."

"Well, don't worry about it. Usually that sort of thing works itself out."

"The Renshaws was comin' to get me, wasn't they?"

"They were coming to get Trisha for shooting that no-good kin of theirs."

"Trisha did it to keep 'em from takin' me."

"I know. I saw it. She's a spunky girl."

"But . . . but Miss Addie had to leave her farm because of me." There was real sorrow in the boy's voice. "She said she didn't, but I think she did."

"It was partly because of you, I guess. But also because Preacher Sikes wanted to get Dillon away from her. He thought she was unfit to raise him because of the men who went out to the house."

"That wasn't her fault . . . or Trisha's. They never let nobody in."

"The talk in the town was that they did. The preacher spoke to the magistrate, after Addie gave him that dressing down, about you going to the Renshaws and after he heard Dillon's father wasn't coming back."

246

"Do *you* believe it?"

"Would I have taken her for my wife if I thought she was a loose woman?"

"I . . . had to ask."

"It's all right. You can ask me anything."

"Miss Addie didn't tell me that old turd was going to take Dillon."

"I guess she didn't want to worry you."

"She was awful worried about you. What happened with the Renshaws? Did you shoot 'em?"

"Naw. It's best not to shoot if there's another way. We tossed them in the creek, made them sit there, and ran off their horses. Buffer was right when he said they were a stupid bunch. They'd not last in the territories. Within a week's time their scalps would be hanging from a lodgepole."

"Ah . . . sir?" Colin's hesitant voice stopped John as he was about to leave. "I was wonderin' if . . . if me and Jane Ann —"

"You and your sister will have a home with us for as long as you want."

John had been raised in the security of a loving family, always knowing that his ma and pa were there to rely on, but still he understood the uncertainty Colin was feeling.

"When I asked Addie to marry me, she told me that she had three children and Trisha. I took it as an honor that she not only trusted her life to me but the lives of her children and Trisha. Addie's children are now my children, Colin. That means you and Jane Ann as well as Dillon. You'll live with me and Addie in our home until you're old enough to take care of yourselves."

"I'll try not to . . . be any trouble."

"Don't try too hard, son. It'll take all the fun out of it." In spite of his exhaustion, John grinned broadly. He clasped the boy's shoulder. "I remember my pa saying that when I was your age he was sure that I didn't have enough sense to come in out of the rain."

"Is he still livin'?"

"Very much so. He'll take to you." John chuckled. "The first thing he'll teach you is how to bring down a turkey or a jackrabbit with an arrow. He'll teach you how to make a fish hook out of a turkey bone and how to creep up on a deer and skin out a rattler. He was raised by the Shawnee and has more woods sense than any man I know."

"Golly," Colin whispered in awe.

"There'll be plenty of time for me to tell you about him before we get home. Go on to bed. I'll be back in a little while."

# CHAPTER

## * 14 *

The coffeepot, blackened by many fires, stood in the coals on a flat stone. John took a tin cup from a sack hanging on the side of the cook wagon and filled it with strong black coffee. Only three men had waited beside the fire. The others had taken their bedrolls and gone off into the darkness, knowing the boss was less than happy about the way his wife had been treated.

John looked across the campfire at the silent men. They were a chosen group, selected because they were experienced and able to face the ordeals and trials of a dangerous journey, and, more important, because they were trustworthy. John would trust his life to any one of them and, at one time or the other, had done so.

Cleve Stark was a lean, cold-eyed man of thirty years who feared God and nothing else. He carried his rifle like an extension of his arm, as indeed it was, and he was the sort of man who would last in any venture. Any softness in him had been drained out of his hard, sinewy body by hard living and hard fighting. His dark red hair and mustache had earned him the nickname Red Dog among the Apache and the Navajo. He was constantly alert, as was common among men of his breed. Had he not been, he would not have survived the massacre of his family during the vicious raids by Mexican outlaws and the final destruction of his ranch by the Chiricahua Apache. He was rawhide-tough and durable and was second in command of the bull train.

The head bull-whacker, Dal Rolly, got up to refill his coffee cup. He was in charge of the bull-whackers and the oxen. One man was assigned to each of the sixteen wagons, with six substitutes in case of accident or sickness. The substitutes worked along with the herders to drive the extra animals and as night herders. As the drivers began their day, the night herders turned in to sleep in the supply wagon. Rolly expected every man to do his work without complaint.

Built like a grizzly bear, Rolly had a face full of barn-brown whiskers but little hair atop his head. He was also the wheelwright. With proper tools and a supply of seasoned oak, he kept the wagons repaired. A skilled packer, Rolly balanced the weight and bulk of goods in the wagons to prevent spillage or cargo spoilage if water entered the wagon box when it forded a stream. Just under six feet tall, he weighed nearly two hundred pounds. He was taciturn, patient, and, like many big men, friendly and even-tempered. He constantly pushed his men to break their record of moving out in less than sixteen minutes after "yoke up" call.

The cook, Bill Wassall, nicknamed Sweet William because of his fondness for pouring molasses or honey on everything from beans to cornbread to buffalo steaks, rose before daylight each morning and pulled the ashes from the coals of his fire, sometimes retrieving a kettle of red Mexican beans he had left simmering through the night. After adding wood to the fire, he would grind a pound of coffee beans and start the pots boiling.

When breakfast was ready, he woke the men by ringing a cowbell and shouting, "Rise and shine! Come and get it or I'll throw it away." Sometimes he would burst into song, usually his own raunchy version of "The Yellow Rose of Texas."

He had authority in the camp area. Gray-haired, squint-eyed, he appeared slow and clumsy, but he knew how to get things done. He took great pride in his work and was considered a first-rate cook, which was one of the reasons why John and Rain Tallman had hired him for the trip. Well-fed men were more content and better able to do the jobs they had been hired to do. Another reason was that Bill Wassall was a tough old bird who could handle himself in almost any situation.

The three men waited for John to speak. They all knew he was angry enough to bite the head off a rattler. A quiet man, John didn't get angry very often, but when he did, he acted with either a cold, biting calm or a hot, quick fury.

When John finally spoke, it was to Cleve.

"You got my message before you left Saint Louis?"

"I got the word. We're to meet a judge and his party here and they'll trail with us to the Santa Fe."

"The man who rode in with me has been hired by Judge Van Winkle to hunt for his party."

"How big is his party, for chrissake?" Rolly asked.

"He'll have six wagons, all in tip-top condition, a total of fourteen people including the judge and his niece — fifteen, counting Buffer Simmons."

Rolly snorted. "No younguns in diapers?"

John turned his cold, hard stare on the bull-whacker.

"Will having the children along keep you from doing your job?"

"Naw. It's jist . . . well —" Realizing he had trodden on dangerous ground, Rolly's reply stammered to a halt.

"I'm thinkin' the judge's party'll not be trailin' us for long. They ain't gonna want to eat our dust," Cleve said, hoping to cover the awkward moment. "More'n likely we'll be trailin' them."

"My cousin, Zachary Quill, served during the war with the judge's brother-in-law, Harold Read. Captain Read saved Zack's life and later lost his own. As a favor to Zack, I consented to let the judge and Read's daughter trail with us to Santa Fe. They'll be a completely separate party from ours, traveling near us for safety's sake."

"I've heard of Buffer Simmons." Cleve pulled a burning stick from the fire to light a fat cigar. "He could take them across the territory without any help from us — faster, too. Does the judge know that we'll do good to make ten or twelve miles a day and that our day starts between three and four in the morning and that we take a break in the middle of the day to rest the animals?"

"If Zack hasn't told him, I will."

Bill Wassall hadn't said a word, but his knowing eyes had caught John glancing toward the tents where the new arrivals were sleeping.

"Tomorrow or the next day," John said, "I'm going into Van Buren to get a rig for my wife and the children. Look over the wagon we came in, Rolly, and do what you have to do to beef it up before we reload it for the trip."

"Wasn't this . . . ah . . . weddin' kinda sudden, boss?" the cook asked.

John's cold dark eyes settled on Bill. "If it was, it makes it no less legal."

"She bein' a widder woman with younguns . . . do make it hard to get along." Bill finished lamely because what he had meant to say was that the widow was lucky to latch on to a man like John.

"The little boy is hers. The other two children are orphans she's taken to raise. The girl has been with her for a long time. They are her family. Mine now. If you have any objection to my wife and family being with us, now is the time to say so."

"Hellfire!" Bill exclaimed. "It ain't no business a ours if'n ya up and marry a . . . widder. It jist — wal, took us by surprise. Nobody knew ya was thinkin' of marryin' up."

"No, it isn't any business of yours or anyone else's."

"The men are eyein' that gal. Pretty a piece as I ever did see," Rolly said. "Could be she'll cause a ruckus once we get strung out on the trail."

"If any man makes a disrespectful move toward that girl, he'll answer to me." John's tone left no doubt as to his meaning.

"About today . . . when she came in —" Rolly wanted to get the unpleasant part of the talk over with.

"Yes. What about that?" John asked, tight-lipped.

Rolly looked at the other two men for help. Cleve lifted his brows in a gesture that said Rolly had stuck his head into the lion's mouth and would have to pull it out. Bill glanced up at the moon hanging above the treetops and refused to look at him.

"She . . . ah . . . came bustin' in, horses lathered and all, and said ya was havin' a little set-to down the road a ways with a few Arkies. Not even askin', mind ya, ordered us to ride on down there and save yore bacon. Course, we knew ya'd not want us to leave the wagons."

"And you explained that to her?" John asked quietly.

"Well, we just said ya'd not need no help —"

"— And that I'd not marry a woman with a 'flock' a younguns."

"I don't know who said that. She warn't takin' no fer a answer. Was goin' to take the whip to us." Rolly grinned before he realized how dangerous it was.

"You laughed at her. I suppose that was when you accused her of trying to draw you off so her friends could steal the freight."

"If ya'd a-been here and seen how it was —"

"What about it, Cleve?" John asked quietly.

"I wasn't here when they arrived, but it's as Rolly said. The woman —"

"— Mrs. Tallman," John interrupted.

"I asked her if you'd sent her to fetch us. She said no. We figured that if you'd needed help you'd've asked for it. She let go and started bawlin' when it was plain we wasn't goin'. We thought it a way to . . . well . . . get us to seein' thin's her way. That's when the boy whipped up the team and took off."

"You let them sit down there all afternoon without food or water. They would have been there all night if I hadn't gotten back." John's voice was getting quieter and quieter, the sign that his anger was rising.

"I tried to talk to 'em. The girl run me

off with the rifle. That gal is feisty as a lone flea on a dog's back."

"She would have shot you; make no mistake about that. She shot a man back in Freepoint who was trying to take Colin, the older boy. It was the man's kin that was after us."

"We meant no disrespect to Mrs. Tallman," Cleve said. "Under the same circumstances ya could'a done as we did."

Cleve Stark was the one man in the outfit who stood his ground against the Tallmans. He was not a man to back up and take water if he believed himself to be right. If there were going to be hard feelings over the way the woman had been treated, he wanted to know it now.

He looked directly at the man whom he loved like a brother. John was fast becoming a legend in New Mexico. The vaqueros who worked his rancho swore that he could hit targets no one else could see and that he could track a horse on a pitch-black night in pouring rain. He was a tough but fair man. Rain Tallman had not only seen to that but had given his son a powerful body, a strong feeling for the underdog, deep-seated respect for women, and stubborn determination. From his mother, Amy Tallman, John had inherited his fierce pride and undying loyalty to his family and friends.

John studied his friend Cleve's confident, tough-looking, windburned face; and, although he was certain he would *not* have acted as they had done when a woman came into camp asking for help, he decided it was time to let the matter drop. How Cleve and the other men treated his family in the future was what was important. He swiveled his head and looked at the cook.

"Is there anyone here you would choose to replace Harrison?"

"I ain't give it no thought. Harrison's a good man, jist got a fondness for the bottle."

"Too fond. I'll not tolerate drink on the trail or a man who drinks himself into such a state that he can't do his job. Harrison goes. In the morning."

The cook shrugged. "Paco'd be a'right."

John nodded. "My wife may want to have her own cookfire. She and the children will not hold up this train or disrupt the running of it. Each of you has your responsibilities. *They* are mine," he said flatly, leaving no room for argument. He stood, rinsed his cup in the pot of water beside the campfire, and dropped it back in the sack. To Cleve he said: "We'd better look for a couple more men between here and Fort Gibson."

"What're ya thinkin', Cleve?" Rolly asked,

a few minutes after John had left the campfire.

" 'Bout what?"

"Ya know. 'Bout John marryin' up with that woman all a sudden an' takin' her and the younguns home with 'im."

"John don't go off half-cocked and do somethin' as final as gettin' married unless he's give it serious thought. He must've wanted her for his wife."

"I remember he talked once a fillin' that hacienda of his with younguns. I thought he was talkin' 'bout *his* younguns." Rolly rubbed his whiskered chin.

"They left Freepoint in a yank." Bill poured dried peaches into a pot of water to soak overnight. "That wagon he brought in wasn't packed for a long haul, that's certain."

"It's not our business, Bill," Cleve said, as he knocked the fire from the end of his cigar and pinched it carefully to make sure it was out, then put it back in his pocket. "John will see to it that his family stays out of the way. You won't even have to cook for them."

"I ain't a-meanin' that," Bill retorted irritably.

"He's touchy 'bout 'em." Rolly stood and stretched his massive frame. "Somethin' more here than him wantin' to get in that woman's drawers. Hell! She'd have to be something

259

special for me to take on three younguns and a girl and drag 'em eight hundred miles across Indian country when I could have my pick of women at home."

"Ya'd be smart to keep your opinions to yourself," Cleve said as he walked away.

"That jist what I'm gonna do. Ya can bet on it. Sure would like to know, though, where he run into that woman and what caused him to up and wed her."

"Dillon! Stay where I can see you." Addie and Trisha were sorting and repacking the contents of the wagon that had been pulled up near the tents. "If I have to draw a line on the ground, I will," she threatened.

A line drawn in the dirt with a stick served as an invisible fence. A step across the line meant going to bed a half-hour early. Once, to test his mother, Dillon had repeatedly crossed the line — and had gone to bed at three o'clock in the afternoon, without his supper. It was a dreaded punishment that put a strong restraint on the younger children.

"Don't draw a line, Muvver. I was gettin' my turtle."

"You was not!" Jane Ann said spitefully. Then to Addie, "He went behind a tree and peed."

"You . . . shut up!" Dillon yelled.

"That's enough. Jane Ann, you mustn't tattle. It's all right if Dillon relieves himself behind the tree. There's no privy here."

"But I saw him . . . do it." Jane Ann's lips quivered.

"You should have turned away quickly when you saw what he was doing."

"She follered me. When I saw her I couldn't stop," Dillon wailed.

"After this come tell me you're going to the bushes and I'll see that Jane Ann stays with me. Go play now. Don't go near the cook wagon, and stay where I can see you. Trisha, don't try to lift that trunk by yourself."

Addie took the end of the trunk and the two women lifted it off the washbench.

"If we hadn't took that churn a milk to that cook man, we could'a drank us a bit of buttermilk and not had to go up thar for supper like beggars lookin' for a handout." Trisha had gone reluctantly to breakfast when John had come for them. "Can't we do our own fixin'?"

"I'm hoping we can get set up for it. Have you ever cooked over a campfire?"

"No. But we'd get the hang of it in no time. I'm thinkin' that cook man ain't wantin' nothin' to do with us a'tall. And I ain't wantin' nothin' to do with *him*. Miss Addie,

261

I feel like we's . . . bein' pushed on folks what don't want us. Like we's . . . throwaways, like Colin and Jane Ann. Colin sure took to that passerby, though. He sticks to 'im like a burr on a dog's back. Where've they gone off to now?"

"Colin's over there with Mr. Rolly. He's taking the wheels off our wagon and doing something to them." Addie looked up as she saw a man approaching. "Here comes Mr. Stark, the man we met this morning. Be nice, Trisha."

"I ain't gonna bite him even if'n I want to." Trisha cast an angry glance at Cleve Stark, then moved away and turned her back.

"Howdy." Cleve removed his hat. His hair was streaked with gray, making him appear much older than when he had his hat on.

"Mr. Stark," Addie replied politely.

"I spoke to John about the sheep. He said to talk to you."

"What about them?"

"Do you intend to take them with you?"

"Well, I'd — hoped to. Mr. Tallman didn't tell me that I couldn't take them."

"They'll have to be watched pretty close. A timber wolf will pull one down the first chance it gets."

"Heavens! I hadn't thought of that. They've been like part of the family."

"Yes'm. Sometimes it don't pay to make pets of yore animals." He was watching her with a curiously expectant expression.

"We don't want to be a bother to you, Mr. Stark."

"It ain't that, ma'am. If John says so, we'll put a man on 'em —"

"No! I don't want him to do that. If they could follow along behind the wagon, Trisha, Colin, or I could walk along with them."

"It's a long way, ma'am. We'll make twelve to fourteen miles a day. I'm thinkin' it'd be hard for 'em to keep up. The night herders keep the oxen bunched, and the mules are picketed. How did you plan to pen your sheep?"

"I'll talk to Mr. Tallman about it."

As Cleve stood holding his hat in his hands, his eyes went to Trisha, who had turned her back, then back to Addie.

"About yesterday. We meant no disrespect. We were taken aback is all, or we'd not have acted as we did. We'd not the slightest notion John had took a wife."

"That was yesterday, Mr. Stark. I try not to look back on what I cannot change."

"Yes, ma'am." He put his hat on and tipped it politely.

"I realize that you and the other men hadn't

planned on having women and children on this trip. As I said before, we'll try not to be a disruption."

"Yes, ma'am."

# CHAPTER

## * 15 *

Addie sat beside John on the seat of the old wagon that had been in her family for years. The tired, swaybacked team that pulled it were like dear friends. She and her new husband were on their way to Van Buren to trade the wagon and the horses for a covered wagon that would take her and the children across hundreds of miles to their new home in New Mexico Territory.

She looked back and waved at the little group standing beside the tents.

"They'll be all right, Addie. Trisha is perfectly able to take care of the children."

"I know . . . but overnight —"

"They'll be safer with Cleve, Rolly, and the others than they would be with us."

"Trisha was scared for me to leave, but she wouldn't say so."

"Don't worry about her being bothered by the men."

"I can't help but worry a little. She's a loyal friend."

"I know. You told me."

"I promised her that she could stay with me for as long as she wants to, not because I owe her a lot, but because I love her as I do Colin and Jane Ann."

"I know that too. She'll be welcome in our home."

"She puts on a brave act, but on the inside she's scared to death."

"She's got grit. She'll make out all right."

"She's afraid she'll end up in a . . . brothel."

"If she does, it will be her choice. She can't hold onto your skirt-tail all her life."

"She doesn't hold onto my skirt-tail!"

"What would you call it? She's like your shadow."

"She has no one else. She's been through a lot."

"So have you and your troubles have made you stronger. Now let's not talk about Trisha. She'll marry someday and have a family of her own."

"I doubt that."

"Buffer Simmons admires her."

"A lot of men *admire* her."

"It's more than that. I think he's really sweet on her."

"Did he tell you that?"

"No. But when a man asks as many questions about a woman as he did, he's got something in mind."

"He's got something in mind all right, and it isn't marriage. He knows she's got colored blood. Preacher Sikes saw to it that everyone in town knew it."

"I don't think that would stop Simmons if he wanted to marry her."

"He only wants what other men have wanted when they saw how pretty she was." Addie glanced at John to see how he reacted to her statement. He was looking straight ahead. "They all had *something* in mind," Addie added dryly.

John was silent. The talk about Trisha had kept their minds occupied while they were leaving. But now they were out of sight of the camp, and at last he had his wife to himself. He wanted to use this time to get acquainted with her, really get to know her. He wanted to know what she thought about, dreamed about — how she felt about him. Even more important, he wanted to know why she had married a bastard like Kirby Hyde.

He turned his head slightly so that he could look at her. She wore the same blue dress as she had the day in town when he saw her for the first time. The morning sun was shining now on her light hair, which she had coiled and pinned to the nape of her neck. Her eyes were large and sad. The dark smudges beneath them only emphasized their brilliant color. She held a stiff-brimmed sunbonnet in her lap.

"Did you make a tracing of the children's feet so we can buy them sturdy shoes?" John asked, hoping to keep her talking.

"Yes. And Trisha's too. I tore a sheet from an old catalog, marked around each foot with a pencil and then cut out the shape. We can use the money I got from the farm to buy the shoes. I want you to keep half of what's left after we pay for the wagon and the mules and the supplies we'll need for the next few weeks."

"The money you got from the farm is yours. I'll buy what we'll need for the trip."

Addie turned her head slowly. "Why would you do that?"

"Because you're my wife. I take care of what's mine."

"Like your horse? Your hat? Your freight train?" Her voice was strained.

"I didn't mean that at all, Addie. If the time should come when we need to use some of your money, my pride won't stand in the way. I'm hoping that you and I can work as a team for the good of our family."

"I'm sorry if I sounded ungrateful."

John slapped the reins against the horses' backs and the wagon rolled down the road.

Addie met his look with unsmiling calm while a frantic uneasiness leaped within her. She felt as if she were in another world. So much had happened in such a short time. Her children and Trisha were back there with strangers. The man beside her was a stranger too. Could it be that less than a week had passed since she had first set eyes on him? Yet, he was her husband and would expect to sleep with her tonight, touch her private places.

*A woman is duty-bound to comfort her husband when and where he needs it.* Kirby had said that.

Would this man be rough or gentle with her? Gentle, as Kirby had been at first, or rough, as Kirby had been after they were wed?

She turned and found John looking at her.

"Are you worrying about tonight, Addie?"

*Lordy! Can he read my mind?* She tried to look away from him, but his dark eyes held hers. She opened her mouth to deny it, but nothing came out. She couldn't lie to him.

"It's . . . been a long time."

"I want babies from you, Addie. But I'll not force myself on you to get them."

She tore her eyes from his and looked straight ahead. "I'm willing to . . . ah, do what's expected."

"You'll do your duty? Is that what you mean?" When she didn't answer, he asked: "Did you love Kirby Hyde?"

"You asked me that once before."

"And you didn't answer me."

"I won't answer you now, either. It's none of your business."

"Everything about you is my business, Addie. But I won't press the point. We've got a lifetime to spend together. I want to know what you want, and I'll give it to you if I can. I want to share the good times with you as well as the bad." *I want us to be like my mother and father. When she comes into a room the first thing she looks for is my father. Their eyes speak to each other. They think and act as one.*

After an uneasy silence, Addie asked, "What do you want to know?"

"Tell me about your parents."

The tension eased as Addie talked of how her mother and father had met when they had been taken in by a farmer in Tennessee to work for their board, much the same as Colin and Jane Ann had done. Both sets of parents had died; Addie didn't exactly know what had caused their deaths.

270

When her father was sixteen, he decided to leave and make his own way. He took her mother with him. They found her mother's brother with another family, and he went with them. They were little more than children when they married. Although life was hard for them, they eventually made their way to Arkansas and took up land.

"Were you the only child they had?"

"They had two before me who died just days after they were born and one after me who lived one year."

"Did you take in Colin and his sister because your parents had been orphans?"

"Maybe at first. Then I came to love them. They needed me," she said almost defensively.

The midmorning sun was hot. Addie fanned her face with the stiff brim of her bonnet. When they came to a small, clear stream, they paused to let the team drink. John jumped down from the wagon and reached for Addie. When she placed her hands on his shoulders, he grasped her waist and easily swung her to the ground.

"Stretch your legs. I'll get you a drink."

When he returned from the stream with a tin cup of water, she drank thirstily, looking curiously at the round cup. It was made of circles of tin that telescoped one into the other when closed.

"I've never seen a cup like this."

"I got it in Saint Louis." He pushed on the top and bottom. The cup collapsed. "It folds to about an inch high. Easy to put in your pocket or saddlebag."

"Better not let Dillon see it." Addie's violet eyes were full of laughter when they looked into his. "He'll wear it out, stretching it out and folding it up."

"That's good to know. If a time comes when I want to keep him quiet, I'll bring out the cup." The look in his smiling eyes was one of conspiracy.

His smile made Addie's heart flutter. She drew the tip of her tongue across her lips and saw his eyes move to her mouth. Being with him and drinking from the same cup as he made her feel mixed up and shaky inside. It felt different to be alone with him out here on this lonely road. He did not seem so stone-faced. He was warmer, friendlier. She wondered if he felt the same about her.

"How much farther?"

"Another hour." He glanced at the sun. "We'll eat at a restaurant there."

He stood looking down at her, his long body relaxed, neither anxious to leave nor indifferent. While he waited for her to speak, time and space seemed to shrink to the small quiet place by the stream.

"I'll be hungry by then."

"I've never seen anyone with eyes the color of yours. Did you know they reflect your every mood?"

"I hadn't thought about it."

"Why are they so sad now?" His tone was soft, intimate. She thought that he was teasing, but he was not smiling.

She turned away, letting her glance move up and down the sparkling stream. She knew she must speak, and speak casually. When she looked back at him, he was watching her so intently that she quickly dropped her eyes. A strange feeling washed over her, as if she lacked breath.

"I don't know why they look sad. I'm not really sad." She paused. "Well, maybe a little." She tilted her head to look at him because he had moved a step closer. "Are you ever sad?"

"Sometimes. I also get tired, hungry, angry, lonely, and scared, the same as you."

"*You* get scared?" she scoffed, wishing that she were less conscious of his nearness.

"Of course. Only a fool isn't scared at one time or another. You've been scared many times, haven't you?"

"Yes. I was scared the night you came to

the farm and ran off those drunken coots! Why did you?"

He stroked his mustache with his forefinger and gave her a leering look.

"Maybe I had plans to *ravish* you myself. Grrrrr . . ." He snapped his teeth together, imitating a hungry wolf.

Addie's expression changed instantly from one of solemn concentration to one of surprise and then to delight. She almost choked on the happy giggle that bubbled up inside her.

"Mr. Tallman! John!" Her laugh rang out. "If you're trying to scare me, it isn't working! Ohhh!" she shrieked as he swept her up in his arms as if she were a child.

"You'd better be scared," he said, and swung her toward the rushing water. "I could drop you right here in the middle of the stream."

"Oh . . . oh, don't —" She grabbed him about the neck.

"If you're properly scared, I'll set you in the wagon."

"As much as I'd love to have a bath, I'm scared of that cold water!" He carried her to the side of the wagon. "And I'm scared because I've never been held like this. Goodness! Put me down. I'm too heavy."

"Heavy, my foot," John said, and set her down on the seat. "You weigh about as much as a sack of feed."

He climbed up the wheel, took his place beside her, and put the team in motion. They splashed across the rocky creek bed and up the bank to the road.

"It isn't very flattering to be compared to a sack of feed." She sniffed in mock disdain, suddenly afraid that she was acting like a witless fool.

"I would have said a sack of potatoes, but they're lumpy. You're . . . soft."

Addie couldn't keep from looking at him. She had never before seen his face so creased with smiles. There were laugh lines at the corners of dark blue eyes which were shining with amusement. They looked at each other, and Addie's soft giggles mingled with John's deeper, hearty chuckles.

The town of Van Buren lay listlessly in the noonday sun. It seemed to Addie larger than Freepoint and much older. Lying on the bank of the Arkansas River across from Fort Smith, Van Buren was the jumping-off place for freight wagons, settlers, and army regiments going into or across the Indian Nations.

Enjoying their easy camaraderie, John told Addie a little about the town as they approached it.

"Thomas Martin, a friend of my father's, came to this place on the Arkansas in 1818 and established a trading post. As settlers came in, a village called Phillips Landing was formed because a man named Phillips had bought up a big chunk of land. Later on the name of the town was changed to Van Buren, for the president."

"Are you known here?"

"Some. Back in the twenties my parents settled about a hundred miles north of here. It's where I was born and grew up. We came here about twice a year for supplies."

"It's hillier than I expected."

"This is hilly country. The stores here are good, but for the amount of supplies we need back home we have to go to St. Louis. The eating places and the hotels are fair; the saloons very good." He grinned at her.

"Of course you would know that!" she said sassily.

John could not recall when he had enjoyed himself more. Time seemed to have flown by since they'd left camp, but in reality they had been on the road almost half a day. Addie Tallman — he never wanted the name Hyde associated with her again — was a delight. She was not only pretty but smart. She had a quick wit and a wonderful sense of humor. She was also a "ring-tailed tooter" when she was mad. He chuckled when he thought of the tongue-lashing she had given the preacher.

"What are you laughing at?" Addie tilted her head to see his face.

"You might be mad if I told you." He couldn't stop grinning.

"Now you've got me curious. You'd better tell me or I'll think the worst."

"I was thinking of you standing in the lane stamping your foot and shouting every swear word you'd ever heard at the preacher." Laughter rumbled up out of his chest. "After seeing that, I don't plan on getting you mad in front of anyone."

Addie's face turned fiery red. "I can't even remember what I said. Trisha said it was things she'd not heard me say before. I was so mad! Why, the idea of that . . . old stink-pot thinking he'd give Colin to that rotten old Remshaw skunk! Course, I didn't know then that he was going to try to get Dillon too. I'd . . . I'd've shot his ugly head off before I gave him my boys!"

"Calm down, honey. I didn't mean to get you riled up again."

As the word of endearment seeped into her senses, she felt a wonderful warm glow of belonging — a feeling of security. She glanced at him and suddenly realized that his head was in constant motion, turning this way and that, but so slowly that the movement was almost imperceptible. He was an extremely alert man, she realized, and beneath his calm manner lay something as inflexible as a stout ax handle.

"Do you think the magistrate has sent word here to arrest Trisha for shooting Ellis Renshaw?"

"If he has, we'll find out about it. Don't borrow trouble. I promise you, we'll take Trisha with us to New Mexico."

He stopped the wagon at the open doors of the livery.

"Howdy, Tallman." The liveryman had a long white beard and wore the gray hat of the Confederacy. He gazed curiously at Addie as John helped her down from the wagon seat. "Have a good trip to St. Louie?"

"Sure did. Take care of the team and wagon, Wally. I'll be back in a little while."

John took Addie's arm as they walked toward the main street of the town, leaving the old man to stare after them before he turned to look curiously at the rickety wagon and the ancient team. He shook his head in wonder that John Tallman would come to town in such an outfit.

"After we eat," John said as they reached the boardwalk, "I'll take you to the hotel so you can rest while I see about getting us a prairie schooner." He hugged her arm close to his side and smiled down at her proudly.

Addie stood at the window in the hotel room and looked down on the street. She was too nervous to rest. Never in her life, unless she was sick, had she rested in the middle of the day. She looked around the room. This was only the second time she had been in a hotel. The room was pretty much like the one she and John had been married in — iron bedstead, washstand, china pitcher and bowl, a table with an oil lamp. Her bonnet hung on the knob of the one chair and the drawstring cloth bag holding her nightdress, comb, brush, wash cloth, and towel was on the seat.

She avoided looking at the bed. It seemed terribly narrow. She tried not to think about her husband's large frame stretched out on one side of it, hers on the other. Instead she thought about how special she had felt when he had ushered her into the restaurant, held her chair for her to be seated, then ordered their meals.

A small voice inside her reminded her that Kirby, too, had been attentive. But that was before they had wed. This was different, her logical mind argued. She and John were already married. There was no need for him to court her. He already had the legal right to share her bed.

Addie looked back down at the street as a portly man in a black serge suit, a high-topped hat, and a gold watch chain strung across his chest came out of the bank with a young lady on his arm. She wore a fashionable pink-and-white–striped dress and a lacy bonnet. Her small waist was emphasized by the yards and yards of fabric in the voluminous skirt. Dwarfed beside the big man, she walked with dainty steps, lifting her skirt when necessary with a gloved hand.

Addie's eyes were not the only ones watching the couple. Men stared; women gawked. A man driving a wagon down the street turned around on the seat so that he could get a better view. The couple seemed unaware of the interest they were creating and continued down the walk to the hotel at the end of the street, where they disappeared inside.

Only mildly interested in the well-dressed couple, Addie pulled the chair to the window and settled down to wait for John.

Van Buren was not only the jumping off place to the West, it was a river town. The streets teemed with a variety of humanity: rivermen, Indians, soldiers, farmers, drifters, and a few Negroes. Deserters from both the northern and the southern armies were coming in out of the hills. While they were eating, John had explained that some were headed south to Texas, others to the far West.

"Anytime you have a war," John had said, "you have renegades. They swarmed over Texas after the defeat of Santa Anna: stealing, picking up the leavings, killing when it became handy. It'll be the same after this war. It'll take a while to clean them out."

"Will we run into them on the way to New Mexico?"

"It's possible but not likely. They usually travel in packs of four to a dozen and prey on homesteads or small trains. That's the reason the judge wants to travel along with us. Don't worry," John had said, when he saw the look on Addie's face. "It would take a small army of them to be effective against us."

Addie's mind was brought back to the present when four riders entered the street from the far end of town. Even from a distance Addie could tell that the men were riding exceptionally fine horses. Their slick dark coats gleamed; their manes were brushed and lay on one side of high-arched necks. They had long, sweeping tails that had been perfectly groomed. The men who rode the horses wore the blue uniforms of the Union Army. They sat straight in the saddles, heads up, shoulders back, as if they were on parade.

As they passed beneath the hotel window, Addie saw that the men were as well groomed as the horses they rode. One man in particular caught her attention. Beneath the dark-brimmed hat, his hair was light, curly, and reached almost to his shoulders. He had a handsome blond mustache and goatee and re-minded Addie of pictures she had seen of General Lee. She was not at all surprised when the soldiers stopped at the hotel at the end of the street and tied their horses to the rail. Three of the men entered the hotel, and the fourth took up a position at the head of the horses, as if he expected someone to steal them.

Addie heard a soft tap on the door and turned from the window. When John entered the room, she stood and faced him and was once again reminded of how big he was. His hatless head reached almost to the top of the doorway.

Had she been able to think clearly, Addie would have wondered why she didn't feel threatened by his size and the fact that they were alone in this small enclosure and he had a perfect right to do with her as he pleased. None of these thoughts, however, entered her mind.

"Did you get a wagon?"

"A dandy." He tossed his hat onto the bed. "It was a stroke of luck that we came today." He poured water into the bowl from the pitcher and splashed his face. "Wally, at the livery, told me about a Dutchman who came to town yesterday in an exceptionally good wagon and wanted to sell it. Wally said that the man had been on his way to Texas when his wife died. He didn't want to continue on with four motherless children." After drying his face, John placed the towel back on the rack and peered into the mirror over the washstand. "I need to visit the barber for a shave and a haircut."

"What will that poor man do?" Addie asked. "Are any of the children old enough to take care of the others?"

"I didn't ask. He'll take his children back to Indiana, where he has relatives."

"He lost not only his wife but his dreams of a new life in a new land."

"Some people aren't suited to blaze new trails. They're better off settling in one place and staying there. The Dutchman is an excellent craftsman. The wagon he built attests to that. But he wasn't trail-wise, nor had he been wise in his choice of companions for the trip. There's a good chance he'd not have made it to Texas, and if he did he might not have been able to stick it out."

"How did his wife die?"

"Snakebite. She was washing in the river and a water moccasin got her."

"Ohh . . ." Addie shivered.

"The wagon is as well built as any I've seen. The Dutchman's taking his belongings out now. We can leave early in the morning and be back in camp by noon."

"Why did you camp so far from Van Buren?"

"The animals had pulled the load down from Saint Louis, and they needed to rest and graze. The area around Van Buren is usually grazed out this time of year because of the number of trains that stop here. We plan to stay for only a day when we stop here to meet up with the Van Winkle party. By the way, the judge is in town. I'll call on him after we visit the store."

Addie put on her bonnet and looped her drawstring purse over her arm. Then John opened the door and followed her into the hallway.

"Addie, we have a good supply of dress goods in the freight we're taking back to my father's store, so you'll not need any more. But I want you to buy anything else you think you'll need for yourself, Trisha, and the children." He smiled down at her. "I don't imagine you'll need to buy stockings. I'll never again wear any but the ones my wife knits. My feet have never felt better."

"You bought the socks from Mr Cash?"

"Sure did. They cost me two bits a pair and are worth every cent."

"Fifty cents?" Her eyes widened in surprise.

"Now you know why I married you: for a lifetime supply of Addie Tallman's knit socks."

As he squeezed her arm, his dark eyes teased her. She walked beside him down the stairs, floating along with him on a cloud of happiness.

He was not like any other man she had ever known.

In the lobby of the hotel, John paused to speak to the man at the desk, then took Addie's arm again and they walked along the street to the big mercantile on the corner.

# CHAPTER

## * 16 *

Addie was amazed at the amount of goods on the counters, the walls, and even hanging from the ceiling of the large store. It must be twice again as large as the store in Freepoint, she thought. It was late afternoon, and there were quite a few other customers in the store. Addie couldn't see them because of the stacks of goods on the tables. In most places they were piled higher than her head. Passing along the narrow aisles, she could, however, hear the murmur of voices.

"Goods were scarce in Freepoint during the war," Addie commented to John.

"Most of what's here has come in from the North since the end of the war."

A young man with a white apron wrapped about his waist hurried toward them. His hair was parted in the middle and plastered down. A waxed mustache adorned his upper lip.

"Mr. Tallman, it's a pleasure to see you. We heard you'd be passing through town."

"Addie, this is Ron Poole. His father owns the store. Ron, my wife, Mrs. Tallman. We're here to buy shoes for our children."

"Your children? Ah . . . well, right this way." He led them to shelves crowded with shoe boxes. "Children's high-tops are on the top shelves, ladies' on the bottom shelves. Boys' boots are at the end of the aisle. Now, what can I show you?"

Addie selected shoes for Trisha and the children, holding the paper tracings of their feet against the soles of the shoes to make sure of the sizes. Then, at John's insistence, she chose a pair for herself, serviceable black shoes that laced to above the ankle. After picking out brimmed hats for the boys and heavy duck britches for Colin, Addie hesitated over a riding skirt for Trisha.

"Trisha loves to ride," she said, by way of explanation, as she placed the skirt on the stack of goods they were going to buy. "The owner of the plantation where she was raised had a large stable. She told me about going out into the pasture at night and riding the horses because she wasn't allowed near them during the day."

"Do you like to ride?"

"I don't know. I've not ridden anything but the workhorses."

"Pick out a skirt for yourself. You'll have

plenty of opportunity to ride when we get home."

*Home.* It was the first time he had used the word in connection with her, and, to her surprise, she began to tingle as if she had been pricked with a thousand needles.

John moved along the tables and shelves selecting many items, much to the delight of the store owner's son, who scurried after him to carry the articles to the counter and add them to the bill he was tallying. Addie lingered beside the table of chalkboards and *McGuffey Readers.* Her fingers caressed the covers of the *Primer,* the *First* and *Second* readers, and the *Speller.*

"Do you want them for the children?" John was close against her back and had spoken softly in her ear.

"Colin hasn't had a chance to go to school. Jane Ann and Dillon are ready to start. I could teach them with these books, but the price is . . . dear." Her voice was as soft as his.

"You can't put a price on education. Get them and the *Fifth* and *Sixth* readers too."

Addie held the four books as if they were treasures. She looked at them, then up at John. Her violet eyes questioned his.

"Will you let me pay for them out of the farm money?"

"I thought we had settled that. What is mine is yours and what's yours is mine." He reached around her, bringing his chest against her back, and took the books from her hand. At the same time he picked up the other two. "You'll need slates and chalk pencils. Get plenty of chalk."

While Addie was choosing the slates, John went to the table where knives of various shapes and sizes were laid out in neat rows. A couple came toward him down the narrow aisle. The man wore the uniform of the Union, the woman a fashionable pink striped dress. John gave them only a brief glance and dismissed them. In the flicker of an eye he had sized the man up as a dressed up dandy, enjoying the war now that it was over. The soldier was giving his full attention to the woman. She was young and pretty and was looking up at him as if he were the only man on earth.

After much consideration, John selected a folding jackknife for Colin, took it to the counter, then went back to where Addie stood beside the books.

"Can't decide on the slates?"

"I have the slates, but I don't know how much chalk to get."

"Two boxes. It won't spoil." He was so serious that she laughed, and her laughter was so infectious that he laughed too. Her musical tones mingled with his deeper, hearty rumble. "I like to hear you laugh, Addie."

John was fascinated by the sparkle in Addie's eyes and the smile on her lips. He failed to see the Union officer and the woman who had stopped at the end of the aisle, nor did he notice the way the man's feet seemed to be frozen to the floor as he stared. Then he turned the lady and urged her toward the door.

"Come on, let's tally up," John said. "I've got a surprise waiting for you at the hotel."

"A surprise? Good or bad?"

"What would you consider a bad surprise?"

"Preacher Sikes or Ellis Renshaw waiting for me."

John laughed.

The store owner winked at his son. John Tallman, usually stern and unsmiling, was plainly smitten with his new wife and was indulging her in whatever she wanted. Too bad, the proprietor mused, that she didn't want one of everything in the store.

On the way to the counter, John picked up a set of toy soldiers, a sack of marbles, and a small glossy-headed doll.

"John! No!"

"Addie! Yes!" He laughed again.

Suddenly he realized that he had laughed

more today than he had during the previous month. The thought sobered him momentarily. Had he fallen in love with this woman? He liked her, admired her, and had married her because at this time of his life he wanted his own family. Also, he felt a certain obligation to her. But love, as his father defined it, was something rare and wonderful and enduring. Had John stumbled into it by accident?

It was dusk when they reached the boardwalk in front of the store. Lamps were being lit along the street.

"We'll pick up our purchases in the morning on our way out of town," John said, and stopped her hand when she moved to put the bonnet on her head. "Leave it off. You have beautiful hair, Addie."

"It isn't really proper to be on the street without a bonnet."

"Being *proper* is something we won't worry about. Shall we eat before we go back to the hotel?"

"I hadn't thought about that. I'm too excited about all the things we bought and . . . the surprise."

"It pleases me to see you happy. You've not had much happiness, have you?"

"Oh, yes!" She looked up at him earnestly. "I was very happy the day I found Trisha in my barn, the day my son was born, and when Colin and Jane Ann came to live with me. I've had a good life, John. I don't want you, or anyone else, feeling sorry for me or my children."

John thought it strange that she didn't mention Kirby Hyde in connection with her happy times.

"I don't feel sorry for you, Addie. I admire your courage. Not many women could have endured what you have and come out of it as sane as you are."

"Sometimes I don't think I'm sane at all. A week ago I was working my garden, hoeing my cotton, tending the sheep, and taking care of my family. And now here I am in a strange place, planning to take my children to a strange land. And I'm —"

"You're what?" John asked quietly.

"I'm not at all afraid that you'll not take care of us." Addie let the words rush out while she had the courage to say them.

"I'll do my best. I swear it." John felt a tightness in his throat. He had never meant anything more in his life.

The lamps had been lit in the lobby of the hotel where they were staying. Two men lounged in the leather-covered chairs reading the newspaper.

"Let's go eat at a place I know. Your surprise will be here when we get back."

"Are you sure?"

"Very sure."

They passed the bank and turned down a side street toward a small stone building with a wooden porch. A sign on a weathered board nailed to a porch post said: BUNG FOD-DER.

Addie read it aloud, then said: "What does that mean?" John leaned down and murmured in her ear: "You don't want to know. It's someone's idea of a joke."

They went up the steps and into a room that had two long tables with benches on each side. A colorful mural of a Mexican hacienda surrounded by blooming cactus plants covered one wall. The back wall had two doors, one curtained and one that opened into a kitchen. A delicious aroma filled the small building.

"Lupe!" John called. "It's suppertime."

"Don't ya be tellin' me what time it is, ya slick-eared son of a mule. Sit yoreself down. I'll be out when I get damn good and ready to serve ya. It be only . . . Oh, Holy Father! John-ny! John-ny, my love! You come to see Lupe!"

The woman who barreled through the curtained door was almost as broad as she was tall. She wore a full black skirt with a red ruffle on the bottom, a white boat-neck shirt, and numerous bright-colored necklaces of various lengths. Black hair that hung to her waist was caught at the back of her neck with a wide red ribbon.

She tried to wrap her arms around John, but her voluptuous breasts were in the way. The top of her head came to the middle of his chest.

"Hello, Lupe." John's laughing eyes found Addie's.

" 'Hello, Lupe.' 'Hello, Lupe.' Is that all ya can say? Tell me I still be your best girl, ya young rooster!"

"If I did that, Lupe, my wife would take a stick to me." He held the little woman away from him and smiled down into her round, jovial face.

"Yore wife? Ya've up and married another woman? Yi, yi, yi!" she wailed. "Ya've kilt me is what ya done." She held her hands to her breast and turned large, sorrowful black eyes to Addie. "Ya've stole my heart," she said dramatically.

"I'm sorry," Addie said, trying desperately hard to keep a straight face. "I didn't know he was spoken for."

Then almost instantly Lupe's face was wreathed with smiles, and she grabbed Addie's hand.

"Tell ya the truth, dearie, I was afeared I'd have to marry up with him. He's been pesterin' me for years. I'm a-gettin' too old to keep them high-steppin' mares outa his stall. Ya 'pear to be young and strong. I'm hopin' ya pack a wallop." She slapped her fist into the palm of her other hand. "He'll be needin' it from time to time."

"Don't take any advice from her, Addie. I've known her since I was knee-high to a duck."

"Ya better pay attention to what I say, John Spotted Elk Tallman. If I can't have ya, I'm glad — What's yore name, hon?"

"Addie."

"I'm glad Addie got ya. Ya be good to her, or I'll beat yore butt," Lupe said sassily. Then: "How's your maw?"

"Amy's fine. Now that the war is over, she and Rain might come back next year for a visit."

"I'd like ta see 'em. Now, tell me about this new wife of yours. How did a ugly old thin' like ya talk her into hookin' up with ya?"

"It wasn't easy, Lupe. How about dishing us up something to eat before the place is overrun with hungry men."

The chicken and rice was delicious. John showed Addie how to butter a hot tortilla and roll it up like a fat cigar.

"Do you like it?" he asked after she had taken a bite.

"Very much."

"Mexicans put meat, chili, or peppers in them. They eat tortillas like we eat bread."

Soon it became too noisy to talk. The tables were filled, and customers waited on the porch. Lupe brought out large platters of food. The men took plates from a shelf and helped themselves, all the while teasing the jolly little woman.

When John and Addie finished eating, John left money beside their plates. Lupe followed them to the porch, hugged John again, then wrapped her short, plump arms around Addie.

"Ya got a good man, Addie. I'd-a dropped Amy in a well and took his pa in a minute if'n he'd looked at me sideways," she teased. "Don't ya tell Amy that, boy," she said to John.

"I won't. Take care of yourself, Lupe. If you get a notion to leave here, load up and hook onto a freight wagon and come on out. You'd be welcome."

"I jist might do that. Go on, now. I got to get back in there or them men'll start chewin' on a table leg."

"Did you like the supper?" John asked on

the way back to the hotel.

"Yes, and I liked her."

"She and her husband came up from Texas just after the battle for Texas's independence. Even though her man, along with quite a few Texas Mexicans, fought with Sam Houston at San Jacinto, many people down there hate Mexicans."

"Has her husband passed on?"

"Quite a few years ago. My folks asked her to come to New Mexico, but she has a no-good son around here someplace and she doesn't want to leave him."

They entered the hotel and went up the two short flights of stairs to their room. Addie's churning thoughts kept her bodily weariness at bay. She'd had an enjoyable day and had become accustomed to John's company. The realization that she was growing very fond of him made what lay ahead less frightening.

John unlocked their door and went into the room to light the lamp while Addie waited in the doorway. As soon as the room was flooded with light, she saw the large tin bathtub.

"I've never seen one before," she blurted. "Only pictures."

She ran her fingers over the edge of the high back of the tub and then touched the soft towel, soaps, and powders on the low stool beside it.

"I've been told that a bath in a tub is one of the things a woman likes best. My sister pestered my father until he had one just like this brought out."

"I've never bathed in anything but a wash-tub," Addie confessed.

"The water is on the way. I'll wait until the tub is filled; then, while you're bathing, I'll call on the judge." John showed her the thick hose hooked over the edge of the tub, and pointed to a covered opening in the wall. "This is where they empty the water down a pipe when you're finished, so they don't have to dip it out and carry it downstairs."

"Isn't that something?"

John answered the soft tap on the door. Three boys came in, each carrying two large buckets of water. Steam rose as the water was poured into the tub. One full bucket remained on the floor when the boys left without a glance at either John or Addie.

"If you want them to empty the tub and take it away before I get back, pull on the cord hanging by the washstand."

"John. Thank you for the surprise."

"You're very welcome. I'm not used to providing surprises for ladies, but I didn't think I could go wrong with this one."

"It was very thoughtful of you."

"Take your time. I'll be gone awhile. Lock the door when I leave, and hang the key there on the nail. I have another key."

Outside the hotel, John stopped to light a thin cigar, then walked toward the hotel at the end of the street. His mind was on the woman he had left in the room. He wasn't sure how to proceed with his new wife. He could feel himself swell just thinking about having her in bed, soft, and warm, and willing. There was no doubt that he wanted her — not just any woman, but *her*. He would go slowly. *Hell, I'm not a randy billy goat,* he assured himself. He stopped at the tonsorial parlor and stuck his head in the door.

"Be back in about a half-hour. Got hot water?"

"Howdy, Mr. Tallman. You betcha. Got plenty."

John nodded and crossed the street.

The hotel was among the most up-to-date in Arkansas. John had chosen the less fancy hotel for himself and Addie because he thought she would be uncomfortable amid such luxury. As for himself, he had stayed in many fine places, and he cared not at all if the hired help looked down their noses at him because of his frontier clothing. Confidently, he opened the door of the hotel. Its beveled glass pane, decorated with an etching of a stag, rattled, and a clerk at a polished counter looked up.

"What room is Judge Van Winkle in?" John asked.

The young man in the high stiff collar eyed him suspiciously with raised brows.

"The judge is dining."

"Where?" John asked.

"Why . . . in the dining room. Where else?"

" 'Where else?' " John echoed around the cigar in his mouth. "I thought he might have gone down to Lupe's."

The clerk formed a horrified O with his thin lips, then he pressed them together forming a line of disapproval.

John turned his back and leaned against the counter for a moment, then took off his hat, tucked it under his arm, and walked across the lobby to the dining room. The manager was at his elbow the instant he stepped into the room.

"Sir?"

"Which one is Judge Van Winkle?"

"The judge? He's the one standing beside the table with the Yank . . . ah, Union man. He was getting ready to leave when the soldier came in."

"Thanks." John returned to the lobby to

wait for the judge.

When Van Winkle came through the door, he was walking behind a young lady and a Yankee captain, the same couple John had seen in Poole's store. The man was dressed as if for a parade, his blond hair, mustache, and goatee perfectly groomed. *A proud, useless peacock,* John thought. This time the woman wore a lavender dress adorned with pieces of lace and ribbon.

The couple stood closely together and looked into each other's eyes as they talked. John watched the man lift the girl's hand to his lips and kiss it. Then, still holding the girl's hand, he spoke to the judge, who slapped him affectionately on the shoulder. The judge and the girl walked the captain to the door.

John moved out from the wall when they came back into the lobby.

"Judge Van Winkle. I'd like a word with you."

"Yes, yes," the judge said impatiently, frowning. "What can I do for you?"

"Not a thing," John replied with equal impatience. "It's about what you want me to do for you. I'm John Tallman."

"Tallman?" He looked at John as if he didn't quite believe him.

The judge was a tall, portly man with sparse

white hair and a thick white beard. The vest beneath his dark serge suit was elaborately embroidered in a scroll pattern. A heavy gold watch chain stretched across his ample girth. He removed the watch now and looked at it as if he had an urgent appointment.

"Tallman," he said again.

"John Tallman. My cousin is Zachary Quill," John added, to jog the judge's memory.

"I know. I know. I just wasn't expecting — Ah, yes, fine gentleman, Captain Quill."

"I think so," John said dryly.

"This is my niece, Miss Cindy Read."

"Ma'am." John nodded.

"How do you do. I saw you today in the store." The girl's large, cornflower-blue eyes focused on John with interest.

"It's nice of you to remember me," John said politely, before turning again to the judge. "The hunter you hired is back at our camp. He said to tell you that he'll join you in a day or two."

"The hunter. Oh, yes. A party the size of mine needs someone to hunt fresh meat."

"Whether you hire a hunter is up to you. One of my men will be in tomorrow to look over your wagons and your stock to see if they're up to the trip and to make sure you have enough extra parts to make repairs. I won't be held up by broken-down rigs or worn-out stock."

"Go on up to your room, my dear." Van Winkle patted the hand on his arm. "Mr. Tallman and I have a few things to settle."

"Oh, pooh! You always send me off when things get interesting." She smiled coyly at John. "Good night, Mr. Tallman."

"Good night, ma'am."

After the girl disappeared up the stairs, the judge moved to the far corner of the lobby so that they would have privacy. John followed, then waited as the man lit a cigar and poked the matchstick down into a nearby urn of sand.

"My wagons and stock are my concern," the judge said, in a tone that plainly indicated that he was not pleased. "The only reason I agreed to go along with you was to provide extra protection for my niece."

"They may be your concern now, but they'll be my concern if you break down and we have to wait for you. How many men do you have?"

"Thirteen, not counting myself or my man."

" 'Your man'?"

"Darkie. Been in my family all his life."

"Thirteen men and six wagons. How many of your men have been out West before?"

"See here, Tallman. I don't have to justify my selection of these men to you."

"Buffer Simmons is the only experienced man you've got. Isn't that right?"

The judge's face reddened. "The recent reports I've heard say that the trip is not as dangerous as it was a few months ago. The back of the South has been broken. The Indians are settling down. They know which side of their bread the butter is on. They'll behave or get rounded up and put in a stockade."

John was still for a moment, his face unreadable. When he felt he could speak without showing his anger, he said: "Your reports are wrong."

"No matter. I've got six seasoned soldiers, all wearing the blue of the Union."

"The uniforms will really impress the renegades who attack your party," John said dryly, and shook his head in disbelief.

"The captain of the patrol is my niece's fiance, a highly respected man who served in the quartermaster headquarters in Illinois. He's been reassigned to Fort Albuquerque."

"A real fighting man."

The judge ignored John's sarcasm. "I have been appointed by the late President Lincoln to take charge of Indian affairs at Santa Fe."

*God help the Indians.*

"I'll tell you this straight out, Judge. I've got twenty-one wagons, fifty-two men, two women and three children. I'm not expecting to find trouble crossing the Indian Nations. My father was raised with the Shawnee and I speak the language of the Choctaw, the Cherokee, and the Creek. I'll be crossing their land, not trying to take it from them or telling them how to live."

The judge snorted. "It's a known fact that someone has to tell them."

"Known, no doubt, by the white man who's stealing their land and who has broken every treaty they've signed." John's words were spit out angrily. "There are hundreds of miles through Oklahoma Territory and Texas flatlands that are called no-man's land. The *strongest* rule there. Comanche and Chiricahua Apache roam that land. Both tribes can be meaner than a bunch of stirred-up hornets. But they are mild compared to the packs of renegades, deserters, outlaws, and, the most vicious of all, the bands of Confederate guerrillas who raid and rob and kill not just for profit but for pleasure."

"Damn Rebels, all of them. Won't admit they've been whipped and whipped good."

"I'm coming through here day after tomorrow. You can follow me out if it suits you. If not, good luck."

John slapped his hat on his head, then his long stride ate up the distance to the door. When he reached the sidewalk, the judge, huffing and puffing, was behind him.

"Tallman."

John turned. "You don't need my help, Judge. Your soldier boys will handle things. But I'll tell you this for the sake of the lady with you — listen to your hunter, Buffer Simmons. If anyone can get a small party through, he can."

"Sorry if you misunderstood me, Tallman. I'll pull out tomorrow and meet you at Fort Gibson."

"I'm not going to Fort Gibson. It's out of my way."

The judge yanked the cigar from his mouth. "The detachment assigned to me has been looking forward to visiting a frontier fort."

"Then by all means let them *visit* the frontier fort. I'm in the freighting business; I don't conduct tours. Time means money."

"It would take but a few days."

"I'm not going to Fort Gibson," John insisted.

"Captain Quill said you usually stop for a few days at Fort Gibson."

"I have on other trips. Zack may have assumed that was the route I would take, but not this time of year. I'm going across the territories along the fastest and safest route I know, which is to follow the Arkansas to the Canadian and take the Canadian west."

"I can show you another way. It's said to be —"

"— Look, Judge, this is the route I'm taking. I've got a hundred head of working stock to feed and water. They need to eat in order to work. In another month, the grass will go dormant and dry up in the hot Oklahoma sun. I've wasted a week waiting for you as it is."

"All right, all right. If you won't reconsider, I'm forced to go along."

"No one is forcing you to join my train. For the record, I'd rather you didn't — and you wouldn't, if not for my cousin Zack."

"We'll be ready day after tomorrow."

"Good night, Judge."

The judge watched the frontiersman cross the street and enter the tonsorial parlor. *Impudent young pup!* He wondered how such an overbearing lout could possibly be related to the mild-mannered, gentlemanly Zachary Quill.

# CHAPTER

## * 17 *

Colin sat beside Trisha, determined not to leave her alone with Buffer Simmons. The boy had stayed near her all day. She had tried to send him and the young ones to the cook wagon for supper, but they had refused to go without her, despite being coaxed by the cook. Shy, and missing Addie, they clung to Trisha.

The cook was preparing to send the food down to them, when Buffer Simmons appeared with two small rabbits, dressed and ready for the spit.

At dusk a small campfire was built between the two tents. Dillon and Jane Ann watched with unconcealed excitement as Buffer hung the rabbits over the low blaze. He was wonderfully patient with the children and allowed them to take turns turning the spit so that the meat would cook evenly on all sides.

After eating the rabbits and drinking the buttermilk the cook had sent down, the younger children had fallen asleep, and Trisha had put them to bed.

Now Buffer poked the fire with a small stick without looking directly into the flame. His eyes circled the camp, always alert, watchful, being careful to stay in view of the men who sat around the fire at the cook wagon. He didn't want Cleve Stark or Dal Rolly to come storming down and frighten Trisha into going into the tent. Buffer had intended to go to Van Buren today to make contact with the judge, but he delayed the trip when he learned that Trisha and the children would be here alone in camp, without Miss Addie or Tallman.

Since the younger ones had gone to bed, Buffer had been entertaining Colin, and he hoped Trisha, with yarns, a favorite pastime for men sitting around a fire. Some of the stories were true. Some were not.

"There was the time when I met up with this kid from Galveston. He was a ganglin' boy, young as ya are, Colin. He was all legs an' thumbs an' elbows. I come on to him down on Red River. He was helpin' a feller skin out a cow. 'Pears he was a-botchin' up the job, or so the feller thought. He jist up and knocked the boy right on his ar— knocked him down." Buffer glanced at Trisha. She was looking off into the distance, but she was listening. "Jist up an' backhanded that kid an' seemed to enjoy it. It jist went against the grain to see a man make a move like that against a boy."

"What'd ya do?" Colin asked.

"Wal, I picked up the boy, saw he wasn't hurt none and set him behind my saddle, climbed on my horse, an' rode off." Buffer threw the stick into the fire. Trisha's golden eyes had turned toward him.

"Ya let that mean man get away with it?"

" 'Twouldn't've done no good to beat the stuffin' outa him. Ain't no way to beat the meanness outa a grown man. When I took the kid, he had to skin out that cow all by his own self. Me'n the boy wintered in the Wichita Mountains with a half-mad trapper named Claytrap Throddle. That crazy old man was the beatenest cook. He cooked coon meat, baked possum and sweet 'taters. The best I ever et.

"Well, that kid was wild as a steer and had about as much sense as a cow pile. Come spring, he stole some money from old Claytrap and lit a shuck. Last I heard he was robbin' stages and stealin' horses. Reckon I should'a let that cow skinner have a go at tryin' to knock the meanness outa *him*."

The firelight played on Buffer's ruddy features beneath his shock of brown hair. It curled down onto his forehead and around his ears. It was impossible to tell his age because his thick beard almost completely covered his face. His teeth were even and white, which seemed to indicate that he was not yet forty.

Buffer waited, afraid that Trisha would go into the tent before Colin gave up and went to bed. Since morning the boy had been her shadow. Buffer watched the lad's head nod. He was a tired little duffer, but he was trying to hold on, to do what he considered his duty, guarding Trisha.

She sat on the ground with her bare feet toward the fire, her back resting against Addie's trunk. Buffer could scarcely keep his eyes off her. Tight black curls framed her face and cascaded about her shoulders. Since being in camp she had kept her hair skinned back and covered, but tonight she had thrown off the cloth and had dug her fingers into her hair to massage her scalp. Her lashes were so long that Buffer imagined they might tangle when she closed her golden eyes.

He glanced at Colin. The boy was asleep, his head resting against the stump of a tree. Now was the time Trisha would wake Colin and they would go to bed — if she was going to. A cruel, hard life had taught Buffer patience and how to weather disappointment.

If he didn't talk to her tonight, there would be other nights.

"Why ya lookin' at me, brush-face?" Trisha's voice came low, after a glance at the sleeping boy.

Buffer's spirits rose. He decided that honesty was the best approach.

"Because you're the prettiest thin' 'round here to look at."

"Horse-hockey! I've heard plenty o' that bull."

"I could've lied."

"Heard plenty a lies too. Whad'dya look like under that mess on yore face?"

"I don't rightly know. It's been a long time since I had a clean face." Buffer's fingers automatically began to stroke his beard.

"More'n likely ya got a weak chin. That's why yore hidin' it. A man with a weak chin ain't worth the dram of powder an' lead it'd take ta shoot 'im."

"Ya may be right. Have you known a man with a weak chin?"

"I've known 'em. Weak-chinned, weak ever'where 'cepts one place. There, they's strong as a bull." She lifted her chin and glared at him. "Ya hangin' 'round thinkin' to get under my skirt, brush-face?"

"I'd not be human if'n I'd not thought 'bout it. But hell, I ain't no ruttin' moose," he said, snorting with disgust.

"Ya ain't goin' to do it, an' that's that. If I didn't shoot ya, Colin would. If Colin didn't, Mr. Tallman would. He told me I didn't have to put up with no man I didn't want."

"Christ, Miss Trisha. I'll kill a man who'd try to . . . dishonor ya."

"Why'd ya do that for? I ain't nothin' but a nigger."

"Don't say that! Don't ya say that no more! Yore as white as I am. Even if you wasn't, it'd make no never mind. We be all the same under our skin."

"Ya mean under a blanket —"

"I didn't say that, dammit! I noticed ya first 'cause yore the prettiest thin' I ever did see. Then yore bein' pretty didn't matter, 'cause I saw how ya was with Colin and the younguns, how ya stood up to that old Renshaw. That means more than pretty." He poked at the fire angrily, and sparks floated upward.

After a long profound silence, Trisha said: "That don't change nothin' a'tall. Why'd ya stay here? Why didn't ya go on?"

"I . . . I thought I'd get a chance to talk to ya. I've been wantin' to since I saw ya in town. I . . . wanted to court ya then. Now, I've said it, an' ya can laugh yore head off," he finished angrily.

"Climb down off yore high horse. I ain't laughin'. Ain't wantin' no brush-face courtin' me, neither. 'Sides I ain't much of a talker, an' I reckon that's what courtin' is."

"Humph! I ain't seen a mouthier girl."

"I ain't no girl. I'm a woman."

"Ya look like a *girl.*"

"I'll be twenty years come July. That ain't no girl. That's too old for courtin' where I come from."

"Where's that?"

"Orleans," she said and then clamped her mouth shut.

"How long ya been with Miss Addie?"

"None o' yore business."

"I'll ask Colin."

"Ya do, an' I'll shoot yore blasted foot off!"

"It'd be just like ya to do it, too." He picked up a stick and placed it on the dying fire.

"Are ya a *old* man?"

"What'a ya want to know for?"

"I'm a-tryin' to talk to ya, brush-face. Ya don't have to tell. I ain't a-carin' if'n yore old as these hills."

"I'm twenty-five. Five years older'n ya are."

"I ain't a believin' it."

"I been on my own fer half my life. That'll

do two thin's to a man. It'll either make ya strong as a bull, or it'll kill ya. And, missy, I ain't dead." He thumped his chest with his fist for emphasis.

"What's got ya so all het up? Are ya mad 'cause ya ain't dead?" Suddenly a high little giggle escaped her. She covered her mouth with her hand in an attempt to smother it.

Buffer was confused for a moment. Then he chuckled.

"Ya get my dander up quicker'n anybody I ever saw, and I wanna wring yore blasted neck."

Trisha sobered. "Ya better not try it. I got me a stiletto that'll cut yore liver out." She lifted her skirt and gave him a brief view of the thin blade strapped to her calf.

"Christ on a horse! You'll fall on that thin' and cut yore leg off. It ort to be in a scabbard."

"It's a-doin' fine where it is."

Buffer drew his knife from the scabbard at his waist. He held it in his palm, then balanced it on his forefinger. He picked up his hat, flattened the crown, and tossed it into Trisha's lap.

"Sail my hat out yonder away from the tents."

Trisha spun the hat away from her as if it were a disk. Buffer drew back the knife.

As soon as the hat was in the air he sent the blade flying as swift as an arrow. It pierced the hat and fell to the ground. When he brought the hat back to Trisha, the knife blade was still in the crown.

"Tarnation!" she exclaimed. "Ya ruint yore hat."

"It needed another air hole."

"Ya reckon I could learn that?"

"Shore ya could. Could get to be better'n me, an' I'm good. Yore lighter an' quicker — makes for a good knife-thrower. I'll show ya some tricks . . . someday."

"Don't be doin' me no favors, brush-face."

"Don't ya worry none, *sour-mouth*. If'n ya can throw a knife, ya might save one of the younguns from getting snakebit." He snarled, slammed his hat down on his head, and stomped off toward the place where he had thrown his bedroll.

He was smiling.

Addie lingered in the tub until the water cooled. She had soaped herself from head to foot with the sweet-smelling bar and had washed her hair. After drying herself and toweling her hair, she put on her nightdress and her dress over it. It was so bulky that she couldn't button the bodice so she held it together with her hands when the boys came to empty the tub and take it away. Standing partially behind the door, she was relieved when she closed it behind them.

The warm water had relaxed and soothed her nerves enough that she felt prepared for what lay ahead when John returned. She had no fear of her new husband, but she dreaded the act he would commit upon her body. She would welcome him, she thought now as she worked with the towel to dry her hair. She owed the man a great deal. It wasn't as if she hadn't done it before. She only hoped to have it over quickly.

With the lamp turned to a faint glow, Addie sat beside the window and watched the activity on the street below. This was new to her. She was used to the quiet at the farm, and it seemed strange to see people walking about and to hear music coming from the saloons down the street.

The sound of a piano and a fiddle mingled with male voices and drunken laughter. Occasionally she heard loud, boisterous voices and the scraping of boot heels on the boardwalk as men left one saloon and mounted their horses or staggered off to another saloon. She thought about Trisha and the children back at the freight camp and wondered what they would think of the goings-on here.

She missed them. But not as much as she

had thought she would. It had taken all her willpower not to cry when she left the little group standing beside the tents. This was only the third night since Dillon's birth that she had not been able to reach out and touch him — to make sure he was breathing. Mrs. Sikes had told her that sometimes babies stopped breathing in the night. She had worried about that until Dillon was old enough to walk.

Sitting there in the near dark, Addie visualized how happy her children would be when John gave them the presents. Jane Ann had never had a glossy-headed doll. Dillon didn't know there were such things as tin soldiers, and Colin would be thrilled to own a jackknife. Addie had seen John slip in a tin of candy sticks. She had started to protest, then had caught the sly wink he gave the clerk and realized that he wanted to surprise her as well as the children.

She was combing the tangles out of her almost dry hair before braiding it when she heard the soft tap on the door, then the grate of the key in the lock. Her heart picked up speed as she stood, her eyes on the door.

John came in, his gaze finding Addie in the dimly lighted room before he turned and relocked the door.

"Smells pretty in here."

"It's the soap . . . and the powder."

"I see the tub is gone."

"Yes. I pulled the rope and the boys came and got it. Thank you for the bath."

"You don't have to thank me, Addie." He hung his hat on the bedpost and walked toward her.

"I've been watching out the window," she said quickly, and turned to look down on the street. "I can see the other hotel from here."

John moved up close behind her. She felt his hand touching her hair, and despite all her good intentions, she began to tremble.

"Your hair is almost dry."

"I was about to braid it."

"Do you have to?"

"It'll be a tangled mess in the morning if I don't." Addie was as breathless as if she had run a mile.

"If you leave it down, I'll help get the tangles out." John put his hands on her shoulders and pulled her back against him. "Don't be nervous, Addie."

"I'm not."

"Yes, you are. I can feel your trembling and the frightened pounding of your heart." He had lowered his head until his cheek was pressed against her ear. His arms encircled her, crossing beneath her breasts, locking her to him.

They stood silently for a long while, Addie staring out the window, seeing nothing.

"Would you like to sit here until your hair is completely dry?" John asked; and then not waiting for her to answer, said: "You've got your dress on over your nightdress. I'll turn off the light and you can take it off."

When he left her, Addie took her arms out of the sleeves and let the dress fall to the floor. She picked it up and hung it on a hook on the wall. Her nightdress was very modest. The sleeves were elbow-length. She felt to be sure it was buttoned to the neck.

The only light in the room now came from the window. Addie went toward it. John was seated in the chair. He took her hand and pulled her down on his lap. She was acutely aware that only his britches and her nightdress were between his hard thighs and her bottom. At first she sat erect, then gradually the stiffness went out of her spine and she leaned against him. He swept her hair up and spread it out over his arm and shoulder.

"Put your head on my shoulder. You'll be more comfortable."

"I've . . . not sat on a man's lap before."

"I've not held a woman on my lap, so that makes us even."

Her nose brushed his cheek as she laid her head on his shoulder. She smelled a tangy odor and realized that he had been shaved at the tonsorial parlor. She remembered Kirby spending almost the last of their few coins to be barbered and shaved. They had gone without coffee until Addie had knitted a cap and some mittens to trade at Mr. Cash's store.

John's hand worked beneath her hair, his fingers stroking the nape of her neck. It felt so good that Addie almost purred.

"You've had a busy day." The words were murmured as he crossed a leg over his knee to make a nest for her to settle in. "I'd hoped to keep you so busy you'd not have time to miss the children."

"I haven't missed them as much as I thought I would."

"You haven't worried, then?"

"Not really. I wondered mostly about Trisha. She asked me if Mr. Simmons would be there while we were gone. I think that because he came with us from the farm, she would look to him for protection should something happen."

He lowered his head and whispered in her ear: "They're going to have to get used to sharing you with me."

John took a deep breath. Holding this soft, sweet-smelling woman in his arms was sorely testing his control. Part of him was throbbing, painfully aware of what was pressed against it.

"Did you see the judge?"

"I saw him. If he hadn't had a young lady with him, I'd have been tempted to tell him to cut his own trail."

"You didn't like him?"

"He's an arrogant know-it-all."

"Is the lady his wife?"

"His niece. She was nice enough, but the type who's never done a day's work in her life."

"Shame on you," Addie said with a smile in her voice. "Because she can't walk behind a plow or shoot the eye out of a squirrel doesn't mean she's useless."

"Can you do those things?"

"I can certainly walk behind a plow. How do you think Trisha and I got our crops planted? And" — she chuckled softly — "I did shoot the eye out of a squirrel once, but it was an accident. I was aiming at another squirrel."

John laughed. Addie could feel the movement in his chest and the heavy pounding of his powerful heart.

"Addie, you're a wonder." As if to underline his statement, he placed his lips against her hair. "I told the judge that we'll be coming through here day after tomorrow, and he can tag along if he wants to."

"He still plans to go with us?"

"As of tonight, he does. Wait until he hears that we break camp at three in the morning and travel from six to eight hours, rest the animals in the middle of the day, then travel until dark. He's going to roar like a stuck hog."

"Why didn't you tell him that tonight?"

"I had other things to tell him that I thought would discourage him. Maybe when he finds out, he'll head on up to Fort Gibson and wait for another train."

Silence stretched between them, heavy with emotions. John had difficulty grasping the fact that this woman was his wife. *Wife.* She was his, to love and to protect forever or until death parted them. He wanted her; wanted to lose himself in the softness of her body, take comfort from her, and give comfort in return. He didn't want merely to slake his thirst. He wanted to make love to her and to hold her all through the night. More than that, he wanted her to *want* him to love her. Dammit to hell! He wanted it more than he'd ever wanted anything.

Nothing of what he was thinking was reflected in his voice when he spoke. He had been absently stroking her hair. If not for that hand movement and the heavy beat of his heart against her breast, Addie would have thought he was falling asleep.

"Do you want to go to bed now?"

She lifted her head from his shoulder and looked into his face. She had never voluntarily touched him. She did so now, placing her palms against his face, her thumbs touching his silky mustache.

"John, I'm not a young maiden. I know what to expect in the marriage bed. You've given me all that I hold dear in life, and —"

John took her wrists and removed her hands from his face.

"I don't want you to come to me out of gratitude. I've done nothing that I didn't want to do. I'll wait until the time comes when you want me, turn to me, with no thought in your head of what I've done for you."

Addie slipped off his lap and stood beside him. She wanted to cry. What she had intended to say was that she was fortunate to have him for her husband. It had come out wrong. Gratitude was a burden. Having cautioned herself about using the word, she now made a vow not to do so again. But she had said it, and now there was a strained silence between them.

# CHAPTER

## * 18 *

Addie, feeling miserable and not knowing how to undo the effect of her words, went around the end of the bed and slid beneath the thin covering. She stretched out on her back and stared at the dark ceiling, listening to John move about as he undressed. Finally he came to the bed and lay down beside her.

"I'm not wearing a nightshirt, Addie. Don't own one. On the trail I sleep in my britches. At home I sleep naked."

"I don't expect you to change your ways for me," she said in a small voice.

"I didn't want you to think I was going to pounce on you."

"I didn't think that."

"It's going to be a long night for us to lie here afraid we're going to touch each other. I'd like to hold you —"

"I'd like that too."

He slipped his arm beneath her shoulders. With his other hand he turned her toward him. Gently he pulled her against his side until her entire length was pressed against him. Her toes touched his leg above his ankle, and her thighs were against his. She nestled her head against his shoulder.

"That's better, isn't it?"

"I should have braided my hair. It'll get in your face."

He gathered the long silken tresses at the nape of her neck and pulled them over to cover his naked chest. John found her hand and flattened it over his heart, covering it with his own.

"Do you . . . mind being here with me like this?"

Acutely aware of how close she was to his strong, naked body, Addie lay without moving, inhaling the very presence of him, and feeling none of the dread she had expected.

"It's rather . . . nice," she said finally.

"I believe we'll have a good life together, Addie." She felt the caress of his mustache on her forehead when he spoke.

"I hope so. I hope never to disappoint you."

"We may come to love each other in time." He waited anxiously for her reply.

"A dear friend, who has been gone for a long time now, told me that you have to *like* a man first, then be friends with him. If love is to come, it comes after that."

326

"That makes sense to me. I like you, Addie. I like many things about you."

"I like you too."

"What is it about me you like? I'm not handsome, nor am I one to stand and shoot the bull. Days may go by without my saying more than three words."

"I wouldn't have thought *that* about you. You've talked plenty to me."

"Maybe you're just easy to talk to. What do you like about me?" he asked again.

"Well . . . I like the way you look," Addie whispered, and turned her face into the warm skin of his throat because she was embarrassed.

"You're joshing me now!" Silent laughter rumbled in his chest.

"No, I'm not. You're a fine figure of a man. You stand out in a crowd."

"It's my clothes. I won't be so noticeable when we get home."

"You like children, and you're kind to them," she continued. "You look stern sometimes, but you're really not. I like the thought of having someone like you beside me in case of trouble. Not that I like you just for *that*," she added hastily. "You're dependable and . . . a good horse trader, or I'd never have gotten the good team of mules from Mr. Birdsall."

"Addie, are you sure you're talking about me?" There was laughter in his voice — pleased laughter.

"Are you going to get a swelled head?"

He laughed aloud. *Oh, Lord. Where had this woman come from? Amy is going to love her.*

"I might not be able to wear my hat tomorrow."

He laughed again and hugged her, forgetting about the part of him that was reacting to her femininity until it touched her thigh. She appeared not to notice, but he pulled back.

"Do you know *who* I think about when I look at you?" It was easy for her to talk to him here in the dark.

"I'm afraid to ask."

She began to laugh and couldn't stop. She pressed her mouth against his shoulder. John's hand went to the back of her head. He caressed her hair. She continued to laugh, softly. He remembered hearing that women sometimes laughed like this when they were nervous.

"I've got a feeling that I'm not going to like this," he said with his lips against her temple. "Who do I remind you of that's so funny?"

"I was going to say Quasimodo. To . . . to tease you. It struck me funny that if there was ever anyone *not* like Quasimodo, it's you."

"Quasimodo? The hunchback? Why, Esmeralda, how kind of you." *I have truly found a treasure!* John ran his fingertips over her ribs, and she went into spasms of giggles. "You didn't think I'd know who you were talking about, did you?"

"I . . . didn't think —"

"Your husband is no ignorant lout, Mrs. Tallman. I'll have you know that we have Victor Hugo's entire works at home. My mother read them to us, then we all had to read them ourselves when we were old enough."

"Are you . . . mad at me?" Addie asked when she finally stopped laughing.

"No. Well, yes. I was sure you were going to say Sam Houston, Jim Bowie, or Heathcliff," he said with a low and happy laugh.

"Never Heathcliff! Maybe Sam Houston. When I look at you I think about Hawkeye from *The Last of the Mohicans*."

"That so? Hawkeye? He's a hero. Saves damsels in distress. Never tickles them. On the other hand, I rather like tickling you."

"Don't do it! Please! I do terrible things when I'm tickled."

"Do you do terrible things when you're kissed?" he asked, his voice suddenly strained. Whether by intent or by accident, his hand rested on the side of her breast.

"Not like I do when I'm . . . tickled."

Her voice died away and she lifted her face. Her heartbeat had quickened. The rest of her tingled. Her hand, captured between his and his chest, felt the pounding of his heart. She wiggled her hand out from under his and moved it up to the curve of his neck. Her fingers slipped into his hair.

He held her with gentle strength. Reality was fading. It seemed an eternity before his lips slid across her cheek to her mouth. He made a low groaning sound as he began to kiss her soft and sweetly parted lips. He kissed her tenderly, nudging her lips, stroking them. The softness of his mustache was a silky caress on her cheeks. Then, as if he couldn't get enough of her, he hungrily pressed his mouth to hers and tightened his arms around her.

She wasn't prepared for the warmth or the strength of his hard, muscular body, the long legs against hers, the enormous arms under and around her.

"You're a very kissable woman, Addie Tallman," he said huskily when he lifted his mouth from hers. "You smell and taste like a flower garden."

His hungry mouth searched and found hers again, and held it with fierce but tender possession. His hand moved down to her buttocks and pressed the seat of her femininity tightly to his thigh.

She wanted to speak, to tell him that she was not a girl but a woman, that she was not afraid of giving herself. She opened her mouth, but it was too late. He covered her parted lips, his tongue darting hotly into her mouth and out again, exploring lips that trembled beneath his demanding kiss. She moaned gently and panted for breath.

"Addie, sweetheart!" he whispered between kisses. He wanted to be closer to her soft body, to hold her against him so tightly that their flesh would become one. *She's not a whore*, he told himself sternly. *She's known you for less than a week.* "I'm trying to stop." He gasped. "But you're so sweet . . . a sweet, soft woman. I want to touch you . . . everywhere."

"You can." She pressed herself wantonly against him.

"No." He fell away from her. "I promised you I'd not force you to accept me."

Even as he spoke, her hands clutched him closer, her stomach muscles tightened, and her breathing and heartbeat were all mixed up. *Oh, dear heaven!* she thought wildly. *I love him! How did it happen so fast?*

She leaned up so that she could peer down into his face.

"If I didn't want you, you'd know it damn quick," she said angrily, then dropped her face down to his chest, wadded her fist, and hit him on the shoulder. "See what you've done? You've made me make a fool out of myself."

To say that John was stunned would be to put it mildly. He didn't know that she was crying until he felt her tears on his skin. He tried to lift her face, but she held it tightly to his chest.

"Addie, honey. I don't know what you're talking about."

"I've . . . disgusted you," she said between silent sobs.

"Where in the world did you get such a ridiculous idea?" He pushed the hair from her cheeks with fingers that shook.

There was a long silence. When she spoke, she seemed determined to say the words.

"Because . . . because I was acting like a . . . bitch in heat. That's why! Nice ladies don't act like that. Whores do."

John drew in a deep, shaky breath as his mind grappled with what she was saying.

"Where did you get that idea?" he asked again. "Hellfire, sweetheart. The reason I stopped was because I didn't want to push myself on you, make you feel obligated to let me love you. I want you to want me as much as I want you."

"I . . . didn't want you to stop. But —"

"Honey . . ." He kissed her forehead as if she were a child. "Why were you afraid to let me know that you liked to be kissed, and touched, and made love to? It's certainly nothing for you to be ashamed of." Her silence spoke for her. "Did Kirby Hyde tell you that a *lady* lies like a lump of flesh and lets her man satisfy himself on her body?" When Addie remained silent, John felt fierce anger toward the man. "If he told you those things, he was a stupid, ignorant son of a bitch!"

John's arms closed around her and he held her so close that she could barely breathe. When his fingers raised her chin, she snuggled her cheek against his shoulder. John's thumbs stroked the wetness beneath her eyes.

"You have such beautiful eyes. I've never seen any as beautiful. I don't like to see them filled with tears. Honey, it's just as natural for a female to want to mate with her man as it is for a man to feel the urge to mate. A man who has a woman who wants to join her flesh to his, to take pleasure from him as he does from her, is a very lucky man."

Addie kept her eyes tightly closed. They

lay quietly, as Addie felt the thump of his heart against her palm. When she spoke, words that she had no intention of saying just flowed out on a sob.

"I . . . don't know what's wrong with me. I think I . . . love you."

John caught his breath. "Sweetheart! I had hoped you would . . . someday."

"But it's too soon!"

"It happens like that sometimes. I may have fallen in love with you when I saw you that day in the store. Something drew me out to your farm."

"You can't —"

"Can't love you? Why not?"

"Because I'm . . . plain. And I've got three children."

"Addie, my love, you're far from plain. I've never met a woman who made me feel as you do, or who I wanted to be with . . . all the time. And those children are just an added bonus."

He hugged her so hard that she began to believe it could be true. She lifted her face to his. Their lips came together. Hers were soft, while his were hard and insistent. Her reaction to the kiss was instantaneous. Her lips parted, her whole body shivered, and her arm crept up and around his neck. Naked heat built in both of them. He breathed the fragrance of her skin, her hair, felt himself flame and harden. His arms and legs began to quiver.

His hands moved down her body. The nightdress was unbuttoned and swept away without her being quite aware of it. She returned his kisses with innocent hunger. The long, hard rod pressed to her belly thrilled her. The rough, seeking touch of his callused fingers, stroking her from her nape to her shoulder to cup her breast in his huge hand, sent delicious shivers throughout her melting flesh. His mouth was hard yet wonderfully warm and sweet. A joyful desire burned within her. She closed her eyes in ecstasy.

"Touch me, too, sweetheart," he whispered softly, placing her hand palm down on his abdomen.

The need for him blazed through her body and mind. She stroked him from his throat down over his shoulder to his lean rib cage, flat belly, and taut buttocks. His breathing came fast and irregular as her soft hand glided over his flesh. His whispered words were muffled as he kissed her lips and his tongue probed at the corner of her mouth. He held her breast in his hand as he lowered his head to nuzzle it and take the nipple into his mouth.

It was all so sweet, so much better than

she had ever imagined it could be. He was unhurried, gentle, his stroking hands and warm mouth sending waves of awakening pleasure up and down her spine. She arched against him, tugging at his powerful body as his hands slid under her, lifting her to him. She opened her thighs and welcomed him. He slid into her, filling her. There was a frenzied singing in her blood, and it grew with such rapidity that words beat against her brain: "I love you . . . I love you . . ."

She heard his smothered groans as if they came from a long way to reach her ears; and then the pleasure rose to intolerable heights, and she was conscious of nothing but her own sensations. She clung to him as an intense tide of feeling washed over her.

"Addie, sweetheart, I've —"

What he was about to say was never said. He began to move within her in a fevered rhythm, each breath a soft, stirring gasp.

Soaring, they held on to each other fiercely, as they ascended into ecstasy.

"Oh, Lord!" he cried, clutching her against him.

Addie's heart raced, her mind whirled. Her arms and body were deliciously full of him. John's head had dropped to her shoulder, and she delighted in the weight of his body on hers. Love for him filled her heart. She was sharing his pleasure, and he was right — there was no shame in it, just joy.

John turned on his side, bringing her with him, wrapping his powerful arms around her, pulling her thigh up over his so that they could stay united. The swift honesty with which she had given herself overwhelmed him. He had no words to tell her what her sharing of this sweet intimacy meant to him.

"Sweetheart, will you like this part of our married life? Lord, my heart is racing like a runaway mule. I wanted you to — feel what I did."

"It was grand. I felt as if I went out of my body for a little while. Is that what you wanted me to feel? I didn't know it could be so pleasant."

"Always tell me how you feel. If a time comes and you're not in the mood to do this, you only have to tell me. I can wait."

His hand moved down to her hips and pressed her soft down tightly to his groin. The part of him inside her swelled and hardened again. He hesitated for a moment, a long moment to see if she would pull away. Then with a quick intake of breath and a hungry, eager, forward motion of his hips, he moved in that slow, ecstatic rhythm of love.

Addie's mouth was as eager as his. She

invaded his mouth with the tip of her tongue. A small sound of pleasure came from deep in his throat at the sweet entry. As she met his thrust, a flame was rekindled in her belly. The flickering fire went on and on. The widening circle of pleasure was so profound that it sucked her into a swirling eddy where she thought she would drown. She sobbed his name as together they let go and moved into another world.

Drained, Addie turned toward him when he fell away from her. She reflected with wonder at what had happened. She couldn't get over the tempest of fiery emotion that he had aroused in her or how sweetly he had doused that fire.

His heart was quieter now, his breathing slower. She lay cocooned in his arms, her arm twined around his neck as his hands stroked her back and buttocks, and wondered if she had ever been happier in her life. She had meant to give this strong, wonderful man comfort in payment for what he had done for her. It had turned out so differently from what she expected.

She had found heaven.

# CHAPTER

## * 19 *

John and Addie met the Dutchman at daylight to take possession of the prairie schooner he had built to serve as a traveling home for himself, his wife, and six children. It was forty-two inches wide, fourteen feet long, and designed with a chuck box extending three feet across the back end. A lid, which was as large as the front of the box, was hinged to the bottom. It was designed to be raised to close the box, and when it was let down, it became a table.

The box was equipped with all the cooking utensils a family needed: an iron pot big enough to hold two gallons of water and with two bail handles so that it could be hung over a campfire; an iron skillet for frying; a Dutch oven with heavy iron lid for baking; and a coffeepot. There was a space to hold eating utensils and staples, even a built-in salt box.

On top of the three-foot-high sides of the

wagon, boards were nailed crosswise. These crossboards began behind the wagon seat and extended back six feet. A mattress rested on them. John explained that this was called an overjet. Beneath the overjet was room for another mattress. Attached to the wagon bed on all sides, rolled up and tied, was heavy canvas. This canvas could be let down and staked to make a snug tent beneath the wagon.

Four bows arched over the wagon, covered by a huge sheet of heavy duck from the front to the back with enough left over to draw together at the end.

On the outside of the wagon were shelves for a water keg, a water bucket, kerosene lantern, ax, scrub board, laundry tub, and other necessities.

Yesterday's purchases from Poole's store had already been brought to the wagon, as had supplies from a list Bill Wassall had given John.

Addie's eyes were bright with excitement as she looked over the wagon. She came back to stand close to John. He introduced her to the Dutchman and she told him how sorry she was that he had lost his wife.

After the Dutchman left, John grabbed Addie's hand and pulled it into the crook of his arm.

"Do you like it?"

"It's grand. But, oh, that poor man. You can see that he put his heart into that wagon."

"We gave him a good price. He can take his family back to where he has friends and relatives and have enough left over to give him a start. Do you know what I like the best about the outfit?"

"The chuck box?"

"I didn't even notice that." John grinned. "I like it because at night I'll have you all to myself. The family can sleep in the wagon, you and I under it. With the sides let down, we'll have our own tent."

Addie's cheeks turned rosy. She shuttered her eyes until he wiggled her chin with his thumb and forefinger. Then her eyes, shining violet pools, smiled up at him.

On the way to Lupe's for breakfast, they stopped at the corral so that Addie could say goodbye to the two faithful animals who had been a part of her life for so long. She rubbed their noses and patted their necks.

"What will the liveryman do with them?" she asked.

"Someone will come along who'll want good old horses for light duties. They'll be all right."

" 'Bye, Betsy. 'Bye, Martha." Addie turned away quickly and walked with John to the eatery.

Lupe was as boisterous this morning as she had been the night before.

"Yi, yi, yi. My eyes is lovin' what I'm seein'. Johnny, ya look like a fox a-comin' outta a chicken house."

"You look good too, Lupe." He grinned at the little woman. "How about some tortillas and eggs?"

"Tortillas and eggs for the lovers," she teased, disappearing into the kitchen. She returned with a platter of food and placed it in front of them. "Eat," she commanded. "I go to feed my babies."

"My wife is a sheep lover too, Lupe."

"Yi, yi, yi. Before ya go ya must see my pets."

Later, after they had said their goodbyes and were on the way back to the livery where the new wagon awaited, John said: "If you decided not to take your sheep, Addie, they would have a good home with Lupe. You can see how she dotes on hers."

"I've been thinking about what to do with them. I don't want them pulled down by wolves. What do you think I should do?"

"They're your sheep. If you want to take them, we'll try to drive them with the extra stock. But I must tell you, it will be hard on them. They probably won't make it."

They walked in silence. Addie didn't speak

until they had almost reached the livery.

"I'd rather Lupe have them than for them to die."

"If that's what you want, we'll drop them off when we come this way tomorrow."

A team of huge gray mules was hitched to the wagon. While John walked around the mules inspecting the harnesses, Addie waited beside the wheel and watched him. This wonderful man was her husband. It had all happened so fast that it was hard for her to believe it was real. She admired his patience and resourcefulness, his confidence. Just looking at him put a song in her heart.

*Dear God, you have been so good to me that surely you have forgiven me for the things I said to Preacher Sikes.*

This morning a nibbling on her ear and a large, callused hand cupping and caressing her breast had awakened her. Her back was pressed tightly to her husband's warm naked chest. Her buttocks were nestled in the cradle made by his torso and thighs. She could feel the bold urgency of him.

When she stirred sleepily, he buried his face in the curve of her neck.

"Who is this pretty woman in my bed?"

"Who are you, sir? A *passerby?*" she answered sleepily and covered the hand on her breast.

"Nay, sweet lady. I'm Hawkeye, looking for damsels in distress."

"Look no farther, my love."

She turned, laughed against his face, and twisted her fingers in his hair. Wrapping her arms about his neck and sliding her legs between his, she lifted her mouth. His kisses were warm, devouring, fierce with passion. Her ragged breath was trapped inside her mouth by his lips. After long, hungry kisses, he lifted his head and looked into her face, his hand gentle at the back of her head.

"You've become very precious to me," he whispered.

"I'll be loyal and true, my Hawkeye, and love you . . . always."

He made love to her slowly, kissing her temples, the curve of her cheeks, the corners of her mouth. He closed her eyes with gentle kisses. His large, firm sex was throbbing against the thigh pinned between his. Addie moved her hand down over the smooth flesh of his flat belly. Fingers that had lost their shyness closed around his erection. A low moan of pleasure came from his lips when she touched him, teasing his hardened flesh and then guiding him into her.

He had not expected this sweet willingness or the passion that lay slumbering behind Addie's calm, beautiful face. As on the night before, she held back nothing from him, and he held back nothing from her. The swift honesty with which she offered herself delighted him. The gentle, reverent way he took what she offered delighted her.

Brought back from her daydreaming by the sound of horses approaching and a shout of laughter, Addie watched two horsemen, trotting side by side, approach the livery. She recognized them as the Yankee soldiers she had seen ride into town yesterday while she was looking out the hotel window.

The riders passed on the other side of the wagon without noticing her. Addie moved around the end of the wagon for a better look at the magnificent horses just as the soldiers dismounted. One of the horses was jittery and danced at the end of the reins. The Yankee began to speak to him, attempting to soothe him.

"Cool down, big fellow. Cool down . . ."

The voice and the words hit Addie like a dash of cold water. For a moment she was stunned.

"Now . . . now . . . cool down. You wantin' me to rub you a little?"

A tingling sensation washed over her, as if she were being pricked by a thousand needles.

*Cool down, little filly, cool down.* The voice

and the words echoed in her mind. She had heard the words many times when she had nagged Kirby to help her do some chore that needed to be done.

The Yankee soldier's back was to her. His blond hair was longer than Kirby's and curled down to the collar of his blue Yankee uniform. She remembered Kirby as being smaller than this man. Yet, when she closed her eyes, the voice rang in her ears.

Was she going crazy? Kirby had not been a Yankee soldier; he had joined the Confederate Army. *Kirby was dead.* She had not heard his voice for four years. How could she think it was his?

When she opened her eyes, the Yankee soldiers had entered the livery and John was at her elbow to help her climb the wheel to the wagon seat.

"You all right, honey? Light hurting your eyes?"

Addie smiled. "Just a little," she lied.

The Yankee soldiers came out of the livery as the big wagon moved away. Addie's head was turned toward John, and she didn't see the blond man pause to stare after them, his eyes hard, his fists clenched. His companion, a few steps ahead of him, turned.

"Coming, Kyle?"

"Of course I'm coming. Where did you

think I was going?" he snapped.

"What in hell's got into you? Do you know those folks?"

"The man in buckskins was in the hotel last night. I'm wondering if he's the John Tallman the judge has been waiting for."

"The freighter? Could be. He looks the part — big enough to whip a bear with a willow switch. Don't worry, Captain, he's not Miss Cindy's type. Anyhow, he's got a woman. She's a little old for my taste, but I reckon she suits the freighter. It's a long way across the territories. You'll have plenty of time to court Miss Cindy."

The blond man had heard only snatches of what his friend was saying. The last, however, caught his attention.

"Yes, I'll have plenty of time," he murmured, but his thoughts were not on Miss Cindy Read.

The spring seat with its high back made the return trip to camp more comfortable than Addie had thought possible. An hour before noon they neared the knoll where the freight wagons were parked.

Addie looked questioningly at John when he stopped the team and wound the reins around the brake.

"Come here, honey." He slid his arm across

347

her shoulders to pull her close. "You've been awfully quiet. Did I tire you out last night?"

Addie's arms encircled his waist and she hugged him as if he were a stout log she clung to to prevent her being washed down-river by a flood. She didn't dare tell him that the Yankee soldier back at the livery was so like Kirby that she had feared she was losing her mind until logic had forced her back to reality. Kirby would not have come back to life as a *Yankee,* even if such things were possible. He despised Yankees, or so he had said. Of course, long before he had left her she had come to re-alize that Kirby sometimes said whatever he thought someone wanted to hear — true or not.

"I'm anxious to see the children," Addie murmured with her lips against John's cheek. "But — I've loved every minute of the time we've had together."

John kissed her gently, lovingly. "I've loved it too, Addie girl. We'll not have much time to be alone from now on. I'll be pretty busy getting you and the children and the freight wagons home. Kiss me again, then I'll get these mules headed on down the road."

He kissed her nose; she kissed his lips again and again. They sat looking at each other. She couldn't keep from smiling. His dark eyes adored her. It was pure magic to be here with him, their arms around each other, their minds attuned.

"I'm acting like a callow youth who's just discovered that girls are different from boys," he confessed.

"I'm acting like a silly schoolgirl."

Their soft laughter mingled as they shared one last kiss.

The camp seemed almost empty as they approached it. The cook and Paco stepped out from behind the cook wagon and waved. John drove on toward the tents, where Trisha stood waiting alone, her arms folded across her chest, a frown on her lovely face.

"Trisha!" Addie called before John stopped the wagon. "Is everything all right?" She began climbing down as soon as the wheels stopped rolling. Her heart began to thump painfully when she heard one of the children crying. "Trisha, what's wrong?"

"I'm glad yore back, Miss Addie. It's Dillon. I can't do nothin' with him. The turtle's gone off, for one thin'." Trisha's golden eyes were sad. "And this mornin' one of them ornery mules . . . kicked Bucket to death. Dillon and Jane Ann saw her hangin' up an' one a them Mexican fellers skinnin' 'er out. Dillon run at 'im, kicked 'im, and hit 'im. He's awful stirred up about it, and so's Jane Ann."

"Oh, my goodness!" Addie ducked into the tent.

"Anything else happen, Trisha? Were you and the children treated all right?" John asked.

"We was treated like we was tryin' to 'scape on the underground railroad or somethin'. Them fellers watched so good, me and Jane Ann was afeared to go to the bushes."

John grinned. "Is Buffer Simmons still here?"

"He lit out this mornin'. Cleared the air, if ya was to ask me."

"Did he bother you?"

"Naw. He was a'right that way. Last night he cooked rabbit for the younguns. They thought it a lark." Trisha eyed the wagon. "That what we goin' in?"

"That's it. I'll unhitch the mules and leave it here. You and Addie put in the things you'll need for the trip. The rest" — he gestured toward the pile of household things — "will be put in the other wagon."

"Can we all sleep in thar?"

"Sure can. Addie'll show you."

She gave him a sideways glance. "You, too?"

"No. Addie and I will sleep *under* the

wagon." Leave it to Trisha, John thought, to get to the point. "Where's Colin?"

"Down there with that Gregorio. He's been showin' Colin how to throw a rope over a fence post. Colin's havin' hisself a high old time."

"He's a different boy now that he's out from under the threat of going to that bastard Renshaw. He can thank you for that, Trisha."

"You done it." Trisha tossed her head and looked away. " 'Twarn't nothin' I done."

"I've got a new, light rifle. As soon as we get strung out on the trail, I'll teach you to shoot it and to hit what you shoot at."

The girl's golden eyes came alive. "Old brush-face is gonna teach me to throw a knife so I can kill a snake. You gonna show me how to shoot the gun. My, my, I gonna be one of them holy terrors if'n ya don't watch out."

John smiled. "You already are."

Trisha smiled back. "I guess I is, if'n ya say so."

Inside the tent, Addie sat on the mattress, holding Dillon on her lap and snuggling Jane Ann close to her side. The sobs of both children had turned to sniffles.

"It's sad to lose Bucket, but we wouldn't have wanted her to live with broken legs or a cracked head. She would be happy to know

351

that you'll have her warm coat. You can snuggle down on it and remember her."

"That Paco said they'd . . . eat her." Jane Ann began to cry again.

"We eat chickens that we've known. Remember the pig we fattened so that we'd have bacon and ham and lard?"

"But the pig didn't have a . . . name."

"She did to other pigs. Now dry your eyes and come see our new wagon. John bought new clothes and presents for everyone."

Both children sat up and dried their eyes on their sleeves.

"Me too?" Jane Ann asked.

"Why, of course. You're our little girl, aren't you?"

It was evening. The tents had been taken down, the canvas rolled and stored. The new wagon was now home. They all climbed inside and Addie opened the bundles from the store. The children and Trisha were delighted with their new clothes. Shoes were tried on after Addie dug into her trunk and brought out a supply of new stockings she'd been planning to trade at the store. The gifts, she hid away until John could be there to present them.

When the other wagon was brought up to be loaded with the rest of Addie's possessions, Colin sat beside the driver wearing his new shoes, duck pants, and straw hat. The new clothes seemed to imbue him with new pride. He no longer looked like the scared little boy he had been back at the farm.

The floor of the wagon had been water-proofed with tar and canvas. This time, with careful rearrangement of the things Addie had brought with her, there was space left over. It was quickly filled with a couple of spare wheels, buckets of tar to be used as lubricant, extra yokes, and a number of spare axles. A heavy tarp was spread over the load and tied securely to the sides of the wagon.

Gregorio explained in his broken English that strapped beneath each wagon was an extra tongue and that each wagon carried a water keg fastened on the side that would be filled at every watering place. There was also a chip sack hanging on a hook on the side of each wagon; this was filled with buffalo or cow chips collected during the day to be used for the evening campfire.

Shortly before dusk, Bill Wassall strolled down to the new wagon.

"Howdy, ma'am. This shore is a fine schooner. Don't know as I ever saw a finer one."

"Mr. Tallman was pleased to find it."

"Well, if'n anybody knows what'll go over the trail, it's John. Ah . . . ma'am, I jist want ya to know I'm plumb sorry 'bout the

353

other day. Me an' the fellers was as surprised as all get-out. If —"

"Let's forget about it, Mr. Wassall. I try never to look back and dwell on what's over and done with."

"I'm not wantin' no hard feelin's."

"Let me assure you there are none."

"I'm plumb relieved to hear it. Now, ma'am, there ain't no use in you cookin' tonight. Me an' Paco got a big mess of catfish bakin' in the pit. Paco stirred up a batch of tortillas and patted them out real thin like an' they been cookin' all day. Them Mexican fellers can shore chaw down on a pile of tortillas. Y'all come on up and hep us eat 'em."

"Thank you for the invitation, but I'm not sure it's a good idea tonight. Jane Ann and Dillon are still upset over the death of our ewe. It would have been wasteful not to use the meat, but I don't want them to see any part of it."

"The critter is still a-hangin' out there in the woods. Gregorio skinned her and stretched the hide on the side of the wagon. We thought you'd want the pelt. Later tonight, after she's cooled out some, I'll salt her down."

Addie winced at the matter-of-fact way he spoke of Bucket, the sweet little lamb that

354

spent the first few weeks of her life in Addie's kitchen.

"Got catfish, tortillas, and peach cobbler." Bill patted his plump stomach and grinned.

He really was nice, Addie thought. His eyes were twinkling.

"Mr. Tallman told me you were called Sweet William. How in the world did you cook peach cobbler over a campfire?"

"Wasn't nothin' to it a'tall. I got a big iron pan." He spread his hands to show the size. "I jist put the peaches, flour, sugar, and — Oh, shoot, I'll show ya how sometime."

"I would appreciate that. I don't know much about cooking over a campfire."

John walked up behind Addie and put his hand on her shoulder.

"Get settled in?"

Before Addie could answer, Dillon and Jane Ann ran to him.

"Lookee at my new hat!" Dillon put both hands to the round brim. "Lookee at my new shoes!" He stood on one foot so he could lift the other.

"Do they fit?" John squatted down and pressed his thumb to the end of the shoe.

"I got new shoes too," Jane Ann said, lifting her skirt to her knees and looking anxiously at John.

"So you have. Do yours fit?"

"They're big. Miss Addie says I'll grow."

"And you will." John took the end of the child's braid and tickled her nose with it. She giggled and shied away.

"I want shoes like yours." Dillon had squatted in the dirt and was fingering the lacings on John's knee-high moccasins.

"Me too!" Jane Ann echoed.

"We'll get you both some when we get to New Mexico. For the trip you need heavy shoes."

The children scampered away to tell the news about the moccasins to Trisha, who was still in the wagon.

"I held back the other . . . for you to give them." Addie waited until Bill had left them to say this. "And I thought that maybe you should wait awhile. They're so excited about the new clothes and the trip —"

"Spread out the joy a little, huh?"

"Something like that."

"I'm sorry about the ewe."

"I know. I didn't want to leave them at the farm. The Renshaws would have killed them out of pure meanness. The sheep helped to get us through the war. I'll always love them for that."

Bill rang the supper bell.

"Call the children, Mrs. Tallman. It's suppertime."

Later, drifting down from the breathless heights of pleasure, Addie lay as if in a trance. Her body nestled against John's, a warm soft thigh between his legs, one arm across his chest. John's strong fingers worked the muscles of her back and shoulders.

He had brought a ground sheet and a feather tick, and showed Addie how to lower the canvas and fasten it to the wheels. He had also looked into the wagon and said good night to Trisha and Jane Ann, who were going to sleep on the overjet, and to Colin and Dillon, who were sleeping under it.

"Where's Muvver gonna sleep?" Dillon had asked.

"She'll be here with me under the wagon."

"Under the wagon? That's funny," the boy had shouted.

Then Trisha had shushed him, and soon all was quiet.

John continued now to rub Addie's back. She stretched like a contented kitten, and a throaty moan escaped her.

John laughed softly into her hair.

"John, sometimes I'm afraid." His fingers stopped and she hurried on: "Afraid this is a dream and I'll wake up back there at the farm with the Renshaws, old Preacher Sikes,

357

and nothing but bleak years staring me in the face."

"It isn't a dream, sweetheart. Although at times on the trail you may wish it were. It's not an easy trip — dust, wind, rain, breakdowns, rivers to cross."

"I'll not worry because we'll be with you. I used to worry about what would happen to the children and Trisha if something should happen to me."

He shook her shoulder gently. "Shhh . . . Don't talk like that."

"I know you would take care of them, or see to it they were cared for."

"Of course I would. Now, hush up and go to sleep. This train rolls at dawn."

Addie snuggled against him, but she couldn't sleep. In the back of her mind was the image of the Yankee soldier she had seen at the livery, and uneasiness stirred within her.

# CHAPTER

## * 20 *

When Buffer Simmons left the freight camp, he backtracked as far as the stream where he and Tallman had dumped the Renshaws, looking for a trace of them. It would have taken a while for them to round up their horses; but two days and two nights had passed, and if they were still trailing, they were too dumb not to have left some sign. Buffer had no doubt that one or the other of them was still dogging Trisha's trail.

Riding along, looking for tracks of sloppily shod horses, Buffer mused that people as low as the Renshaws had to find someone they considered lower than they were. In this case it was Trisha. From the bits of news he had picked up in Freepoint, it was Preacher Sikes who had passed the word that Trisha a Negro. He had declared her to be a runaway slave. Up until that time, she had been presumed by the townsfolk to be a distant relative of Miss Addie.

What the hell difference did it make if Trisha's great-grandma came over on a slave ship? Buffer's own grandpappy had been plucked out of Newgate Prison and sent to the New World. He thought of the time he had spent with Trisha, the firelight shining on her face. What he had told her was the truth. He had first noticed her because she was pretty, but there was more to her than her looks — much more. She was spunky, loyal, dependable, and tough as a willow switch. She would be one to winter with. There would be no dull days with her around. Buffer chuckled as he remembered her asking if he had a weak chin. *"Is that why you cover it with brush?"*

He fingered his bushy beard. One of the first things he was going to do when he got to Van Buren was to visit the tonsorial parlor. He usually let his whiskers grow in the winter and shaved in the spring. This year he just hadn't gotten around to it.

Buffer completed the circle without finding a track he could tie to the Renshaws, so he took the trail along the river to Van Buren, arriving there about noon. He ate beans and tortillas served by a jolly little Mexican woman in a brightly painted eatery. When he entered, the two tables were full except for one place on the end. As he filled his plate from the bean pot on the table and forked several hot pickled peppers onto his plate, he felt the intense gaze of a man at the other end of the table. Buffer let his eyes pass over the starer as if he hadn't noticed the man's interest.

He was tall, Buffer judging by the way the man's shoulders rose higher than those of the diners on either side of him. His black beard reached the third button on his shirt and his black eyes, separated by a beak of a nose, were ice-cold. A vulture was what he resembled, Buffer thought. The man ate only beans, slurped his coffee, and spoke to no one.

Passing the time of day with the others at his table, Buffer hedged when asked where he was from and where he was going. His built-in survival instinct warned him that the *vulture* was listening to all the conversations going on around him.

On leaving the table, Buffer jollied for a moment with the woman called Lupe, then left the building and headed for the mercantile, dismissing the *vulture* from his mind.

Several hours later, after a bath, a shave, and a haircut, and dressed in clean buckskins and a new shirt, he went back to where he had left his horse. On his way out of town, he stopped again at Poole's store. He bought himself a new hat and the smallest pair of buckskin breeches they had in the store, although he figured even then they would be too big for Trisha. He wasn't sure why he had bought them or the scabbard and belt. Before mounting his horse, he added them to the roll tied behind his saddle along with his bedroll.

Buffer was almost through town when the black-bearded man came out of a doorway and walked toward the store. He was thin to the point of gauntness, his shoulders were narrow, and his arms and legs were long. He carried a long-barreled rifle and wore an old, black, high-crowned hat. He walked along the street ignoring the curious stares of those he passed on the boardwalk.

About three miles out of town Buffer found the judge's camp. Before riding in, he pulled his horse to a halt, leaned on the pommel, and studied the scene. He thought that he had seen every manner of train that had crossed the territories, but one of the six wagons in the semicircle was a sight he'd not encountered before. It was a caravan with wooden sides and a shingled roof out of which extended a tin chimney. A white canvas canopy, covering the length of the vehicle, was attached to the side and supported by poles on each end. Seated in the shade of the canopy were a man and a woman with a small table between them. The caravan was painted a soft yellow and decorated with blue and green scrollwork designs. Steps led up to its back door.

Two of the wagons were prairie schooners, apparently new, judging from the gleaming paint and snow-white canvas stretched over the bows. A Negro man sat beside one of them, polishing a pair of boots.

The next two wagons were heavily loaded freight haulers with high sideboards and dark canvas covering the loads. The fifth wagon was the type used by the army to carry men and supplies. An extra wheel was attached to the tailgate. The sixth was the cook wagon. Beside it, a colored man was working over a smoking campfire.

Shaking his head in dismay, Buffer was sure that there was not one spare axle, wagon tongue, or double-tree in the camp, and that the only spare wheel was the one attached to the back of the army wagon. The freight wagons had two barrels for water on each side, and one water barrel was attached to the side of the cook wagon; no barrels hung from the sides of the prairie schooners or the caravan.

Buffer's eyes wandered to the meadow where the stock was grazing. In an area off to the side were some of the finest horses he had ever seen. They were Thoroughbreds, from the look of their shiny coats, long slim legs, and high arched necks. Aside from the Thoroughbreds, there were six draft animals and a dozen head of mules and horses.

Taking off his hat, Buffer scratched his head. He let the warm sun beat down on his face, the lower part of which felt almost naked, having been sun-shaded by his beard all spring. The thought came to him that getting this flashy outfit past renegades and others looking for easy pickings would be about as easy as stretching a bluejay's ass over a water barrel.

Several Yankee soldiers lounged beneath a pecan tree, and a couple of men on horseback circled the grazing stock. A colored woman came from the caravan, walked around to the far side, and shook a cover of some kind. She wore a black dress with a white apron tied about her waist and had touches of white at her neck and wrists. Buffer had not seen one before but he reckoned she was a "lady's maid."

He debated turning his horse around, going back to Tallman's freight camp, and asking to sign on. Hell, he'd work his way across for his grub. He sat for several minutes and thought about it. Finally he came to the conclusion that he owed it to the men in Fort Smith who had recommended him that he at least speak to the judge and give him a chance to hire another hunter.

A suspicion began to form in Buffer's mind. Why would the judge need a hunter for a party this size? It seemed to him that one of the soldiers could go out once in a while and bring in fresh meat.

After folding up the front of the brim of his new hat and securing it to the crown with the silver pin he took from his old one, Buffer slapped it on his head and put his heels to his horse. He rode slowly into the camp. Before he neared the wagons, the soldiers moved quickly from beneath the pecan tree and intercepted him. One stepped up beside his horse and took hold of the cheek strap.

"What's your business here, mister?" he demanded in the harsh, clipped accent of the North.

"What's it to ya?"

"We saw you sitting off out there watching our camp. What do you want?"

"Ya been a-fightin' in the war?" Buffer asked softly.

"Of course I have. What about it?"

"Didn't nobody ever tell ya not to come up to a mounted man and take hold a his bridle like yo're doin'? Yo're primed to get the toe of my boot right under yore chin. Seen a few fellers lose teeth that way and one that bit his tongue right off."

"I'm asking what your business is here."

"It ain't with you, sonny boy, and that's a fact. I'm here to see the judge."

"What about?"

"Gawddammit!" Buffer's temper flared. His booted foot shot out of the stirrup. "If ya don't get outta my way, I'm gonna get off this horse and kick yore ass up so high yore damn head'll be ridin' on it."

"You're taking on the United States Army, mister."

"I'm takin' on a puffed-up, brayin' jackass and two other jacks, if they deal in."

"Back off, Shipley. The captain told us the judge had hired a hunter. Might be this is him."

"If he is, why didn't he say so?" Red-faced, the soldier backed away.

The instant the man let go of the bridle, Buffer gigged his horse. The animal shot ahead. A sharp tug on the reins spun it around. Just as Buffer had expected, Shipley had his hand on his side arm. In a lightning-fast move, Buffer pulled his knife from its scabbard.

"Ya gonna bet ya can shoot me 'fore I

put this knife in yore throat?" He spoke calmly as he tossed the knife up and caught it by the tip of the blade between his thumb and forefinger.

"The judge is yonder by the caravan." The man who spoke was holding Shipley's arm.

"Thanky kindly." Buffer slid his knife back into the scabbard, rode the short distance, dismounted, took off his hat, and dropped the reins to the ground. The ground-tied horse stood perfectly still.

The man who came forward to meet him had white hair and a flowing white beard.

"I assume you are looking for me."

"If'n yore Judge Van Winkle, I am. I'm Jerr Simmons, known in some places as Buffer."

"Glad to meet you." The judge held out his hand, and as Buffer shook it, he noticed that it was as soft as a woman's. "You were having words with my escort," the judge observed.

"If ya mean by 'havin' words,' was I 'bout to kick his teeth out, I guess I was."

"I'll have discipline on this trip. The contingent of army personnel have been given complete authority to keep order and protect this train. You will make your reports directly to the captain of that detail; and if there is anything worthy of my attention, they will inform me."

"Well now, Judge, I got a whole bunch a respect fer a man who comes right out with plain talk. Reckon we see eye to eye on that. I'll just put my cards on the table. If it be that them tinhorn, bunghead, half-ass soldier boys ya got out there is runnin' this show, it ain't no place for Buffer Simmons. I'll say good day to ya, Judge." Buffer slapped his hat back onto his head and was halfway to his horse before the Judge recovered from his shock.

"Just a minute. You hired on to do a job."

Buffer turned. "I just quit. If ya get on down to Van Buren, ya might hit it lucky and find ya a hunter who'll kowtow to them know-it-all pissheads ya call fightin' men. It ain't gonna be Buffer Simmons, that's certain."

"I was told at the fort that you were a level-headed man who could be trusted to do a job. They told me that you knew the trail across the Indian Nations and Oklahoma Territory as well as any man."

"I know that trail. Ya ain't needin' a scout or a trail boss, Judge, if yore gonna hang tight to Tallman's bull train. And, to my way a thinkin', that's the onlyest way ya'll make it across."

"Nonsense. I've got the best wagons money can buy, the best animals, drivers, and herders. And six seasoned soldiers to escort us."

"Six soldier boys? Haw-haw-haw! Ya ain't got nothin' to worry 'bout 'cepts losin' yore hair." Buffer turned to his horse.

"Wait. Tallman's bull train will make only ten or twelve miles a day. I'm told that with these wagons, my dray animals and mules, we can make half again as many miles a day as he can. I need a scout to lead the way."

Buffer's jaw dropped. "Ya mean strike out with this outfit?"

"That wasn't the plan at first. Since coming to Van Buren, I've been speaking to men who have been over the trail with bull trains. They tell me that the dust those trains raise is stifling, and on a clear day it can be seen for twenty miles. They say that bull-whackers and lowlifes who hire out on the trains are scum of the worst sort and will steal a man blind. They're said to be not much better than Indians and other undesirables that prey on travelers."

"Ya thinkin' yore wagons won't raise dust?" Buffer asked, knowing that there was no reasoning with the man on any part of what he had said.

"Not as much."

369

"I ain't never heard nothin' as harebrained as that."

"Now see here —"

"Judge, ya ain't never seen nothin' as sickenin' as a train of folks that's been overrun by a bunch a murderin' cutthroats. There ain't no Indians I know of that'll hold a candle to renegade whites and Mexicans when it comes to pure-dee old meanness. Most of them outcasts was suckled on wolf's milk. There ain't nothin' human 'bout 'em."

"I'm well aware of the hazards."

"Hazards, hell! Them fellers get a look at that woman and they'll have her, come hell or high water. They'll have her till she's bleedin' from ever' hole she's got and ain't nothin' but a pile a bones, meat, and hair. An' that ain't all, Judge. They'll cut yore pecker off an' poke it in yore ear, that is, if'n they don't roast it over a fire while it's still on ya!"

"That's enough! I'll not listen to such crude talk!"

Buffer mounted his horse. The woman had come out from under the canopy and stood waiting for a soldier who was approaching. She was young and pretty, and it was a pity what awaited her if the judge struck out without waiting for Tallman. A rich outfit like this stood no chance at all of getting across

370

the territories without being attacked. Buffer liked his skin on the outside of his bones and his head on his shoulders too much to take a chance like that.

"Judge, I'm tellin' ya fer the sake of that woman, wait fer Tallman. Ya might think them bull-whackers be a bunch a low-down greasers, but they're fighters. Most of 'em would die tryin' to keep that woman over thar outta the hands of a pack a outlaws."

The judge stepped back, the posture of his whole body conveying his contempt. He fixed Buffer with a piercing eye.

"You coward! Get out of my camp."

"Callin' a man a coward is a invite to fight. If ya wasn't such a dumb-ass old man I'd take ya up on it." Buffer whirled his horse and rode toward the road, passing the soldiers without a glance.

Judge Van Winkle watched him go, then turned back to the caravan where his niece and her Captain Forsythe waited.

"Who was that man, Uncle Ron?"

"The man I was told could lead us to Sante Fe."

"Why is he leaving?"

"We had a disagreement about discipline." The judge moved behind his niece and met the eyes of the young officer.

"Honey, does Ivy have any more of that lemonade?"

"If not, she'll make some." Cindy clasped the captain's arm with both her white hands and looked up at him adoringly.

"See about it, sweet. I'll wash up and be right back."

"You and Uncle Ron just want to get rid of me so you can talk," she said, pouting.

"That isn't so, and you know it. Who in their right mind would want to get rid of a pretty little thing like you?"

"When there's something serious to talk about, you always send me to do something."

"Run along, Cindy," the judge said curtly. "I need to talk to Kyle."

"Oh, all right."

Kyle walked with her to the steps of the caravan, holding onto her hand until she threw him a kiss and disappeared inside. He joined the judge and they walked along the line of wagons, stopping beside the colored man polishing the boots.

"Get Captain Forsythe some wash water, Saul."

"Yassah." Saul took a bucket from the end of the wagon and hurried away.

"I didn't let that ignorant lout know it, Kyle, but he threw a scare in me about our going on ahead of the bull train."

"What did he say? The usual about renegades and wild Indians? Judge, I've talked to men who have been over that trail, and all they encountered were small groups of Indians armed with bows and arrows."

"I don't know. We don't have a scout now. You know I hired Simmons as a hunter because I didn't want word to get out that we might want to strike out ahead of Tallman."

"We can go to Fort Gibson and pick up a scout there."

"I thought of that, but Tallman refuses to go to Fort Gibson. He's an overbearing bastard." The judge was thoughtful. "So is this fellow Simmons. I think this country breeds overbearing bastards," he finished bitterly, and cast a wary eye at the Negro who had returned with the water and lingered beside the wagon. "Don't you have anything to do, Saul?"

"Yassah."

"Then do it," he ordered curtly, and watched the man scurry away.

"Blasted coloreds. They're good for only one thing: listening and repeating what they hear."

Kyle carefully combed his hair and smoothed his mustache before he spoke.

"Is Tallman married? From Cindy's description of him, I think I saw him in the mercantile and again this morning with a woman."

"His wife and three children are with him."

Kyle poured water into the wash pan and splashed his face with his cupped hands. After using a towel, he tossed it down beside the basin and turned to the judge. His handsome features were creased with a worried frown.

"I'm eager to get to Albuquerque and take up my post. The sooner I'm settled, the sooner Cindy and I can get married."

"I take up my duties at the Office of Indian Affairs in three months' time. I figure that if we travel with Tallman we'll make twelve or fifteen miles a day. Figuring at twelve, we'll arrive with only about a week to spare."

"That's cutting it tight," Kyle replied. "My men and I are expected two weeks after that."

"A post like this is something I've wanted all my life," the judge confessed. "Still, if something happened to Cindy, I'd never forgive myself. She's all I've got."

"She's all I've got, too, Judge. I love her very much. Always have. I had to wait for her to grow up."

"Come on, Kyle." The judge slapped him on the back. "You had to go out and sow a few wild oats."

"That too, sir."

"Tallman will be coming through tomorrow. I think for a while we'd better let him think we're joining his train. In the meantime, we'll watch for a chance to break off and head for Fort Gibson. We'll get good trail information there and maybe hire another scout."

The two men walked back to the caravan. The judge was deep in thought, and Kyle Forsythe wondered what the hell he was going to do now. His "wild oats," as the judge had chosen to call his activities before the war, were coming back to haunt him.

# CHAPTER

## * 21 *

Addie was awake when the clang of the cowbell announced the first appearance of the
new day. A short while before, snuggled securely in John's arms in their bed beneath
the wagon, she had felt the gentle caress of
his lips on her cheek and had turned to slide
her arms about him and return his kiss.

"Mornin'," he had whispered. "Sleep
well?"

"Mmm . . . like a rock."

"You don't feel like a rock." One hand
moved up and down her back, the other
cupped and squeezed her soft breast.

She nestled her face in the curve of his
neck. She loved the masculine scent of his
skin, the rasp of his whiskers on her cheeks,
the hardness of the arms holding her.

"Do you have to get up now?"

"Uh-huh, but you don't have to until Bill
rings the bell. It'll take half an hour to yoke
up." He kissed her, then rolled out from

under the covers and put on his britches and shirt. He turned back and leaned over her. "I think I like married life. You washed my socks." He pulled the cover up over her shoulders, dropped a kiss on her nose, and was gone.

Addie was still smiling when the cowbell rang again. She dressed quickly, rolled up the side canvases and fastened them, then folded the mattress and the covers.

Trisha, silent as a shadow, came out of the wagon.

"This is the first day of our journey, Trisha. Are you excited?"

"I am, Miss Addie, but I been worried 'bout ya."

"Why?"

"Him. That passerby."

Addie laughed. "Are you still calling him that? He hasn't forced himself on me, if that's what's worrying you. Under that rough exterior is a sweet and gentle man. I didn't know there were men like John Tallman. It's a miracle that we found him, Trisha. Or that he found us. I love him."

"How ya know that already?"

"I just know." Addie had brushed the snarls out of her hair and was swirling it so that she could fasten it to the top of her head and cover it with her bonnet.

"Are we goin' now?" Colin climbed down out of the wagon.

"In a little while. Go on up to the cook wagon, Colin. Mr. Wassall will give you some cold meat and biscuits. John told me the first meal of the day will be cooked when we stop in Van Buren shortly before noon. We'll start up again in the middle of the afternoon and travel until after sundown."

"Gregorio told me that too." Colin popped his new hat on his head.

Addie saw that he had turned up the front of the brim and pinned it to the crown with a pheasant feather. If Trisha noticed that the boy had copied Buffer Simmons, she didn't comment on it.

"Mr. Wassall told me last night that there would be morning coffee. Take the little syrup bucket, Colin, and bring back some for me and Trisha."

When the wagons moved out, John, mounted on Victor, led the train out onto the main road, while his second in command, Cleve Stark, directed the order in which they traveled. Addie's wagon, driven by Huntley, a short, bowlegged man who had an engaging grin even though his teeth were stained brown by tobacco, was second in line behind the lighter wagon carrying her possessions. Colin sat beside Gregorio on the seat of that wagon.

Looking back, Addie could not even see the end of the train, it was so long. The bull-whackers walked beside the oxen singing a chorus of "Get up Baldy, Go 'long Gert, Geehaw Ranger, and Wo-ah thar Sugar Tit!" The *pop! pop! pop!* of the bull whips could be heard clearly in the still morning air. The lash of the whip was coiled and thrown around and over the bull-whacker's head, then shot straight out and brought back with a quick jerk. The result was a cracking sound like that of a revolver shot.

When Addie mentioned this to Huntley, he told her that each lash was from fifteen to thirty feet of braided rawhide and on the end was fastened a buckskin popper.

"A good bull-whacker don't hardly ever strike an ox. Could nip the hide like a knife if'n he had a mind to. Sound of the pop is 'nuff to keep 'em humpin'."

There was plenty of room on the seat for Trisha, but she chose to sit on the overjet behind the seat, where she and Jane Ann had slept. Dillon had crawled out of his bed when the wagon began to move. He and Jane Ann had dressed and were watching, wide-eyed, out the back of the wagon.

When the trail curved, Addie could see across a field where the extra stock were being herded behind the train. She felt sad about leaving Mr. Jefferson and Dolly. John had told her they had found a place for them in one of the freight wagons, and when they reached town one of the men would take them to Lupe.

"This be a mighty fine wagon, ma'am," Huntley said. "Jist like sittin' in a rockin' chair."

"I don't know much about wagons. Mr. Tallman thought we were lucky to get it."

"An' ya were. Nice high back. Spring seat."

"Have you made the trip before?"

"Second trip. Ain't goin' to go on no more, that's certain."

"Why is that?"

"Don't like a city or city folks. Too many of 'em. Purty country around here, but ain't no place purtier than home."

John was leading the train in a wide loop around Van Buren when Buffer Simmons came up through the trees to ride alongside him.

"Gawdamighty! I'd not've known you if not for that turned-up brim. Your damn face is as bare as baby's butt."

"Ya didn't know I was purty, did ya?" Buffer rubbed his fingers over his smooth cheeks. His thick brown hair had been

380

trimmed, and he wore a new shirt beneath his cowhide vest.

"You're about as pretty as the north end of a southbound mule." Buffer was younger than John had thought him to be. "What are you doing here? Why aren't you down there getting the judge ready to head out?"

"I quit. I guess I ort to tell you why — 'cause I want to sign on here and work my way across."

"Because of Trisha?"

"Why'd ya say that?" Buffer's face lost its friendly smile.

"Hell, I'm not blind. When you're near her, you moon around like a dying calf."

"If ya don't like it, now's the time to say so." Buffer's tone was sharp.

"Pull in your horns. It isn't up to me to like it or not." John's reply was equally curt. "Say your piece."

"I didn't quit Van Winkle because of Trisha. I could still see her if the trains ran together. Truth is, that stupid son-of-a-bitchin' judge wants to go on ahead. I could tell right off he didn't hire me to hunt, he hired me to scout. Christ on a horse! It'd be like throwin' a babe to a pack a wolves."

"You told him that?"

"Damn right. I told him he'd be easy pickin's, and I told him what'd happen to that woman if he was overrun. Old fart didn't turn a hair. Called me a yellow coward and told me to get out. I'd-a cleaned his clock then and thar, if he'd not been so damn old."

"A remark like that can get a man killed in the country where he's going."

"He's a mouthy old bastard. I was quittin' even 'fore he told me he wanted to strike out alone. He come right out an' said the soldiers was runnin' thin's. I was to report to 'em. Hell, Tallman, ya should'a seen 'em. They're dumb enough to kick fresh turds on a hot day."

"What's he gonna do?"

"Hell. Yore guess is good as mine. I never saw such a outfit. Wait'll ya see it, an' tell me if it ain't the dangedest sight ya ever did see."

"How long have you been out of the Nations?"

"Couple months. Wintered down on Wolfe Creek in Oklahoma Territory. Texas is fillin' up fast with homesteaders. The Indian Nations and the territory is fillin' up with outlaws lookin' for easy pickin's. They do their meanness and blame it on the Indians.

"I come over to Boggy Depot, then up the Shawnee Trail. Cattle outfit I was with took the east trail to North Fork. By then I'd had my fill of chasin' wild steers and come on into Fort Smith. Feller I knew there told me the judge wanted a hunter. They said the pay was good. I got me a little poke, but could always use more."

"I'll not match Van Winkle's pay."

"Ain't askin' ya to. No pay is 'nuff fer me to kowtow to them army bastards. If I'd-a wanted to a-done that I'd-a signed on to their war."

"We needed two more men. Go tell Cleve we've hired one of them."

In a grassy meadow, a half-mile beyond the Van Winkle camp, John formed his wagons in a semicircle. The teams were unhitched and the oxen unyoked. The equipment was placed in the center, preparatory to hitching and yoking up in the middle of the afternoon. After the stock was driven to water, they were herded to a place where they could graze. Each man tended the animals assigned to his wagon. Not until Huntley led away the team of gray mules did Addie allow the children to leave the wagon.

Bill Wassall and Paco immediately began to cook the first meal of the day. A large sheet of cast iron was placed over the fire and slabs of meat began to sizzle. Paco stirred while Bill mixed the ingredients for flapjacks in a large vat. Addie could smell the meat frying while she was still trying to start a cookfire.

John and Dal Rolly came walking down the line inspecting the wagons and the loads. Dillon ran toward John, shouting: "Mr. Tallman, Trisha says —"

"Dillon!" Addie hurried to head him off before he could reach John. "He's busy now."

"I'm not that busy. I'll be down to the supply wagon shortly, Dal. Come here, tadpole, what's this important news you have to tell me?"

"Trisha said you're my papa. I ain't never had a papa before. Muvver said I had one, but he didn't come back from the war. Them damn Yankees shot 'im."

"Dillon, for heaven's sake! He picks up everything he hears."

"That's how he learns." John lifted the boy to sit him on his arm. "Trisha's right. When I married your mother, it made me your papa. Is that all right with you?"

"Yeah! You ever had a boy?"

"No, but I've got one now. As a matter of fact, I've got two boys — you and Colin."

Jane Ann tugged on his hand. "Have ya got a little girl?"

John looked down into the child's face, her eyes full of yearning. He stooped and raised her to sit on his other arm.

"I have now. Her name is Jane Ann."

Jane Ann put her arms around John's neck and her lips to his ear. "Can I call you Papa, too? Colin said not to ask."

"I'd be proud if you called me Papa — all of you."

"Trisha, too?" Dillon asked.

"If she wants to." John set the children on their feet.

"I'll tell Trisha. She went to the bushes," Jane Ann shouted over her shoulder and ran toward the bushes that lined the clearing.

"Well, that's settled." John went to stand beside Addie. He was still astounded by the force of his desire to be with her, to touch her. Life had taken on a new meaning for him since he had met her.

She turned to look up at him. Tears shone in her violet eyes. "You're a wonderful man."

John smiled, his mustache lining his wide, firm mouth.

"I think so too." His words had the effect he'd intended.

"Oh, you!" Addie laughed and poked him in the ribs with her forefinger.

"Bill thinks you're out of sorts with him, and that's the reason you don't go up to the cook wagon."

"I'm not out of sorts with Mr. Wassall. I'm —"

A piercing scream cut off her words. Another scream followed. John and Addie ran to the side of the wagon as Jane Ann came running from the bushes, screeching at the top of her voice.

"Tri . . . Tri . . . sha! Pa . . . pa! Tri— !"

John reached the child yards ahead of Addie and grabbed her shoulders.

"What about Trisha?"

"Back — back . . . there —"

"Go to the wagon, honey. *Now!*"

John plunged into the bushes. By the time Addie reached him he was in a small clearing, kneeling beside the unconscious girl. He lifted her and quickly unwrapped the thin, tight strip of leather from around her neck. Her face had started to darken; blood flowed from a gash above her temple, and her arms, legs, and face showed marks from a whip.

"Oh, dear God! Dear God! Dear God!" Addie couldn't take her eyes off Trisha's face.

John threw the whip aside, straddled Trisha, and began to lift her arms up over her head in an attempt to pump air into her lungs.

"Please, please, God . . ." Addie wasn't even aware of what she was saying. She dropped to her knees and pulled Trisha's dress down over her legs, which were crisscrossed with bloody whip marks.

"Who would do this? Who would do such a thing?" Addie murmured over and over.

"She's breathing! She's breathing! Thank God." John ran his fingers lightly over Trisha's throat. "We got here just in time." He lifted her hair to look at the gash on her head. "It's bleeding a lot, but head wounds usually do. She was whipped as she lay on her side after being struck on the head. The son-of-a-bitchin' bastard!" he mumbled through clenched jaws.

"Trisha would have fought him like a wild-cat. He must have sneaked up on her."

Buffer Simmons came charging through the brush like an enraged bull. Cleve was a few steps behind him.

"What the hell? Jane Ann said —" Buffer dropped down beside the girl on the ground. "Who did this? *Who the hell did this?*"

"We don't know. We've got to get her back to the wagon so Addie can take care of her." He turned to Cleve. "Does the whole camp know about this?"

"Simmons and I come to find ya. The little girl told us you were here. I don't think anyone else knows."

Buffer gently lifted Trisha in his arms. Addie hadn't recognized him until she saw his cowhide vest. She led the way back to the wagon. John picked up the whip. He and

387

Cleve carefully scanned the ground for tracks, then followed.

"I'll need hot water," Addie said, after Buffer had eased Trisha down on the overjet.

"Will she be all right, ma'am?"

"The cuts from the whip will heal, but I don't know how serious this cut on her head is . . . or if the lash around her neck did damage to her throat."

"A lash around her neck?"

"John got it off so she could breathe. He said we got there just in time. We can thank God that Jane Ann went looking for her."

Buffer picked up Trisha's hand and held it in both of his.

"I'll kill the man who did this to you," he whispered to her, then quickly left the wagon.

John pulled the two young children out from under the wagon. Jane Ann was sobbing. She wrapped her arms around his leg. Dillon was crying because she was.

"Jane Ann, honey. Did you see the man?"

"I . . . was callin' Trisha — and listenin' for her to say somethin'. But she was falled down dead."

"She isn't dead. Did you see anyone?"

"Just Trisha. She looked dead!"

"She isn't. She's going to be all right. Don't cry. You did just right. You came for help.

That's my girl." John lifted the hem of Jane Ann's dress and wiped her eyes. "Buffer is starting a fire. You and Dillon see if you can help."

Buffer set the children to gathering sticks for the fire but cautioned them to stay close.

"Look at this whip, Cleve. It's not a bull whip."

"Overseer on a plantation uses a whip like this. It didn't come from this camp. I know every man jack that's signed on except Simmons. None of 'em ever used a whip like this."

"Buffer's so moony-eyed over the girl, he can't see straight."

"He was with me. That leaves someone from the Van Winkle train or from town."

"Pass the word quietly to the men. Tell them what happened and ask them to keep their eyes open. It's clear the son of a bitch was watching the wagon and waiting for a chance to get one of the women. He got his opportunity when Trisha went to the bushes."

"Get the women a slop jar." Cleve met John's surprised look. "I know 'bout women-folk. I had one once."

"I know ya did," John said gently, remembering Cleve's slain family. "Somehow I'm thinking it was Trisha the man was waiting for."

"Why?"

"There's things about the girl you don't know, Cleve, things beyond her control. She's a good girl. Addie has vouched for that."

Cleve shrugged. "Simmons told me you took him on."

"Where do you want to use him?"

"Me and him can take turns scoutin' and ridin' tail. That'll keep you close to the train."

"I was thinking something like that myself. I doubt if any of us know the territory like he does. He should know what to expect and where it's coming from."

"Tallman!" Buffer called loudly. "Yo're bein' honored by a visit from them brayin' jackasses what calls themselves fightin' men."

John turned to see the Union soldiers approaching; backs stiff, elbows in, boots shining, saddles gleaming. Their belt buckles were polished and their hats set at the regulation military angle. The Thoroughbred horses they rode looked as if they had just been washed down and curried. Their long flowing tails were free of even a dried blade of grass.

The bull-whackers had stopped working to gawk at the spectacle. Well aware of the attention they were creating, the two soldiers held a tight rein to force their mounts' heads up, causing them to prance and sidestep.

"Gawdamighty," John said. "Look at that. Betcha two bits I can see my face in their boots."

"Ain't they a sight?" Cleve chuckled, something he seldom did. "They jist got done with one a them military schools for boys and is showin' off."

John stepped away from the wagon. He stood with his legs spread wide, his arms folded across his chest, his hat pulled down low on his forehead. The soldiers pulled their mounts to a halt.

"Are you the man in charge here?" one asked crisply.

"I am."

The soldier alighted from his horse and handed the reins to his companion. As he approached John, he removed his wide-cuffed gloves, placed the palms together, and secured them under his arm. He stood at attention before John, his body ramrod straight, his head back.

"Lieutenant Bradford Shipley with a message from Judge Ronald Van Winkle."

"Spit it out." John looked the man in the eye and wondered how in the hell the North had won the war.

"Judge Van Winkle sent his request in writing."

The lieutenant drew a sheet of folded paper from his pocket and handed it to John. John scanned it and handed it back.

"Tell the judge that I'll be here until three this afternoon."

"The message states that the judge requests a meeting at his camp site at thirty minutes past one this afternoon." Shipley spoke as if he was sure that John had been unable to read the message.

"I guess you didn't hear me, mister. I said I'd be here until three this afternoon. At that time we'll be pulling out. Tell the judge that if he wants to be a part of this train, he is to have every member of his party here at exactly thirty minutes past one. As wagon boss, I'll be making a few things clear, such as laying down the rules and establishing the punishment for those who break them."

As John spoke, the lieutenant's eyes began to blink, his lips to twitch, and his face to redden. By the time John had finished, the young man was so enraged he could barely unclench his jaws to speak. He opened his mouth to make an angry retort, but looking into the dark blue eyes beneath the brim of that leather hat was like looking into the double barrel of a shotgun. The lieutenant's face was tight with fury, but some vague intuition cautioned him to speak calmly.

"I don't believe you understand the situation, Mr. Tallman. At this time Judge Van Winkle is the highest-ranking government official in this area. He is a very important man, an appointee of the United States Department of Indian Affairs."

"Let me assure you, I understand the situation perfectly. The judge may be an important man *somewhere,* but not in this camp. I'm the one who's important here. I run this train. These men work for me. I don't take orders here; I give them. Is that understood?"

"That's your final word?" Shipley was trying to keep his composure. Behind him, his supposedly perfectly mannered horse had become frightened and was dancing at the end of the reins. The confusion was not helping matters.

"It's my only word."

"Very well." The lieutenant jerked his gloves out from under his arm and put them on. "I'll take your message back to the judge."

"You do that." John held up his hand as the soldier began to back away. "Watch your step, Yank, unless you want to get those shiny boots all nastied up. There's a pile of horse shit behind you."

# CHAPTER

## * 22 *

Addie had bathed Trisha's wounds and covered them with a salve that Buffer had given her. It was made from the aloe plant and had been a gift to him from a Mexican woman trained in the arts of healing. He swore that it helped to speed the healing of open wounds. Addie was grateful for the salve.

John climbed up into the wagon as Addie was placing another wet cloth on Trisha's head.

"How is she?"

"Still unconscious. I cut her hair around the wound. It doesn't seem very deep."

"He hit her with something blunt, like the stock of a rifle. He could have killed her with that blow. I'm wondering if she saw it coming and rolled her head. She's lucky, too, that all that thick hair helped to cushion it."

"Who would do this?"

"Not any of our men, Addie. The lash

wrapped around her neck wasn't a bull whip. Cleve said it's the kind an overseer on a plantation would use on field hands."

"Do you think he was trying to *kill* her?"

"Yes, I do. I think that he had twisted the lash around her neck and was going to drag her deeper into the brush when he heard Jane Ann calling. He ran out of time and probably slipped into the brush just as Jane Ann got there."

"Why didn't he just shoot her if he wanted her dead?"

"A shot would have drawn attention."

"Maybe it was me he was waiting for."

"I think he was one of the Renshaws. They want Trisha, not you."

"They wouldn't still be following, would they?"

"We'll know for sure after we cross into the Indian Nations. Honey, Colin is hanging around outside. He's worried sick about Trisha. Can he come in for a minute?"

"Of course. He can empty the wash pan and get some fresh water. Where are Dillon and Jane Ann? I forgot all about fixing a meal."

"Cleve took them up to Bill. He'll see that they're fed."

"Oh, no! The men have their own work. I don't want the children underfoot." Addie started to get to her feet, but John pressed her back down on the chair.

"They're not underfoot. Cleve knows about children. He had some of his own once. Bill isn't as grumpy as he appears. Old codger probably has a whole passel of younguns scattered around the country that he doesn't know anything about."

"What a thing to say." Addie couldn't help but smile.

"Dillon and Jane Ann are all right. If they get troublesome, Bill or Cleve will sit them down." He paused for a moment.

"When Trisha wakes up, she's going to have a hell of a headache. Try to keep her head still. Pack something on each side of it. It'll be pure hell for her when we start moving, but laudanum will help. I've brought some from the medical box. Give her two drops at a time in a little water. It'll dull the pain and let her sleep."

"I wish she'd wake up."

"She will. You're doing all you can for now. The wet cloth on her head will help keep the swelling down."

"She was so excited to be going to a new land — where folks wouldn't know her. It's unfair, John. She's pretty and sweet, and because she's admitted to having Negro blood, people treat her like dirt."

"Have you told the children and Colin not to mention that to anyone?"

"I told them. But Buffer Simmons knows."

"He'll not say anything."

"She's so proud," Addie said, smoothing the hair back from Trisha's face. "She's always saying, 'I is what I is.'"

"We've got to admire her for that. Honey, I'm going to grab a bite to eat. I'll tell Colin he can come in."

"Has he had anything to eat?"

John squeezed her shoulder. "Ever the worried little mother. Yes, he ate with Gregorio and the other men. After he's seen Trisha, send him up to the cook wagon. Bill will fix a plate for you."

"Do you think whoever did this will come back?"

"If he does, he's in for a big surprise. From now on we'll keep a close watch."

Trisha woke slowly. Her eyelids fluttered, then opened completely and she looked wildly about.

"Don't be scared." Addie bent over her so she could see her face and held tightly to her hand. "You're here in the wagon with me. Lie still."

"Addie . . . Oh, my head —" Trisha's voice was hoarse, and she reached for Addie with her free hand.

"It worried me that you didn't wake up. Can you drink some water?"

"Oh, yes," Trisha licked her puffy lips as if unaware of how the whip lash had injured them.

Addie slipped her arm under the pillow, tilted Trisha's head, and held a cup to her lips. She had already added the two drops of laudanum to the water. Trisha held the water in her mouth for a while before swallowing slowly. Her eyes clung to Addie as she sank back against the pillow.

"Trisha, honey, who did this to you?"

"Don't know if it was real. Saw a dream. My head pop—" Her voice cracked, and she lifted her hand to her throat.

"Jane Ann went looking for you. She saw you lying on the ground and came for us. Buffer carried you back here to the wagon."

Trisha opened her eyes. "Old . . . brush-face?"

Addie smiled. This was the old Trisha.

"Yes, old brush-face. Now sleep. I'm going to put pillows on each side of your head so you won't move it. Sleep now, honey. I'll be right here."

"Don't go . . . Miss Addie . . . please . . ."

"I won't go. Someone will be with you all the time."

A short while later, Buffer came to the end of the wagon.

"Miss Addie, has she waked up yet?"

"Come on in." The wagon rocked gently from Buffer's weight. "She woke up. I gave her the two drops of laudanum and she went back to sleep."

"Will she be all right?"

"John thinks so. Her throat is sore. It's hard for her to talk or swallow." Addie dipped the cloth in the basin of water and squeezed out the excess before placing it on Trisha's head.

"Did she say . . . anythin'?"

"That what she saw wasn't real. It was a dream. Then her head 'popped,' she said. But she may not have been fully awake."

"Ma'am, can I sit with her a bit? I'll keep the cloth on her head."

"I don't know. She asked me not to leave her. Trisha seldom asks anyone for anything."

"If yo're thinkin' it ain't proper, I'll open up the whole back of the wagon."

Addie looked up at him and smiled. "That's kind of silly, isn't it?"

"Yes, ma'am."

"I think Trisha would feel safe with you here. I'll take you up on your offer."

"John's gettin' ready to call his meetin'. You might want to be there."

Addie looked down at the sleeping girl, then back at Buffer.

"Thank you," she said with genuine warmth.

Addie stepped down into the sunshine and looked for her son and Jane Ann. Catching a glimpse of Jane Ann's blue dress, she walked quickly toward the cook wagon and found the two of them sitting on a box in front of a table where the cook was dressing wild turkey. Each of the children had a turkey foot.

"Looky, Muvver." A huge smile covered Dillon's freckled face. "Looky what Mr. Wassall gived me." He held up a yellow foot, pulled on the white tendon, and watched in fascination as the toes curled.

"Mine does it too," Jane Ann chirped happily.

"That's very . . . interesting. Come along with me now. You've bothered Mr. Wassall enough."

" 'Twarnt no bother a'tall," Bill said, and slammed the meat cleaver down through the turkey's breast.

"Thank you for feeding and looking after them."

"How's the girl, ma'am?"

"She's hurting, but she'll be all right."

Bill Wassall shook his head. "It's beyond

me how and who," he said cautiously, looking down at the children. He carried the turkey halves to an iron roasting pan, dumped them in, and covered the pan with an iron lid. After washing his hands in a basin, he took out his pocket watch and flipped open the lid. "All right, Dillon, it's time." He reached into the wagon and brought out a large cowbell. "I told Dillon he could call the men to the meetin'."

"Me too?" Jane Ann asked.

"Yup, you too, missy."

Addie now looked at the pudgy little man in a different light. The bitterness she had felt toward him since the day they arrived had vanished. She stood back and watched a grinning Dillon vigorously swing the bell. It was heavy and soon his arms tired. Bill took the bell and handed it to Jane Ann. She was able to swing it only a few times before Bill took it and the loud clanging went on.

The men, coming from their various duties, began to gather. Walking with the children back to the wagon, Addie was stopped by a shout from Colin.

"Miss Addie! Looky what's comin'."

Addie turned in the direction of Colin's pointed finger. The sight that greeted her was far grander than the parade that was staged in Freepoint when the war ended.

Leading the procession on handsome horses were a man in a dark suit and a woman mounted sidesaddle. Her riding clothes were hunter green, as was the plumed hat perched on her high-piled blond hair. Behind the pair were six Union soldiers riding two by two. A short distance behind the soldiers was another small group of horsemen. They rode into the clearing, moved back to the tree line, stopped, and sat their horses while they held a discussion, then dismounted.

The herders and bull-whackers gawked at the newcomers as they moved forward to stand in a group apart. It was so quiet that you could hear the cry of a whippoorwill and, from a distance, the sad call of a mourning dove.

John moved out from the cook wagon and held up his hand. When he had the attention of the gathering, he began to speak.

"It is customary that at the beginning of each trip I speak of the routine we'll follow and the rules we'll stick to until we reach our destination. All but a few of you have made this trip with me before, and you know that I do not permit drinking on the trail or in camp. One drunk man could cause half a dozen of you to be killed. If I catch a man drunk or drinking, he'll be forked on a horse and cast out regardless of where we are.

"We will travel eight or ten miles a day until the oxen become seasoned; after that I hope to make twelve to fifteen. The night herders will ride in and wake the camp at three o'clock in the morning. They then sleep while the rest of us yoke up and roll out within thirty to forty-five minutes. At ten o'clock we make camp and have the first meal of the day. At that time the animals will be watered and staked out to eat. Repairs, if needed, will be made during the midday stop.

"In the middle of the afternoon we yoke up again and travel until after sundown. The wagons will be circled every night to form an improvised fort in case we are attacked, or a corral to hold the stock during a storm. A favorite time for an attack is in the morning when we're yoking up. During the confusion and distraction, hostile Indians or renegades hope to catch us unprepared. In the evening when the train is going into camp is another moment of opportunity for them. We will be especially watchful during those times.

"It will take the combined efforts of all of us to get this train safely across the territories. We have the best wagons made — Espenshieds, built in Saint Louis, and the best head bull-whacker in the business, Dal Rolly. Cleve Stark, assistant wagon boss, has made this trip more times than I have. He knows what he's about. Listen to what he tells you. If we reach our destination without the loss of a man or a wagon, a bonus awaits you.

"I will be available at any time to hear your suggestions or your grievances. One more thing. We have provided you with the best cook between the Mississippi and the Rocky Mountains. From time to time you'll see game along the trail. We kill nothing we don't eat. Bill will pass the word when he needs fresh meat."

When John finished speaking he wondered if he should have mentioned the Van Winkle party. If they were joining the train, the men were entitled to know. While he was mulling over the thought, the men began to break up into small groups and move back to lounge beside the wagons they were assigned to. John spotted Addie and the children and moved toward them. He was intercepted by the judge.

"Word with you, Tallman."

"Go ahead."

"Private word, if you please."

John moved into the shade of one of the freighters. The judge followed.

"Have you decided what you're going to do?" John asked bluntly.

"I have no choice but to go with you."

"You can wait here for another train to come along. There should be one or two more this season."

"I cannot afford to wait. I'll be late for my appointment as it is."

"Then go to Fort Smith and hire a guide."

"I thought I had one."

"Buffer Simmons? You lost him when you let those dressed-up jackass soldiers insult him. He wouldn't have taken you across anyway without my train. He knows the dangers."

"Did I understand you to say you start the day at three in the morning?"

"You did. Each one of my wagons weighs three tons. I don't work my oxen in the heat of the day."

"You're not making it easy for us, are you?"

"Why should I give you any slack, Judge? You sure as hell wouldn't give me any." John lifted his hand and motioned to Addie as she was passing. "Come here, honey." Addie came to him. He took her arm and proudly drew her to his side. "This is my wife, Mrs. Tallman. Honey, Judge Van Winkle."

"How do you do, sir?" Addie extended her hand.

"Ma'am." The judge removed his hat during the introduction, then took Addie's hand.

Although his manners were faultless, Addie

405

had the impression that the judge's interest lay elsewhere.

"Excuse me." She looked up at John. "Dillon slipped away from me, and I don't want him to get near those excitable horses."

"Go find him, then. I'll see you in a little while."

Addie moved away. When she did, she saw her son heading for the Union soldiers as fast as his short legs could carry him. She hurried after him and reached him just as he stopped in front of the officer standing beside the woman.

"Are you a damn Yankee?" he asked, looking up at the man. His little-boy voice carried to a group of bull-whackers who hooted with laughter.

"Dillon! You shouldn't say such things." Addie grabbed his hand, looking up as she did, an apology forming on her lips. All thought but one died within her when she looked into the man's face. Standing before her was Kirby, her husband — her *dead* husband. His eyes were the same, his face the same except for the mustache and goatee. The blond wavy hair was longer. His shoulders were broader. He was older. But it was Kirby, and he was looking at her as if she were a complete stranger.

"Don't worry about the boy, ma'am. I've

been called worse than a damn Yankee since I've been in the South."

The voice, with its slight northern twang, was Kirby's. Addie stared at him. He looked her straight in the eye without one flicker of recognition.

"You've got a fine boy," he said at last.

"Yes, I have." Addie turned, pulling Dillon with her, and headed back across the clearing, focusing her dimmed, agonizing sight on her wagon, a place where she could hide.

Behind her, the woman laughed softly, looking up at the captain with a teasing light in her eyes.

"You dazzled that poor woman, Kyle. She couldn't take her eyes off you. Should I be jealous?"

"I want you to be jealous of every woman who looks at me," he said softly and squeezed her fingers. "Then I'll know you truly love me."

"Pooh, darlin'. You know *that* already."

The two were so engrossed in each other that they didn't see the judge approach until he spoke.

"Kyle, are we ready to pull out?"

"You're going with him?"

"For now, anyway. I'm hoping that later we can peel off and go up to Fort Gibson. By Gawd, when I get to Sante Fe, I'll use my influence to get even with the bastard. He's going to find out who is important and who is not."

Addie sat beside Trisha as the train rolled west alongside the Arkansas River. The quivering inside her had not subsided. Now she felt a new wild rage. *How dare Kirby Hyde be alive.* Every instinct within her told her that the Yankee officer was Kirby Hyde, the man she had married, the father of her son. But questions nagged at her logical mind. Kirby had joined the Confederate Army. He had come home from town and told her he had enlisted. How could he suddenly appear as a Yankee captain?

The war between Addie's intuition and her rational thinking went on and on. She tried desperately to remember if anyone else had gone to join the army at the same time as Kirby. She had been so unhappy, and so scared of being alone with a baby coming, that months had gone by and she hadn't spoken to anyone other than the neighbors who dropped by. Reason told her that the Yankee captain just *looked* like Kirby. She had heard that everyone had a double somewhere. Maybe Kirby had a twin brother she didn't know about.

In the short time they had been together,

Kirby had said that he had no relatives. Then one time during a rambling conversation he had mentioned an uncle at Jonesboro. When she had asked him about the uncle, Kirby had said they didn't get along very well. It was to Jonesboro that she had sent the letter telling Kirby he had a son.

Oh, God! If the officer *was* Kirby, how could he look at Dillon, his own flesh and blood, and reject him so completely? She remembered how sullen Kirby had become after she told him she had missed her monthly flow and could be with child. She had been so happy and had wanted to share the good news. She realized now, as she had then, that Kirby would not have been a good father. He had been selfish, deceitful; and although he had worked hard at first in order to gain her affection and assure himself a place at the farm, he had later become uninterested and lazy.

What could she do? she pondered. If the Yankee captain was Kirby Hyde, that meant she was not married to John. Should she tell John now, or wait until she had some proof? *Proof!* How could she prove this Yankee was Kirby Hyde? It would be his word against hers. He would make her look ridiculous not only in John's eyes but in the eyes of everyone on the wagon train.

★ ★ ★

At dusk the wagons formed a circle for the night. Huntley had explained that camp sites were usually chosen earlier in the day by the scout or the wagon boss. They were late reaching this one because of the extra time it had taken to ford a tributary of the Arkansas River. The freight wagons circled, he said, not because they feared an attack in this area but because the wagon boss wanted the stock to get used to the maneuver.

Trisha had slept throughout the day. Had she awakened, Addie would have given her another drop of the laudanum. Addie silently thanked Bill for the turkey feet that had kept Dillon and Jane Ann amused during the early part of the afternoon. The latter part they had spent on the wagon seat beside Huntley.

Now that the wagon had stopped, Addie was almost afraid to leave it for fear that she would come face to face with the man she believed to be Kirby Hyde. But when she did step down, she realized that the Van Winkle party had camped a short distance away and that she was unlikely to encounter the captain. She also realized that Gregorio, with a rifle in his hand, had taken up a position with a view of the back of their wagon.

During the day, Addie and the children had used the slop jar that the thoughtful

410

Dutchman had provided for his family. It needed to be emptied before nightfall. Dillon and Jane Ann had scampered away with Colin, who had promised to keep an eye on them, leaving Addie free for the moment. Taking the jar from the wagon, she hurried toward the foliage that lined the small stream.

"Miss Addie! Wait!" Buffer Simmons's call was urgent. Addie turned to see him coming toward her on horseback. "Don't go into the bushes until I take a look," he said sternly, then rode into the thick copse of gooseberry bushes, myrtle grass, and willows.

Addie set the chamber pot on the ground and tried to hide it with her skirt. Embarrassment had reddened her face and quickened her heartbeat. It seemed forever before Buffer reappeared.

"Don't go in more'n ten feet, ma'am. I'll wait here."

"Thank you, Mr. Simmons." Too embarrassed to look at him, Addie hurried past.

When she returned, Buffer, leading his horse, walked with her back to the wagon.

"John put a watch on the wagon."

"I see he has."

"Miss Trisha wake up again?"

"No, but when she does, I'd like for her to eat something."

411

"Do you reckon she can tell us what she saw?"

"I don't know. It wasn't Ellis Renshaw, that's sure."

"It must've been one a his kin. I'm tryin' to figure which one a them muddle-headed ninnies is smart enough to slither 'round here and not be seen by nobody. Nobody on this train's seen a stranger 'bout."

"Trisha said that what she saw just before her head popped was a dream. I don't know what she meant by that."

When they reached the wagon, Buffer took a bundle from behind his saddle while Addie was putting the slop jar back in the wagon. She was terribly conscious of the guard watching her.

"When Miss Trisha wakes up give her this." Buffer held out the belt and scabbard he had bought in Van Buren. "It's for that pig-sticker she carries."

Addie took it from him and stared up into his sincere brown eyes. He looked so much younger without the beard, and his face was pleasant, if not handsome. He was a man of massive strength, yet so gentle.

"You . . . know that Trisha has admitted —"

"I heard all that in Freepoint. It don't mean nothin'. What's bloodline, anyhow? Is Renshaw blood better'n Trisha's?"

"You . . . care for her?"

"Yes, ma'am."

"You'd marry her?"

"If'n she'd have me, I'd be proud."

"She's proud. Proud as a peacock."

"Yes, ma'am. She's got more pride than sense." Dimples appeared in Buffer's cheeks when he smiled. Addie placed her hand on his arm.

"I wish you luck with your courting."

"Thanky, ma'am."

# CHAPTER

## * 23 *

Addie thanked God for Colin and Bill. Colin
had taken Dillon and Jane Ann to the chuck
wagon, where Bill had fed them even as he
was preparing the evening meal for the men.
When they returned, Colin was carrying
plates of food for her and Trisha.

Trisha awakened with such pain in her head
that she was sick to her stomach and unable
to eat. Addie held her head over the slop
jar while she emptied what little she had in
her stomach. When she stopped vomiting,
Addie gave her more laudanum in a sip of
water and she went back to sleep.

A lantern hanging on the end of the wagon
cast a dim light inside where Addie washed
the two younger children and put them to
bed. She did not admit even to herself that
she was exhausted in both mind and body.
The first day of this eventful trip had taken
a toll on her strength in ways she had not
imagined.

414

When Addie stepped down out of the wagon, she knew that somewhere out there in the darkness Buffer and Colin were watching. The big man had been visibly shaken by the attack on Trisha. When he had spoken of it to Addie, he had said that he thought the Renshaws had given up after they were dumped in the creek. His being wrong had put Trisha in danger, and he felt responsible.

Word of the attack had spread among the bull-whackers. They were angry and embarrassed that a woman in their camp had been subjected to such treatment. If the attacker was found, John said, he was not sure he could prevent the bastard from being hanged on the spot.

Leaning against the wagon, out of the circle of light, Addie gazed across the expanse of darkness at the well-lighted Van Winkle camp. Buffer had told her that the woman had a colored maid, and the judge had a colored man who performed personal services for him. These people were from a world that Addie knew nothing about — a world of servants, fine clothes, and beautiful homes. Was that the world Kirby had come from? If so, why had he been walking down a road in the Arkansas hills looking for work?

What troubled Addie most was how she was going to tell John that she suspected her first husband was not buried in that grave near Jonesboro and that her marriage to him was not legal in the eyes of God or man. It was morally wrong for her to be with him in that intimate way that had been so heavenly when she may still be married to another man.

Mr. Cash had said that the man who brought the news of Kirby's death was a Confederate officer. He would have had to be a terribly cruel man to bring news to a widow that her soldier husband was dead unless he was sure of the fact.

It occurred to Addie that she should be glad Kirby had not been killed — for his sake. On the heels of that thought came another: How could a man look down into the face of his son and deny him? The only resemblance between father and son that she could see was that they both had blond hair. It was not unusual for a child only four years old still to have blond hair, though it might darken later.

Addie's thoughts were interrupted by the sound of John's voice.

"Simmons?"

"Yeah?"

"Go on to bed. I'll be here for the rest of the night unless something comes up."

"We should'a hung ever' blame one a them

gawddamn Renshaws when we had the chance."

"We didn't have a reason before. We do now."

"I'm hopin' he makes another move."

"He may have hightailed it when he saw what he was up against."

"Colin is gonna bed down with me under that wagon ahead. My new partner's got a good set a ears. He can hear a owl pissin' on a . . ." Buffer's voice faded.

Addie was coming out of the wagon where she had gone to see about Trisha when John called her name.

"Addie? How's Trisha?"

"Still sleeping."

"Come here, sweetheart. I've not seen much of you today." With his hands at her waist, he lifted her down, then turned the wick of the lantern to put out the light. "I don't want everyone in camp to see me kissing my wife."

Addie's arms went around him. She pressed her face against his shirt, savoring the familiar, smoky, male smell of him. He held her tightly; she could feel his strong heartbeat. They were content to hold each other quietly for a long while.

As the events of the day came rushing at her, her arms tightened about him. She held him as if she couldn't get close enough. Earlier tonight, she had felt like she'd been caught in a whirlwind, swept away like a leaf from a tree. Here in John's arms she felt safe, protected. He was all that was certain and secure.

His lips nuzzled her ear.

She held on to him with all her strength. "I can't let you go! I can't let you go!" she whispered against his throat.

"What did you say, sweetheart? When you tell me sweet things, I want to hear them." He laughed softly, his lips in her hair.

"I'm glad you're here. I know you've got a big responsibility and I'm . . . grateful for the time I can be with you." Her voice grew weaker and weaker and then ceased altogether.

"It'll be this way for the next seven or eight weeks. Some nights we may not even have these few hours alone. I've got a very important reason right here in my arms to get this train safely home."

"I was . . . proud of you today."

"I was proud of you too, Mrs. Tallman. Kiss your husband. He's been looking forward to it all day."

He lowered his mouth to her upturned lips and kissed her with a hunger that left her mindless. Her body quivered; her resolve to hold herself apart from him receded and dissolved into submission to his deep, starved, unrelenting kiss.

"Come to bed with me, love. I want to hold you, and . . . love you —"

"I . . . should stay with Trisha."

"Later. I need you now."

"I'll always love you." Desperation was in her voice, indecision in her heart. Inside her a voice whispered, *He wants you. He needs you. Take what you can, you'll have sweet memories.* To her surprise and dismay, a tear rolled unheeded down her cheek. Another quietly followed.

"Trisha . . . might wake up." She made one more attempt to do what was right.

"We'll hear her."

She allowed John to pull her down onto the bed beneath the wagon that she had laid out for him alone. Mindlessly she removed her dress and chemise while he took off his shirt and britches. It wasn't until they lay down and he wrapped her in his arms that he felt the tears on her cheeks. He went still.

"Addie, sweet. Why are you crying?" he asked helplessly. "Are you regretting —"

"Never! Never that! It's just that so much has happened today."

"I thought maybe you were sorry you jumped into marriage with me." Relief lowered his voice to the mere breath of a whisper.

"I'm going to love you so completely that you'll forget about what happened today. You're going to forget everything but me."

Soon Addie's senses were singing with uninhibited desire. She moved her mouth from his to kiss his jaws, under his ear, his chin. Her lips moved over his face almost frantically before seeking his again, kissing him with prolonged hunger, tasting his mouth, loving the feel of his mustache, his strong, rough hands stroking up to her smooth shoulders and then down her bare arms to her hips, returning to her breasts, stroking, kneading.

Impelled strongly by remembered frenzies of delight, her hand slid down between them to find him, hold him, feel him expand in an arousal equal to her own.

Poised in a kind of wonder, John reveled in the feeling of her soft breasts against his chest, her small, strong fingers caressing him. This wondrous, loving, giving wife of his excited him, confounded him, thrilled him. He treasured her shuddering, leaping response to his caresses. He raised himself above her, entered her quivering softness, and made her forget everything but him.

Four days out of Van Buren they made night camp in a long valley beside a small tributary that flowed into the Arkansas River.

Addie had become reconciled to the fact that she could not cook meals over a campfire for her family that halfway equalled the ones Bill Wassall cooked for the men. For the past two days she and Colin had gone to the chuck wagon at noon and again at night and tried to make themselves useful to Sweet William Wassall, the chubby little man who was swiftly becoming a dear friend. At the noon camp she peeled potatoes for soup and made biscuits for bread pudding to serve at the evening meal. Sweet William, as she now teasingly called him, openly enjoyed their company. Colin's help freed the grateful Paco for other chores.

Trisha recovered more quickly in body than in spirit. The second morning after her attack she was up, but she refused to see Buffer or leave the wagon even though the mark on her lip and cheek had receded to a dull red. When she became aware that she had been whipped while she lay unconscious, she felt an overwhelming shame and wouldn't even allow Addie to treat or see the welts on her arms and legs. When asked about the attack, she refused to talk about what she had thought was a dream just before she was hit on the head.

It was dark when Trisha stepped down out of the wagon, the rifle in her hand. Colin had brought her a plate of food, which she had eaten without enjoyment because her throat was still sore when she swallowed. She couldn't shake the fear that traveled down her back when she thought of the lash that had sliced through the air to cut her flesh, or of the man who had wielded it.

She settled down on the grass with a wagon wheel at her back and had been there several minutes when Buffer Simmons came out of the darkness. She had known he was there, had located him before she left the wagon, and was comforted by his presence.

"Miss Trisha. It's me, Buffer."

"I know it's you. Don't know nobody else who'd come flyin' outta the dark like a turpentined cat."

"How're ya feelin'?"

"Strong enough to spit in a bobcat's eye."

"That's a pile a — !"

"If ya knowed so much, why'd ya ask?"

"I'm saying ya ain't up to snuff yet."

"Ya don't know nothin' 'bout me."

"I know yo're balky as a mule."

"— And ya ain't got no faults a'tall."

"Yore a sour-mouth, is what ya are," Buffer said impatiently. "Times yo're like a bobcat with bristles on its belly."

"If I'm a sour-mouth, balky bobcat with

bristles on my belly, why're ya here? Jist get yoreself gone. I ain't askin' ya to stay."

"I'm stayin', if'n ya like it or not."

"Why'd ya shave? I woke up oncet and saw a bare-ass naked face a-lookin' at me. I was gonna poke it with my knife till I saw that silly vest ya always wear."

"Why didn't ya let on ya'd waked up?"

" 'Cause I wanted to see if ya was sorry as I thought ya was."

"Yo're sneaky too."

"— And good at it."

"Was ya sleepin' when I kissed ya?"

"Ya what?" Trisha jerked her head around so fast that she gasped from the pain.

"Don't get all het up now," he said with a chuckle. "I was funnin' ya."

"Ya got a poor way of funnin'."

"Did Miss Addie give ya the scabbard?"

"Yeah."

"Why ain't ya wearin' it?"

" 'Cause it'd go 'round me 'bout three times."

"Hell. I can cut it down and punch in a few more holes."

"How'd I know that?" She turned her golden eyes on him. "Guess I can't call ya brush-face no more. Why'd ya shave for?" she asked again.

" 'Cause I wanted ya to see my weak chin!"

A snorting sound came from her, then: "Fiddle-faddle."

" 'Sides, I shave every spring. Jist hadn't got 'round to it."

"Guess that's the only time ya take a bath, too."

"No. I take one at Christmas if I get to stinkin' real bad." He heard a whisper of a giggle, which gave him the courage to say: "Get the belt and scabbard. I want ya to wear that knife where ya can get at it."

Without a word she went to the back of the wagon and climbed inside. Buffer followed and waited, his back to the wagon, his eyes searching the darkness.

She had no trouble locating the treasured gift in the dark and was back almost immediately, slapping it against his chest as if it were of no consequence to her.

"Here. I ain't doin' ya no favors for it."

"Dad-blame it! I don't recall askin' for any favors. Put it 'round yore waist where it'll ride comfortable so I'll know where to cut it off." She fumbled to put the belt around her waist while still holding the rifle. "And put down the gun! Ya'll shoot yoreself or me."

"I ain't got but two hands," she snapped.

Buffer leaned his gun against the wagon and yanked the belt from her hands. Kneeling in front of her, he swung it about her slender waist.

"Where do ya want it?" he asked crossly.

She moved the belt down to ride just below her waist.

"Right there . . . bung-head!"

"I need a light," he grumbled.

"Ya ain't gettin' one here and that's that."

"I already seen that mark on yore face, if that's what's got yore tail over the line. Ya think ya ain't pretty no more an' ya don't want me to see ya."

Trisha stood as still as a stone. It took Buffer a full minute to realize that she'd not had a sharp comeback. He looked up and saw that she had turned her face away. She had not taken his words as lightly as he'd meant them. Her silence became a cold and alien thing that clamped around him, making him feel like he had just kicked a puppy or stepped on a baby chick. He stood for a minute or two and then began talking, hardly knowing what he was saying.

"I'll mark this an' fix it tomorrow. Rolly's got a leather punch. I'll get a loan of it an' put in more holes. Did I tell ya that I'm dickerin' with a feller for a throwin' knife like mine? It's a mite smaller is all, and lighter. Just right for ya. That pig-sticker ya carry would be handy for close in, but ain't much good for throwing. It ain't heavy enough. I'm thinkin' ya'll take to knife-throwin'. By the time we get to Santa Fe, ya'll be pinnin' a fly to the wall."

She didn't move or speak. Buffer couldn't tell if she was annoyed. It wasn't like him to rattle on, and it wasn't like her not to have a comeback. He shuffled his feet and took a quick glance around the camp site. Still she didn't speak or move. The silence went on for so long that Buffer began to feel desperate.

"Trisha, ya mean more to me than anythin' in the world," he blurted. "I'd cut off my right hand 'fore I'd say or do anythin' to hurt ya."

He waited in the long quiet that followed his outburst. He waited with his heart in his throat for her to laugh or make a witty retort. He heard a small sound. When it came the second time, he realized it was a sniffle. Hesitantly, he put his finger to her cheek. It was wet.

"Gawdamighty, Trish. I'm jist a dumbhead. I ain't used to talkin' to women. I didn't mean nothin' by saying ya wasn't purty. You're the purtiest thin' I ever did see."

"It ain't that. I wish I was ugly as a . . . mule's ass."

"What is it then? What's got ya so all tore

up? I'll make it right, if I can."

Up out of the depth of her came an agonizing sob. Then came words that stunned the man beside her.

"I'm . . . so . . . scared!"

"Ah . . . don't be! Don't be!" Buffer opened his arms and she flung herself against his chest. He held her tightly, protectively, while small, miserable, choking sounds came from her.

"Darlin', sweet girl. My darlin' sweet girl . . . " he crooned. "Ain't nothin' ever gonna hurt ya."

"He'll be . . . back. He don't give up."

"Nobody's gonna hurt ya. Nobody." Buffer's arms held her close, his hand stroking her dark hair.

"I was thinkin' he'd not find me. It's been so long —"

"Can ya tell me which'n it was? I'll cut the bastard's heart out."

"I knowed it was him when I saw the marks. It wasn't no dream."

Over Trisha's head Buffer saw John, Addie, and the children coming toward them. He picked up his rifle and kept one arm about Trisha to urge her along the side of the wagon to the front of it.

"John and Addie comin' back," he whispered in her ear. "Stay with me. Please stay a while." Buffer took her silence for consent and called out to John: "Trisha's with me. We're goin' to walk a bit."

"I hear you. Behave yourself."

Buffer waited, afraid that Trisha would bolt. But she stayed within the circle of his arm and walked beside him to the next wagon in line.

"Will ya let me sit ya up on the seat?"

"I ain't crippled. I can climb up." She put her foot on a wheel spoke and pulled herself up onto the seat.

"I know ya ain't. I was lookin' fer a chance to lift ya."

"What fer?" Trisha asked, and moved over to make room for him to sit beside her.

"Hell! I don't know." He placed the rifle in easy reach and propped his moccasined foot on the footboard.

"Mr. Tallman wears shoes like that." Trisha bent over and wiped her eyes on the hem of her skirt. "Where'd ya get 'em?"

"From a Indian."

"Ain't ya 'fraid of 'em?"

"Some of 'em. There's the good 'uns and the bad 'uns, jist like white folk. If we run into some Choctaws, I'll get ya a pair."

"Don't do me no —"

"— Favors? I ain't. Will ya do me one?"

"What?"

"Tell me 'bout what yo're scared of. It ain't no Renshaw, is it?" Buffer wanted to move closer to her, put his arm around her, but he didn't dare. "Tell me 'bout where ya come from. Who yore folks are."

"Why'd I do that? Ya ain't told me where ya come from. Who yore folks are."

"I will. I'll tell ya even the parts I'm 'shamed of. Some of my kin is so dad-blamed low-down they'd not have to take off their hats to walk under a snake."

Even in the dark, Buffer could see the distinct outline of her profile. She was so still. There was something in the tension-charged atmosphere when he was with this woman that compelled him to irritate her and act the fool. It was purely crazy, he thought. She threw his mind for a loop. He wanted to reach out and slide his fingers along her cheeks and into her hair. *Trisha, Trisha, sweet girl . . .*

# CHAPTER

## * 24 *

"My granny was a quadroon, my mama a octoroon. My own daddy was white, but I don't know what I is." The words came out in a rush.

"I know what ya are. Yore a spunky slip of a girl what's had a heap of trouble."

She turned her great golden eyes on him, then looked up at the heavens and began speaking slower.

"Me and Mama had a pretty little house in Orleans. We even had a darkie to do for us. Mama had been brought up ladylike and Daddy doted on her. When he come, he brought us presents and said we was his special ladies. Mama played the spinet. Daddy'd set me on his lap and we'd sing. He was proud of her. Sometimes he walked her out to show her off 'cause she was the prettiest thin' in Orleans when she was dressed up."

Trisha's eyes were fastened on the cloudless, star-lit sky as she remembered.

"Daddy said he wedded that woman to get a heir 'cause niggers can't own land. It hurt Mama, but she knowed how it was. He come ta see us more'n ever after that. Then Mama died."

"How old were ya then?"

"Ten years. Daddy give her a big buryin', then took me to Satinwood Plantation, but not to the big house. Old Amelia, Daddy's wife, wouldn't have me around. I stayed with Mammy Orkie in the quarters and worked in the kitchen. Miz Amelia hated me. She hated all of Daddy's younguns cause Daddy treated us good and got a teacher to teach us to read. I called her the witch woman.

"Amelia's Hector was a sickly, ugly-lookin' pup. I hope he died!" She turned her golden eyes to Buffer. "He was meaner'n a dog with a belly full a cockleburs. He didn't have none a Daddy in 'im far as I could see."

Buffer wanted to ask questions, but he didn't dare for fear that she would stop talking.

"Daddy went off to the war and I ain't knowin' where his boys went. The witch woman might'a let the devil man have 'em. Them two was thicker'n thieves. Old devil man did her nasty work. She ran to 'im when one a Daddy's boys looked crossways at Hector. He'd give 'im a whuppin' and put 'im on bread and water. The boys was older'n me. I hope they run off where that devil man couldn't find 'em. He worked 'em hard, whipped 'em, and . . . starved 'em." She shuddered. "He liked it when a nigger run."

"Is that what you did?"

"I didn't get no chance to. Mammy Orkie was gettin' me ready ta run, when that witch woman sold me to a riverboat man who had him a whorehouse."

"Gawddamn!"

"I didn't do no whorin'," she said quickly. "I rode with 'im on the boat a ways 'cause I had to. First chance I got, I cut that sucker with my knife and jumped in the river." Trisha's voice sank to a whisper. "River was dark and cold. Old darkie pulled me out. I stayed with 'im till I heared that riverboat man was lookin' for me. I was scared he'd hurt that old darkie.

"Some folk didn't know I was a nigger an' let me work for 'em, cookin' or washin'. Oncet I fixed hair for whores while they was comin' upriver to Little Rock. When we got there, they didn't want me hangin' 'round, so I left. Comin' up over them hills, I got good at stealin' somethin' to eat. Had to, or lay down and die. I warn't goin' to do that. Ended up in Miss Addie's barn. Bestest thin' I ever did."

"Is it that devil man yo're scared of?" Buffer asked quietly. "Are ya thinkin' he found ya?"

She turned to him and for a long moment stared into his face, making no attempt to mask her naked fear. In some way she had changed since she'd started telling her story. She didn't move any part of her body, but her brilliant eyes held the look of resignation of an animal caught in a trap.

"Before I was popped on the head, I saw a flicker of somethin'. I knowed it wasn't no dream when I saw where he'd whupped me. Miss Addie showed me the lash. 'Twas his. He makes 'em hisself."

"If he's got any sense a'tall he's gone by now. There's men here who'll tear him apart if they catch him. Course, they'll have ta get in ahead a me."

"He ain't goin' till he knows I'm dead. He ain't found no buryin' hole, so he ain't gone."

Her quiet mood puzzled and then irritated Buffer.

"Ya givin' up?" he asked.

She brushed her hand over her eyes, as if forcing them to stay open. She looked straight at him. Her lips moved. It required great effort for Buffer to hear her.

"Ya ain't knowin' him."

"I know me, Buffer Simmons. And I know that bastard ain't touchin' a hair on yore head!" Angered, he reached for her and, without giving her a chance to hold herself away from him, drew her close and wrapped his arms around her. "He ain't touchin' a hair on yore head!" He felt the quaking in her slender body and pressed his cheek tightly to the top of her head. "Now . . . now . . . don't shake so, and tell me what this devil man looks like."

She didn't answer him at once, but Buffer was encouraged by the small hand that crept under his cowhide vest and burrowed beneath his arm. A minute later he felt the stiffness go out of her body and heard her take a deep breath.

"Black-haired. Beard 'round his mouth. His eyes is mean. Mammy Orkie said he could have nigger blood, is why he hated darkies so. His brag was that no nigger ever got away from Satinwood and lived." Her voice was shallow and toneless.

"Will yore daddy look fer ya when he comes home from the war?"

"He ain't comin'. He was soldierin' at a place called Gettystown, or somethin' like that. They all got shot all to pieces. Poor Daddy. I reckon he didn't care much."

Rough fingers lifted her chin, gently but

insistently. She felt his warm breath on her cheeks.

"Look at me, Trisha."

She tried to hide her tear-wet face against his shoulder.

"Don't be 'shamed a cryin'. Ya've had plenty to cry about. Ya got more guts than any woman I ever did see. Most women would'a caved in a-fore now." Buffer held her close and stroked her hair. "I'll be lookin' out for ya from now on. Ya ain't to worry 'bout that old devil man or nobody else."

"Ya ain't . . . meanin' that?"

"I am meanin' that. That devil man makes a move and I'll kill him quicker than ya can blink them purty eyes of yores."

"I mean ya . . . ya can't mean from now on!"

"I shore do! If ya'll have me, we'll find us a preacher —"

"We . . . can't!"

"Sure we can, if yore willin'." He tilted her head back against his arm and looked her in the face. "Folks might not think I'm much 'cause I've roamed a lot. I ain't got no book learnin' to speak of, but I'll take care a ya if ya'll let me. I got a little poke salted away. Maybe it'd be enough to start us up a place out in the New Mexico where you'd be near Miss Addie."

She stopped his words with her fingers against his lips. She felt his heart beating strongly and heard the anxiety in his voice.

"I'm proud. Purely proud ya asked me. But we can't."

Heavy lashes lifted from tormented eyes only inches from his, and the look she saw in them was not the one of lust she had come to expect from men. It was a look of such yearning that it broke her heart to have to deny him. If at this moment Buffer had asked her, she would have given him ten years of her life, but she couldn't give him what he was asking.

"Ya don't like me . . . enough?" he whispered hoarsely.

She lowered her face to his shirt, and her voice, when it came, reflected her misery.

"We can't." She rolled her head from side to side in an agony of denial. "I'm a — I'm . . . a —"

"Don't say that!" He grabbed her upper arms and held her away from him. "I ain't carin' if ya was black as the ace of spades! Hear me?" He shook her and glared into her face. "Yo're white as me, as Miss Addie. Yore blood's red, like mine. Why do ya keep sayin' that?"

" 'Cause it's what I . . . is!"

"It don't matter. I swear it don't."

He pulled her into his arms and kissed her hard on the lips. Then the anger seemed to go out of him. He gathered her close and kissed her again, but now his kisses were soft and gentle. He lovingly caressed her mouth with his.

Trisha had never known the *gentle* touch of a man's lips. Strength flowed into the hopeless void she had carried within her for most of her life and filled the hollows her despair had dug. Hope blossomed in her heart and began to grow. He lowered his head and kissed her again, this time reverently, as though she were something fragile and precious. She was consumed with love for this big bear of a man who had accepted her for what she was.

Then sudden fear for him swept over her. She saw him ringed by the darkies who had been summoned to watch the flogging. He was stripped to the waist and hanging from a limb by his bound hands. The devil man with a smile on his evil face uncoiled his whip and drew it back. *No! No!* her mind screamed repeatedly. She wrapped her arms around him and held him with feverish desperation, wanting to shield and protect him.

Not knowing what was in her mind, Buffer hugged her and crooned to her.

"We gonna have us a good life, little bird,"

he said softly, his lips in her hair. "And lots of purty little younguns." He chuckled happily. "We gonna make us a home on a mountain top . . ."

Buffer talked on and on. In the shelter of his arms, wrapped in the velvet darkness of the prairie night, Trisha began to believe that what he was saying could really come true.

At the other camp, Judge Van Winkle paced alongside the parked wagons. He was restless and impatient, finding fault with everyone from his man, Saul, to the cook, the driver, and the herders. So far his wrath had not come down upon the head of the patrol.

The trip so far had not been the adventure he or his niece had anticipated. It was hot, dirty, uncomfortable, and at times downright miserable. All of this could have been endured if not for the humiliation of being forced to take orders from an inferior. Today he had ordered his party to drop back a half-mile. The dust was still stifling and the pace so slow it seemed they had gone no distance at all when the signal was given to make camp.

Cindy's voice, shrill with anger, broke the silence.

"You miserable girl!" Cindy snatched the hairbrush from her maid and pulled the blond

438

strands of hair from the bristles. After twisting them around her fingers, she poked them into the hole of a china bowl. "I've got enough hair in that hair-saver to make a full wig. You've pulled out a handful every day since the beginning of this hellish trip."

"I's sorry, Miss Cindy. It . . . it so tangled up." The maid sniffed and tears formed in her eyes.

"Don't bawl, Ivy," Cindy demanded. "Dammit, I've enough to put up with without having to listen to your sniveling every time I correct you. Just look at my face! The wind and dust is ruining my skin. Oh . . . why didn't I have sense enough to stay home? If I were home I could be having a bath, drinking iced lemonade, and going to parties."

The judge stood beside the caravan and listened to Cindy railing at her maid because of the dust on the coverlet of her bed and swearing because she couldn't remove the cork from the bottle of olive oil she put on her sun-dried face.

"I swear, Ivy. I don't know what you're good for. I should have brought Bethel with me. At least she didn't bawl all day every day."

"I's sorry, Miss Cindy."

"If you say that again, I'll slap you! I know

439

how sorry you are. You're a *sorry* maid, is what you are. Now get out of here before I take this hairbrush to you."

Ivy came out the back door of the caravan, her hand over her mouth to silence her sobs. She disappeared in the darkness to cry and to wait for Cindy's temper to cool.

With his head bent, the judge walked down the line of wagons to where Captain Forsythe sat with the men of his patrol.

"Word with you, Forsythe."

"Yes, sir." The captain got up and followed the judge back toward the caravan.

"I do not intend to eat the dust from that freight train another day. A man of my position should have some consideration from that uncivilized lout."

The captain waited for the judge to say more, not knowing if an answer was required.

"Well?" the judge snapped. "Do you not agree?"

"Absolutely. There are two things we can do, sir. Fall farther back or go on ahead."

"We can't afford to fall back and waste time. Did either one of the new men you hired have scouting experience?"

"To find a scout, we'll have to go to Fort Gibson. I hired night herders and extra guns in case of attack. Both men are crack shots."

"I'm glad to hear that. How many more

days until we reach the trail to Fort Gibson?"

"Three or four at the rate we're going. I heard that from one of the bull-whackers. I strongly urge you to turn north to Fort Gibson, Judge. Even if it means we will be a few days late reaching Albuquerque."

"I've been thinking that myself. That man Rolly is nosing around our wagons telling the drivers to grease this, grease that. They resent it. I feel trouble brewing between our men and that crew of miserable bull-whackers. Meanwhile, we'll not be reduced to the status of beggars and *allowed* to follow this train and eat their dust. Tomorrow our wagons will go to the front of the line or I'll do everything in my power to ruin that bastard when I get to Sante Fe."

"It might be better," the captain said hesitantly, "if we just hung back rather than rile Tallman. A few more days and the trail will split. We'll have some relief from the dust tomorrow. The wind switched around to the south late this afternoon. It should hold for a day or two."

"Hell and damnation, Kyle. What's the wind blowing from the south got to do with anything? Cindy is having the screaming trembles. At this rate she'll be a wreck by the time we get to Fort Gibson and will be nagging to go back home."

"Do you think that's a bad idea? I could escort her."

"Of course it's a bad idea. I'll not hear of it. I'm Cindy's guardian. She goes where I go."

Kyle Forsythe didn't dare say the words that sprang to his mind: *Cindy's fortune goes where you go!* The greedy old bastard didn't dare let her go back home. He'd lose control of thousands of Yankee dollars.

"I'll talk to her," Kyle said, bringing his thoughts back to the present. "Maybe I can persuade her to ride in the caravan during the day."

"I tried that. She won't leave the windows open in the caravan because of the dust, and she won't stay inside because of the heat." The judge turned and looked toward the freight camp. The only light was the small campfire in front of the cook wagon. "He keeps a tight camp even here where the Indians are supposedly friendly."

"Our camp is well secured. The only light is Miss Cindy's. The guards take three-hour shifts so that every man gets his rest and is alert on watch. Judge, we can go on ahead and find that cutoff to Fort Gibson. I'd rather not have a confrontation with that high-handed savage if there's a way around it. He could cause us a lot of trouble if he had a mind to."

"Such as?"

"He has more than twice the men we have, for one thing. And, for another, I heard plenty about him at the livery in Van Buren. His father was Rain Tallman. Have you heard of him?"

"Some. What'd you hear?" he asked impatiently.

"Rain Tallman was raised Indian. By the time his sons, John and Mac, were knee-high, they spoke Shawnee. Tallman sent his boys out to live with the Shawnee for months at a time. They learned the Indian ways. The Tallmans can hunt, track, use a bow and a knife as good as an Indian. John is known as Spotted Elk, named for Rain's Indian father. Mac is known as Stone Hand. I suspect both of them are as mean and as sneaky as the Indians who trained them."

The judge turned slowly to stare at the captain. "You scared of him, Kyle?"

"Hell! What gave you that idea?"

"It's plain that you don't want to go up against him."

"I don't want any unnecessary trouble. I'm suggesting that if we can't go on ahead, we should make the best of it until we can split off from them."

"Once you start caving in to these people

443

out here, you lose your authority."

"If I learned one thing during the war, Judge, it's when to stand and when to retreat."

"You learned that handing out supplies at quartermaster headquarters in Illinois?" A sneer colored the judge's voice.

"I was trained for combat before I went to headquarters," the captain said with restrained anger.

"Kyle, I'm well aware that you may have had some basic trainin', but you've had very little, if any, combat experience. It's of no consequence to me. You're the one Cindy wants, and I've accepted that. You handle your patrol, and I'll handle the politics necessary to get us to our destination."

Kyle Forsythe was grateful that the darkness concealed his livid face and the fists he clenched in anger. The potbellied old fool had never spoken to him in that contemptuous tone before. He had to exercise considerable self-restraint to keep from pointing out to the judge that he put up with his arrogance and stupidity only because of Cindy and what she could bring to their marriage.

*Damn him to hell!*

Kyle stayed where he was when the judge left him to walk down the line to his wagon. He was on shaky ground here and he knew it. He had planned so carefully, and now something he'd had to do to survive had come back to plague him.

Kyle stared at the freighter-camp clearing visible in the moonlight. He had been in tight spots before — plenty of them — and brazened his way out. There was no reason why he couldn't do it again. It all boiled down to her word against his. All he had to do was deny everything.

With that resolve in mind, he headed for his tent without, as was his habit, stopping by the caravan to say good night to his fiancée.

# CHAPTER

## * 25 *

This was the fifth day on the trail. The sun sent heat waves shimmering down on the train as it moved sluggishly across the prairie of sparse grass and baked earth. When John signaled the lead wagon to turn in for the midday rest, the cry "Swing in!" was echoed down the line. The bull-whackers guided their oxen into a wide curve and stopped them when the wagon boss signaled. By the time the last wagon was in place, the oxen pulling the first wagons had been unyoked and were being led to water.

Addie and Colin went to help Bill prepare the first meal of the day, while Trisha stayed to tidy the wagon and watch the two younger children. She wore the new riding skirt Addie had bought her and a shirt tucked neatly into the waistband. Her hair was pulled back and secured with a ribbon at the nape of her neck. Addie refrained from commenting on her appearance for fear that Trisha would be embarrassed and go back to her old ragged skirt and loose shirt.

Trisha was unusually quiet, which led Addie to believe that something had happened last night between her and Buffer Simmons. This morning she stayed out of sight inside the wagon when he came by to pass the time of day.

"Dillon, I got to wash yore face and hands."

"Ah . . . Trisha —"

"Yore mama said ya can't go eat if ya ain't washed and your hair ain't combed."

Trisha was washing Dillon's face when Buffer rode up and dismounted. On the point of going to her, he saw her eyes drop and her hands still for a second. A mighty upsurge of confidence filled him, and he looked at her with a slow smile. He understood that it wasn't easy for her suddenly to let down her defenses and be easy with him. He stood waiting for her to look at him.

"Hello, Mr. Buffer." Jane Ann came out of the wagon. "You gonna go eat with us?"

"Howdy, Miss Janie. Yore lookin' chipper."

"What's that? You mean I'm a bird?"

"Yup." He glanced at Trisha and saw her smile. "A purty little wren."

"Hear that, Trisha. Mr. Buffer said I was pretty like a bird."

447

"For once, I think he's right." Trisha looked at Buffer, her eyes mirroring her pleasure. "Maybe he'll teach you to whistle like one."

"I'm not much of a whistler." Buffer slapped the belt he had cut down for Trisha lightly against his thigh.

"You gonna whup somebody?" Jane Ann asked anxiously. She shied away from him.

"Naw. This is for Trisha."

"Are ya gonna whup Trisha?" Jane Ann put her arms around Trisha's waist.

"Christ on a horse," Buffer muttered.

"He ain't meanin' that, honey." Trisha hugged the little girl. "He fixed it so I can wear it an' have my knife handy ta get a splinter outa yore finger, or cut ya some flowers."

Buffer knelt down and swung the belt around Trisha's waist. He fitted the strap into the buckle, then settled the belt to ride above her hip bones and the scabbard against her thigh.

"Where's that pig-sticker of yore's?"

She stepped into the wagon and returned with it fitting snugly into the scabbard.

"That'll do till I get ya a good throwin' knife."

Buffer's hand caressed her shoulder and arm. It was something he had to do. He had to touch her this morning to make sure that what had passed beween them last night was real and not a dream. She didn't flinch away, and his heart soared.

"Where's Dillon?"

"There he is!" Jane Ann shouted, pointing toward where the stock was grazing. "He's way over there."

"Lord have mercy!" Trisha exclaimed. "That little devil is faster than scat! Stay here, Jane Ann —"

"I'll get him." Buffer mounted his horse. "Keep the younguns close to the wagons, Trisha. This is a good place for prairie rattlers."

A minute later, Trisha and Jane Ann watched as Buffer leaned from the saddle and swept the boy up to sit in front of him on the horse. He held Dillon to him with an arm clamped about his waist.

"Ya ever seen a rattler, boy?"

"A snake? Colin killed one with the hoe."

"The rattlers here on the prairie are big enough to swaller ya up whole. There's dens of 'em. Ya stay near the wagons, hear? Snakes scatter away from the oxen 'cause they don't want ta get stepped on. If ya run off again, I'll tell yore pa and he'll tan yore hide."

Back at the wagon he set Dillon on his feet. The boy ran to Trisha and wrapped his arms around her thighs.

Buffer sat his horse and looked at her. His heart swelled with love and pride. It was a miracle that now she looked upon him with favor. He'd been alone since he had been Colin's age. He'd had no one to look out for but himself. No one had really cared for him, or depended on him, until now.

*Trisha, Trisha. I'll spend my life keeping you safe.*

"Stay in the open, sweet girl," he said softly. "I'll be watchin'." He rode away still looking at her over his shoulder.

Trisha combed Jane Ann's hair and waited for the sound of the bell to call them to the cook wagon. It had been an ordeal for her to go among the men, but this morning her heart fluttered only when she thought of Buffer Simmons and what he had said to her last night.

"Howdy, missy. Howdy there, young scutters. Grab ya a plate and get ya some flapjacks," Bill called cheerfully as they approached.

He was pouring batter from a pitcher onto a flat iron griddle set up on legs over the fire. At another campfire, Colin turned slabs of meat with a long fork. Addie dipped coffee from a large round pot with a long-handled ladle.

This was the time Bill liked best. He ragged the men who came with their plates, calling them hogs and accusing them of having hollow legs. They grinned, knowing that if it were not for the ladies present, Sweet William's language would not be so sweet.

Each man washed his own plate, cup, and spoon with a mop in a large pot filled with warm sudsy water, then rinsed them by holding them in hot water with a pair of pliers. Afterward they were set on a table where Addie dried them and stored them away for the next meal.

The men had become used to her and Colin being there. They teased Colin and passed a few shy words with Addie. Today a few of them paused and spoke a few words with Trisha, then hurried away.

"Glad to see ya doin' all right, miss."

"We find who hurt ya and he'll get ripped, that's certain."

"Ah . . . señorita. Sad we are for what happen."

"We catch the *perro*, we keel him!" The Spanish word, meaning "dog," was hissed through the young Mexican's tight lips.

Trisha glanced at each man, murmured her thanks, and looked down at her plate.

Addie was anxious at first, fearing that Trisha would bolt when the first man approached, then was relieved and proud. When the last man left the cook area, the girl's golden eyes sought Addie's. She smiled.

They both knew that Trisha had passed a test . . . of sorts.

It was high noon. John, with Dal Rolly, was making the round of the wagons to check the loads and the wheels, looking for signs of possible breakdowns.

"I'm just now knowin' why Simmons signed on. He's sweet on that gal." Rolly cut a slice from a plug of tobacco and poked it in his cheek.

"You'd have to be blind not to see it. Simmons is a good man. I'm glad we've got him with us."

"Damn good at readin' sign, so Cleve says. He oughta know, 'cause he ain't no slouch hisself."

"Got any ideas how a man could've got in that copse and waylaid the girl without being seen by someone?"

"The only thin' I know is that it wasn't one a ours. It's gotta be somebody who rode out from town. Tell ya one thin', the men would'a strung him up and skinned him if we'd caught him." Dal spat in the grass. "It's a downright insult to 'em to let it happen."

"Cleve backtracked and saw no sign. Simmons has been nosing around too."

"Shitfire! Here comes the judge and that damned stiff-necked Yankee captain."

"They'll be complaining about something."

"Ain't they the damnedest know-it-all bunch ya ever did see? They've not tarred a wheel since they left Van Buren. When I told 'em that sand was gettin' in the hubs, they didn't bat a eye. Just sat right there on their arses like I didn't know what I was talkin' 'bout."

"I hope we'll be rid of them in a few days."

"I'll pray on it," Rolly murmured, turned his back and poked at a rim on a wheel as the riders approached.

"Word with you, Mr. Tallman."

"Step down, Van Winkle."

The captain dismounted also, even though he had not been invited. Van Winkle removed his hat and wiped his forehead with a pristine white handkerchief.

"Hot day."

"It'll get hotter . . . and drier."

"I understand you'll be crossing the Arkansas in a few days to follow the Canadian River west. Captain Forsythe and I are considering going ahead of you tomorrow and on to the fort."

"Tomorrow?" John lifted his brows.

"We've seen nothing since leaving Van

Buren to indicate there are hostiles about."

"Did you expect to?"

"We've seen none of the roving bands of savages and outlaws you said were in this area. If they are here, they've left no sign."

"They've left signs. Yesterday we passed within a mile of a freshly abandoned camp. Not an Indian camp. Indians clean their camp sites before they leave."

"It could have been an army camp — a patrol out of Fort Gibson."

John laughed. "Not likely."

"Who, then?"

"Renegades. Mexican outlaws. Confederate bands that refuse to admit the war is over."

"How many days to the fort from the fork of the rivers?"

"Two. Maybe three. The closer you get to the fort, the less likely you are to be set upon."

During this exchange the captain had remained silent, as if he were not interested in the conversation. John directed his next remarks to him.

"You'd be smart to advise the judge to hang with us until we reach the cutoff, then follow the Arkansas and run hell for leather for the fort. That outfit of his is like a hunk of bread being dangled before a starving man. You can bet it's been spotted. News travels fast, even out here."

"We're not afraid of being overrun by a rag-tail bunch of misfits."

John shrugged.

Dal Rolly spat a stream of yellow tobacco juice into the grass and shaking his head in disgust, walked away.

With his foot on the tongue of the wagon, John leaned his forearm on his thigh and wished the judge and his captain would mount up and leave. Addie and the children were coming from the cook wagon and he wanted some time with them.

Dillon broke loose from Addie's hand and ran to him. John scooped him up to sit on his arm. Dillon put his face close to John's.

"Papa! Mr. Buffer said you'd tan my hide —" Suddenly aware of the strangers, the boy became bashful and hid his face against John's shoulder.

The smile died on Addie's lips when she and Jane Ann rounded the wagon and she saw the judge and the captain standing in the shade of the freight wagon. She felt as if she were going to suffocate. Her eyes went to the captain's face. She saw it clearly in her mind without the mustache and goatee. *It was Kirby's face. The mole on his chin was covered by the goatee.* Dear God! It was *him.* The man looked at her and away, then turned to fiddle with a strap on his horse's bridle.

John saw the look of shock on his wife's pale face, saw her lips tremble, saw her suck air into her open mouth. Instinctively he knew that she had known Captain Forsythe in the past or thought she had. Forsythe's face, however, gave no indication that he'd ever seen her before.

"Captain Forsythe, have you met my wife and son?" With Dillon still on his arm, John reached out with the other and drew Addie close to him. "And my daughter, Jane Ann?" he added as the child leaned against his knees.

"Yes, I met Mrs. Tallman and the boy the first day out. It's nice to see you again, ma'am." Kyle Forsythe looked Addie in the face and spoke quietly, politely. There was not the slightest tremor in his voice. But Addie knew it was Kirby's voice, even though the northern accent was more pronounced.

Without uttering a word, Addie lifted Dillon from John's arm and set him on his feet. Taking his and Jane Ann's hands, she went around the long, high vehicle and hurried down the line to where Colin and Trisha were sitting in the shade of their wagon.

"I'm confident the captain's patrol, backed by my men, can see to our safety," Van Winkle said, taking up the conversation as if it hadn't been interrupted.

"Get to the point, Judge. Is that all you wanted to tell me?" John said impatiently. His mind was on the stricken look that had come over his wife's face when she had seen the captain.

"We'll go with you to the fork, then follow the Arkansas River to the fort."

"Suit yourself."

"But —"

"Yes?" John had turned away, but he turned back.

"I insist that our wagons be brought up from behind. We're being stifled by your dust."

"You insist?" John straightened to his full height and folded his arms over his chest. "You have no right to insist that I do anything."

"You've had the same two wagons at the head of the line since we left Van Buren."

"I'm not obligated to tell you this, but I will," John said, holding a tight rein on his rising anger. "The first wagon in my line sets the pace." He spoke in harsh, clipped tones. "It is driven by a man who has been over this trail six times. The second wagon carries *my* family. I will remind you once again that you are free to take off on your own any blessed time you choose."

"It isn't fair to put us to the rear. My

niece is very distressed —"

"What in hell do you want me to do about your distressed niece?"

"I want our wagons brought to the front of the line. We've been at the back for almost a week. We should be at the front for the next few days."

"No! I will not break up my train to accommodate you."

The judge's face turned a dull red, and his jowls quivered.

"Don't you talk to me like that . . . you bas—"

"Watch yourself, Judge. You call me that name and I'll flatten you like a pancake, I don't care how damned old you are."

"I'm the highest government official in the territory and I demand respect."

"Demand? Hell!" John's temper made his voice oddly soft. "I don't care if you're Christ on a horse," he said, borrowing Buffer's favorite expression. "A man doesn't demand respect. He *earns* it."

"You're being unreasonable and dictatorial because you have the men to back you up. It's no more than I should have expected from your kind."

"Call it what you want. Dust is always a problem on a train. If you didn't know that when you started, you do now. You can move off to the side, you can go ahead, or you can lag farther behind. It makes no difference to me. I'll not have your wagons mixed in with mine. That's all I have to say about it."

The judge was so angry he looked like a puffed-up bullfrog.

"You'll regret these insults."

"They're not insults. They're common sense. Your dray animals and mules do not set the same pace as my oxen. Plain and simple — they won't mix."

The judge turned to his horse. "This isn't the last you'll hear of this. I have influence and I'll use it when I get to Santa Fe."

"At the moment, I have doubts you'll ever get there," John commented dryly.

At that instant Addie stepped around the end of the wagon and faced the captain. Determination was etched in every line of her face. She had watched and waited for the right moment to call out to him.

*"Kirby! Kirby Hyde!"*

The captain put his foot in the stirrup and mounted.

"I know it's you, Kirby!"

"Are you speaking to me, ma'am?" the captain asked calmly.

"You know damn good and well I am. You're Kirby Hyde."

"I'm Kyle Forsythe, Mrs. Tallman. You've confused me with someone else."

"What's this? What's this?" the judge sputtered.

"The lady has mistaken me for someone else." The captain put his fingers to his hat brim. "Good day, ma'am."

Judge Van Winkle frowned down at Addie before putting his heels to his horse.

Addie stared after them, her fists clenched, her eyes too dry for tears. She was more convinced than ever that Captain Kyle Forsythe of the Union Army was Kirby Hyde, who had ridden away from her farm to join the Confederate Army.

"Addie . . . honey —" John was beside her, his arm around her. "What's this about?"

"Oh, John! I'm sorry! I'm . . . so sorry!"

"About what?"

"Everything. I've made such a mess —"

"Nothing we can't handle. What's this about Kirby Hyde?"

Addie's mouth opened and closed, then opened again. Before she could utter the hateful words, the sound of a shrill whistle commanded John's total attention. Waving his hat, Cleve rode toward them on his big gray horse. He pulled the animal to an abrupt stop beside John.

"A party of thirty or forty headed this way.

They're a mile, maybe a little more, behind that rise." John's eyes followed Cleve's pointed finger.

"Indian or white?"

"Indian."

"What tribe?"

"Couldn't tell. They were too far away."

John turned to Addie and kissed her hard.

"Honey, get the children and stay in the wagon out of sight." He issued the order crisply, jumped over the wagon tongue, and ran for his horse.

Cleve put his fingers to his lips and whistled a long blast followed by two short ones. A few seconds later, he repeated the signal. Men rolled out from beneath the wagons where they had been resting. Bull-whackers shouted, and their long whips began driving the stock into the semicircle made by the wagons. After sending a man to advise Van Winkle to gather his stock and set up a defense should one become necessary, Cleve rode the outer circle giving orders to string chains between the wagons to tighten the corral.

Both camps were suddenly alive with activity.

Astride his horse, John paused beside the wagon where Colin stood with Trisha's rifle in his hand. The children were inside and

Addie was handing up the water bucket to Trisha.

"Just because they're out there doesn't mean they'll ride on us. They could be friendly. Addie, you and Trisha and the children stay out of sight. If you hear gunshots, lie down on the floor of the wagon."

"John, be careful, and don't worry about us."

"Take care of our women, Colin."

John was gone before the boy could answer, but Addie saw the pride on his young face, and she had yet another reason to love John Tallman.

# CHAPTER

## * 26 *

Having Buffer and Rolly to see to the defense,
John and Cleve rode out from the camp. They
galloped to the rise, where they stopped and
John lifted the glass to his eye. Indians, no
more than a half-mile away, were studying
tracks. A few had dismounted and were walking their ponies; the others followed well to
the side so as not to disturb the sign should
the trackers want to backtrack. As John
watched, the trackers mounted up again and
the party headed their way.

"They're Comanche." John handed the
glass to Cleve. "One of them is called Wild
Horse."

"Friend a yores?"

"Not exactly, but not an enemy either."

"It ain't no huntin' party."

"We might as well give them a greeting."
John waved his rifle over his head, acknowl-
edging their approach, then shoved it back
in the scabbard.

He counted more than thirty young warriors riding small, swift horses. He recognized Wild Horse as the brave he had seen once with young Quanah Parker, subchief of the Quohada band of Comanche. Parker was becoming known not only for his leadership but for his raids on cavalry camps. The Comanche's hatred for the horse soldiers was well known.

"They're lookin' for someone, that's sure," Cleve murmured.

The Indians approached at a gallop. As they neared, Wild Horse held up his hand. The braves stopped. Most of them were young. Their dark eyes were alive with suspicion, and they looked long and hard at John and Cleve.

Alone, Wild Horse walked his horse to within a few yards of where John and Cleve waited. Long white feathers hung from the Indian's thick braids, which had become streaked with gray since John last had seen him. A large round amulet hung from a thong around his neck.

"Wild Horse." John held up his hand, palm out.

"Spotted Elk." The Indian returned the greeting. "You pass over Indian land with your wagons." His English was better than John remembered.

"My father, Rain Tallman, pays your people with cattle, food, and medicine for the right."

"It is known to me." The Indian's eyes honed in on Cleve. "You are known as Bloody Knife. Stone Hand say you friend of Comanche but not of Apache or Kiowa."

"That is true."

"Stone Hand is with Quanah on big hunt."

John smiled. "My brother, Stone Hand, is a longtime friend of your young chief."

"Stone Hand say you pass this way. He say Spotted Elk give Wild Horse bullets and tobacco."

"I will honor my brother's promise."

"We look for white men who steal our horses, kill two of our women, steal two more. They come this way."

"They may have. But we have seen no man."

A murmur of disbelief rose from the riders grouped behind Wild Horse. He turned, spoke a sharp word, and the grumbling ceased. When he spoke again it was to the braves.

"Spotted Elk, Stone Hand, and their father Rain Tallman do not lie. He says he sees no man. He sees no man." He turned back to John. "Young braves. Hot blood."

John nodded his understanding. "We will smoke and talk while my friend" — he nodded toward Cleve — "gets tobacco and bullets from the wagons."

Wild Horse nodded and, to John's surprise, kicked his horse and led the way toward the freight camp. He glanced at Cleve, who had been in enough tight spots to reveal nothing of what he was thinking.

John had begun to plan how he would keep the band of warriors outside the circle of wagons, when the Indian leader stopped on the flat prairie a few hundred yards from the freight camp. He spoke rapidly in Comanche to his braves. John understood enough to know he was telling them to stay and build a fire, and that when he returned with Spotted Elk they would smoke. The young braves dismounted immediately and Wild Horse continued on toward the freight wagons with John and Cleve.

John's eyes scanned the camp. Buffer or Rolly had seen them coming. Some of the men leaned casually against the wagons, while others appeared to be working on a wheel or a tongue. To John's relief, there was no show of firearms.

Wild Horse took in the scene inside the circle where horses, mules, and oxen milled about.

"You think we steal your horses, Spotted Elk?"

John caught the look of amusement in the Indian's eyes.

"We didn't know you were friends, Wild Horse. You could have been horse soldiers dressed as Indians."

The Indian's mouth didn't smile, but his eyes did. "It is wise to be ready."

As they rode down the line of wagons toward the one that held goods for occasions such as this, Rolly, bouncing on the back of a horse, came toward them. It was unusual to see the big man on horseback. He hated riding.

"Dal, this is my friend, Wild Horse, of the Quohada Comanche."

"How do?" Dal held out his hand. The Indian grasped it and gave it a downward shake.

Dal wasn't sure how much English the Indian understood, but what he had to tell John had to be said.

"I'm havin' a hell of a time with them half-ass Yanks in the other camp. Better get over there, John. They're fixin' to mount up and ride on the . . . enemy."

"Enemy?" Wild Horse caught the last word. "Spotted Elk got enemy? We help you kill."

"The men of whom we speak are their own enemy. They are stupid men who do not know our ways," John explained.

Then he groaned inwardly as he saw the Yankee patrol, followed by a dozen armed men, ride out from the judge's camp and head toward Wild Horse's hot-blooded young braves. Seeing the soldiers, the braves ran for their horses.

"You have horse soldiers!" Wild Horse spat the words.

"They're with the other camp. I will stop them."

John gigged his horse and Victor sprang forward. At the same time, another horse jumped a wagon tongue and sped toward the patrol. Buffer Simmons, too, was trying to head off the disaster.

Buffer skidded his horse to a stop in front of the captain's high-strung mount.

"What the hell are you doing?" the captain shouted angrily after he got his mount under control.

"I'm stoppin' ya from startin' a ruckus with the Comanch that'll get ya kilt. I ain't carin' 'bout ya, I'm carin' 'bout the other folk of this train."

"Get out of the way. I'll have you clapped in irons for interfering with an officer of the United States Army."

"It's plain ya've never fought Indians. They'll flank ya and half of ya will be down 'fore ya can swaller."

John rode up and jerked Victor to a halt.

"You gawddammed fool! Get your men back to that camp and stay there before you get them killed," John snapped.

The captain's face was a dull red. "You've no authority here. Move out of my way, or I'll order my men to remove you."

"Try it." Buffer snorted. "Hell. Ya couldn't haul a sick whore off a piss pot."

"The judge is in charge of Indian affairs —"

"Not here. They're on their own land, you stupid jackass. Conducting their own business. They would like nothing more than for you to fire on them. It would give them an excuse to wipe you out."

"Let them try. They're nothing but a bunch of savages."

"They may *look* like savages, but they're shrewd fighters, Forsythe. I could put all the brains you've got in a gnat's eye." John pulled his rifle from its scabbard and placed the barrel an inch from the head of the captain's horse. "Unless you want me to blow the brains out of this high-prancing fancy horse the judge is so proud of, get your patrol back to your camp and stay out of sight."

"You've no right to interfere. This is army business."

"It's my business when it'll mean my men will have to try to save your ass!"

John turned to Buffer. "Tell the captain's men what they're in for."

Buffer rode down the line of horsemen who waited behind the patrol. He looked each of them in the face.

"Don't let that duded-up flitter-head get ya scalped. Them Comanch braves are fighters. One of 'em can outfight three white men."

"Don't look much like fighters to me. Look like skinny, shitty younguns a-tryin' to act big." The man who spoke was big and burly with a mean face and a large lump of tobacco in his jaw.

"They might be skinny and shitty, but 'fore ya blink a eye, they'll make ya a new mouth under yore chin. Ya'll not have to spit out that wad yo're chawin' on." Buffer moved on.

"Is it true Injuns is bad shots?"

"Maybe. But I've seen 'em bring down a jackrabbit with a arrow and both of 'em a-runnin' full speed. That ain't *bad* shootin' to my way a thinkin'."

"I ain't wantin' to fight no Indians if I don't have to." The man who spoke had a thin beard and wore a straw hat that had seen better days.

"Ya sure as hell don't have to this time unless ya push 'em. Their leader is being friendly with Tallman."

"Old judge'll have a fit if we don't stand with the blue bellies." This was muttered by another man in a low voice.

"It's better old judge has a fit than fer ya to be staked out fer the rattlers to gnaw on."

"Hell. That Yank ain't no Indian fighter. I knowed right off when he couldn't tell them Indians was Comanch."

"If the Comanch is a friend, he's a friend." Buffer looked the man in the eye. "But if yo're his enemy, he's a mean son of a bitch. They hate horse soldiers worser than anythin'."

"Reckon if we back off we'll get shot in the back."

Buffer snorted. "Judge ain't gonna shoot all of ya. He needs ya to drive them wagons."

Buffer rode on down the line, speaking to the men. At the very end was a man on a long-legged black horse. Buffer looked at him, then looked again, as something about him caught his eye. It wasn't the black beard or black hat, which were ordinary. It was the way he sat his horse, tall in the saddle, his narrow shoulders, his long arms. The man's head was tilted, his face turned away. Buffer rode around him, aiming to get a better look, but then one of the soldiers shouted something. The man wheeled his horse, as did the others in the line, and headed back to their camp.

"Dumb bastards won't live to get to Sante Fe," John said. "He finally admitted the *judge* told him to chase the Indians away. *Miss Cindy* had had a screaming fit. Lordy, I'll be glad to see the North Canadian River and the last of them."

"I'd-a not butted in, but I was 'fraid any minute they'd sound the bugle to charge. One a them fools was unrollin' the flag. Can ya beat that?"

The midday stop lasted two hours longer than usual. The "yoke-up" call came when the Comanch mounted their ponies and, leading a horse loaded with gifts from the freight wagons, rode away.

It had been a long, worrisome afternoon for Addie. Keeping the children close at hand became her first concern. She had kept them in the wagon until the stock had once again been let out onto the prairie to graze.

The slates and pencil chalk were a blessing. Although Addie knew that Trisha could read and write, she was surprised at how easily she went about teaching the alphabet to the younger children and later to Colin.

Dillon's attention lasted through the letter *B*. After that he was interested only in covering the slate with white chalk lines and was a distraction to Jane Ann and Colin.

Addie took him up onto the wagon seat and gave him a book to look at. Her mind was full of misery and the dread of telling John about Kirby. Thinking about it made her stomach roil. There was absolutely no doubt in her mind that the "captain" was Kirby Hyde. His mouth had tightened and his nostrils flared just as they had done four years ago when he was angry with her. Oh, he was Kirby, and she could prove it if he shaved off the goatee and exposed the mole on his chin.

It was almost a relief to Addie when the call came that they would be moving again.

"I learnt to make a *A* and a *B* and a *C*, Miss Addie. Trisha knows all of 'em. She'll write my name next time." Colin was far more interested in learning than Jane Ann was.

"He learns fast," Trisha commented, after Colin left to help Gregorio hitch their team to the wagon. She wiped the slates with a cloth and put them away. "He'll know more'n me in no time a'tall."

That afternoon they crossed a vast space of prairie land. Dust rose in a cloud over the wagon train. The oxen moved with slow, ponderous steps over the almost treeless prairie.

Addie had chosen to stay in the back of the wagon. Trisha and Jane Ann sat on the seat beside Huntley. Dillon was riding with Colin and Gregorio in the wagon ahead. She had not seen John, Buffer, or Cleve since the train had moved out from the noon camp.

Her mind kept returning to her confrontation with Kirby. She had thought to catch him unaware when she called out to him, but he hadn't hesitated for even a second. He had mounted his horse and turned when she called out the second time. *He was expecting me to confront him.* So many questions filled her mind. What was he doing in a Yankee uniform? Who was buried in the grave that was supposed to be his? She understood why he wanted her to think he was dead: He wanted to be rid of her.

The sky was darkening. Long ago the shadows that followed the train had disappeared. There was dampness in the air and the smell of trees and water. The call came to "swing in," and Cleve guided the lead wagon into the large arc. Going down the line was the order to "tighten up." The drivers left only enough space between the wagons to unhitch the teams.

Addie dreaded going to the cook wagon to help with the evening meal. She felt much relieved when Bill told her that the long noon rest had given him time to prepare it and all he had to do was make the coffee. Addie went back to her wagon and reached it just as Buffer appeared. Pleading a headache, she asked him to take Trisha and the children to eat, then crawled into the back of the wagon and sat there in the dark. She wasn't sure how long she had been sitting there when John arrived.

"Addie?"

"I'm here."

"You all right?"

"Well, yes . . . and no." She stood for a minute with her forehead against his chest after he had helped her down. "Have you had supper?"

"No, but it won't hurt me to miss a meal. I asked Buffer to stay with Trisha and the children. Come on. We've got to talk." Holding her elbow firmly in his hand, he led her down the line to a large freight wagon; the wheels were as high as her head. John reached into the back, brought out a piece of rolled canvas, and spread it on the ground.

"We watched you ride out to head off that patrol," Addie said as she settled down on the canvas, trying desperately to think of something to say before John began his questions.

"It's been a long time since I've seen as stupid a move as they were about to make. Thank the Lord, they'll turn north to Fort Gibson in a couple of days. Come here, honey." He put his arm around her and pulled her to him. "I'm not alone with you near enough. I don't want to waste a minute." He lowered his head and kissed her so lovingly that she immediately burst into tears. "What's this? Tears from my Addie?" He held her and let her cry.

Finally, she moved out of his arms, lifted the bottom of her skirt and dried her eyes. She settled back against him and wrapped her arms around his waist.

"I never thought I'd cry because someone *wasn't* dead." Her face was against his neck. "I love you, John Tallman. I love you so . . . much." She felt her throat close as more tears filled her eyes.

"I love you too, Mrs. Tallman —"

"Oh, but . . . I'm not!"

"Now what, Addie girl?"

476

"Not Mrs. Tallman. That . . . captain is Kirby Hyde. That means I'm still . . . married to him."

"I know you think that, honey. I saw the look on your face today when you first saw him."

"It wasn't the first time. I saw him the day we left Van Buren and again the day we started the trip. Each time I became more convinced. It's him. I know it sounds crazy because Kirby joined the *Confederate* Army."

"Addie, it isn't him. Kirby is dead. Won't you trust me in this?"

"I wish I could. I've dreaded that he'd come back. It was sinful, but I didn't grieve for him when I heard he was dead."

"Do you want to tell me about him?"

"I was so lonesome," she began, and went on to tell him about Kirby's coming to the farm and working for her. Embarrassed, but determined to tell all, she told John how she had fallen for Kirby's charm and had allowed him to seduce her. Feeling guilty and fearing she might have a child, she had nagged at him until he agreed to have Preacher Sikes marry them.

After they were wed he had gone to town frequently. Then, out of the blue, he had come home one day and told her that he had enlisted in the Arkansas Regulars. He left the next day and she had not seen him again, until that day in Van Buren. She told John how shocked she had been when she heard his voice and his words, "Cool down, little filly." She had at first thought her mind was playing a trick on her.

"It's him, John. I don't know how he got into the Yankee army, and as an officer at that. The only relative he mentioned was an uncle in Jonesboro. That's where I sent a letter telling him that he had a son. I don't suppose he ever got the letter. But that man is Kirby, and he knows that Dillon is his son. I understand that he could deny me, but how can a man deny his son?"

"Because, Addie, he is *not* Kirby."

"Why are you so sure? You've never met him. All you have to go on is the judge's word that his name is Forsythe." Addie sat up and looked into John's face. "I wish it weren't true." Her arms moved over his shoulders and around his neck. "I can't begin to tell you what being with you has meant to me. I never even dreamed a man could fill my heart so completely. Regardless of what happens . . ."

"Nothing is going to happen, sweetheart." John kissed her lips and tried to pull her into his arms. She resisted and framed his face with her palms.

"Please believe me."

"I know you think the man is Kirby, but he isn't!"

"How do you know that?"

"Because I killed him, Addie. I killed Kirby Hyde."

Addie's mouth dropped open. She looked at him in stunned silence. When she came out of her shock, she uttered two words:

"When? Where?"

# CHAPTER

## * 27 *

*He woke with the cold blade of a knife against his throat.*

Since leaving Quill's Station on the Wabash, John had met hundreds of Yanks and Rebs on their way home from the war. Now, he realized that he should have pushed on instead of bedding down at this crossroads where a dozen men had stopped for the night.

John Tallman was a sucker for the poor fools who had been led to the slaughter by the politicians, and he had shared what food he had and his coffee with a couple of them.

Hellfire! He didn't want to kill the war-weary bastards.

"Whatcha waitin' fer? Kill 'im. He's a ridin' a mighty fine horse an' he ain't givin' it up less'n he's dead." The whispered words came from out of the darkness. "Ya wantin' to walk while all them other fellers is ridin' past ya?"

"I've never killed a man in cold blood."

"Gawdamighty!"

"It was your idea —"

"Ya said ya'd kilt plenty a Yanks."

"That's different."

"Hell, it ain't no different. A killin's a killin'. If ya ain't got the stomach fer it, get the hell outta the way."

*The sons of bitches! The murdering bastards!*

A coldness grew at the back of John's neck. He knew with certainty they meant to kill him for his horse. He waited a few seconds, letting his nerves grow quiet and his senses poise for the action he would have to take to save his life.

When he moved, it was whiplash-fast. He grasped the wrist of the hand holding the knife and pushed it from his throat. At the same instant his other hand brought up his rifle. The butt smashed into the side of the man's head with such force that he heard bones crack. Then John flipped the barrel and fired point-blank at the second figure, who was jumping at him with a blade in his hand. The blast threw the man back.

John was on his feet before the jumper hit the ground. His eyes swept the clearing where men had sprung up out of their bedrolls. He was only vaguely aware of the sharp sting of the cut beneath his jaw and the blood that ran down his neck.

"Don't shoot." Several men stepped forward. "They're not with us."

"Never saw them before we rode in to bed down."

"Figured them Rebs for back-stabbers."

"You a Reb?" one asked.

"No."

The man laughed. "Got to be a Yank, then."

"No."

"No?"

"Any of you men planning to take my horse?" John stood ready to bring his rifle into play.

"We got horses, but we'll take him if you're givin' him away."

"I could use a shovel. I've got one man to bury — maybe two."

"Hell, man. You don't have to bury them Rebs. Leave 'em for the wolves and the coyotes."

In the silence that followed, John let his gaze travel over the Yankee soldiers — what he could see of them.

"Would you want a pack of wild dogs gnawing on you?" John's voice was nearly a snarl. "They're men, even though they're rotten, murdering ragshags. I'll bury them."

The quiet rage in his voice whipped one

of the men into speech.

"I'll get ya a shovel."

"Thanks."

John looked down at the man he had cracked in the head with his rifle. His skull was caved in, and his eyes were open and staring. John did not like to kill, nor did he want to be killed.

"This one's dead, too." He moved to the body with the gaping hole in the chest and stooped to search the clothing. "Check the other one's pockets and see if you can put a name on him," he said to no one in particular.

One of the men went down on one knee beside the body, then stood, holding a letter in his hand. He struck a match on his bootheel, sheltered the flame with his hat, and began to read.

" 'To the uncle of Kirby Hyde, Jonesboro, Arkansas. From his wife.' "

"Shit!" John snatched the letter from the man's hand and crammed it into his shirt pocket.

"That's what it says." The Yankee's voice was not quite steady. "I'm glad I'm not the one to break the news to his widow. It's a shame to come through the war and get yourself killed on the way home."

Without a word, John took the shovel,

walked a few paces, and began to dig in the soft river sand.

The breeze died down with the coming of dawn. The silence was eerie as John read through the letter, pocketed it, then carefully printed the name of the dead man in his hat and tied it to a stake he drove into the ground. When he was finished, he leaned the shovel against a tree where it would be easily found, and without a glance at the men sitting around a small fire he saddled his horse and rode away.

Addie had been quiet, scarcely breathing while John talked. Now she stirred restlessly.

"Addie, Kirby is dead. I'm sorry he had to lose his life that way. But he was going to kill me."

"I can't imagine Kirby killing a man with a knife. He didn't even want to kill a chicken. In the back of my mind I thought of him as kind of . . . cowardly."

"I don't think he wanted to do it. I think he was pushed into it by the other man."

"Who was he?"

"There was no name on him. Only a picture of a woman bare from the waist up."

"That was the only letter I wrote to Kirby. I thought he should know he had a son. I wasn't sure it would even get to him. I guess it did."

"I didn't want to tell you this."

"Why?"

"I didn't know if . . . you cared for him. You had his son."

"Yes. I had his son, and no, I didn't care for him . . . after a while. He just used me. I've thought about it a lot, and I think he was hiding from something or someone when he came to the farm."

"You may be right. Are you convinced now that the captain isn't Kirby?"

"Oh, John, I don't know. The man you describe doesn't seem to fit the Kirby I knew. But it's been so long, and war can change a man."

"I've got the letter in my pack back in the storage wagon."

Addie was quiet. After a while she drew back from him so she could see his face.

"Why did you come to Freepoint?"

"I had some time. I was going to leave word to be passed to the Hyde family, but someone had already brought the news to the store. I heard the storekeeper tell you about it when you came in that day."

"You heard talk about me and Trisha, too, didn't you?"

"Yes. I saw you and didn't believe a word of it."

"Did you marry me because you were sorry you had to kill my husband?"

"Addie, love, I married you because I was determined not to let you get away from me."

"It's hard to believe that you'd . . . want me . . . for myself."

"Believe it, love. I killed that man before he could kill me. I hated the thought that he left a wife and a son, and that might be the reason I went to Freepoint. I was going to leave a little money with the store man if you were in need."

"Is that why you were in the store?"

"I was nosing around to see what I could find out. I heard him call you Mrs. Hyde. After you left, I hung around and talked to him. He let me know that he thought you were too good for the likes of Kirby Hyde."

"Not many people knew Kirby —"

"I liked what I saw of you that day, liked you even more after I heard you talking to the two drunks that came to the farm that night. It was the first I'd heard anyone cussed out in such ladylike language." He chuckled. "Even when you got warmed up, you couldn't think of anything worse to call them than chicken-livered polecats."

Addie hid her face against him. "I was so mad!"

"I was fascinated with you after you invited me in to breakfast, and when I heard you finally break out into real profanity when you were raking the old preacher over the coals, I was so smitten with you I hated to leave you to go back to town to see the magistrate. I hurried back the next morning."

Addie wrapped her arms around his neck. "I love you, you know. Please don't ever leave me."

"Ah . . . sweet girl. You'd have a hell of a time getting rid of me." His big arms squeezed her, his lips nuzzled her neck. "You are my Addie girl. I'm going to tell you I love you every day for the rest of our lives."

Sheet lightning played in the clouds continuously the following morning. By the time the wagons circled for the midday stop, bulging gray clouds were being nudged along by a brisk wind, and thunder had become a constant rumble of sullen threats. A chain of lightning came sputtering down, as if tearing itself loose from the heavens.

The big wagons had formed a tight corral to hold the stock being unhitched and to give them protection from the storm. The belt of rolling white and gray clouds that bore down on them from the southwest reached eagerly forward. Below the roiling clouds was a solid expanse of color, a dark dirty gray tinged with green.

To Buffer Simmons, riding with the herders circling the extra stock, the green-tinged cloud meant only one thing. Hail. The huge rumbles of thunder reverberated, making the ground tremble. The nervous stock was milling about. Buffer heard the rush of wind overhead. A big drop of rain spattered against his hat. He thought of Trisha in the wagon with Miss Addie and the kids and hoped that she wasn't scared.

The wind and the rain hit quickly and with surprising violence, as if it meant to snatch the clothes from his back. A tremendous clap of thunder broke overhead with a burst of light. It shook the earth. Darkness closed in and it wasn't even noon. The intense flashes of lightning emphasized the darkness. Rain came down in sheets. The cattle milled but were holding, then suddenly the signal passed through them. The oxen bawled, the horses whinnied, and the mules let out frightened snorts.

A herder wrapped in a poncho passed Buffer, his hat brim pulled well down on his head, protecting his face. Buffer turned his horse to ride counterclockwise around the herd. The raindrops, driven by the wind, felt sharp as hail against his back. Through the rain and the gloom, he noticed that the rider who had passed him veered off toward the circle of wagons.

The horse had carried Buffer fifty feet before the thought came storming into his brain. The rider who had passed him was wearing a poncho but not a round-brimmed Mexican sombrero. Gawdamighty! The man was sitting too tall in the saddle to be a Mexican.

Buffer yanked his horse around, dug his heels into its sides, and raced toward the wagons. The rider was out of sight, but instinct told Buffer where he was heading. A cold band of dread settled around his heart. Trisha had been so sure the "devil man" would not go away as long as she was alive.

*He found no buryin' hole. He won't go till he knows I'm dead.*

John reached the wagon as soon as it had stopped and the mules had been unhitched.

"Don't be afraid. This is a good heavy wagon. Huntley and I will make sure the canvas is tight. If you light the lantern, Addie, put it out when the wind comes up."

"We'll be all right."

"Papa, is it gonna storm?"

"I reckon so, son, but it's nothing to be

scared of. Colin isn't here, so you're the man in charge. Take care of Jane Ann, your mother, and Trisha."

"I'll take care of 'em." Dillon looked proudly at his mother. He already loved John dearly.

"Shall I give them the presents?"

"Presents?" The word was echoed by both children.

"That's a good idea. I think you could even break out the candy sticks, Addie."

"Candy?" both shrieked.

Trisha and Addie laughed.

"They'll be a-wishin' for a storm every day, Mr. John."

"I hope they don't get one every day. I'll keep an eye on the wagon." John leaned from the saddle and kissed Addie.

"Put on your slicker —"

He laughed. "Yes, *Muvver.*"

Jane Ann was speechless when Addie handed her the doll. When finally she could speak, she whispered, "She's mine."

"Yes, honey. John bought her for you."

The child's eyes were as bright as diamonds. "He *is* my papa, ain't he?"

"Yes, he is, honey."

"Looky, Trisha. Looky at her dress. She's got fingers!"

Dillon was interested in the doll until he

saw the tin soldiers. The look on his face was one of awe. The box held ten brightly painted soldiers; five in the uniform of the North and five in the uniform of the South. He grabbed a Union soldier from the box.

"Look, Muvver! This is like that man." He was so excited he could scarcely talk. "See, Trisha?"

"Did Papa get Trisha a present?" Jane Ann asked.

"He bought her some ribbons for her hair. I'll get them out later."

"He didn't do no such, Miss Addie," Trisha whispered.

"How do you know, Miss Smarty?" Addie put her arm around her friend and hugged her. "Oh, Trish, we're so lucky to have John. I think of the time back on the farm as a nightmare."

"It wasn't bad, 'cept there at the last. Mr. John come in the nick a time."

"And Buffer did too. Remember when we first saw him in town? He collared those two drunks and sent them sailing out into the street. He liked you even then."

"But he . . . knowed —"

"It's all the better. He liked you in spite of that. You do like him, don't you?"

"He's all right now he's got that brush off his face."

"John says he wants to marry you."

"He . . . can't!"

"Trisha, it's one thing to be proud, it's another to be so stiff-necked proud that you ruin your chance to be happy. I know you're not ashamed of your colored blood; but you've got far more white blood than colored, so go with what you've got the most of."

"I was thinkin' it was red!" Trisha giggled.

Addie laughed. The wind hit the wagon with a force that rocked it.

Addie hurried to put out the lantern. Trisha tied down the back flap. A tremendous clap of thunder broke overhead, and Jane Ann let out a little shriek. Trisha reached for the child as the wind-driven rain struck the tightly stretched canvas. Addie held Dillon and his precious tin soldiers in her arms and wondered if John and Colin were out in this heavy downpour.

The wind slackened some, but rain continued to pour out of the sky. Inside the dark wagon, there was just enough light for the two women holding the children to see each other. Water began to come in around the front flap. Trisha moved Jane Ann close to Addie and hurriedly removed the mattress from the overjet and placed a rag rug beneath the leak to catch the water. Then she went back to sit on the trunk with Jane Ann.

The noise made by the driving rain against the canvas prevented Addie from hearing the voice that called out to Trisha from the end of the wagon. But Trisha heard it, and fear spread through her brain like a writhing serpent. She reached for Addie's arm, squeezed it, and put her finger to her lips.

"Come outta thar, girl!"

"It's him!" Trisha mouthed. Then, hearing a sound from Jane Ann, she clamped her hand over the child's mouth.

"Shhh . . . honey," she whispered against her ear. "Go get under the overjet. Hurry!"

It took less than half a minute for the women to shove the children under the over-jet and to lift the trunk and place it in front of them. Trisha motioned frantically for Addie to get under the jet with them, but she shook her head.

"I'll empty both barrels in thar if'n ya don't come out."

Addie looked for a weapon. The old buffalo gun was under the wagon seat. Colin had taken Trisha's rifle. The knives were in the chuck box, but its door was outside.

The rumbling thunder was constant now. Addie looked across at Trisha. She stood poised, one hand on the bow of the wagon, the other clutching her knife.

A sudden *rip!* Through a yard-long slice

in the canvas the head and shoulders of a man appeared. Rain-soaked black hair was plastered to his head. A black beard covered his face. His eyes, even in the gloom, shone with the light of insanity.

"Ya ain't gettin' away this time."

Trisha launched herself at him as he was bringing up the double barrel of his gun.

She never reached him.

He was suddenly swept away by a long arm that looped around his throat. The gun he was holding went off, the bullet going through the top of the wagon. The attacker dropped the useless weapon and struggled to reach the knife tucked in his belt. Then Buffer's fist came at him with such force that his head snapped up and his body arched back. He staggered, but when he righted himself he had a knife in his hand.

"Come on, ya *vulture!*" Buffer roared, reaching for his own blade. "I'll cut yore gawddamned heart out!"

The huge man was wild with rage. The bearded man knew that this would be a fight to the death.

"She ain't nothin' but a split-tailed nigger!" he sneered. With hot fevered eyes on Buffer, he began to sidestep to force Buffer against the wagon tongue.

It was a mistake. The instant the intruder's

back was to the wagon, Trisha launched herself through the opening in the canvas. With all the strength she possessed she plunged her knife into his back. She fell to the ground and bounced back to her feet like a cat. The black-bearded man staggered, then stood motionless for a few seconds. He turned slowly as if dangling from a string, his eyes wild, his mouth open.

"Nigger bitch! I'll whup the meat off yore bones!"

Trisha backed away. Vaguely she could hear Buffer calling her name and then his arms were pulling her back, shielding her with his body.

As the bearded man stared at her, the stiffness went out of his legs and his knees folded. His hate-filled eyes never left Trisha's face as he sank slowly, his knife hand reaching out for her. Then he was on his face, Trisha's knife protruding from his back. Buffer stepped forward and kicked the knife from his hand, then bent and yanked Trisha's out of his back.

The man screamed.

"Shit!" Buffer muttered. "The bastard ain't dead!"

The rain had waned to a fine drizzle, but no one noticed. Addie stood in the back of the wagon looking down on the scene. She couldn't believe the risk Trisha had taken to jump out of the wagon and sink her knife between the shoulder blades of the man who had come to kill her.

Addie heard a shout and saw John running toward them.

"Addie?" His voice was filled with anxiety. "I heard a shot. Are you all right?"

"We're all right. See about Trisha."

Buffer's arms were around Trisha, her face against his wet shirt. She was quiet and appeared calm.

"I knowed it was him . . . that *devil man!* I wasn't going to let him cut ya up, Buffer. He's . . . so mean —"

"Sweet girl. Ya scared the hell out of me." Buffer's arms cradled her. "Don't ever do that again!" he said gruffly. "I'll do the fightin' for both of us. Hear?"

"I wasn't gonna let him cut ya, Buffer," Trisha said again.

She stood still in Buffer's arms while he told John what had happened. Buffer blamed himself for not keeping a closer watch.

"Trish said he'd be back to finish the job. Guess I got careless, thinkin' he'd not come out here." His arms tightened around Trisha. "Damn vulture was in the judge's camp all this time."

John knelt beside the man on the ground.

"He isn't dead!"

"I can fix that!" Buffer's blood was still at the boiling point.

John turned cold eyes on Buffer and said curtly: "No, you won't! That would be murder, and I'll not stand for it."

"Gawddammit, John. The son of a bitch was gonna use that scatter gun. He wasn't carin' who he hit, just so he got Trisha. He tried to kill her . . . twice! He ain't fit to live!"

John ignored Buffer's outburst and showed no sign of how shaken he was to learn that the man was going to fire into the wagon.

"Throw out a ground sheet, Addie. We'll get him under the wagon out of the rain." John unlaced the back flap and swung it open.

"Get in the wagon, my sweet brave girl," Buffer muttered for Trisha's ears alone as he lifted her up in his arms and carried her to the end of the wagon. "Put on some dry clothes. Me an' John'll take care of this heap a horse dung."

Huntley, Paco, Colin, and Cleve arrived in time to help lift the man who had been rolled over on the ground sheet. They placed him beneath the wagon. Cleve looked at him and shook his head.

"He'll last an hour, maybe two. The knife went into his lungs. They're fillin' up with blood. Should I notify the other camp?"

"Let him die first," John said without feeling. "They can come get him and bury him. How is the stock doing?"

"They stirred a bit, but held together. That was some turd floater. The stream ahead will be out of its banks till mornin'."

"Guess we've gone as far as we'll go today. Any of the freight get wet?"

"Rolly's checkin' it."

The dying man beneath the wagon lay alone, gasping for breath. John ducked beneath the wagon to speak to him, not out of compassion but decency.

"How did you find her?"

"Wasn't hard. Missed her at Freepoint. Some fellers . . . told me some gal had crippled a man . . . she'd gone with a bull train. Knowed it was . . . her. Almost got 'er . . . once."

"The Renshaws?"

"Didn't ask 'em no . . . names. Hee-hee-hee! Told me to bring 'em a ear . . . they'd give me a . . . horse."

"You're not going to make it, you know. Is there anyone you want notified?"

"Never . . . thought I'd be brought down . . . by a damned nigger wench!" Blood trickled from the corner of the man's mouth and disappeared in his thick black beard.

"If you'd shot into that wagon and hurt my wife, my kids, or Trisha, I'd not have waited for you to die. I'd have stomped the life out of you where you lay."

"Big talk. Ya ain't . . . got the guts fer it," he said with a sneer.

"You tried to kill Trisha in Van Buren. What's she done to you that you'd follow her all the way out here to try it again?"

"She's a nigger! And she run!" Black brows drew together. "Ain't never . . . lost one. I always get 'em. Miss Amelia had to give . . . the buyer his money back, 'cause the bitch run."

"The war is over. Slaves are free people now."

The man's face was ashen, causing his eyes to look brighter. His lips curled again in a sneer.

"They ain't got sense . . . enough to be free! They're dumb animals. Only good to . . . work. Some ain't worth feedin'."

"You're the sorriest piece of shit I've come onto in a long time. If you weren't dying I'd be tempted to kill you where you lie."

The dying man gave a derisive snort and blood came out of his mouth.

"Miss Amelia'll send somebody else to get that . . . bitch."

"Let her try. They'll get what you got."

"I got them . . . other bastards . . . them high-yeller boys. I made sure they knowed . . . it was me that . . . got 'em. If I'da got *her*, Miss Amelia's Hector would have all a Satinwood Plantation, best cotton . . . land on the river."

"You didn't get Trisha. Trisha got you." John's voice was heavy with contempt.

"I . . . ain't never failed Miss Amelia." The dying man's voice was weakening.

"You did this time."

"Gawd! I hate them white niggers. They . . . so . . . uppity. Mr. Du Bois . . . ride 'em and get more white niggers . . . outa 'em. He call the wench *La* Trisha . . . like she was . . . somethin' grand." He lifted a bony hand and clutched at his chest.

"Du Bois is dead?"

"In the . . . war." His head and shoulders heaved as he struggled to breathe. "Left Satinwood to Hector and them . . . three nigger bastards. It wasn't right a'tall. Ah . . . poor Miss Amelia. I got them . . . studs. Almost got the wench. Tell Miss Amelia, I almost . . . got the —"

Blood gushed from his mouth. His eyes remained open and staring.

John waited.

To be sure he was dead, John moved one

500

of the man's eyelids with the tip of his finger. It stayed closed. The other remained open. He closed it and placed the man's hat over his face.

# CHAPTER

## * 28 *

The wind blew away the clouds and the sun came out. The rain had washed the dust from the white canvas tops of the wagons, and now they gleamed in the sun.

Colin took the two younger children to Bill to stay until the dead man could be removed from beneath the wagon. Addie reminded them to thank John for the presents. Afterward they insisted on giving him big kisses on his cheeks. John was wonderfully patient with them. He smiled up at Addie, clearly enjoying hearing them call him "papa."

After the children left, John repeated word for word his conversation with the dead man.

"What's his name?" Addie asked.

"I didn't think to ask him."

"It's . . . David Blessing." Trisha's golden eyes had a sparkle when she looked at Buffer. "Nobody ever called him that but Miss Amelia. Us slaves said, yassuh, nawsuh. But when he wasn't around we called him devil man."

" 'Blessing' certainly doesn't fit the man from what you've told about him," Addie commented before turning to John. "Does that mean that Trisha owns half of a large plantation?"

"I reckon it does."

"I ain't goin' back there!" Trisha's voice rose. "I ain't wantin' any a that Satinwood." She turned pleading eyes to Buffer. "Ya said we'd fix us a place —"

"We'll do it if that's what ya want."

Trisha was close to tears.

"I'm goin' with ya, Buffer. Hector and old Amelia can have it all. Them folks that work it hate 'em both. They'll go somewhere else. Let nasty old Hector hoe cotton in the sun till he's so tired he can't eat." A smile came into her golden eyes. "I hope he has to slop hogs, cut cane, and carry out the slop jars too."

"We'll start us up a little place, sweet girl." Buffer's voice was husky with relief. He'd had a moment of panic when he realized that Trisha could claim part of a big plantation. "We ain't gonna have no *big* place —"

"I ain't carin' about no *big* place, Buffer." She held on to his arm with both hands. "I ain't never goin' back to Orleans or Satinwood. I was thinkin' ya was tryin' to back out on . . . on . . .' "

Buffer grasped her shoulders with both hands. "I ain't never backin' out on what I tell ya. I just want ya to be shore ya won't be sorry 'bout missin' out havin' . . . all that."

"All that *misery?* All them folks lookin' down on me? I ain't never gonna miss *that.* 'Sides, Buffer, ya promised to show me how to throw a knife so . . . it'll be easier for me to stick folks." She failed in her attempt to get him to smile.

"I'm goin' to. Lord, ya scared the water outta me when I saw what ya was up to."

When Buffer realized what he had said, his face turned fiery red. He could feel the laughter in the girl snuggled close to him and wanted to shake her.

"If you can take your eyes off Trisha for a minute, Buffer, we've got one more thing to decide." John's serious tone drew their attention. "I don't think anyone outside the four of us and Cleve knows why Blessing was after Trisha. I told Cleve after she was attacked. You can trust him not to say anything." He looked at Trisha and she nodded. "I don't think Blessing would have told anyone at the other camp because he wanted to get away after he had done his dirty work. He seemed to be quite taken with his Miss

Amelia and wanted to get back to her."

"They was thick as eight in a bed," Trisha commented dryly.

Addie frowned. "That's right. What reason can we give the judge for his trailing Trisha and trying again to kill her? Her background is her business . . . and, I think now, Buffer's."

John's dark blue eyes twinkled with love for her. His Addie took everything in stride. She, Trisha, and the children had just escaped death at the hands of a madman. No screaming, no crying. Calm . . . and beautiful. Lord, how had she become so important to him so fast?

With an effort John brought his mind back to the conversation.

"I agree, honey. Why don't we say the man was obsessed with her. It's true that he was . . . in a way. They'll think he was captivated by her beauty, and that when she would have nothing to do with him, it drove him crazy."

"I go along with that." Buffer grinned at Trisha. "I can see how she'd drive a man outta his mind."

"Some men ain't even got one, so they ain't got nothin' to worry 'bout." Trisha tilted her chin at a sassy angle and gave Buffer a side-long glance.

Buffer Simmons, the big bear, was clay in the hands of this slip of a girl. John shook his head in amazement.

"Let me say one thing, then we'll drop the matter. When you get to New Mexico, Trisha, there may be a few people, a very few, who will be interested in whether you're a full-blooded Caucasian. A lot of white folks out there are part Indian or part Mexican. Go with Buffer. Be happy and be proud of *yourself*."

It was as if a weight had been lifted from Trisha's back. Her eyes sparkled when she looked at Buffer. He looked at her as if she were the most precious thing on earth. They would make a great pair — if they didn't end up killing each other. Addie stifled a giggle at the thought.

John decided that this wife would make a terrible poker player. He could read every expression that flickered across her face. She turned her beautiful violet eyes toward him, and he felt something warm deep inside him. He looked at the sun and wondered how long it would be until he could be alone with her. When he spoke, his words were miles from his thoughts.

"I went through Blessing's pockets. He had a little money and some papers. Nothing of interest. But he had this." John took a heavy gold watch from his pocket. "It's got the name Paul Du Bois engraved on it. I thought Trisha should have it."

"Daddy's watch." Trisha reached for it. "He let me play with it when he came to see me and Mama." She held the watch in both hands and looked at it lovingly before she pressed the stem. The cover on the face popped open and she read the words engraved on the inside: " *'I'll always love you.'* Mama had that put there one time when Daddy left his watch at our house. He was . . . so tickled." Trisha looked off into the distance, her eyes misting as she remembered the happy times of her life.

John's eyes sought Addie's.

"We'll have to get some canvas and fix those holes in the top before it rains again. Come on, wife. Let's leave the lovers alone. I've got to send someone to tell Van Winkle to come get his man and bury him."

Trisha and Buffer, standing close together, their heads bowed over the watch, were not aware of their leaving.

The scowl on the judge's face should have been a warning to Addie that he intended to raise serious questions about the death of one of his men. It had not occurred to her that he and the captain of his patrol would accompany the men who came to take away the body.

John and Buffer were repairing the wagon top when the judge, the captain, and two other men rode up leading an unsaddled horse. They dismounted. The captain stooped and lifted the hat from the face of the dead man.

"It's Hopkins," he informed the judge. "One of the last men we hired."

"His name isn't Hopkins," John said to the judge, ignoring the captain. "It's David Blessing."

"How do you know that? Did he tell you?"

"No. Trisha, my wife's stepdaughter, did."

"Her stepdaughter?" The captain looked from Trisha to Addie.

"Her stepdaughter," John repeated smoothly. "Do you have a question about that?"

Forsythe shook his head.

"How does she know that?" the judge demanded.

"He's been following her for . . . about a year. He's the one who tried to kill her back at Van Buren."

"Why?"

"Look at her and look at him."

"Stop talking in riddles. Someone here

killed one of my men and I want to know why."

"He was determined to have her. She didn't want him."

"Seems clear to me, Judge." Forsythe was anxious to leave. Addie had not taken her eyes off him. Sweat rolled from his temples down the sides of his face.

*Damn her!*

"I'll report this to the commanding officer at the fort. Which one of you killed him?" Van Winkle's eyes went first to John, then to Buffer.

"I did it." Trisha spoke up before either of the men could speak. She took a step out from the wagon and faced the men, her hands on her hips. "I kilt the nasty old pile a . . . horse-hockey! I'm glad 'twas me. I stabbed the sucker in the back. Same as he's done to lots of other folks."

"Trisha . . ." Addie said softly. She feared the girl would reveal too much.

"I did it, Miss Addie, and I'm glad I did. I ain't carin' if this puffed-up bullfrog knows it."

Buffer grinned.

John's eyes sparkled with amusement when he saw the look of outrage on the judge's face. He doubted if he had ever heard anyone refer to him as a "puffed-up bullfrog." Van

509

Winkle was trying hard to maintain his stiff-necked dignity.

"What's your name, girl?" Van Winkle took a pencil from his pocket, then an envelope, and began writing on the back of it.

"Trisha."

"Well — ?"

"Trisha Hyde. Spelled *H-y-d-e*," Addie cut in quickly, looking directly at the captain. She saw him clench a fist and was pleased that he was bothered.

John's insides began to quake. *Addie still isn't convinced that the captain is not her dead husband.*

"How long have you known Hopkins . . . er, Blessing? Have you been leadin' him on?" Van Winkle's demanding voice broke into John's thoughts.

"That question is unnecessary, and you know it." John spoke firmly, looked at Buffer, and hoped he would keep his mouth shut. "Blessing followed her to Van Buren. He almost killed her there. You hired him, giving him another chance at her."

Ignoring John, Van Winkle looked at Addie and continued his questions.

"Did her pa die in the war?"

"Yes." Addie's eyes were on the captain. "His name was Kirby Hyde."

The tension was heavy. Only Addie, Forsythe, and John were aware of what Addie was doing.

"All right. Get him out from under there." The judge put the envelope and pencil back into his pocket.

The men went to the other side of the wagon and pulled on the ground sheet, bringing the body out into the bright sunlight. At John's suggestion, they rolled the dead man in the canvas. While they were doing this, the captain managed to move his horse into a position that blocked Addie from the others. He reached out and grasped her arm.

"If you ruin things for me, Addie Faye, you'll be sorry!" He stepped away, leaving Addie stunned.

Up until that moment she had not been *absolutely* sure that the man was Kirby. John's story and the letter he produced had caused her to believe that she might be mistaken. The captain *could* be someone who looked like Kirby — a rare coincidence, one of life's strange little quirks.

Addie felt a numbness start at her knees and work its way up to form a cold ring around her heart. She was married to that cold-hearted man. *Addie Faye. Addie Faye.* The Kirby she had known had teased her when he found her full name written on a sampler her mother had made when she was a baby. The precious keepsake was still in her trunk.

She went into the wagon and sat down. She didn't want to bring the matter up to John again. But how could she not? She couldn't live the rest of her life not being sure that the man she loved with all her heart was her legal husband. She pressed her palm against her stomach.

*Our children would be . . . bastards.*

"Ya in here, Miss Addie?" Trisha stepped up into the wagon. "Well, they've gone. Ain't that judge the beatin'est? Things don't go to suit, he swells all up." She puffed out her cheeks. "He shore do look like a bullfrog." She leaned down and peered into Addie's face. "Ya tired, ain't ya, Miss Addie?"

"I reckon I am. We've had lots of excitement the last couple of days."

"Ya sit right here. I'll go get the younguns and keep 'em outta yore hair while ya rest."

"Thank you, Trisha. Give me an hour and I'll be all right."

Addie closed her eyes. She wasn't sure that she'd ever be all right again.

Captain Kyle Forsythe was almost sick with worry. He went through the motions of overseeing the burial, leaving most of the details to Lieutenant Shipley. They buried the man, still wrapped in the ground sheet, on a small rise where the earth was not rain-soaked. After the judge said a hasty prayer, one of the men threw a loop around a dead tree branch and dragged it up to cover the grave.

On returning to camp, Kyle dismissed the detail and went directly to the wagon he shared with Lieutenant Shipley. The four enlisted men shared the other wagon. The burying had interrupted a card game Shipley was having with two of the enlisted men and a driver. Kyle was relieved when the lieutenant went back to it. He needed time alone. He had to think.

He sat down on the shelflike bunk that served as his bed, rested his elbows on his thighs, his head in his hands, and stared at the floor.

Unless he did something to stop her, that blasted woman was going to ruin the best chance he'd ever had to be somebody.

The farm had been a good place to bide his time. Seducing Addie had been as easy as falling off a log. The country girl had never heard sweet talk. She fell for him and opened up like a ripe melon. In order to stay at the farm until the way was clear for him to go back to Illinois and pick up his commission, he had let her drag him to that hill preacher and go through the mockery of a wedding.

What a farce that was!

Hell! He couldn't let his big chance blow up in his face.

The damn ridge-runner had gone to Freepoint and found Addie. Why had he married her, for chrissake? If he'd wanted to bed her, all he had to do was sweet talk her a little. It wasn't very flattering to learn that his "widow" hadn't grieved for him but a few weeks before she took another man.

Kyle didn't know where the girl Trisha had come from. Lord, but she was a beauty. Cindy would be green with envy if she saw her. He had been getting aroused just looking at her, then Addie had knocked the props out from under him when she said the girl's last name was Hyde. Damn her! She was trying to trip him up.

What to do now? He would deny, deny, deny. It was her word against his. He had to keep telling himself that. He couldn't let anyone or anything get between him and Cindy.

Kyle got off the bunk, washed his face, combed his hair, and left the wagon. Walking on the outside of the circle to avoid Van Winkle, he went to Cindy's caravan and tapped on the door.

"Who is it?"

"Me, Kyle."

"Let him in, Ivy, then get out."

"Yas'm."

The maid opened the door and slipped out.

Kyle stepped in and threw the latch, locking the door. The window was open and a cool breeze came through. Still the place smelled deliciously like a woman. Cindy, wearing a loose robe with ribbons at the neck, put the novel she was reading aside when he entered.

"Hello, my sweet and beautiful girl." He stood with his back to the door and looked at her for a long while.

"I've missed you."

"I've missed you too. Your uncle is a demanding fellow."

Cindy held out her hands. "Don't waste time," she whispered.

Kyle sat down beside her and scooped her up to lie across his lap.

"I stayed away as long as I could. I'm going to have some of your sweet kisses and I don't care if your uncle pounds the door down." He buried his face between her breasts and nosed aside the opening of her robe. He stroked her soft skin with his tongue. "Mmm . . . you taste good enough to eat."

She gave a wanton little cry, wrapped her arms around his neck, and pressed herself against him.

# CHAPTER

## * 29 *

Trying to keep uneasiness about Addie from his mind, John rode ahead of the train, his eyes searching for a cloud of dust, a startled animal, or the sudden rising of a flock of birds. His experienced eyes scanned the ground from fifty feet ahead of him to the horizon in all directions, looking for a sign that they were not the only humans on the vast prairie. He saw only prairie grass, jack oak, and every now and then a clump of cottonwoods.

He had waited until daylight to move the train out and cross the rain-swollen stream. Thankfully, the stream was rock-bottomed and not much trouble to cross. Later on, when they reached the wider sand-bottomed creeks flowing into the Canadian River, the bull-whackers would hitch extra oxen to the freight wagons to pull them across.

Because of the late start John decided to cut out the midday rest and travel until late afternoon. He had sent Buffer back to let the cook know the change in plans.

His disturbing thoughts of Addie persisted.

Last night, for the first time since they had married, she had not slept in his arms for at least part of the night. He had missed not only the sweet agony of losing himself in her warm woman's body, but the smell of her hair, the soft kisses, the whispered words they always exchanged before falling asleep. She had become not only his lover and wife but his friend. They had shared many confidences, but not since he had told her he had killed Kirby Hyde had they spoken of him. John frowned over the knowledge the man had come between them.

Addie had laid out their bed beneath the wagon as usual, but then had asked him if he would mind if she slept inside with Trisha and the children. At first he had thought she didn't want to sleep in the place where a man had so recently died, but as he lay alone, looking out at the star-filled sky, her motive became clear: She was holding herself away from him because she still believed that she was married to another man.

John looked back at the ribbon of wagons stretched out for a mile behind him. Following the wagons were two groups of stock, his and the judge's.

Tomorrow they would reach Webbers Falls and part company with the Van Winkle train. John would lead his freight wagons across the Arkansas River and follow the Canadian River. The judge would follow the Arkansas north to the fort. John had looked forward to the day. But now he realized that things must be settled between Addie and Kyle Forsythe, or the opportunity would be lost — perhaps forever.

He wouldn't allow the shadow of another man to stand beween him and his wife for the rest of his life. He muttered an expletive. It was time the air was cleared.

It was not yet five o'clock when John gave the order to "swing in." The animals had been working for ten straight hours with only a half-hour stop for rest and water. He left the placing of the wagons to Cleve and rode Victor down the line to where the Van Winkle party had already began to turn in for the night.

John reined up beside Captain Forsythe. He lifted his arm and pointed to a clump of cottonwoods a quarter of a mile away.

"Be over there in a half-hour."

"What the hell for?"

"To clear up whatever is between you and my wife."

"There's nothing between me and your

wife. I . . . never saw her before."

"You're lying. Be there, or I'll bring Addie here and we'll say what we have to say in front of the judge and his niece."

"God damn you!"

"God damn you for whatever it was you did to Addie!"

"All right. I'll be there."

John nodded and rode back to his camp.

Addie was perfectly miserable and had been since learning for certain that Captain Kyle Forsythe was the Kirby Hyde who had come to her farm, married her, and fathered her child.

It had been a long day. Crossing the swollen creek had been scary. It would have been worse but for their driver, who seemed to think it was nothing at all. Nevertheless, Addie and Trisha held on to the children, and Addie worried about Colin in the wagon ahead.

During their one brief stop, they had all had a drink of water and Addie had handed out the candy sticks, insisting that even Trisha and Huntley each take one.

"Seems a shame, ma'am, to be wastin' this on me," Huntley drawled. "The younguns oughta be havin' it."

"There's plenty. The candy will help tide

you over till supper."

Knowing that Addie was troubled, Trisha had worked hard at keeping the children amused. She cast worried glances at her friend who sat at the back of the wagon staring at the plodding beast pulling the wagon behind them.

Addie's mind went over and over the events that had led to this crushing despair. John had been so sure the captain was not Kirby Hyde when he brought her the letter taken from the dead man. Even then there had been a small doubt in her mind, but one she could live with.

Now, she had to tell him that their marriage was not real. That her real husband was Captain Kyle Forsythe, the man she knew as Kirby Hyde.

She thanked the Lord when the order came to swing in. While the wagons circled, Addie brushed her hair and rebraided it. They all climbed down as soon as the wagon stopped. It was good to have their feet on solid ground. The children chased each other while Addie washed the dust from her face and hands and prepared to go to the cook wagon to help Bill with supper.

John rode up on Victor.

"Trisha, Colin is coming to take charge of Dillon and Jane Ann. Will you take Addie's place helping Bill with supper? She's going with me."

"Where are we going?" Addie turned an anxious face up to his.

He looked down at her for a moment. She was beautiful, but that wasn't the reason he had lost his mind and fallen so completely in love with her. It was her inner beauty that reached out to him. He had never thought to meet the likes of Addie. When she was old, that inner beauty would still be there. He had no doubt that as the years went by, she would become ever more precious to him.

"John —"

He took his foot from the stirrup. "Put your foot in there, honey, and I'll lift you up. We're going to take a little ride."

"Can't we walk?"

"No, sweetheart. Come on, I'll not let you fall."

The anxiety was still on her face as she obeyed his instructions. He lifted her and settled her on his lap. She wrapped an arm about his waist and held on to him. His arms enclosed her, sheltering and protecting her. He could feel the frightened trembling in her body. She was so damned sweet and giving. He wanted desperately to kiss her and ease the worry from her mind, but that would have to wait.

Sometimes it was necessary to be cruel in order to sweep away doubts and distrust.

He turned the horse and they rode toward the clump of cottonwoods on the rise. John knew that his wife was worried. He wanted to hold her, to hug and kiss her, and to tell her that even if Kyle Forsythe was Kirby Hyde they would find a way to be together.

The thought had come to John today that he could kill the captain and then their troubles would be over. But it had been only a thought, quickly dismissed. He couldn't deliberately kill the father of Addie's son.

John put Victor into an easy lope, anxious to get this confrontation over. Addie's cheek was pressed to his shoulder. Her long honey-colored braid hung down over his arm.

"When we get home, I'll pick out a gentle mare for you and we'll ride up into the mountains. It's beautiful this time of day."

"I have things to tell you."

"I know, sweetheart. We're almost there."

John stopped his horse in the shade. He sat looking down at Addie, then lifted her chin with his fingers. He looked into the violet eyes that had fascinated him since that first day at the store. He lowered his head and placed his lips against hers. The kiss was long and deep and satisfying. As he looked into her eyes, they began to mist.

"I had to do that," he said huskily, and smoothed an errant strand of hair over her ear. "I missed you last night."

"I missed you —"

John lifted her down and dismounted. He saw a horseman leave the Van Winkle camp and head their way. Knowing he didn't have much time, he grasped her shoulders and looked down into her face.

"Addie, love, believe this — I want you and the children with me regardless of whether our marriage is legal. You *are* my wife in my heart. Nothing will take you from me. Captain Forsythe is coming. We're going to get everything out in the open before we leave here, if I have to beat it out of him."

She hung her head. "Then . . . what?"

"Then we're going home to New Mexico."

The captain stepped from his horse and carefully tied the reins low on a bush so that the animal could easily crop the grass. During that small space of time Addie's fighting spirit took over. She moved a step away from John. This was something she had to do alone. Anger at the carefully groomed Yankee captain swept over her. It stiffened her back and heightened her resolve to make him admit who he really was so that they could decide what to do about it.

"Hello, Kirby," Addie said as he turned toward them.

"Ma'am, my name is Kyle Forsythe."

"Very well, I'll call you that. Kyle, how did you know my name is Addie *Faye?*"

"I don't know that."

"You called me Addie *Faye* yesterday. You said that if I ruined things for you, I'd be sorry."

"I said no such thing, Mrs. Tallman."

"Wait a minute. Shall I hit you first for threatening my wife or for calling her a liar?" John asked.

"I'm saying she's mistaken." The captain's face turned a dull red and he began to sweat.

"I am not mistaken, Kirby . . . ah, Kyle. I want nothing from you except for you to admit who you are."

"I've told you." He turned his back, folded his arms across his chest, and looked toward the camps.

"Kirby, did it not mean anything to you to see your son, that precious little boy who thought you looked so grand in a captain's uniform?"

No answer.

"That little boy means the world to me. I can't even hate you for leaving me to fend for myself that long, cold winter, because you gave him to me. My baby and I would have died if not for a young girl who was so skinny a wind could have blown her away. She worked her fingers to the bone taking care of us."

No reply.

"I wasn't heartbroken when you didn't come home from the war. I was dreading it. I knew the kind of man you were even before you left me. But still, I didn't want you dead."

He leaned against his horse and remained silent.

"I can prove you are Kirby Hyde." He whirled to look at her. "You've got a mole on your chin under that goatee."

His only response was to pound a clenched fist on his saddle.

"You can always shave and prove you're not Kirby Hyde," John interjected.

Kyle's control snapped. His handsome face became etched with lines of anger and frustration.

"What the hell do you want from me?"

"I think it's obvious. If you're Kirby Hyde, you owe Addie an explanation."

"All right!" he shouted "I've gone by the name of Kirby Hyde, Kent Wood, and several others. But my real name is Kyle Forsythe."

Addie leaned back against John and closed her eyes. He put his arms around her waist and held her close.

"You've got about a minute to start talking, Forsythe, or I'll start taking strips of your hide and hanging them on that bush."

"You could probably do it," Kyle said, sneering. "I learned how to sweet-talk the ladies, but I never learned to fight dirty. *Gentlemen* don't indulge in the sport."

"What brought you to my farm, Kirby?" Addie's voice was calm and quiet. "Why in the world would you play such a cruel game with another person's life?"

"Hell!" His cold blue eyes fastened on Addie. "You've always been poor, so you wouldn't know what it's like to be a rich aristocrat one day and a poor one the next."

"No, I wouldn't know that."

"I got an education because I was a Forsythe, which came in handy when I applied for a commission. Along with the education, I got lectures from everyone even remotely related to the Forsythes on how a *gentleman* should behave. Lectures and handouts are the story of my life."

John gave a derisive snort.

Kyle's eyes fastened on him. "You think I'm not worth much, but I've done pretty well for myself considering my circumstances.

"My mother never got her hands dirty in her life. My sister cried if she had to wear

526

the same ballgown twice. I was pushed into marriage with a horse-faced, nagging bitch so that they could keep up appearances."

"You married her before you married me?"

"Yes. She's dead, thank God. She made my life hell!"

The hatred on his face made Addie's heart throb under her ribs in a strange and urgent way. Unconsciously, she reached for John's hand.

"Everything about you was a lie, wasn't it, Kirby? You never joined the Arkansas Regulars."

"Hell no! I suppose you'll not be satisfied until you hear all the wretched details of my life."

"That's what we're here for." John held Addie protectively to him, her back against his chest.

The captain couldn't seem to stand still. He walked up and down, never looking at them. A few times while he was talking he pounded his fist into his palm, or let out a derisive, snorting laugh.

"A few months before the war broke out, I was forced to leave Vandalia until a stink I had created died down." He didn't seem in the least embarrassed to admit this. "I'd already applied for a commission and decided to *visit* an uncle down in Jonesboro while I waited for it to come through. My uncle had gotten hard-nosed since I'd seen him last and insisted that I work for my keep. Hell, I hadn't been brought up to lift flour barrels, cotton bales, and syrup buckets. But I did it, and did a damn good job, too."

He looked at Addie over the back of his horse.

"I never had any trouble getting a woman. The only trouble I ever had was getting away from them. I couldn't help it if a silly town girl lifted her skirts the first time I crooked my finger. She got the crazy notion that I should marry her because I'd fucked her."

Addie closed her eyes against the crude word.

"I left Jonesboro in the middle of the night. The next morning I caught a ride on a hay-wagon with a darkie. I'd been in Freepoint only a day when I heard about the woman living all alone on a farm a few miles from town.

"The farm was a good place to spend some time, Addie Faye. Seducing you was as easy as falling off a log." Kyle felt he was damned anyway and held nothing back. He watched Addie's face as he said the cruel words. She showed no emotion at all.

He shrugged.

"In order to stay at the farm until the way

was clear for me to go back to Vandalia and pick up my commission, I let you drag me to that hill preacher and go through a wedding ceremony."

"You really are rotten, Kirby," Addie said.

"I admit that. A man in my circumstances does what he has to do to get along. I racked my brain trying to think of a way to get away without your raising a fuss. Usually, if I wait long enough, the cards fall my way. I heard about the Arkansas Regulars from old Cash at the store. It was a way to get out of a miserable situation. I 'joined' the day I got the letter from my sister telling me that I was no longer being sought by the brothers of the *lady* I was supposed to have violated. The *lady* had run off to St. Louis with a married drummer, and the brothers had been forced to face the fact that their sister was no lady.

"I left Freepoint, made my way to Illinois, picked up my commission, and got myself a soft job that lasted throughout the war."

"You're a real hero," John said dryly.

"At least I'm not dead." Kyle laughed. His face was flushed. He sincerely believed that he had blown his chance with Cindy, so he threw caution to the wind.

"I met Cindy Read six months before the war ended. She's everything I ever dreamed a wife could be: rich *and* beautiful. She's connected in the right places, too. A perfect wife for an ambitious army man.

"Occasionally I do something very stupid. I stopped by Jonesboro on my way out to Fort Smith to meet Van Winkle and Cindy. Uncle Kirby enjoyed giving me the letter from Addie."

" 'Uncle Kirby'?"

"Another stupid mistake. When I got to the farm, Kirby Hyde was the first name that came to mind."

"It meant nothing to you that you had fathered a son?" Addie asked in as cool and steady a voice as she could manage.

"Frankly, no. I've scattered seed around, as have most men."

Now Addie's control snapped. She took the two steps necessary to reach him. Her hand flashed up and she struck him a resounding slap across the face. She was as stunned by her action as the man in front of her and the one behind her. It was something she had never done before and had never expected to do.

Kyle stood motionless. "Do you feel better for that?" When she didn't answer, he said: "I seem to bring out traits in women they don't even know they have."

"You were at the crossroads the night I

killed the Reb." John reached for Addie and pulled her back away from the captain.

"Yeah. When you asked for someone to put a name on him, the opportunity fell right into my lap. A way to put Kirby Hyde to rest. I took the letter out of my pocket and gave it to you."

John's eyes narrowed as he studied Kyle's face. "You're different from that man."

"The mustache and goatee do wonders." He fingered the short beard on his chin. "I recognized you the night we met in the hotel in Van Buren. Same hat, same clothes, same long black hair. When I saw you again the next morning, Addie was with you." He laughed. The sound was short and dry. "I thought, well, Kyle, if you get out of this one, you should get a medal. You know, Addie, it wasn't flattering to find out that my *widow* hadn't grieved for me very long."

Addie felt choked with bitterness. She allowed her lips to form a contemptuous sneer, then realized the futility of the gesture, for it was completely lost on this self-serving man.

Behind her, John took her shoulders and moved her aside. Before she or Kyle knew what he planned to do, his fist slammed into Kyle's face. The blow sent him staggering backward, then he fell heavily to the ground. He lay there fingering his split lip.

"What was that for?"

"For deserting a little boy — one of the 'seeds' you so carelessly spread around."

Kyle got to his feet, pulled a handkerchief from his pocket, and dabbed at his lip. The instant he returned the cloth to his pocket, John's rock-hard fist slammed into his face again. The blow rocked Kyle's head back and knocked him to the ground. Blood spurted from his nose. He lay there holding the cloth to his face.

"Goddammit! Are you going to keep this up?"

"I don't have enough time to give you what you deserve. It'll be dark soon. But that was for the Reb lying in a grave near Jonesboro. His folks will never know what happened to him."

"He was trying to kill you, for chrissake."

"He was human. Some take life. Others, like you, take a person's self-respect."

"Hell, I haven't killed anybody."

"John." Addie put her hand on his arm. "Hurting him won't help. I can't believe I'm married to such a sorry piece of trash."

Kyle got to his feet, keeping a wary eye on John.

"I'm not married to you! Do you think

I'd tie myself to a farm woman who doesn't know a napkin ring from a mule's ass?"

Addie held John's arm to keep him from lashing out. Her heart was beating wildly. Unconsciously, she raised her hand to press against it.

"What do you mean? You said your wife died."

"She did. She killed herself the day I returned to Vandalia. She thought I'd come back to her. I was married to the bitch when I married you."

"Oh . . ." Relief so acute that it was painful washed through her. "Oh," she said again, and yielded to the arms that came from behind her and pulled her back against a hard, warm chest.

Obviously unconcerned with her feelings, Kyle had taken a canteen from his saddle and wet the cloth he was using to wipe the blood from his face.

"I suppose your revenge will be to go to Judge Van Winkle and ruin things for me there." Kyle scrubbed at the blood on his coat.

It was John who answered him. "No, we won't do that. I think you and the judge deserve each other. I do feel somewhat sorry for his niece, though."

Kyle's laugh was a snort. "Don't. Cindy

can take care of herself. She's got the instincts of a barracuda."

Addie turned questioning eyes up at John. "A man-eating fish," he explained.

Addie turned back to Kyle and wondered how she could ever have been so blind as to believe he had a sincere bone in his body.

"Kyle Forsythe." She shook her head as she said his name. "My hope is that I never hear your name or see your face again as long as I live." Her expression and tone told both men that she meant every word.

Kyle shrugged. "Fine with me." He stepped to his horse, took the reins, and prepared to mount. John's voice stopped him.

"There's one more thing."

"What now?"

"Stay away from Dillon. Don't come near him or speak to him or about him. If you do, I'll kill you."

"Fine with me," Kyle said again, and stepped into the saddle.

John had one last word. "A little advice for the sake of the men on your train. When we split off tomorrow, push those wagons from daylight until dark, and even longer if you can. Get to the fort and don't leave it until you have a good-sized escort."

"How many is that?"

"As many as you can get. Not less than fifty."

"Thanks." Kyle gave a half-salute, turned his horse, and left them.

Addie stood within the circle of John's arms and watched Kyle ride down the slope toward the camp. She was wrung out emotionally, but happy that it was over. John turned her to face him.

"You were never married to him, Addie. Even if he hadn't been already married at the time, I'm not sure that it would have been legal with him using a false name."

"You must think me a fool, to have allowed him to . . . do what he did."

"I think nothing of the kind. He's smooth. He took advantage of you. I think he's relieved to get that part of his life behind him. Now he can concentrate on making someone else's life miserable. I'm kind of hoping it will be Van Winkle's."

"I never knew a person could be so completely selfish, so self-centered."

"There are plenty like him. You just haven't met them."

"Do you think Dillon will . . . be like that?"

"Of course not. We'll teach him to have respect for other people. Dillon is my son now. Dillon Tallman. I never want the name

Hyde or Forsythe mentioned in connection with him."

Addie slipped her arms around his neck. "I love you."

"I love you, Mrs. Tallman. I can hardly wait to get you in our bed beneath the wagon. I intend to make you pregnant before we get home."

"I won't be alone this time."

"A team of mules couldn't pull me from you while you're having my child. I'll be the first to hold him . . . or her."

Addie looked lovingly into her husband's eyes. Her fingers smoothed his silken mustache down each side of his mouth.

"I was so . . . miserable last night."

His smile was full of tenderness. "I'm glad. I'd hate it if I were the only one who suffered. Kiss me, sweetheart. It's got to last a while."

They stood close together and so still that a mockingbird settled in the cottonwood above their heads. They stayed until the light faded in the west and Victor had cropped all the grass within his reach. They realized his impatience when he snorted and pawed the ground. Lights from lanterns appeared at the cook wagon and at Addie's wagon, where Trisha was putting the children to bed.

"You missed your supper," John murmured against her kiss-swollen lips.

"I don't care. I'm hungry for something else." She laughed against his cheek. "Come on, you . . . *passerby*. You've got work to do if I'm going to be pregnant by the time we get home."

# Epilogue

Exactly eighty-eight days after Addie had left her farm in Arkansas she arrived at her new home in the mountains of northern New Mexico. John was eager to show Addie her new house and to see his parents, who were waiting there. He drove one of the wagons, followed by Trisha and Buffer in the other, through the densely wooded Cimarron Valley and on to Elk Mountain.

Sprawled out in the sunshire was a low adobe dwelling, built in the shape of a U with a courtyard and many rooms. Addie clapped her hands in delight at the scenic view that spread out before her. The house and the courtyard were surrounded by a solid rock and adobe wall.

Heavy wooden gates stood open in welcome.

As John stepped down from the wagon, a tall, slim woman came running from the house. Holding his arms wide, he went to meet her. Squealing with laughter, she threw herself into his arms. Long, thick, silver and gold hair, clasped at the nape of her neck, sparkled in the sunlight. She wore a skirt that ended halfway between her knees and ankles, and on her feet were soft leather moccasins. John whirled her in the air. She squealed and demanded to be put down.

Addie's attention went to the smiling man who stood nearby. His clothes were identical to John's; his hair, not quite as long, showed streaks of white. The woman stepped away and the two men shook hands, then hugged. They were of equal height, although the older man was somewhat heavier. The thought came to Addie that this was what John would look like thirty years from now.

As they came toward the wagon, Addie smoothed the skirt of the best dress she owned; she wanted to look presentable when meeting John's parents.

"I've got a surprise for you, Amy."

"It's no surprise, you rascal." Her voice was young, her laughter ready, belying her silver hair. "Have you forgotten you sent Anselmo in two days ago? He couldn't wait to tell us the news, and we could hardly wait to meet our new daughter, could we, Rain?"

John lifted Addie down from the wagon. With his arm around her he proudly introduced her to his parents.

"This is Addie Faye. Addie, my parents, Amy and Rain Tallman."

The welcome she received brought tears to Addie's eyes. She got a hug from a smiling Amy and a warm handshake from the tall man who stood behind her.

"Anselmo didn't tell you that you have three new grandchildren, did he?" John had a smug smile on his face. He went to the back of the wagon, where he had told the children to hide so that they would be a surprise to their new grandmother.

Amy squealed with delight and raced around to help John lift the children down.

"This is Colin. He's going to make a top-notch hand, Pa. He's shouldered his share of the work all the way across the territories."

Colin offered his hand to Amy, who ignored it and gave him a hug. Rain took the boy's hand, then held it to keep him beside him.

"Here's Jane Ann." The child was clutching the doll John had given her. Her frightened eyes went to Addie, who nodded, before she allowed herself to be drawn into Amy's embrace.

"A little girl! Oh, how pretty you are."

"This rascal is Dillon." John lifted the boy to sit on his shoulders.

"My name's Dillon Tallman," Dillon announced proudly. "I'm four." He held up four fingers.

"Almost," John added with a wide grin.

Amy clapped her hands. "I've waited a long time for this. You do things up right, don't you, Johnny?"

"Of course, Mother. Did you doubt it?"

Trisha and Buffer arrived and were made welcome.

"We stopped at Adobe Walls Mission long enough for these two to be married," John announced.

"We've planned a celebration for tonight." Amy turned to her husband. "Rain, it'll be a *double* celebration. Do we have enough of everything?"

"Yes, love." Rain chuckled and ran a finger down his wife's soft cheek. "You've asked me that only six times today."

Addie loved everything about her new home — the warm sunny days, the cool nights. Amy came often and took the children to stay with her for a few days. Jane Ann adored her. The little girl blossomed under Amy's love and attention.

One of the first things John did was to get Addie a half-dozen sheep. Dillon promptly named one of them Dipper.

By fall, Addie had lost her waistline and

John accused her of swallowing a melon. They eagerly looked forward to spring and the new addition to their family. A beautiful baby girl with dark hair and eyes arrived in time for Easter. John caught her when she came from her mother's body and then had to be forcibly removed from the room by the new grandmother so that the baby could be washed and dressed. They named her Liberty, after John's aunt, but she soon became known simply as Betty.

Buffer and Trisha started their "little" place. Trisha was happy as a lark, and Buffer was proud as a peacock of his beautiful wife. Trisha wore the leather britches Buffer had bought for her at the store in Van Buren and soon was riding and shooting and throwing a knife as if she had done it all her life. The first year, the Simmonses became the parents of a big, husky boy.

The Van Winkle party came through the territories with another train and an army escort. On a recent trip to Sante Fe, Rain and Amy learned that due to Rain's influence, Judge Van Winkle had been removed as Indian agent — recalled, after a year of service, for inappropriate behavior. Strings were pulled so that Captain and Mrs. Forsythe were able to accompany the judge back East, where the captain was reassigned to a quartermaster post.

The night John told Addie the news, they were lying in bed.

"Forsythe will earn every penny he gets out of Van Winkle and Cindy. Not many men would put up with that pompous old goat." John was lovingly stroking Addie's belly, which had begun to swell again.

"I'm glad . . . ah, you-know-who is hundreds of miles from here."

"Be Christian about this, Mrs. Tallman. Without that clabber-headed, stinking polecat, you might not have met me. I'd have never gone to Freepoint. I'd never have seen you in that store. Think what you would have missed."

"That's true. But *you* should thank your lucky stars too. If not for that worthless buzzard bait, whom I refuse to call by name, you could be wearing socks with holes and sleeping alone in this bed."

His sigh was long and dramatic. "I'm not real sure I should thank him. Maybe you should show me why." He was trying to tease her, but his voice sounded gruff.

She flopped over onto her stomach, her elbows on his chest, and began to kiss and nibble on his chin.

"Sure now?" she asked, and ran her fingertips across his ribs and flat belly.

"Well . . . ?" He drew the word out. "I don't know."

"Mr. Passerby, you're getting hard to please." She lowered her hand into the thick hair surrounding his sex.

"I like that," he said quickly.

"I thought you would."

A second later he was in sweet agony.

"You lustful wench!" He rolled her onto her back. "I'm afraid I'm going to have to keep you!"